I05938833

CONDUIT

K.F. BRADSHAW

Conduit

By K.F. Bradshaw
Published By
Wishbox Press
Copyright © 2018 by K.F. Bradshaw
ISBN: 978-0-9987518-3-2
First Edition, 2018
Cover by TS95 Studios

All Rights Reserved. This book or any portion thereof may not be reproduced or used in any manner whatsoever without the express written permission of the author except for the use of brief quotations in a book review.

www.kfbradshaw.com

To my wife…and all the readers who gave *Enchanters* a chance.
Conduit is for you.

THE ENCHANTERS TRILOGY

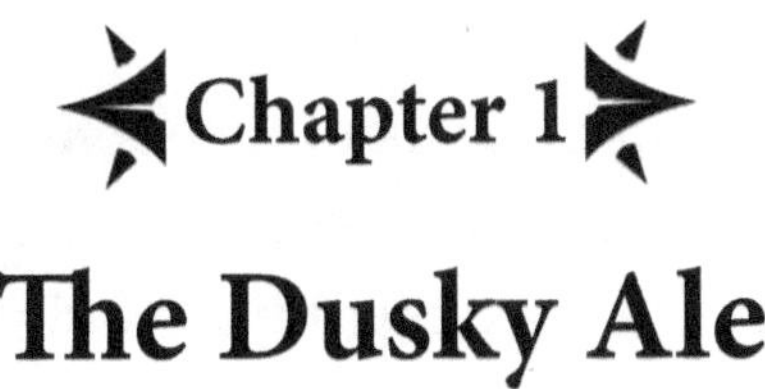

Chapter 1
The Dusky Ale

Damea, 224 2nd Era
Sadford, Azgadaran Empire

"Here you are, Taryn." The metal tankard—desperately in need of a polishing and filled to the brim with the town's seasonal spring brew—came down with a heavy thud on the worn down wooden countertop.

Taryn glanced up at the barkeep in confusion. Her dark eyebrows arched up over her small grey eyes as she pointed at the drink. "I didn't order that."

The barkeep shrugged, a crooked smile crossing his rough features. "Looks like you have a new friend." Taryn followed his gaze toward the back of the tavern. In the far corner lit only by the glow of a few dying candles sat a hooded woman. It was hard to get a good look at her from where Taryn sat, but she could just make out leather armor underneath the woman's olive-green cloak.

"Suppose I should say thank you," she said as she turned to the barkeep. But he had stopped paying attention to her and was now serving other patrons. *Right, let's see what this is about.* She hopped off her stool, the chain links of her Legionnaire armor clinking as she grabbed her drink from the counter and pushed through the other soldiers and guests lining up to give their orders. The collective murmurings of various conversations united in a dull hum throughout the room. She was grateful her commander had released her from her shift early so that she could beat the late-evening rush to Sadford's only tavern.

As Taryn approached the stranger's table, she could see that the woman was only a few years younger than her. Her height was difficult to discern as she was sitting down, but the way her armor fit her form—not to mention the sheathed dagger peeking out from beneath her cloak—suggested that this woman was trained in combat. Upon seeing Taryn, the woman removed her hood, revealing dirty blonde hair—a bit above shoulder length and shaved close on the sides—which had been pulled back with a few wisps of it framing bright blue eyes. A thin scar was faintly visible on her tanned skin and ran just above her eyebrows, which rose at Taryn in amusement.

"I didn't know what you liked so I guessed," was her opening line. She gestured for Taryn to sit, offering her a sly smile—as though there was some inside joke between them that Taryn did not remember being part of.

Strange accent. "Good guess, and thank you. It's much better than last year's, for sure." Taryn tried to get a closer look at her new acquaintance's clothing to see if she could find a crest, a symbol—anything that might give some clue as to where she was from—but there were none in sight. She wasn't ordinarily so suspicious, but it was not every day that someone like this walked into the Dusky Ale and bought Guardswoman Taryn of the Azgadaran Legion a drink.

She noticed the woman did not have a mug of her own. "You're not having anything?"

"Nah," came the blunt reply, accompanied by a half shrug. "I'm not really a fan of the menu here to be honest. I'm Cassie, by the way." She extended a gloved hand, which Taryn clasped after a brief hesitation.

"Taryn."

Cassie withdrew her hand before giving Taryn a quick inspection. "Nice outfit. Where do I get one?"

Taryn could not help but grin. *Funny, if a bit odd.* "Standard Legion attire, of course. They even gave me a sword," she said, patting the sheathed weapon that hung from the belt she wore around the black, gold, and blood-red garments of her uniform.

"Don't suppose you have any extras lying around, do you?"

Ah, should have known better. Taryn cursed inwardly. Why else would an armed woman seek her out at her usual drinking spot after her shift to buy her a drink? *Better luck next time, I suppose.*

Or...she could have a bit of fun with it. *And she is pretty cute...*

"Let me guess—they told you I was the one to talk to about recruitment?"

Cassie put her hands up. "Hey, I was just following directions. I didn't mean any harm."

Of course she doesn't. Technically, Cassie had been informed correctly—after a few years of service to the Legion she was finally in a position to influence recruitment. Still, she would not have said no to one evening free of her duties and responsibilities to the empire. "It's no bother. You seem experienced by the look of you."

"I've been in a fight or two, yeah."

"But," Taryn motioned at Cassie's hood, "why the secrecy?" She took a sip of her drink and lowered her voice to just above a whisper. "You on the run?"

Cassie raised an eyebrow. "Lived in the western realm for years. Would you believe me if I said I was bored and needed some excitement in my life? Also," she pointed a thumb toward the door, "it's chilly out there."

Taryn laughed. "Not a very compelling reason for my commander, but say I believe you. The Legion is built upon loyalty. How do I know you're not just going to desert the moment your 'boredom' strikes again?"

"That's not what I heard."

Taryn frowned. "Say again?"

"The loyalty thing. Or was that just a rumor about the empress's bodyguard?"

Ah, that. She ran her hand through her short black hair. "What sort of rumors have you heard?"

"Oh, come on," Cassie said. "Like there's anyone not living under a rock that doesn't know she betrayed the empire and killed General Cadar in Gurdinfield." She leaned in, lowering her voice. "And you guys *still* haven't caught her? How is that even possible? I mean, you're the *Legion!*" She glanced down at the table in obvious disappointment.

"All right, all right—not so loud!" Taryn hissed. She knew discussing this was against regulations, but if she could restore Cassie's confidence in the Legion perhaps she could convince her to apply. Taryn's commander would be happy for a recruit with combat experience—perhaps even recommend Taryn for promotion next year. "Look, she's been apprehended." She chuckled. "We found her *here* of all places. It's almost as though she had been *trying* to get caught."

Cassie's eyes lit up. "Uh...wow. I mean…" She cleared her throat. "That's pretty impressive. Maybe you guys *are* as tough as everyone says you are."

Taryn swelled with pride. "So, you're interested, then?"

"I might be," Cassie said. She glanced past Taryn before meeting her gaze again. "I uh…wouldn't end up stuck guarding a door or something, right?"

Not much I can do about that. "It would be difficult to guarantee where you might end up, but I could recommend a post for you to my commander."

"As long as I don't end up dead because that traitor got free."

"Hah! No need to worry about that one."

Cassie leaned in again. "Why not?"

Taryn finished off her drink. *Commander Eron will kill me if he gets wind of this, but soon all of Azgadar will know anyway.* "Got her locked up right here in Sadford. We're taking her to Azgadar tomorrow."

"Oh! Well, I guess that makes sense," Cassie said. She pointed at the empty tankard. "How was it?"

Taryn smiled. Perhaps this was going better than she had first thought. "Sorely needed, thank you again. Anyway, I can give my commander your name or, well, I'll be stationed in Azgadar for a bit after we finish up our transport." She hesitated. "If you wanted, you could always find me there. All the new recruits have to train there."

"Yeah, I'll think about it," Cassie said. "Thanks for your help—and the opportunity. Nice hair by the way." She pushed the chair back.

It's now or never. Or a long time from now, assuming she actually goes to Azgadar. Taryn took a deep breath. *Still, no harm in trying.* "You know, I'm off duty until tomorrow evening. If you wanted to…to stay and talk some more where it's not so loud, I have a room rented until I leave for Azgadar."

Cassie's eyes widened for a moment and Taryn could swear she saw her tanned cheeks grow pink as she rubbed the back of her neck. "Ah…yeah. Sorry. I mean, you seem pretty nice but I'm, uh, spoken for."

Of course she is. She forced a laugh. "I don't see a bracelet." It was crude and probably inappropriate, but the sight of this woman squirming was too entertaining to pass up.

Cassie exhaled sharply, her nervousness obvious. "It was nice meeting you, Taryn. Thanks again." She offered a final smile as she stood up and straightened her clothing before walking past Taryn and disappearing into the crowd of patrons near the bustling entrance of the Dusky Ale.

Chapter 2
Breakout

The breeze of a spring Azgadaran evening made Cassie shiver as she stepped outside, the heavy wooden door thudding shut behind her. The town of Sadford was quite a bit calmer than it had been when she arrived earlier in the afternoon. Nearby, merchants were packing up their wares from the trade carts that dotted the town's marketplace. Only a few people remained on the dusty, lantern-lit main street, most huddled in small cliques. Cassie took a deep breath, enjoying the much-needed fresh air after being stuck in that dingy tavern for so long.

"Did you get it?"

Cassie tensed up as the voice's owner stepped into the yellow light given off by the lantern hanging outside the tavern. He was one of the tallest men she knew and sported the lean build of an archer. His auburn hair was pulled back into a low ponytail that reached just past his shoulders.

"You scared the crap out of me, Victor," she breathed.

Behind Victor, a bald, dark-skinned giant of a man gave a booming laugh, setting Cassie's nerves at ease. "Sorry, Cass. I forgot you were afraid of the dark," he said with a scarred grin, revealing several gaps where teeth should have been were it not for the violent fistfights he often wound up in before joining the Guardians of Gurdinfield. Once the trusted protectors of Gurdinfield's royal family, the Guardians had been exiled during the land's twenty-year civil war, when they were reduced to a rebel militia. Now, with the war over and a new queen on the throne they were once again serving their ruler by defending her and, on occasion, carrying out reconnaissance missions.

"Oh, ha ha," Cassie said with a roll of her eyes. "That's *almost* funny every time you say it, Roe."

"You *did* jump pretty high when you saw that rat, Cass," Victor said. "Need to be prepared for anything if you're going to be a Guardian." They walked toward the main road, staying to the side to avoid catching the ears of the townspeople who were still out.

Cassie narrowed her eyes at him. "Right. 'Prepared'. You want to talk about being prepared? Could have told me up front that Miss Legionnaire in there was looking for a *date*."

Victor and Roe exchanged amused glances. "Well, yes," Victor said. "We needed that information and Guardswoman Taryn is known for opening up to…the right people. Why do you think we sent you in instead of one of us?"

Cassie blinked. "So I've been demoted to bait. Great."

"It worked, didn't it? And you got it? You have the info?" Victor asked again as they reached the town stables, where their horses had been kept for the day.

"Yeah, I got it," Cassie grumbled, giving Victor's horse a brief pat on its neck before checking the saddlebags. "She's here, actually. They're keeping her at the Legion fort."

"Right here in Sadford?" Roe asked, mounting his own horse. Victor followed suit and Cassie, who still was not comfortable riding a horse on her own, clambered on behind him.

"Right here," she confirmed. "They're going to hold her until tomorrow. Then she's off to Azgadar." She held onto Victor as the three of them headed out of the stables and made their way toward the Legion fort on the outskirts of town. Her stomach lurched, reminding her why she hated traveling on horseback.

"Can't believe she got caught," Victor said, shaking his head in disbelief.

"Yeah, the girl in there seemed just as surprised," Cassie said. Glancing over at Roe, she shot him a roguish smile. "So…we're going to get her out, right?"

Roe hesitated. "I don't know, Cass. A lot could go wrong, and—"

"Oh, come now, Roe!" Victor said. "This isn't just any old mission. Can you imagine the look on the queen's face when we return our dear friend to Gurdinfield where she belongs?"

Roe raised an eyebrow. "Is this before or after the captain skins our hides for going against a direct order?"

"Come on, Roe!" Cassie joined in with Victor. "We didn't come all this way for nothing."

"I don't know…the queen was pretty clear that we were to return with the information."

"Which is exactly what we're doing," Cassie said as they passed the town border. Up ahead, the stone walls of the Legion fort were just visible against the dark horizon. "And as a bonus, we'll be bringing back her favorite grumpy Legionnaire."

"Hmph. Assuming we don't get ourselves run through by some guardsman's sword," Roe said.

Victor groaned. "You're quite dull, you know that? But… maybe he's got a point, Cass. And you're already in hot water. You sure you want to do this?"

But Cassie dismissed their concerns. "Guys, it was *one* tiny incident and I'm sure Diana's forgotten all about it by now."

"You let three goats into the palace during the captain's birthday party when you should have been keeping watch," Roe reminded her.

"It was Kye's idea! Well, kinda…"

"And they crapped all over the floor in the throne room," Victor continued.

"Okay, but Andrea figured out how to use magic to clean it so it was fine."

"And then we all had to listen to her yell at you for the rest of the evening," Roe said.

"Ha! That's right—Her Majesty didn't even *need* to say anything to you," Victor laughed.

"We can return the information to the queen and perhaps she can reason with the empress," Roe suggested.

Cassie shook her head. "If you hadn't noticed, the empress isn't exactly the type to be reasoned with. She locked up Andrea for wearing a *necklace.* She invaded another country because she wanted magic." She looked out at the Legion fort ahead.

“No, we’re doing this tonight.”

* * *

Glancing up from her dinner, Elisa watched with mild interest as a rat scurried across the cracked stone floor of her cell, its path lit only by the glow of the sconces that lined the corridor of the jail. The rat hesitated before wandering over to her and grabbing one of the crumbs of stale bread that made up her meal.

Tossing the piece in her hand to the ground, she leaned back against the wall and muttered, “You can have the rest, but don’t be surprised if it’s inedible.” The creature jumped back, but then with a cautious step forward it sniffed the bread as though pondering how it was going to get the food back to its nest.

“Wasting food again, are we?” A guard’s voice sounded behind Elisa on the other side of thick, iron bars.

“Would hardly call it food. Even *he* doesn’t want it.” She pointed at the rat, who had decided to leave the bread behind and was now heading back to the tiny crevice in the wall it came from.

The guard was unamused. “Were it up to me, I’d let you starve. Fortunately for you, Her Majesty wants you alive for some reason.”

“Well then, I suppose you’ll just have to fetch me something else for dinner.” Elisa fidgeted with her wrist guards and adjusted a few buckles on the black leather armor she wore.

"Preferably something *not* disgusting."

"You should be executed for your crimes to the empire," the guard spat.

Elisa made an affirmative noise as she pushed herself up off the floor and dusted her clothes off before walking up to the cell door. The torchlight illuminated her pale green eyes and copper-red hair which, usually braided, fell just past her chin in a tangled mess. She wrapped her hands around the cold bars and leaned forward, almost touching noses with the guard, who held his glare at her as his lips tightened.

"What's wrong?" she drawled. "Nervous to be so close to the woman who killed your great general?"

The guard drew his sword and held it up to the door, its blade inches away from Elisa's throat. "Back away from the door. *Now.*"

Elisa stared at the sword for a moment before bursting into laughter. "Go on," she said with a taunting grin. "Surely your empress will understand how you had *no choice* but to run the most wanted criminal in the empire through with your mighty blade."

He held the blade steady, hesitating, before swallowing and sheathing the weapon. The sneer remained in his tone. "I hope Her Majesty orders a slow death for you, *traitor.*"

"Yes, yes, now fetch me that dinner. I'm quite hungry." Elisa released the bars with a sigh and took a step back. The guard grumbled something under his breath before turning on his heel and walking out of view. Seconds later, a muffled yell filled the corridor followed by a pained grunt and the sound of a body crumpling to the floor.

"Ha! Well done! Pretty sure that one's going to be out for a while." Elisa thought she recognized the man's voice.

"Did you find it?" another, deeper voice said.

"Hang on, hang on. Give me a second—you two are so impatient...there we go!" A third voice—this one female and *definitely* familiar.

Elisa stepped up to the door again and peered out into the corridor. Her eyes widened when she saw the guard who had threatened her only moments earlier sprawled on the floor, unconscious. His assailants stood over him, one of whom was holding what appeared to be the key to the cell.

"Cassie? What are you doing here?" Elisa exclaimed.

Cassie stepped over the guard and inserted the slightly bent metal key into the lock. "Oh, I see how it is," she said, shaking her head. "It's 'what are you doing here' when it *should* be 'oh, wow, Cassie—thanks for saving me!'" The lock made a satisfying click and the door swung open.

"You have my eternal gratitude," Elisa said, eliciting chuckles from her other two rescuers. "Victor and Roe. Why am I not surprised?"

Roe bowed his head. "Good to see you again, Lady Elisa."

"We obtained these at the door." Victor held up a worn-out backpack from which a sheathed sword of Azgadaran make and two long daggers hung.

Elisa tilted her head as she reached out to take the bag. "The door? Am I to assume you've taken care of the other guards, then?" She slid the daggers into the sheaths on her belt and slung the backpack and the sword over her shoulder.

"Yeah, though there were only a few of them. I guess they don't post a lot of security here at night," Cassie said as she led the group down the corridor.

"Most likely you only handled the guards at the front but there are bound to be more further in," Elisa said as she stepped over the guard, who was still out cold. "Legion forts are a bit like anthills that way."

"Hey, I'm fine not fighting hordes of them. If you want to stay, though…"

"No, thank you," Elisa said. "I've had more than my fill of Legionnaire arrogance for the day—probably for the week." They passed through the prisoner receiving area at the front of the fort, where three more Legionnaires lay unconscious on the floor amid scattered papers and weapons. "How did you find me? Did the queen send you?" she asked, keeping her voice down in the event more soldiers heard them. She knew it was only a matter of time before someone walked by her cell and saw she was missing.

"Some recon work," Cassie said as they left the jail, following Roe to their horses. "But yeah, Diana wanted to know what happened to you." She shrugged. "Apparently, you stopped writing."

Elisa sighed. "It hasn't been *that* long." She did some minor calculations in her head. *It's only been three, no, four weeks…oh.* "Eh, perhaps it has." She climbed onto Roe's horse as Cassie did the same with Victor's. Moments later, they were riding away from Sadford in the direction of the City of Towers.

"I didn't get a letter," Cassie accused.

Elisa snorted. "I could say the same thing to you."

"You didn't exactly give an address where I could send it to."

"You could have asked Her Majesty."

"Been kinda busy with stuff."

"Indeed. On that note—Andrea doing well, then?" The tease in Elisa's voice was obvious. Both Victor and Roe erupted into laughter.

They had been riding northeast for several minutes in silence save the solid impacts of the horses' hooves against the dirt road when Victor spoke up. "You don't think this'll cause a stir with the empress, do you?"

"What's she going to do? Invade Gurdinfield *again?*" Roe scoffed.

"With the way things in the empire are going right now, I wouldn't rule anything out," Elisa said. The interested expressions from the others did not go unnoticed by her. "But that information is for the queen's ears first. I'm sure the three of you will hear about it from Jacob."

Cassie looked out at the road ahead. "Then let's get home."

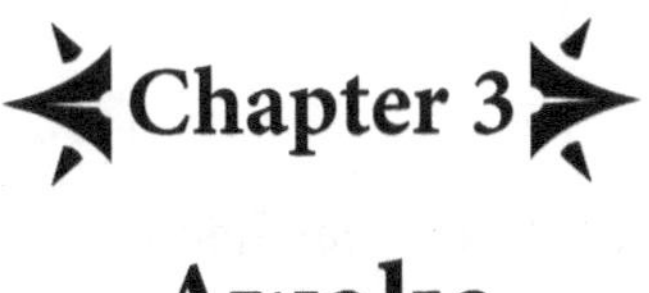

Chapter 3

Awake

The Black Forest

Richard blinked. Then again. His blue eyes struggled to focus, the world around him still a dark blur. The first things he noticed once his vision had returned to normal were the obscene number of cobwebs on the ceiling above him, and the ache in his limbs from lying on a cold metal table. He was clothed only in a pair of loose-fitting pants and a dirty, white sheet that had been draped over him, stopping just below his shoulders. The table beneath him was vibrating slowly and a low hum filled the room.

He was weak, that much was certain. There was a dull, painful throbbing behind his temples and his mouth was dry, as though he hadn't had anything to eat or drink in…

No.

It took all his strength to push down on the table with enough force to lift his upper body so that he was sitting upright, the sheet falling into his lap. The air around him was dank and heavy. The steady drip of water sounded from somewhere behind him, accompanied by the squeaks of a mouse as the creature scampered across the stone floor. *This isn't the cellar.*

By the looks of the dark corners, the dreary cobwebs that coated the rafters and the walls, and the lack of windows anywhere, Richard knew he was in *a* cellar. But this was not his home in the City of Towers.

Meredith.

The memories surfaced. They had been eating dinner—was it the leftover stew? The civil war had been dire enough in the city that it was difficult to get to the market without being harassed by a Moore or a Harrington soldier, or the thugs and looters that often took advantage of the deteriorating situation in the capital city.

They had forced their way in. Thieves, robbers—whoever they were. *Somehow, they found us out.* Remaining in the City of Towers during the chaos of the civil war was probably the worst idea he and his wife, Meredith, had come up with. The men had knocked on the door, masquerading as beggars, and like a fool, he had opened the door for them. They had overpowered him within seconds. His wife, Meredith, had held back from using her magic on them, but Richard had flung lightning with every bit of energy he could grasp. Moments later, he lay on the floor dying, the invaders sprawled lifelessly around him and Meredith leaning over him. She helped him drink the vile concoction that would slow both the illness and his aging until she could find a way to cure his ailment and wake him up.

But where was Meredith? He took a moment to study the room more closely.

It was definitely an enchanter's laboratory, though from the looks of it, it had been abandoned weeks ago, months even. The torches that lined the walls had long since gone out and the only light was a faint white glow that came from the large, cracked glass tube on the floor. A few other broken tubes were scattered across the lab. Pieces of clothing—a cloak, some shirts, a pair of boots—lay on the alchemy table a few steps away. A pile of books collected dust nearby. Richard recognized some of the titles. This wasn't just any enchanter's lab—it was Meredith's.

He tore the sheet from him, sending a cloud of dust into the air, and cast it to the floor before swinging his legs over the side of the table. Wherever he was, he needed to find Meredith and find out what had happened. He reached his hand up and touched his face, discovering a short but even beard. The blond hair on his head was still mostly neat, as he preferred it, but a quick run-through with his fingers told him that although the potion had slowed its growth, he was still in need of a trim.

"Meredith?" he called out, the sound bouncing back at him as it echoed against the walls. *She's not here.* There was no way someone as meticulous and diligent as his wife would leave her lab in such a mess. Panic rose within him. *She's all right—she has to be.* Somehow, after the incident, Meredith had managed to get him here. More perplexing was the fact that other than feeling parched, Richard felt *well.*

Could it be? He held out his hand, feeling the warmth of magical energy flow through his arm as he channeled a ball of blue light. It was small and only lasted a moment, but it was all he needed. He gasped. If he had in fact contracted the illness that befell enchanters who overextended their resources, he had somehow been cured of it. And since the lab he now sat alone within had clearly been untouched for quite some time, there was only one logical conclusion he could make.

Magic had been restored to Damea.

* * *

So bright.

The magic was just as Andrea had imagined it. Cassie's map had shown it to her, albeit it had been on a much, much smaller scale.

She was alone, her footsteps echoing in the enormous cavern as she approached the sphere before her. It pulsed—a beacon of blue radiance—and its steady hum filled the room, making the rocky ground tremble beneath her boots.

But there was something unsettling about it. She swore she had been here before, but had she really? She felt…odd, but she knew she needed to focus on the incredible phenomenon in front of her.

Then why did it seem like nothing made sense anymore?

"There's nothing we can do. The illness…it is fatal. No doubt it's accelerated as well, given where we are," the voice called out, but there was no one in the cave with her.

Something else, though. Something had changed, and it was impossible to tell what that meant for her…and for Damea.

"The magic is right there! Use it and fix this!" *Cassie. It had been such a long journey. The Black Forest. Azgadar. Gurdinfield. And finally, Rhyad. They had been through so much—the fighting, the arguments, the sheer stubbornness that delayed them almost every step of the way.*

The lies Andrea had told.

Cassie had been so angry when the horrible truth had been

revealed—that there was no way to send her home. But that did not matter. Nor did Cassie's anger. That was why Andrea had to cast the barrier—to stop the rocks. Cassie was the key to it all, yes, but she was so much more than that.

The hum of the sphere grew louder and the room began to shake. The odd sensation amplified into a debilitating weakness that spread throughout her body. As she grew weaker, the sphere pulsed more brightly .

"...enchanters are the reason for every *problem in this land!" Her father's angry words. She had never let them go. Perhaps she never would. What would it take? They had found the magic—what else was left for her to do?*

It had been unstable, though. The magic, those rocks—the entrance to the cave, its collapse imminent.

Cassie had been right there. It could have been the end. It would have been.

No. *Not if Andrea could help it.*

Damea would be all right. Her friends would be all right. Cassie...she would be all right, too. She would be safe.

Andrea's heart ached as a scream rang out—not her own—sending wave after wave of nausea through her until she could stand no more and was thrown to her knees. The sphere shook violently—its radiance encompassing the room in a blinding flash of blue light—before finally exploding, and Damea's magic was released in a violent blast that would change the world forever.

* * *

Her eyes opened, the world around her a haze of blurred colors. It took a few seconds of blinking for Andrea of Ata, Royal Enchanter of Gurdinfield, to recognize the spacious bedroom around her.

There was no cave. No sphere. She did not feel weak at all—on the contrary, Andrea felt quite rested. *Just a dream. Again.* The dream was always different in some small, meaningless way, but it was always about Rhyad, where she and her friends had released the magic trapped there and restored it to Damea. The strange part was that most of the dreams were of events that only Cassie and Meredith, her former mentor, had been conscious for. Cassie had explained everything later, but Andrea was always surprised at how vivid her dreams were.

Sitting up, she yawned and attempted to run her fingers through her dark hair, grimacing at the chaotic frizzy mess it had evolved into after a night of tossing and turning. *Without fail.* She looked over at the empty space next to her and sighed. Cassie would no doubt have poked fun at her bird's-nest hair, as she did most mornings when it occurred.

But she's not here. It had been less than a month since Cassie had left with Victor and Roe on an important reconnaissance mission, though to Andrea it seemed longer. As proud as she had been that Cassie joined the Guardians, Andrea knew that even with magic restored, Damea still had its dangers. Bandits, especially bandits hunting for enchanted artifacts—which were still rather valuable considering how rare enchanters still were even after the Restoration—still prowled the roads of Damea day and night, looking for an easy target. Andrea was confident in Cassie's ability to defend herself and trusted Victor and Roe, but she would have been more at ease had Queen Diana just allowed her to accompany them.

She swung her legs over the bed, squinting through the bright streaks of sunlight that peered in through the edges of the deep blue floor-to-ceiling curtains. Andrea shivered when her bare feet came in contact with the wood floor. It was late spring in Gurdinfield, but even so, the early mornings remained chilly. She and Cassie used to have a rug that lay underneath the large bed they shared, but Cassie had spilled hot soup all over it when she had, against Andrea's advice, brought dinner to their room. The rug had been sent downstairs to be cleaned at Diana's request and Andrea had been meaning to check on it since Cassie left on her mission, but…things had gotten busy. *She* had been busy.

Cassie. Andrea often cursed under her breath whenever she caught herself getting lost in the giddy thoughts she associated with her partner—or "girlfriend" as Cassie had made a point of calling herself. Their journey together had taken them from fighting to friends to…more.

"I think I love you." She hadn't remembered saying that until after they had returned to the palace and settled in, but the dormant memory of her last words to Cassie before she lost consciousness did eventually surface. To make matters more complicated, Andrea did not remember Cassie returning the sentiment, assuming she even had. Andrea was certain about one thing—her words had been true. She had never told another person she loved them and she certainly wouldn't have thrown the words out of carelessness or desperation—especially not to

Cassie. *Does she feel the same way? What if we're moving too quickly?* How would she even begin to go about finding out?

The subject was a difficult one to ponder and Andrea had dared not bring it up, in part because she was afraid of what Cassie would say and also because she was not sure what would become of their relationship if Cassie did not feel the same way.

Refusing to let her runaway thoughts and a cold floor impede on her morning routine, Andrea grabbed a brush from the adjacent nightstand and set to working out the tangles in her wavy hair before getting ready for the day. *Shouldn't worry about this now. Maybe I can talk to her when she gets home.* There were other, more important matters anyway. Matters she wished were not on the agenda.

But that could definitely wait until after Cassie returned.

She made a point of drawing the curtains back to let light into the room to help her wake up. Her bedroom was on the second floor of the palace and overlooked the City of Towers, giving Andrea a sweeping view of the winding cobblestone roads that ran from the top of the steep hill upon which the palace was built down to the newly repaired city gates, flanked by the white stone walls and three watchtowers that protected the city. Beyond that she could see nothing but the rolling green hills that eventually stopped at the edge of the Gurdin Woods.

She dressed in her usual dark leggings and a loose white blouse. Diana had offered her an appointment with one of the city's most notable tailors, but Andrea had declined. In her line of work, fire, lightning, and at times messy alchemical ingredients were often involved, so simpler clothing was best. She did make sure to throw on the blue enchanter's robe Diana had made for her—a symbol more than anything, complete with gold trim and the crest of Gurdinfield, a proud lion with three towers behind it, sewn into the right shoulder—before making one last pass at the large mirror near the door.

She had never put too much thought into her day-to-day appearance, but since being appointed Gurdinfield's official source of knowledge on all things magic-related, Andrea found herself double—and sometimes triple—checking herself to make sure she was presentable for an audience with the Queen and any other visitors to the royal court.

She made some last-minute adjustments to her shoulder-length hair, pushing back the more stubborn strands that insisted on falling in front of her hazel eyes, and was pleased to see that the scars she had received from the great battle at the City of Towers months earlier had all but faded from her fair complexion. The deeper ones which ran from just under her eye and down her cheek were there to stay, though.

Andrea shrugged. *At least I still look somewhat "like a badass."* Cassie's words, though Andrea knew she said it to make her feel better, considering how close she had come to not living to tell the tale of how she acquired those scars.

I suppose that's the risk one runs when using a magical barrier to stop a giant ball of fire from destroying a city. She tried to shake off the memory—the soldiers screaming, the nauseating scent of melted metal and burnt bodies—and turned to open the bedroom door. Humming a happy tune from a song that her friend, Kye, had written and performed just the other night, she headed downstairs to the throne room, where she was certain the queen and prince consort would be at this hour.

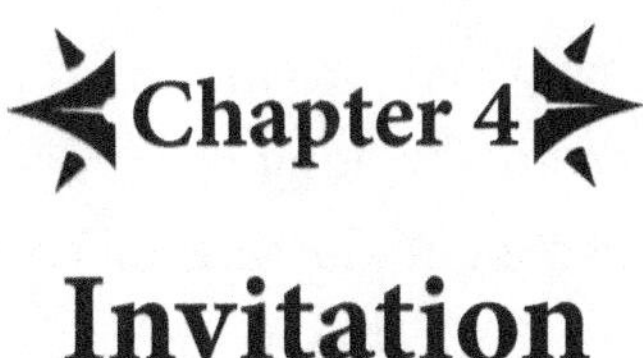

Chapter 4
Invitation

"'...that we resolve this matter. Therefore, I would like to invite you and your council to Azgadar with the prospect of opening up discussions that could help both nations as we adjust to our changing land...'"

Lydia Diana Taylor's stern voice could be heard all the way down the main corridor leading to the throne room, and Andrea could tell right away that the Queen of Gurdinfield was not happy. Diana was never the cheerful type, but it had been sometime since Andrea had heard her friend this upset.

She entered the throne room—a spacious, well-lit hall situated under a tall arch of old wooden rafters and flanked by close to a dozen blue, white, and gold banners embroidered with Gurdinfield's lion crest. Diana sat on her throne, gripping a long piece of parchment in one hand and rubbing her temple with the other. Andrea surmised she must have been out in the training courtyard earlier as Diana and her husband, Jacob, who was standing on her right, were both wearing combat leathers. Diana had been one of the leaders of the Guardians before becoming queen and Andrea was not surprised she still spent the early morning hours keeping her fighting skills sharp.

She *was* surprised, however, to see that standing before the throne were none other than Cassie, Victor, Roe, and...*Elisa? What's she doing here? Where was she?* All four of them appeared weary—no doubt from the long journey—and their clothes were all covered in a light dusting of dirt and grass stains. Victor looked guilty and Roe remained straight-faced and attentive. Cassie had the expression of someone who wanted to be anywhere else, while Elisa just seemed amused by everything that was happening. She knew Elisa's correspondence to Diana had ceased weeks prior, which was why Diana had sent the Guardians to Sadford in the first place. But seeing her friend now standing in the throne room of the City of Towers was not something Andrea expected to wake up to.

"'...and of course, to prevent incidents such as this from occurring in the future I would ask that you cease any and all operations near Legion forts and outposts. It has also come to my attention that there are a number of convicts in Gurdinfield's custody that are wanted for various crimes against the empire. I would also ask that these individuals be returned...'"

Andrea took her place on Diana's left and glanced down at the parchment before catching Cassie's gaze. Cassie flashed her a brief, playful smile that Andrea would have loved to return had she not been afraid of Diana noticing.

"'I look forward to meeting you in person, where I hope we can forge the beginning of a powerful alliance. Sincerely, Her Majesty Ithmeera Cadar, Empress of the Azgadaran Empire.'" Diana let out an exasperated sigh as she bowed her head and let the parchment hang down, her long dark hair falling on both sides of her tanned face. "Would one of you care to explain to me which part of 'reconnaissance mission' was not understood?" She stared at the three Guardians, brown eyes narrowed. Her cold expression and the slight reverberation the acoustics in the throne room gave her voice made them all cringe.

No one spoke. Andrea tried not to appear as uncomfortable as she felt. She really disliked confrontation, especially if it was between her friends.

"Her Majesty asked you a question," Jacob said, his green eyes devoid of their usual humor. He seemed tired, and his shaggy blonde hair was still damp from exercise. Like his wife, he appeared quite displeased with his fighters.

Andrea held her breath, suspense exacerbating the tightness of her throat.

Roe was the first to step forward, hands behind his back. "Apologies, Your Majesty. We reached Sadford as you instructed and were able to ascertain the location of Lady Elisa by questioning one of the Legionnaires off duty."

"That does not explain why half a dozen Legionnaires were disabled, or why this letter was sent to me by the empress herself," Diana said, standing up and holding out the parchment. "For the first time in decades, the kingdom is united and its people have hope. I refuse to let another incident with the empire get in the way of that!"

When Roe did not respond right away, Cassie spoke up. "Diana—"

"'*Your Majesty*,'" Jacob corrected with a harsh glance at her.

Diana's face softened. She took a moment to adjust the

enchanted, multi-colored woven bracelet she wore—a symbol of her marriage to Jacob—before lowering her voice. "No, no. It's fine. We're all friends here." She smiled at Jacob before turning to Cassie. "I'm not angry. I'm just…a bit disappointed is all. This was supposed to be a simple investigation and what happened was...unexpected. But please. Go ahead and explain yourself."

Cassie cringed a bit and Andrea could not help but feel bad for her. "Er, right, sorry," Cassie said. "Look, *I* made the call to get Elisa out of that prison once we found out where the Legion was keeping her."

"Be that as it may, Roe was the commanding officer on this mission—not you," Jacob said.

"And he disagreed with my idea, but I pushed them to do it anyway." Andrea had to struggle to not shake her head. This was not the first time Cassie had gotten into trouble as a Guardian, and Andrea worried that Diana and Jacob's patience would run out eventually. While she was not opposed to the idea of spending more time with Cassie, she knew the training and the missions made Cassie feel helpful—something that had been important to her ever since she had lost her magical abilities.

"I apologize for that, sir," Roe said. "Cassie was very helpful in obtaining Lady Elisa's location, and it made sense at the time to attempt to free her. No trouble from the Legionnaire we questioned, either—in fact, she was quite loose with the information."

Jacob cast a disappointed look at Roe. "You had *Cassie* question the Legionnaire? A new recruit who only began her training months ago? That is a task I would expect her *mentors* to take on."

Roe cleared his throat. "With all due respect, sir, Cassie was far better suited for this particular task than either myself or Victor."

"And why is that?" At Jacob's words, the entire room stared at Roe as the poor man side-eyed Victor for assistance.

Victor chuckled. "Well, for one thing, she was definitely more our friendly Legionnaire's type."

Silence.

"And much better-looking than us as well," he added.

Diana blinked in Cassie's direction. "What sort of questioning…tactics did you employ, Cassie?"

It was Andrea's turn to look at Cassie, who rolled her eyes in frustration while Elisa stifled a snicker. "You have *got* to be kidding me. I asked her about Elisa and she told me where she was. That was it."

"Well, she also asked you to her room," Victor pointed out.

Now all eyes were on Cassie, who shot Victor a dirty look before taking a deep breath. "Irrelevant, and I turned her down. Look, if we had waited any longer, they would have taken Elisa to Azgadar and we all know that we wouldn't have stood a chance at getting her back. Can we all just be happy that no one died and we got Elisa back here safe and sound?"

The room went silent again as everyone waited for Diana's judgement. Finally, a smile graced her face. "We can. Elisa, I am beyond relieved to see you alive and safe. It is wonderful to have you back. I believe we have a lot to discuss over breakfast, if you would join us?"

Elisa gave a short bow. "It would be my honor."

"Wonderful. As for the three of you, this has unfortunately escalated to a level that I can't ignore." Diana exchanged pensive glances with Jacob before turning to the Guardians again. "Roe and Victor, I expect better leadership from the both of you. I trust you'll remember that for future missions."

"Yes, Your Majesty," Roe and Victor replied in unison.

"Please, enough with the 'Your Majesty' nonsense. You two are dismissed. Now, Cassie," Diana began after Victor and Roe bowed and left the room, "I believe it might be in the best interest of both you and the kingdom if we were to focus your tasks on something more suitable to your skills."

Andrea's heart fell as she saw Cassie lose some of the color in her face. Her question came out in a mumble. "Are…are you saying I can't be a Guardian anymore?"

Both Diana and Jacob laughed, making Andrea sigh with relief. "Of course not!" Diana exclaimed. "But we've a trip to Azgadar approaching."

Andrea raised her eyebrows. "Your Majesty? But the letter—"

"Oh, enough with the formalities, Andrea! Do not worry about the letter—I will take care of that. I will brief you when I know more details, but in the meantime know that we will be heading west when the Grandmaster of Gurith's Merchants' Guild departs next week after his visit. Don't worry, this should not affect your upcoming personal trip too much."

"Cassie, you'll be accompanying us and will be filling the role of personal guard," Jacob said.

Andrea tilted her head. Cassie as a bodyguard? For whom?

"Andrea will be your charge," Jacob finished.

Oh. Andrea wasn't sure whether to be elated or concerned. On one hand, this arrangement would no doubt lead to more time with Cassie, which was something Andrea had no issues with whatsoever. On the other, was that even what Cassie wanted? What if their relationship posed a distraction to Cassie being able to do her job? If Cassie made a mistake, would Diana make her leave the Guardians?

She tried to gauge Cassie's thoughts on the matter, but her partner's expression gave little away. "Sure thing. I mean, um—yes, sir," she said. Jacob gave her a reassuring smile and Andrea was relieved when she saw Cassie's shoulders relax a bit.

"Excellent. Now, there's a lot to go over I imagine, Elisa," Diana announced.

"There really is. If you don't mind, I'd like to get cleaned up. It's been a long journey," Elisa said.

Andrea seized the opportunity. "Your Majesty—I mean, Diana," she corrected upon Diana's pointed glare, "might I borrow Cassie for a bit?" She saw Cassie arch her eyebrows at the question.

Diana exchanged amused glances with Elisa before giving Andrea a warm smile. "Of course. We will see you at dinner, then?"

Andrea answered in the affirmative before bowing and met Cassie's puzzled gaze once more. "Please meet me in my laboratory when you're ready, Cassie."

Reunited

Andrea hurried through the palace toward her laboratory—which was actually a study that had, on Queen Diana's order, been converted for the exclusive purpose of enchanting. It was here that Andrea spent most of her time conducting research and experiments in the hope that she might be comfortable enough one day with the state of magic in Damea to recommend the reopening of the Enchanters' Academy, which had been closed for the last twenty years.

With Cassie several paces behind her, Andrea pushed open the heavy double doors and strode into the dark room. The only light came from the dim green glow of the philters on the alchemy table in the far corner, upon which a heaping pile of parchment covered with scribbled writings sat. A small couch and a few chairs were situated on the right wall. Sure, she could pull back the heavy curtains that framed much of the room's walls to brighten things up, but Andrea dared not let in more light and risk ruining the experiment that had taken up most of the month.

When Cassie had nearly caught up, Andrea waved her over. "Come on, now. Hurry up."

Cassie gave her a look. “I’m coming, I’m coming.” She quickened her step as she entered the room, grumbling as Andrea closed the doors. “Okay, I’m here,” she said, looking around. “Nice to see you, too. What the hell was so important that you couldn’t wait five minutes—”

Surprising herself at her own boldness, Andrea grabbed the collar of Cassie’s shirt and pulled her close in a fevered kiss. A surprised squeak escaped Cassie before she wrapped her arms around Andrea in a crushing hold. They stayed that way for a bit, Cassie slowly tracing the embroidery of Andrea’s blouse as Andrea rested her hands on the sides of Cassie’s face, making gentle strokes with the tips of her thumbs. Cassie moved forward, pressing herself against Andrea and deepening the kiss for just a moment before Andrea tilted her head down, breaking their momentum.

They continued to hold each other, their shallow breaths and the steady drips from the alchemy table the only things filling the silence in the room.

Cassie offered a light laugh that sounded almost nervous to Andrea. “Um…hi.” She relaxed her arms, hands coming to rest on Andrea’s hips.

Andrea let her thumb trace over Cassie’s eyebrow and her barely visible forehead scar, keeping her eyes locked with Cassie’s the entire time. “Hello.”

“Miss me?”

“Mm…maybe a little.” She gave Cassie a final kiss before releasing her. “You’re covered in dirt.”

Cassie snorted. “Uh, yeah. That’s a thing that happens when you’re traveling a lot. Especially in dusty places.”

"Such wit," Andrea said, remembering with fondness a time when she hadn't appreciated Cassie's sarcasm nearly as much. She approached the alchemy table. "Speaking of dusty places," she mused as she observed the philters, "what's this about a Legionnaire in Sadford? How did Victor put it—you were 'her type'?" She took a moment to grin teasingly at Cassie before returning her attention to the experiment.

Cassie was unfazed. "You're cute when you're trying to be funny." She faux-yawned. "Might want to leave the humor to the professionals, though—it takes time and dedication that I just don't think you have."

But Andrea would not go down without a fight. "Really now? And are Legionnaires in random taverns suddenly worthy of your time as well, then?" She expected Cassie to get annoyed at her comment—a sign of victory if there ever was one, as Andrea had discovered just how much *fun* it was to get a rise out of Cassie—and was startled when familiar arms snaked around her from behind.

"The only Legionnaire in Sadford worth my time was a pissed-off lady in a jail cell, and even with that one I'm not so sure. Besides, you're not *jealous,* are you?" Cassie said, her lips hovering just next to Andrea's ear. She held her, the occasional nuzzle making its way to Andrea's cheek, as several seconds of silence went by and Andrea sniffed the air, a distinct unwashed odor disrupting her peaceful moment. It was a wonder she had not smelled it earlier. *Just as I was getting comfortable, too.*

She freed herself from Cassie's embrace and took her hands as she faced her. "Why don't you go wash up so that I can finish this? Then we can have breakfast."

Cassie's eyed widened in obvious excitement at the mere mention of food. "Bath can wait. I'm hungry."

Andrea knew she had to level with her. "You smell like a barn, Cassie."

"Whatever. You're mean." She pointed at the alchemy table. "What are you working on, anyway? Another experiment?"

"Oh." Andrea shook her head. "It's just something I started after you left. One moment, just need to get this on heat again," she said, adjusting the flame underneath one of the draughts. "There. Right, so it's just a theory I'm working on. I want to see if I can store magic like this."

A vacant expression crossed Cassie's face as she stared at the setup. "Um…like what? In glass containers?"

"In liquid," Andrea explained. "It's a potion. I still don't really know how releasing the magic in Rhyad affected everything and I want to be prepared in case…" She let herself trail off.

"In case it didn't really work?" Cassie finished solemnly .

Well, I didn't want to put it that *way.* In the days after the Restoration, Andrea had been delighted to be living in a world where the scarcity of magic was no longer an issue. But if the journey had taught her anything, it was to never take things like that for granted. "Exactly. It's more difficult to store than in traditional objects like jewelry or weapons, but it's a bit more potent."

"So, what—you drink it if we run out of magic?"

"That's the idea. I haven't tested it yet and it's most likely very dangerous in its current state."

Cassie hesitated. "Uh, you're not planning on testing it on

yourself, are you?"

Andrea was not sure how to respond, but she could not help but be a little annoyed by the question. Cassie had grown increasingly protective of her ever since the events in Rhyad, and oftentimes Andrea found herself having to remind her that she was entirely capable of doing magic without getting hurt or ill. "Cassie, we've talked about this—"

"Yeah, yeah—I know." Cassie's concerned expression gave way to a guilty smile. "Sorry."

Andrea could only smile back—she knew Cassie meant well and she could tell she was still somewhat shaken by all that had happened during their journey. She grasped Cassie's arm. "It's all right. Just…I'm fine. Releasing the magic in Rhyad worked and we're *here* now."

Cassie bit her lip. "Right. 'Here'. Speaking of being here, I guess that's not going to be the case for much longer. Did I hear right—we're going to Azgadar of all places?"

"You heard right, yes," Andrea said. "Though, I'm not sure how Diana is planning to deal with the fact that both Elisa and I are wanted by the empress."

"'*Wanted'?*" Cassie said with a chuckle. "Ithmeera locked you up and was probably going to torture you for information, and who the hell knows what she'll do to Elisa if she gets her hands on her. I think 'wanted' is a bit of an understatement."

"We'll be fine," Andrea insisted. "The empress wants an alliance now that magic has been restored. Plus…" She pulled Cassie in close. "I have my own personal Guardian now. That has to count for something, right?"

Cassie cleared her throat. "Uh…yeah. Sure. I'm certain

Ithmeera and her giant army will take one look at me and instantly change their minds about you."

Andrea cast her a knowing glance. "You *did* take out quite a few of the empress's soldiers." She immediately regretted her words when she saw how uncomfortable Cassie looked. "I—sorry. I didn't mean to bring up—"

Cassie shrugged. "It's fine, Andrea. You're right. I mean, that's what happened isn't it? Besides, not like I can do that kind of stuff anymore."

"No." Andrea reached up and kissed Cassie on the cheek. "And you shouldn't have to."

Cassie seemed to relax. "Hopefully we won't have to be there long. After all," she said with a teasing smile, "we already have a trip scheduled."

Ugh. "I have no idea what you're talking about."

"Andrea…"

"Did I mention how nice your hair looks this way?" Andrea mused as she let her fingertips graze the shaved sides of Cassie's head.

But Cassie would not be dissuaded. "Ha. Nice try. Come on, they wrote you back, didn't they?"

"I don't see how that's relevant. The letter from them was nothing more than an acknowledgement that they received mine."

"Well, yeah. I mean, you left out pretty much all of the important crap and didn't tell them about us…"

"I told you—it's better if I tell them in person." Andrea sighed. Was Cassie really going to push this matter again?

Cassie blinked. "Andrea, the letter had the royal seal of Gurdinfield on it. You're the royal enchanter now. Why *wouldn't* you want them to know that?"

"We've gone over this already," Andrea exclaimed, not understanding why Cassie had to keep pushing the issue. "It's just—my parents aren't exactly fans of magic. It was *because* of magic that I left."

"You can explain this away however you want, but we're going to Ata when we're all done with this Azgadar nonsense. Assuming Ithmeera doesn't have us all killed, of course," Cassie said.

"Right. Of course." Andrea shifted her weight from one foot to the other. *Should I talk to her now?* Cassie had only just returned—perhaps this was not the best time to bring up her words in Rhyad. *But if not now, then when?*

No. She refused to put this off any longer. Cassie had made it clear—if they were going to be together then there could not be secrets. Not that this was a secret—Andrea *hoped* Cassie felt the same way, but she wanted certainty. "Cassie?"

"Hm? What? Going to tell me I need to bathe again?"

Andrea fumbled with her words. "No, no. Well, yes, I mean you should probably go wash up but, ah…I was wondering if I could talk to you about something." She met Cassie's eyes. "It's important."

Cassie's grin dissipated as she wrapped her arms around Andrea's waist again. "Everything okay?"

"I…" Why did this need to be difficult? *Just* tell *her!* "Back in Rh—"

A low and rather loud rumbling interrupted her.

"Oops." Cassie gave her a sheepish grin and looked down at her stomach. "Hungry. Tell you what—why don't I go get this 'barn' smell off me, as you so *nicely* put it, and then we can eat and you can tell me anything you want."

While she was a bit disappointed, Andrea figured she could probably use the extra time to work on the potions before breakfast. "All right. I'll be here until you're ready, then."

"Deal," Cassie said, moving closer. "I'll come get you once I'm done." She pulled Andrea in and kissed her again—this time with so much enthusiasm that a brief rush of dizziness overcame her when Cassie released her. "I really did miss you."

Grateful the low lighting in the laboratory prevented the heat in her cheeks from being visible, Andrea gave Cassie a gentle push. "I missed you, too. Now, go get cleaned up."

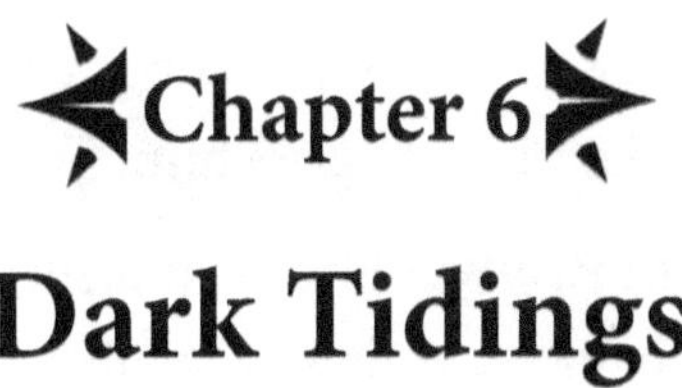

Chapter 6

Dark Tidings

When Diana took her seat in the dining hall, servants were already setting platters of food down on the table. She normally did not make breakfast a large affair, but when the tower watchmen had reported seeing Elisa and the other Guardians approaching earlier in the morning, she had asked the palace chef to prepare food for her Legionnaire friend.

Jacob took a seat on the bench next to her and Alexander sat across from her after he entered the room a short time after she had.

"Good morning, Your Majesty."

"Please, Alexander—I appreciate you taking on the role of royal advisor, but I've had my fill of unnecessary formalities between friends today. It is even less necessary from family," Diana said, annoyed that the day had only just begun and she was already mentally exhausted.

"Long morning?" Alexander smiled at Diana, but the concern in his voice was obvious and his smile only made the wrinkles around his eyes more visible. He had gone grey years ago, but as of late he seemed more tired than Diana remembered seeing him.

She held up the parchment containing Ithmeera Cadar's letter. "The Guardians responsible for *this* returned this morning."

"With extra baggage no less," Jacob joked, not noticing the dismayed head shake his wife gave him.

"'Baggage', Jacob? Really?" Elisa strode into the room wearing a fresh tunic and leggings and gave Jacob and the others a bow of greeting before taking a seat next to Alexander. Her hair had been washed and now fell damp against her face and the back of her neck. "Apologies for keeping you waiting, Your Majesty. Took a while to clean off all that filth."

"No need to apologize, Elisa," Diana said. She murmured a "thank you" to the servants who had brought breakfast and piled food onto her plate. The others followed suit. "As I said earlier, I'm glad to see you safe. We were worried when you stopped writing."

"Understandable." Elisa dug into the piece of ham on her plate.

Jacob leaned forward. "How exactly did the Legion get their hands on you?"

Elisa swallowed the bite of food in her mouth and took a sip of the water that had been placed in front of her. "Right to the point, then."

"We would not pry if it wasn't important, Elisa," Diana said with an apologetic smile. "You know that."

Elisa paused, a grim expression taking over. "I know. Look, my family owns a home in Sadford. Well, *owned*."

Diana understood. "I assume the Legion seized the house?"

"Oh, they certainly did. I broke in anyway," Elisa said with unapologetic confidence. They can keep the furniture. But there were a few...family mementos that I needed to retrieve." She looked away, and Diana thought she heard emotion creep into her friend's voice. "I had to make multiple trips and must have gotten careless on one of my visits."

"So they caught you," Jacob said.

"They had been watching me for a while. No doubt about it. On my third visit they found me out and threw me in a cell."

Alexander folded his hands together. "Nobody's perfect," he said.

"Agreed," Diana added. "You mentioned there was some information you wanted to share with us, Elisa."

"There is. My hope is that it will help the current situation, but I worry there is a larger problem brewing," Elisa said.

Jacob tensed. "A larger problem?"

"First, the information. Apparently, since the Restoration there have been a number of incidents involving enchanters in Azgadar."

"What sort of incidents?" Diana exchanged curious glances with Jacob before returning her attention to Elisa.

"It was just murmurings and rumors at first," Elisa continued. "Things I picked up after being in town and around the Legionnaires. But as it turns out, Prince Marco showed signs of having magical abilities after our friends released the magic." She bit her lip. "Not everyone in Azgadar is pleased with how the empress has handled the return of magic, and there those who are upset with the fact that the heir to the throne is a potential enchanter."

"As strict as the magic regulations were, the empress has never shown ill will toward enchanters. Not to mention Ithmeera has always had the loyalty of her people," Alexander said. "What has changed?"

Elisa met his eyes. "*Everything* has changed." She turned to Diana. "Azgadar has functioned for two centuries with the strictest laws on magic conservation. With magic no longer scarce and morale still shaky from the failed invasion of Gurdinfield, the empire is struggling to adjust."

"If I recall, Ithmeera lifted many of the regulations to make the empire more welcoming toward enchanters," Diana said. "Is that no longer the case?"

"Well, that's the thing. The issue is, well, the enchanters themselves."

"How are *they* an issue?" Diana asked.

Elisa leaned in. "For one thing, we still don't know what caused the magic to gather in Rhyad."

Diana frowned. "Andrea and Cassie told us, though. The device they found had absorbed all the magic, remember?"

"The origin of that device is still unknown," Alexander pointed out. He looked at Elisa. "I believe I understand where you are going with this."

Elisa took another sip. "Precisely. There are still those in the empire that blame enchanters for the loss of magic, even the ones living in the city legally. With the number of potential enchanters on the rise and the laws keeping them from receiving training gone, these people are worried about another

Starving. And," she added, "rumors that you're going to reopen the Enchanters' Academy are only making these people more worried."

Diana sighed. "They think we shall be dragged down into another Starving." She shook her head in disbelief. "But that's… paranoia! Unfounded paranoia!"

"They are fools, then. People fearing what they do not understand," Jacob said, disappointment in his tone. "An enchanter helped save magic and yet it is enchanters who are still looked upon as a threat."

"As upsetting as this is, I can only help the potential enchanters in Gurdinfield," Diana said to Elisa. "You said this information might help the situation with the empress. How?"

"There have been a small but noticeable number of attacks on known and potential enchanters occurring throughout the capital city. Small things," she said, "mostly vandalism, robbery, and the occasional assault. The Legion is beginning to believe it is these people who are behind it—that they are organized and seek to threaten the empress herself if things do not change soon."

Jacob chuckled. "And you heard all this from your prison cell?"

"I told you—I spent some time wandering about town and picking up on conversations. Also," she said with a shrug, "I'm an excellent spy, and bored Legionnaires have a habit of not keeping their mouths shut."

"Explains a lot," Jacob said with a wink.

Elisa raised her eyebrows, unamused. "Your humor has

worsened considerably since I was last here, Your Highness." In the background, Alexander laughed quietly.

Diana could only offer a strained smile as she tried to remain focused on the topic at hand. "What are you suggesting, Elisa?"

"The empress has many things, Your Majesty—an army, land, the loyalty of most of her people—but what she truly needs right now are allies," Elisa said. "Allies who can help her convince the people of the empire that enchanters are not a threat just because magic has returned."

Diana was confused. "How does that help Gurdinfield?" She pointed to the letter on the table. "Obviously, the empress is unhappy with what happened in Sadford. She knows we're harboring you as well as Andrea—possibly even Kye. Gurdinfield is still rebuilding, Elisa. We cannot afford another war."

But Elisa shook her head. "Trust me, Your Majesty. Ithmeera would not have written that letter if she was planning to invade again. I believe Gurdinfield has the upper hand here."

"Empathize with her and the empire's issues," Alexander said. "Use them to get what we need. The Legion's loss here must have taken a serious toll on their morale and the Azgadaran people's confidence in their empress. Don't be afraid to use that to your advantage."

Diana closed her eyes and buried her face in her hands. As relieved as she was that her friend was safe, she would have preferred to build a relationship with the empire at her own pace instead of having her hand forced like this. *Perhaps it will be better this way.* The strands of an idea formed. *Perhaps…*

She looked up at the others, her brown eyes bright and hopeful. "I think I may know a way to secure the alliance with Ithmeera *and* clear everyone's name. Even Kye's."

Elisa and Alexander stared at her in surprise. "What is it, love?" Jacob asked.

The strands wove together with rapid finesse. "I believe Elisa is correct—the letter is nothing more than bravado masking an offer of peace. I propose we do exactly as Ithmeera asks—we go to Azgadar and bring Elisa, Andrea, and Kye before her."

Elisa finished the last of her drink before setting the mug back on the table. "All right. But I assume you have a plan that doesn't involve our necks meeting a Legionnaire's sword?"

Diana placed her hand on Elisa's wrist. "Trust me, my friend. Have I ever led you wrong?"

"Of course not, but these days I try to avoid potential suicide missions if I can."

Jacob laughed and slammed his fist on the table, causing the plates and cutlery to shake as everyone else jumped. "Ha! That's a lie if I've ever heard one!"

"Remind me why you picked this one again, Your Majesty?" Elisa asked Diana with a grin.

Diana feigned a long-suffering sigh. "He has his positive qualities, I suppose," she said while beaming at Jacob.

"With your permission, I can handle the day-to-day duties here while you are away," Alexander offered. "Though I highly advise you to take a group of Guardians with you."

"Agreed," Diana said. "Inform Kye that he will be joining us as well." She turned to Jacob. "I'll leave it to you to pick the

Guardians you want to bring."

Jacob winked. "Only the best. Actually, I suppose they're *all* the best. Hmm," he pondered, stroking his beard, "this might prove difficult."

Diana laughed. "I believe in you. Now, with that out of the way, I believe we have guests arriving from Gurith soon."

"That we do," Alexander confirmed before beginning his brief on what Diana could expect from the long-planned visit of the Grandmaster of Gurith's Merchants' Guild.

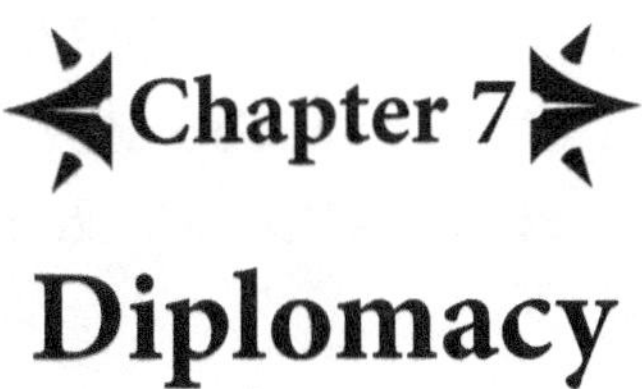

Chapter 7
Diplomacy

"It's too tight!"

"Have you always been this whiny or is this a recent development?" Cassie asked, leaning against the heavy wardrobe she and Andrea shared as she watched Andrea adjust Kye's collar. "You're worse than Andrea."

"I am *not* whiny." Andrea was less than pleased with Cassie's comment, but she was too busy helping Kye to really do anything about it. She looked at the full-body mirror in front of them to observe her work. Kye stood much taller than her despite being a few years younger; the dark dress shirt and suit coat flattered his lanky upper body better than it had a month earlier when Andrea had taken him to a boutique in the city to purchase it. His curly blond hair had finally been cut short, preventing it from falling in front of his light brown eyes as it often had, especially during his performances at the Lion's Den. "There. You look perfect. Now," she said and turned around to face Cassie. "Black or blue?"

"Green."

Andrea shot her an unamused look. "Green is not an option, Cassie. Blue is one of Gurdinfield's colors and black is the only other option." She held up the two choices of robe she had been debating between for the welcome dinner honoring Gurith's diplomats, which would be held later that evening. The Grandmaster of the Merchants' Guild, along with a rather impressive company of bodyguards and associates, had arrived in the City of Towers earlier in the day, where they were greeted at the gates by Alexander. "Now, black or blue?"

"You look nice in green."

This could be interesting. "You're saying I *don't* look nice in black or blue?" she asked in a light voice that held more danger than sweetness.

Cassie frowned. "That's—that's not what I said!"

Kye sniggered. "Someone's in trouble."

"You do know I have a sword now, right?" Cassie threatened, pointing to the sword that hung from her belt. She was already dressed in a brand-new, custom suit of leather armor on top of her dark blue ceremonial Guardian uniform. The pieces were dyed black, the gold and blue sigil of House Taylor adorning the upper-right corner of the chest piece as well as the shoulders. "And don't you have your own room to get ready in?"

Kye put his hands on his hips and thrust out his chest. "I've been working on my barrier and I've nearly got it, so your puny sword will soon be useless!"

Cassie drew her sword enough for the start of the blade to be visible. "Want to test it out now?"

Without hesitating, Kye held out his hands in surrender. "Erm…it's not quite there yet! And Andrea said she'd help me get ready."

"That I did," Andrea said as she ignored their threats and glanced at the robes again. Finally, she let out a frustrated huff and glared at them. "If one of you does not tell me 'black' or 'blue' in the next instant I swear I will set you *both* on fire."

"Blue!" Cassie and Kye both exclaimed at the same time.

Andrea gave a satisfied hum before setting the robes back down on the bed. "I'm going to get ready." She walked over to Cassie and kissed her cheek. Between a rushed breakfast, additional briefings with Diana, and Cassie's mandatory Guardian training, Andrea had not gotten the chance to speak to her partner. She hoped to fix that after dinner. "Wait for me outside?"

Cassie cleared her throat, her visible nervousness and subtle smile all Andrea needed to feel like she had accomplished *something* for the evening, even if the dinner did not go well. "Uh, yeah. I will." She recovered fast. "I mean, I have to follow you everywhere now, right?" she teased.

Andrea laughed. "Maybe not *everywhere*."

Cassie gave herself a final check in the mirror before stepping out of the room, Kye following close behind her. Andrea couldn't hold back a grin upon hearing their exchange before the door closed.

"You two always act like you'll never see each other again whenever you're in a room together," Kye said.

Cassie scoffed. "Don't act like you're not jealous."

* * *

"Grandmaster Balos, may I present Gurdinfield's Royal Enchanter—Andrea of Ata."

Balos was not a large man—indeed, he stood a few heads shorter than Jacob and several of the other Guardians standing behind Diana in the foyer outside the dining hall of the palace. His jet-black hair was straight and neat, framing his dark skin and amber eyes, and pulled back into a short, low ponytail. He was well built, with the gait of someone who had military training, and wore the dark brown and gold-trimmed suit that high-ranking Gurithians often did. His kind smile and calm mannerisms, however, were not really what Andrea envisioned the secretive leader of the Merchants' Guild of Gurith to be like. He extended his hand, bowing deeply.

"An honor, Enchanter Andrea," he offered in an accent that Andrea had only heard once or twice in her travels across Damea. Meredith had never taken her to the Gurith Coast—they had typically shuttled between Gurdinfield and Azgadar during her three-year tutelage—but from her studies Andrea knew it was by far the most diverse region in Damea, with people from all over settling there to take part in the rich economy and its pleasant coastal weather.

She clasped his hand firmly as she bowed her head in return, a custom that mixed both traditional Western Hills and Gurithian greetings. "The honor is mine, Grandmaster, and please, just Andrea is fine."

Balos flashed her another white smile and did not release her hand. "Then you shall call me *just* Balos." He turned to Diana. "Your Majesty, I was not aware your royal enchanter was from

Ata. Beautiful place." His eyes met Andrea's. "Quite a long way from the City of Towers, no?"

"Andrea joined us nearly a year ago. Her knowledge and experience have been a monumental aid in our efforts to rebuild the kingdom," Diana explained, and Andrea struggled not to blush at her words.

"Then I commend Your Majesty for your wise decision to employ such a talented individual." Balos let go of Andrea's hand and gestured with a sweeping wave of his arm to the armed entourage standing behind him. "My attachés from the Guild. We are always looking for strong enchanters to join our ranks." He seemed to realize he had overstepped and bowed again to Diana. "Forgive me, Your Majesty. It was not my intention to offer your enchanter a job. At least, not in front of you!"

Diana laughed, and while Andrea thought the conversation between them was genuine enough, she couldn't help but feel just a bit uncomfortable at the exchange. There were a number of things that made the Gurith Coast attractive—trade, fishing, pleasant weather—but the region was also notorious for hosting some of the seedier elements of Damea. The city of Gurith itself was infamous for its economic inequality, with the elite few of the Merchants' Guild holding most of the wealth. Street gangs ran rampant, maintaining the trade routes for magical items that found their way into the black market of the Azgadaran Empire. They were also known for leading the gladiatorial rings that preyed upon desperate and adrenaline-driven enchanters willing to risk their lives for money and glory in the deadly Shadow Arena tournaments, where they would go head-to-head with other enchanters or even non-magic users like Legionnaire deserters or wild animals.

Andrea did her best to keep her smile on as she tried, without being too obvious, to find Cassie in the formation of Guardians behind Diana. Jacob and Alexander had taken their places in front of the fighters, who all stood at attention beside their queen. She spotted Cassie behind Roe and Victor, but like the other two, Cassie was staring straight ahead and Andrea could not make eye contact. *Probably for the best, anyway.* She did not want to get Cassie in any more trouble. Despite the teasing between them, Andrea was quite proud of how well Cassie had acclimated to her role as a Guardian. Jacob praised her performance in training often, and Andrea knew there was no one she'd rather have protecting her.

Except maybe Elisa, since she can probably kill a man with a table fork and one hand behind her back…or just by giving them a dirty look.

Dinner was announced and all the attendees moved through heavy wooden double doors into the dining hall. A long table with benches and place settings had been arranged for tonight's meal, with Diana, Jacob, Alexander, and Andrea sitting in the middle section across from Balos and his top diplomats. The Guardians took their posts behind the royal family, where they would stand for the entirety of the meal. It was an old tradition Diana's father, Caleb, had practiced, and Alexander had advised Diana to do the same. At the end of the room, in front of a large blue and white banner emblazoned with Gurdinfield's Great Lion, hanging down from the rafters stood Kye, lute in hand, performing the first of many songs.

"That looks good," Cassie whispered behind Andrea once

the palace servants set the plates containing the main course, a cut of venison with sliced potatoes, down in front of the guests.

She cut herself a piece of meat and found it cooked and seasoned to perfection. "It is," she whispered back. The wine was good as well but she knew better than to tell that to Cassie, who refused to try anything else since she had declared that foul Fimen's Fire her alcoholic drink of choice.

"I'm going to have to get me some later."

"This is exquisite, Your Majesty!" Balos proclaimed before shoving another bite of steak in his mouth. "Trust me, we know our fish in Gurith but meat like this is rare in the west."

"We will have to do something about that, then," Diana said, and Andrea noted Alexander's nod of approval a few seats down.

Balos dabbed at the corners of his mouth with his napkin. "Ah, yes, the trade routes. We shall have plenty of time to go over how exactly we can reestablish those." He gestured to the Gurdinfielders . "Of course, we would be grateful for the pleasure of hosting Your Majesty in our humble city, should you wish to inspect the routes and our industries for yourself."

Diana seemed excited at the prospect. "We would very much appreciate that, Grandmaster."

Andrea remained quiet, looking back and forth between Diana and Balos. Seeds of worry were planted in her mind at the idea of visiting Gurith. *I wonder which routes he's referring to—the legal or illegal ones.* She was curious as to just how Balos and the rest of the Guild made their money. Back in the Black Forest, it was rare for Meredith to discuss anything other than enchanting, but her tone was always lined with disgust whenever Gurith was brought up.

Dinner continued into the evening as the guests finished off the sixth and final course and Kye ran out of songs to sing, switching over instead to instrumental strumming to fill the hall. Balos finally excused himself and his diplomats and Diana offered to have the Gurithians shown to their rooms, with the promise of discussing the details of their trade alliance in the morning.

"That was...*exhausting*," Diana concluded once their guests had retired for the evening. Jacob had dismissed the Guardians and Kye as well so they could eat.

"You did well," Alexander said. "Tomorrow will be more difficult. Balos will try to get the best deal possible and he will use all of his charm and wit to accomplish that."

Jacob slapped Alexander on the back and laughed. "Ah, those tricks don't work on Diana. Trust me, I've tried."

"Such an attempt would require actually having charm and wit, Your Highness." Elisa finally emerged from wherever it was she had been hiding all evening and went to stand next to Diana. "They've all gone to bed," she reported. "I was worried I'd have to round them up—they kept admiring the architecture. By the way, his second-in-command snores like one of those magic-powered plows they started using in the fields last week. I could hear him through the door!"

Andrea giggled. "We had one of those on my family's farm. I never did get to see it work," she added with a half-shrug.

"Perhaps you will when you return home, Andrea," Diana

said. She yawned. “I am tired beyond words.” She linked her arm with Jacob’s and looked up at him. “Sleep?”

“Right there with you, love,” Jacob replied before addressing the others. “Good night, all.”

Andrea also said her good nights and headed back to her quarters with the balcony in mind. After so many hours sitting in the warm, stuffy dining hall, she found herself in desperate need of fresh air.

I still need to talk to Cassie. She pondered how she might bring up the topic as she passed her laboratory on the way to the stairs leading to the second floor where their bedroom was. Should she keep it casual? Cassie usually didn’t like formal declarations, but Andrea did not want to offend her by dismissing it as “not a big deal,” as Cassie would say.

She regretted consuming so much bread as she climbed the final step and walked the last few lengths down the hallway before finally reaching her room. An orange light flickered from underneath the door, indicating Cassie was already in there.

She took a deep breath and turned the doorknob. *Here we go.*

The breeze from the balcony cooled her skin immediately, a welcome change from the dining hall. The glass doors leading outside had been opened, the sheer curtains swaying in front of them.

A small lantern, its candle burning low, sat on the bedside table next to Cassie’s side of the bed, where Cassie herself was sprawled out on her back, still in her uniform, fast asleep. Her sword and armor were scattered on the floor and across a nearby chair.

Andrea smiled. After traveling, training, and working the ceremonial guard shift, Cassie must have been exhausted. *Suppose we'll just have to talk later.*

She changed out of her formal wear and climbed onto the bed before draping a light throw blanket over them both. Cassie stirred, but to Andrea's relief she did not wake.

Moving closer, she wrapped her arm around Cassie's middle and nestled her head on her shoulder, grateful that they were together again after so many nights of sleeping alone.

She closed her eyes. "I love you," she whispered, as Cassie's rhythmic breathing brought her closer to sleep.

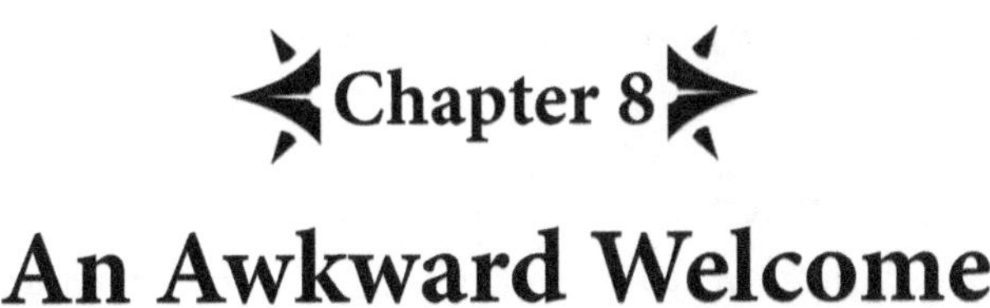

Chapter 8

An Awkward Welcome

Azgadar, Azgadaran Empire

A light, warm wind came in through the open window and ruffled the pages of the short stack of parchment that lay on Ithmeera Cadar's oak desk in her study. Most Azgadarans would have been grateful for the respite from the heat wave the region was experiencing, no matter how small.

But the Empress of the Azgadaran Empire could not have cared less, for as she buried her face in her hands, her long dark curls spilling over her face and onto the desk, she could only guess at just what else could possibly go wrong that day. Preparing for the Queen of Gurdinfield to arrive for what would probably be very uncomfortable negotiations, yet *another* assault on an enchanter in the city followed by heated arguments in the streets between people who supported her new, relaxed laws on magic users and those who were angry at her for lifting the centuries-old restrictions. And now *this*—an aspiring royal enchanter had been injured in an accident during one of the daily lessons held in the palace.

"Your Majesty?" Tobias tried again.

Ithmeera looked up at him. A frail, aging man, Master Tobias had been her late father Nardos' choice for head royal enchanter after his research on magic helped the empire sustain its farming infrastructure for another two decades before the Restoration.

"Your written report says the incident occurred three days ago. It took *three days* to report this accident to me?" she demanded. It was not an accusation but simple fact-gathering. She needed to make sure she knew everything before deciding what to do next.

Tobias dipped his head, the sheen from the midday Azgadaran sun visible on his balding pate. "That is correct, Your Majesty. We—*I* was seeing to my student's recovery. As a result, the report was delayed. My deepest apologies."

Ithmeera bit her lip and folded her hands atop the desk. "I see. And how is your student doing?"

"Better, Your Majesty," Tobias said with a slight smile. "The burn on Luca's arm should heal just fine. I am sure he will be honored you asked." He rolled his shoulders and put his hands behind his back. "What would you have me do?"

What, indeed? Fix all of the empire's problems, perhaps? "Thank you for bringing this to my attention. I see no reason not to continue the lessons." She restacked the papers and set them down again. "Accidents happen. Please enforce caution with the students, Master Tobias," she said. "Magic may have returned, but we must remain vigilant of its dangers and unpredictability. *Especially* with our students."

Tobias bowed. "As you wish, Your Majesty. Thank you. I shall—"

"Mother!" A boy of no more than seven with a mop of curly brown hair and the same dark olive skin as his mother ran through the open doors of the study and past Master Tobias. "Come and see what I can do with my new sword!" He gave the short blade in his hand a few clumsy swings.

Despite the urge to chastise him for bursting into her meeting, as she had reminded him on several occasions not to do, Ithmeera couldn't help smiling widely at Marco. She offered Tobias an apologetic look. "He has a new sword, I'm afraid. Petra gave it to him for his birthday."

Tobias chuckled. "Ah, lovely! I shall take my leave then if that is all right with you, Your Majesty." He gestured at Marco, whose large light brown eyes were eager as he awaited his mother's attention. "Would you prefer I cancel his lessons today, given the—"

"No, no—of course not," Ithmeera said, beaming at her son. "We do not shy away from challenges." She looked at Tobias again. "Thank you, Master Tobias. I suspect there won't be any fireball casting in tonight's lesson?"

Tobias shook his head. "Not at all. Thank you for your time today, Your Majesty." He bowed. "Good afternoon."

Once he had left, Ithmeera pushed her chair back and stood up. She smoothed out her long, sleeveless dark green dress before turning back to Marco. "Is Petra getting things ready for our guests?"

Marco seemed a little disappointed. "She said I wasn't allowed to duel with the Legionnaires."

Ithmeera laughed and knelt before him, amazed at just how much he grew to resemble his father, Philip, with each passing day. "I'm afraid she's right, my dear. The Legionnaires must also prepare for when the Queen of Gurdinfield arrives."

Marco wrinkled his nose. "Uncle Alden says that we shouldn't have the Gurdinfielders here because they can't read!"

Ithmeera rolled her eyes. *Of course Alden would say that. The man has no filter.* Her uncle had been instrumental in advising her on various diplomatic matters over the years, but after the Legion's defeat in the empire's failed annexation attempt of Gurdinfield and the tragic death of its general and her brother, Erik, Ithmeera had asked Alden to resign from his official advisory duties. Despite his elitist attitude toward the other Damean nations, Alden was still family and his decades of experience came in handy from time to time. "He said this to you?"

"No," Marco admitted. "I heard him say it to Councilor Olaro this morning."

"Well, your uncle is quite wrong there." She made a mental note to tell Alden to refrain from such talk in front of Marco and patted her son's shoulder before standing up. "Queen Lydia can read just fine. I hope to become friends with her actually." She smiled again when Marco nodded in understanding. "Come," she said, leading him out of the study with a gentle hand on his back. "Let's go so you can show me your sword moves before it's time for your lessons."

* * *

Diana and Jacob left for the city of Azgadar not long after

the Grandmaster's departure along with Elisa, Andrea, Kye, and a score of handpicked Guardians. All were clad in traveling gear and armor and all were on horseback, much to Cassie's displeasure. She chose to ride with Andrea again, and Andrea was actually impressed by how little Cassie complained about that aspect of the trip. *Everything else, however...*

"I hate the sun."

Andrea was about to reply, but Elisa jumped on Cassie's comment first. "I hate the sound of you complaining, but we all have our burdens to carry on this journey."

"Aw, thanks, Elisa," Cassie said. "I missed you, too."

"Sorry, Elisa, but I think I'm with Cassie on this one," Diana said from the front of the caravan. "The heat is rather unpleasant today."

"Ha!" Cassie stuck her tongue out at Elisa, making Kye snort with laughter. "I win."

"Mm, yes. Well done," Elisa said with a curt nod. Then, in a lower voice to Andrea. "You've found a winner, Andrea. Might as well get the bracelet made now."

Andrea opted not to reply to this particular jest and cleared her throat. "Right. I think I see our destination." She pointed straight ahead.

From atop his horse, Jacob peered out at the distance. "Almost there, friends! Behold! The most uptight place in Damea!" Underneath the bright blue, cloudless skies of the Azgadaran Empire lay the capital city of Azgadar. Great walls of clay and tan stone shielded the city against attacks from any army foolish enough to try to invade it. The spire shot up beyond the top of the wall—the tallest artificial structure in Damea and home of the ruling family: the Cadars, who had been in power for just over two hundred years.

Cassie laughed and tapped Andrea on the shoulder from behind. "Hey! We might get to stay in your favorite dungeon!"

"If Ithmeera has her way, we probably all will," Elisa said, her tone almost as dry as the arid terrain they traveled across.

Kye arched his eyebrows and Andrea pitied him as he actually did look a tad worried. "I hope not. I thought my days of running away from Legionnaires were over."

"Nonsense!" Diana attempted to ease the group's stress about that particular issue for what must have been the fifth time that day. "Trust me—the plan will work."

"Of course we trust you, Your Majesty," Andrea said hurriedly. "Cassie was just joking."

"I was?" Cassie asked. "Hey!" she exclaimed through gritted teeth after Andrea nudged her in the ribs.

Andrea looked back and shot her the sweetest smile she could muster. "Yes, you were."

"Ah. Yeah, totally joking." Cassie released her loose hold on Andrea's waist to stretch her arms out. "Are we really going to be here for a few *weeks?*"

"Azgadar and Gurdinfield have been without a proper diplomatic relationship for twenty years. Renegotiating trade and other matters could take a while," Diana explained. "However, I believe you and Andrea will be leaving us after a few days to go to Ata."

"Right!" Cassie snapped her fingers. Andrea let out a quiet

groan. At this point she couldn't decide which she'd rather endure—the heat of the Azgadaran sun or having to explain to her parents everything that had happened to her.

"Weird," Cassie mused. "By this point in the trip we should have been attacked by some magical rock monster or an entire army or just your everyday crazy person. But we haven't."

"That," Andrea said, struggling to convince herself of Diana's plan as Azgadar grew closer, "doesn't actually happen on *normal* trips."

* * *

The ancient stone steps leading up to the grand main entrance of the palace were impressive on their own. Although the grey rock of each was sprinkled with countless chips and cracks, they held the stories of generations of rulers and their legacies to the empire.

The entrance itself was massive, taller than any doorway Andrea had seen in the City of Towers. She recalled the palace being imposing but between rushing around town with Meredith whenever they visited and sneaking in under the cover of darkness and deception for the Grand Ball, she'd never really had the chance to take in the sheer scale of the architecture and construction of the building. Over five hundred years old, the palace consisted of a spire that overlooked the entire city and smaller towers capped by ornate domes.

Blood-red and gold banners embroidered with the familiar double swords and shield of the Legion hung down from the walls and over the perfect formation of Legionnaires—all armed to the teeth—who stood at the top of the steps to greet the Gurdinfielders.

Andrea shivered as she recalled the last time she was here. If Ithmeera was trying to intimidate them, she was off to a good start.

Diana didn't seem fazed, however. She dismounted her horse and, with Jacob and Elisa at her sides, held her head high as she approached a Legionnaire boasting more decorations on his armor than the rest who appeared to be the commander of the guard. Andrea followed close with Cassie on her right. Kye was flanked by Victor and Roe and the rest of the Guardians stood at attention behind them. For the first since arriving in Azgadar, Andrea noticed the long, sheathed blade Elisa had strapped to her back in addition to the two daggers she typically wielded which hung from her belt.

"Azgadar welcomes you, Queen Lydia," the burly commander said as he bowed before Diana. He appeared to be around Elisa's age and his black hair was cropped short, his small, pale grey eyes standing out against his dark, clean-shaven complexion. A long sword with a gold hilt hung at his side. "I am General Veraun, commanding officer of the Azgadaran Legion. Her Majesty is waiting inside for you." When he noticed Elisa, who shot him a look of pure disgust, his hand shot to his sword . Both the Guardians and the Legionnaires mirrored his action. The two small armies in front of the palace were at a standstill, each side waiting for an order to attack.

"This woman is a known deserter, a murderer, and a traitor to the empire," Veraun spat. "I have been ordered to take her into custody by the empress herself."

Adrenaline fueled Andrea's thoughts. She fought to keep her fear at bay in order to plan what spell she should cast should the worst occur. A barrier was the top candidate, but she wasn't sure just how long she could keep one up for or what its reach could be. She glanced at Cassie who, like the other Guardians, had her hand on her weapon. Her blue eyes were narrowed and her expression was cold and determined as beads of sweat ran down from her temple.

Diana stepped forward while Jacob hovered next to her, his menacing scowl directed at Veraun. Andrea was amazed at how calm Diana was considering the circumstances. "General, we have come at the invitation of the empress. I don't know what kind of crimes my intelligence advisor has committed and to be frank, it is of no concern to me," she said. "Surely Her Majesty has protections she guarantees her potential allies when they visit...as well as their staff?"

Andrea held her breath as Veraun's face twitched before he withdrew his hand and signaled to his soldiers to do the same. "Of course," he said in a tone so strained, Andrea was certain he'd implode on the spot from anger alone. "If you will follow me, I will take you to the empress." He turned on his heel just as Jacob gave the signal for the Guardians to ease off their weapons as well. The entire perimeter of the palace entrance seemed to let out a collective sigh of relief as Diana and the Gurdinfielders followed General Veraun into the palace.

"Whoa." Cassie leaned in and spoke in a voice only Andrea could hear as they passed through the doors. "Elisa sure pissed *someone* off. Didn't she kill the last general?"

"Yes," she said. Remembering she and Elisa were not the only wanted fugitives there, Andrea glanced over at Kye, who seemed about as terrified as she would have expected given the turn of events. She thought she spotted something else beneath his frightened expression—almost as though he had seen or understood something that had been puzzling him.

She tried not to panic too much as they made their way into the enormous throne room and the seat of the Azgadaran Empire, reminding herself she was with friends. *And a small army.* Things would be different this time—at least, she hoped they would.

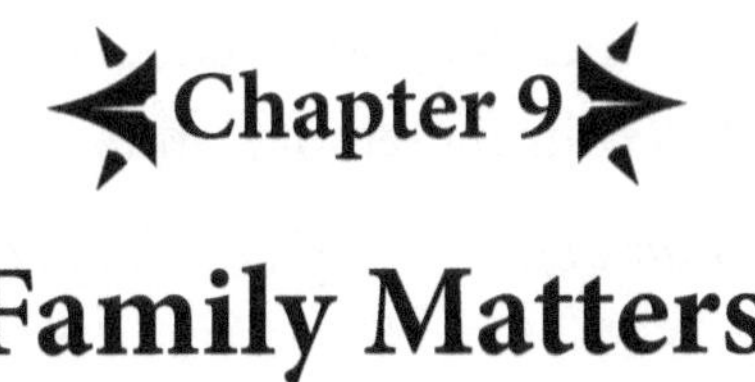

Chapter 9
Family Matters

“Queen Lydia. It is an honor to meet you at last.” The dark red sea of Ithmeera Cadar’s gown rippled over the white marble steps as she stepped down from the landing upon which her throne sat. Andrea could only watch in awe, remembering the paralyzing effect Ithmeera had on people when she entered a room. Her dark hair was pinned back, not unlike how Andrea recalled her wearing it for the Grand Ball. Even the deep green of her eyes shone with so much intensity that Andrea found herself looking away when the empress glanced in her direction. How someone could be so beautiful and so terrifying at the same time was a mystery Andrea was almost afraid to solve.

The fact that they were also surrounded by what appeared to be half the Legion (but was probably less) didn’t soothe her fear. The dozens of banners with the empire’s imposing insignia—a thinly veiled message to any who would dare threaten the security of Azgadar—as well as the flags of what Andrea assumed to be the smaller cities of the empire hung from the high walls and did little to ease her nerves.

She bowed alongside Diana and the others before rising

again on Ithmeera's command.

When Diana spoke, her voice was somehow as calm as it had been during their tense encounter with General Veraun. "The honor is ours, Your Majesty. Thank you for your gracious invitation to visit to your incredible land."

Did she write that before we left, or did Alexander assist her, I wonder?

Ithmeera's eyes went wide when she noticed Elisa and Andrea, but for only for a brief moment. She returned her gaze to Diana and gave her one of her dazzling smiles. "Of course, though if I may speak freely, it appears you employ some interesting individuals."

Andrea held her breath but Diana held her ground. "My advisors hail from all corners of Damea, Your Majesty. I value their experience and their skills."

Ithmeera laughed, startling Andrea and most of the room. "I will be blunt—you employ *criminals,* Queen Lydia. I have asked you here with the hope that we might come to an agreement regarding the reestablishment of diplomatic relations between our nations. As I stated in my letter to you, I am more than willing to forgive the crimes committed by your Guardians in their theft of the empire's prisoners." She gestured to Elisa, Kye, and Andrea. "Yet you bring not only the most wanted woman in Azgadar, but also a murderer and a rogue enchanter into my court."

Andrea felt the color draining from her face. She was certain from the mounting tension in the throne room that a fight was about to break out between the Legion and the Guardians.

But Diana maintained her composure. When she spoke, her voice swelled in strength so that she could be heard by everyone in the room. "Perhaps I was not clear enough in my written answer, Your Majesty," she said, with a firmness that grew with every word. "Your Legion invaded my country and destroyed part of my capital city. Your general threatened the security of our sovereign nation." She took a single step toward Ithmeera, whose smile had vanished. Hands hovered over quivers and swords on all sides of the room.

"Countless men and women loyal to Gurdinfield will never return home to their families simply because your empire wanted more magic," Diana continued. She stared Ithmeera in the eye. "But now that the Restoration has occurred, *I* am willing to forgive the crimes *your* people committed against mine." She stepped back. "I offer you a full alliance, with the added condition that the people in my company are granted full pardons for any past transgressions they've committed."

The room went quiet as both monarchs faced each other with looks that could kill. Andrea waited, knowing the chances of her needing to shield her companions for a battle went up with every anxious second that passed.

It was Ithmeera who gave in first. A chuckle passed her lips as she relaxed, and every Legionnaire in the room relaxed with her. "I agree to your terms, Queen Lydia," she said with a deep nod, her untouchable confidence returning. "I will have my council draw up the paperwork that we shall go over during the next few weeks. You and your Guardians are welcome to stay for as long as you like, as are your...advisors." She cast Elisa an emotionless glance. Andrea was stunned when Elisa averted her eyes.

"I would also like to invite you and your people to join me in a celebration tomorrow night. We are eager to show you our wonderful customs as well as our rich culture," Ithmeera continued. "But I do have one minor request."

Diana smiled, not at all hiding her satisfaction at winning this dispute. "Of course."

Ithmeera's eyes were on Elisa. "With your permission, I would like to speak to my former guard in private. There are… unresolved personal matters between us." She turned back to Diana. "You have my word she will not come to any harm."

"That is up to Elisa." Diana gave Elisa an apprehensive look, but Elisa's subtle nod provided the answer Ithmeera needed.

"Thank you," she said. "I have other matters I must attend to, but my servants will show all of you to your rooms. There are many to choose from, so feel free to pick whichever you prefer." She turned to General Veraun. "General, please have Elisa brought to my study." Then, to the Gurdinfielders, "I wish you all a pleasant afternoon."

* * *

Elisa let out a long sigh as she followed General Veraun away from the rest of the audience. She was not looking forward to this. In fact, this hadn't been her plan at all. Bringing Erik's sword to Ithmeera was supposed to be simple. Any Legionnaire could have taken it from her and brought it to the empress and

Elisa wouldn't have needed to worry about a thing.

Of course, then I would be living out the rest of my days in a jail cell, provided Ithmeera decided not to have me hung in the middle of the marketplace for all to see.

They made their way down a long empty corridor toward the study in silence, their boots clicking on the polished floors. The general must have heard her sigh because he let out an audible snarl. Elisa almost took pleasure in seeing how angry he was at the entire situation. "What? Not happy to see me, Ben?" she asked.

Ben Veraun clenched his jaw. "You murdered my best friend. You should be dead."

"Say what you will, Ben. The only reason we are here is so that you can take me to Ithmeera's study and leave us alone like a good Legionnaire. Have to maintain your honor and all."

His words came out in a bitter sneer. "Ah, yes, honor. Something you would know absolutely nothing about." He grabbed her arm, stopping her in the middle of the corridor. "And it's 'Her Majesty'. You are not to address the empress in any other way. *Her* word is the only thing stopping me from running my blade through you."

Elisa jerked her arm away. "Get your filthy hands off me," she snapped. "My business with the empress is none of your affair. Get that through your very empty head and perhaps we can make it through the rest of the day without killing each other."

"Hah!" he scoffed as they resumed. "You hiding behind that backwater pretender you call a queen does not make you a threat, Elisa—"

Before anyone could react, Elisa threw Ben hard against a stone pillar, her dagger flashing slight movement away from cutting into his throat.

"Go ahead and test me, Ben." She pushed the flat side of the blade into his skin.

Ben craned his neck back in a futile effort to avoid the dagger. "You wouldn't *dare*."

More pressure. "You know I will do it. I have nothing to lose."

"That's enough!"

Elisa turned her head just enough to see Ithmeera approaching in brisk strides, her lady-in-waiting, Petra—a petite young woman with large brown eyes and short blonde hair—trailing just behind. She hailed from a village in the northern part of the empire and had served Ithmeera since before Marco's birth. Elisa had always liked her and had to stop herself from saying hello, instead giving Ben a final shove before she withdrew her dagger.

Ben glowered at her, but Ithmeera didn't seem *too* upset, at least not that Elisa could see. "Fools, both of you. I leave you alone for a few minutes and you're already trying to kill each other. General," she said, "I will take it from here. Thank you."

Furious, Ben rubbed his throat before giving a very stiff bow to Ithmeera. "As you wish, Your Majesty," he said and walked away, his steps heavy with anger.

Once he had gone, Ithmeera spoke. "Petra, would you take Marco to his lesson with Master Tobias? I may be delayed."

"Right away, Your Majesty," Petra replied, meeting Elisa's eyes as she bowed to Ithmeera before she, too, departed, leaving

Elisa alone with Ithmeera.

Ithmeera wasted no time. She pushed past Elisa, refusing to look her in the eye. "The study is right over here."

"I know where it is." She knew she probably shouldn't be testing Ithmeera but after getting caught threatening Ben she really just didn't care anymore. She was here to protect Diana and deliver the sword. All of these theatrics were unnecessary.

Ithmeera rolled her eyes. "Good. Then you can go first."

"Let us make one thing clear," Ithmeera announced when they entered the study, and went to stand behind her desk. "I have refrained from throwing you in prison to rot because an alliance with Gurdinfield is more important than dealing with your thuggish antics." She grabbed some papers sitting on the desk and opened a drawer to her left to file them away.

"I am so grateful."

Ithmeera slammed the drawer shut, making Elisa jump. "You should be!" she yelled. "You cannot just stand there and tell me you feel *nothing* for the murder of my brother."

Elisa swallowed. "I never said I felt nothing."

But Ithmeera was already enraged. "Leaving Azgadar without so much as a letter, stealing my journal, plotting against me—if it was your wish to see me dead, Elisa, why did you leave?" She folded her arms over her chest and moved back around the desk until she stood toe-to-toe with Elisa. "More importantly, why did you come back? To gloat? To see how broken I would be over Erik's death? Or just to test my patience?"

Elisa found herself staring down at the rug on the floor. Despite the inaccuracies in Ithmeera's words, she couldn't bring herself to counter them.

"*Answer* me, Elisa," Ithmeera said, her tone colder than Elisa had ever heard it before. "That's an order."

Elisa took a deep breath. Her heart was pounding; she knew she shouldn't be this nervous, and she shouldn't care what Ithmeera thought. *She'll believe what she wants—what's the point?* She was tired of fighting everyone who refused to believe her. "What is it you want to hear, Your Majesty?" she asked, growing more tired with each passing second of the conversation.

Ithmeera's expression softened. She stepped away, returning to her desk where she sat down. "I just want the truth, Elisa."

Elisa shook her head. "Erik and Be—General Veraun told you what happened. I do not know what else I could possibly add that would satisfy you."

Ithmeera raised her eyebrows. "They told me what happened, yes. But they did not tell me everything."

"I don't understand."

The coldness in Ithmeera's voice gave way to sadness . "Erik was my brother and I loved him. I will always love him. His death was a terr—a terrible event that I will never forget. But… even he had his flaws." She leaned forward in her chair. "Your father. Why didn't you stay to bury him, Elisa?"

Elisa didn't know how to respond. *Does she believe Erik's lie?* "I…was not exactly in a position to, given the circumstances."

"Well, *I* buried his ashes," Ithmeera said. "I know it's not tradition here but it's what your mother would have wanted. That is the Gurdinfielder way, yes?"

It took Elisa a moment to process what Ithmeera had said. "You...you buried him?"

"You left the city before I could have a single word with you about what happened. As for your father..." Ithmeera sighed. "He was Marco's grandfather—of course I buried him. We took the ashes to Sadford."

Tears pricked at Elisa's eyes. The image of her father's shocked expression as Erik ran him through with his sword would forever be burned into her memory. But she had not expected this from Ithmeera. She could feel the icy core of indifference she had carried within her for so long melting away, leaving guilt behind. Elisa blinked, pushing the tears back, and met Ithmeera's gaze again. "Thank you."

"You still have yet to tell me why, Elisa. Why didn't you tell me he was ill? You could have come to me. Instead I received a report that you had been *conspiring* against me?" Ithmeera pursed her lips. "What was I supposed to think? You were gone!"

Elisa looked up at the ceiling. She didn't understand what Ithmeera wanted—why she wanted to talk about this instead of waving her hand, making her judgement, and sending Elisa away like she would any other lawbreaker. *She probably wouldn't be talking to any other lawbreaker in her study like this.*

She couldn't wait for this conversation to end. "I've brought Erik's sword." She reached behind and removed the sheathed sword from over her shoulder before setting it on the desk in front of Ithmeera. "And I'm returning this as well," she said, procuring a thick, dusty book from her pack and placing it next to the sword.

Ithmeera's lower lip quivered, her mouth partly open in shock. "I—I was certain these were lost."

"Well, they weren't," Elisa said brusquely.

"This..." Ithmeera looked up. Her eyes were watery. "I—I need to be alone." She cleared her throat and waved her hand. "Go...go to your queen, Elisa. I will see you tomorrow night."

It was not so much the dismissiveness of Ithmeera's tone that stung Elisa as she gave a final bow and left the study, but the words themselves. *"Your queen"*—how she hated Ithmeera's uncanny ability to tear her apart from the inside with two simple words. *She's the ruler of the most powerful country in Damea—of course she has a way with words.*

The memories of better times with Ithmeera were there. Elisa could recall dozens of times when the two had shared secrets with each other, carried out scandalous pranks and enjoyed inside jokes throughout formal dinners, and even the simplest of days when they would take long walks in the palace garden together, admiring the roses while Marco ran around with a toy sword, declaring war on every plant in the vicinity.

But no more. It was more than the marriage between Philip and Ithmeera that had bound Elisa to her sister-in-law. Ithmeera was her charge and she'd sworn an oath to protect her. She thought she had broken the oath when she ran away to Gurdinfield, but she was wrong. Ithmeera had in two words dismantled that oath—their bond.

Ignoring the stares of the guards and servants she passed in the hallway on her way to find her companions, Elisa tried with all her might to push down the crushing sensation of failure to her father, her empress, and her country.

But she failed.

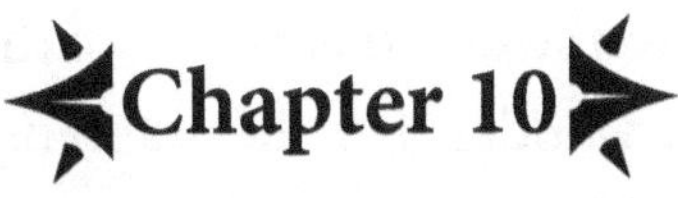

Chapter 10

Preparations

Cassie groaned as she spit out more dirt than was probably healthy to inhale and pushed herself up. *Whose stupid idea was it to have so much* dirt *here?* The training courtyards in the City of Towers had far more grass, which in this situation would not have been *too* much better, but anything was better than eating dirt three times in a row.

It had been a grueling morning, and the sweltering heat wasn't helping. They had only been in Azgadar for little over a day and Cassie was already over the weather.

"That was the sorriest excuse for a block I've seen all day," Jacob barked at her as she picked up her sword and faced him. "Now, *again.*"

Cassie wiped her brow. "Seriously? We've done this a million times already." She knew her whining wouldn't get her very far with Jacob—it never did—but it really did seem like they had been repeating the same drill all morning. Not to mention it was approaching lunchtime and she was *starving.*

Jacob was not convinced. "Ha! Were that true we wouldn't be having this conversation, because you'd actually be *blocking* my attacks instead of welcoming them with open arms." He sheathed his sword. “Fine, fine. Go get some water. We’ll give it another go before we break.”

Cassie didn’t have to be told twice. Dropping the sword again, she jogged to the one shady spot of the courtyard where her gear sat on a wooden bench, grabbing her canteen and taking a long drink before pouring some water over her head to cool off.

“Getting ready for the ball already, Cass?” Victor shouted across the yard as he and Roe paused their own sparring. “There’s training to be done, you know!”

Ha. Cassie pretended to be in thought. “Well, I mean, my date would prefer I don’t smell like dirt and sweat tonight. Yours would probably agree.” She paused and gave Victor a wide grin. “Oh, wait. That’s right! You don’t *have* a date!”

Roe rolled his shoulders back and cracked his neck while Victor let out a fake sob. “So true,” he wailed. “I’m afraid I’ve found no one who thought me worthy enough to be in their company this evening!”

Roe clapped a beefy hand on Victor’s shoulder, a satisfied smile crossing his scarred face when Victor winced in pain. “*I’ll* be your date.”

Victor tore away from Roe’s grasp. “You most certainly will *not*—you dance like an oaf and I have delicate feet!”

Jacob brought a swift end to the conversation by yelling at all three of them, “No one will be attending tonight’s event if they do not show me acceptable progress *today*.” He side-eyed Cassie. “That includes those of us with dates.”

“Coming!” Cassie tossed her canteen on the dirt and ran

back to the center of the courtyard where Jacob was waiting for her. She picked up her dusty sword and waited as Jacob took a moment to shield the woven bracelet around his right wrist with his sleeve.

"Probably should have taken it off in the room. Ah, well."

"What do the colors mean?" She had been there for his and Diana's wedding and understood the general importance of the bracelets, but the actual meaning of the colors was still a mystery to her.

Jacob glanced down at his wrist and smiled. "They mean something different for everyone, really. I chose the blue and gold for Diana's family."

"And the red?"

He looked back at her. "I'm afraid that's something I can't share." He chuckled, keeping his voice low enough for only Cassie to hear. "You, ah, thinking of—"

"W-what? I—um, no. No, I was just asking." Cassie wasn't sure just how she had become a fumbling mess in a matter of seconds over a bracelet, but she was not a fan of the ridiculous squeak that had somehow made its way into her voice. "Sorry, didn't mean to pry."

"You are fine, my friend." He patted her shoulder, his green eyes kind and understanding, and she relaxed a bit. "The colors could mean anything, but they're really like a promise," he explained.

"Uh, how?" Cassie asked, wondering if getting into this conversation was even wise. What if he told Andrea? Was there an expectation for her to get one of these made? What colors would Andrea want? *No wonder she gets all flustered whenever someone brings it up.*

Jacob seemed amused by her curiosity. "They represent what you swore to protect in your life. That's all the bracelet is, really," he said as he took up his sparring stance. "A promise."

Cassie decided to push this from her mind and not think about it anymore. *Focus on training, go to the ball, have fun…or as much fun as one can have hanging around a bunch of people that clearly hate each other.*

She reset her stance and looked to Jacob. "All right," he said. "Just as before. Ready?"

"Yeah," she said. "Let's do it."

Cassie had to give herself some credit—it took much longer this time before she was on the ground again. She succeeded at dodging Jacob's lunge from the left and swung down with her sword to keep him at bay in a failed effort to disarm him. A well-timed push from him combined with a shoulder charge brought the fight to a swift end. Despite the pain that she knew she'd feel later, Cassie swelled with pride, although part of her wished that Andrea had been there see it. *At least I've still got my sword this time.*

"Well done," Jacob praised as he pulled her up. "Your footwork needs improvement, and I can tell what you're thinking well before you actually execute it. But that was much improved." He ran a hand through his damp hair. "I think we're done here for today. I will see you tonight, I hope?"

Cassie sheathed her sword as they walked back to the shade. "Yeah. I don't really know what I'm supposed to do at this ball, though."

Jacob let out a deep laugh. "Other than protecting your charge? Rumor has it one is supposed to enjoy themselves at them. The food here is terrible, though, and I would prefer not to be in the company of that Veraun fellow if I can help it."

"Oh, that guy? Seems like a jerk," Cassie said. She picked up her canteen and slung her backpack over her shoulder.

"I don't know the man well, but he's loyal to the empress and we are their guests," Jacob sighed. He signaled to the other Guardians to finish up. "Might as well make the most of it. I've heard there's to be dancing," he added with a wink.

Cassie's eyebrows went up. *Dancing. Of course. It's a ball—why wouldn't there be dancing?* "Can't we just eat the free food and make fun of the Legion like we do every other time we have the night off?"

But Jacob's thoughts appeared to be elsewhere as they left the courtyard together. "Ah, I still remember before our wedding Alexander had to actually give Diana and me lessons so that we wouldn't embarrass the crown too much during our first dance. She performed far better than me, of course. Lovely time, that was."

Cassie grinned, remembering the day in vivid detail. How the entire city and even citizens from other towns showed up to see Diana and Jacob wed and the week-long celebration that followed. It had all been a blur, but she recalled Andrea having a good time (or as good a time as Andrea could have at a large gathering), especially since the magic had just been restored and their duties had been light following their return from Rhyad. "I don't know—I thought you did pretty well."

He gave a dramatic bow once they reached the door to the palace interior. "Why, thank you, Cassie. Now, I must leave you here to go prepare for later."

"All right, see you tonight," she said as the realization that she had no idea what to wear that evening dawned on her.

* * *

"Correspondences for today, Your Grace."

Ithmeera looked away from her reflection in the full-length mirror long enough to take the stack of envelopes from Petra's hand. "Thank you. Anything of note?" she asked as she flipped through the letters. She glanced up at her lady-in-waiting with a warm smile. "That dress looks positively lovely on you, Petra."

Flustered, Petra ducked her head and touched the silky fabric of her midnight-blue sleeveless gown. "Oh, t-thank you, Your Majesty. I've been waiting for the right occasion to wear it."

"Well, it's perfect," Ithmeera said. "And I am sure Queen Lydia will be honored that you chose blue." Her brow furrowed as she sorted through the letters. "Are these *all* from Sadford?"

Petra laughed softly. "Most of them, my lady. There are a few from the north, too. If I may speak freely, you look quite radiant yourself, Your Majesty," she added, gesturing at the amber-colored dress Ithmeera wore. It was one of Ithmeera's favorite gowns for evening affairs, with long, loose sleeves that hung from her wrists and an intricate lace overlay that fell over the darker billowy material underneath. She had finished the outfit off with an ornate golden belt encrusted with rubies that matched the heavy necklace she wore.

Ithmeera beamed at Petra from the mirror as she double-checked that her dark curls framed her face in the exact way she wanted. "Thank you! This is one of my favorites, I think."

Petra lowered her voice. "There was…something else you should know."

Ithmeera rolled her eyes. *Always something.* "Why can't we just have a ball without any incidents? I tire of all these deaths and spies."

"Actually, the spy has been invited to this one, Your Majesty."

Right. "Ah, of course. Then we are set!" She put the envelopes down on the nearby desk where she kept her diary and sometimes conducted her work from when she felt like staying in her quarters for the day. "I have to keep telling myself that this will be the greatest alliance in the history of the empire whenever I remember that I pardoned those three." She turned to Petra once more. "I'm sorry—what was it you wanted to tell me?"

Petra seemed nervous. *But then again, she always is.* "My lady, you asked me to inform you whenever I noted anything… suspicious from your uncle?"

Oh no. Ever since she had forced Alden to resign from the council that advised her on the day-to-day issues of the empire, he had been more reclusive—sometimes not seeing her or Marco for a few days—and taking more frequent trips to other regions of Damea without more than a day's notice. Her senior councilors had advised her to keep an eye on him as a precaution, but Ithmeera never thought she would actually have to worry about being betrayed by her own family, ambitious as he was. "Go on."

"There was a letter addressed to him. I gave it to him and when he opened it he seemed…alarmed."

Ithmeera rubbed her temples. "Did he say anything to you?"

Petra shook her head. "Just his thanks, Your Grace. But I have delivered letters to him many times and…you should have been there, my lady. His face was so *pale.*"

What could that letter have possibly said? Maybe—no. No, she was going to ignore this and enjoy herself tonight, if only for Marco's sake. Her son was old enough to attend the balls now, though Petra promised she would take him to bed when he grew too tired. "Thank you for telling me, Petra. I am almost done here." She straightened up and faced the mirror once more. "If you could make sure Marco is ready, that would be wonderful. I will see you in the throne room."

Petra bowed. "Of course, Your Majesty." She closed the door, leaving Ithmeera alone to finish getting ready before she would meet her guests for what she was hoping would be a wonderful—if interesting—evening.

Chapter 11
A Formal Affair

So strange to be back here and wearing this, *too.* Andrea frowned at herself in the mirror.

"What's the matter?" Kye sat on a chair on the other side of the generous bedroom Ithmeera had given Andrea and Cassie for the duration of their stay. The room did not have a balcony, but it did have a bay window with a wide sill that provided a breathtaking view of the city of Azgadar. Hugging one wall of the room and accompanied by beautiful, intricately carved wooden nightstands was a large bed—bigger than the one Andrea shared with Cassie in Gurdinfield.

"I feel so…out of place." She looked back at the dark green long-sleeved dress that had taken her longer than she would have liked to admit to put on. A thin silver necklace graced her neck—a gift from Diana. Her hair, which she preferred down most of the time, had been pulled into a braided coil wrapped up in a tight bun with the aid of Ithmeera's servants.

It was strange having so many servants around in the first place. Andrea was used to doing everything herself, as she had done most of her life. Even Diana didn't keep that many servants, and the ones she did were quite friendly and chatty, whereas the Azgadaran servants were quieter and far more serious. They didn't seem to have much sympathy for Andrea, either, as they had poked her scalp more times than she cared to count with what must have been a hundred pins.

The dress reminded Andrea of the one Elisa had loaned her for her ill-fated mission to distract Ithmeera while Cassie and Kye stole her diary. This one fit her much better, as it had been tailormade by Diana's favorite seamstress in the City of Towers. Normally, Andrea would not have invested so much in a dress, or would have worn something blue that she already owned to represent Gurdinfield, such as her royal enchanter robes. As far as formalwear went, dresses were more common in Azgadar and the western regions of Damea than in Gurdinfield, but Andrea preferred the look of them over the stiff suits that most Gurdinfielders wore on special occasions.

Hopefully Cassie will, too.

She noticed Kye tug the collar of his shirt. "Oh, you don't need the top button if it's too tight," she told him.

Kye sighed with relief as he undid the button closest to his neck. "Ah, much better. Felt like I would run out of air by the night's end."

Andrea laughed while Kye straightened out the rest of his suit. She thought he looked quite handsome, much better than the old rags he had worn when they first met in Azgadar nearly a year ago. He had made some progress in learning to control his abilities under her mentorship, but it was still too often that he cast an unintentional fireball that burned hotter than any Andrea had ever seen. She was proud of him, but they had a long way to go before his abilities could be deemed stable.

"No offense," she said, "but it would probably be a better fate than whatever the Legion had planned for you before the empress pardoned us."

He held up his pointer finger as a crooked smile took over. "True! And you'll get to actually enjoy the entire ball without being thrown in prison!"

She looked over her outfit one last time. "Pardon me if I'm still not completely convinced that won't happen. All right," she breathed and spun around to face Kye. "Well, how do I look? Prison-worthy enough?"

Kye did his duty and looked her over. Andrea's first thought: *I feel like an enchanted heirloom up for auction. What if it's not appropriate for a ball? What if Diana disapproves? What if Cassie doesn't like it?* Her anxiety over her outfit turned into nervousness over the event itself. She knew Cassie wasn't a fan of extravagant things in general, let alone a formal ball hosted by a woman who used to be their enemy. Still, Andrea couldn't help but be a little excited for it. She wanted to impress Cassie, even if it meant wearing this silly dress.

And maybe we'll finally get to talk later.

She had spent most of the day accompanying Diana to various meetings with Ithmeera and her council of advisors to come up with an outline for the terms of their new alliance. Cassie had gone to train with Jacob and the other Guardians in the morning, and they hadn't seen each other since. When Andrea had returned to their room, Cassie's pack was open and some of her clothes were gone. She'd also found a note that had been slipped under the door. The paper was splattered with ink blotches and the words *"Cassie with us. See you later"* were scribbled on it, followed by Roe's signature.

Kye took longer than Andrea thought he would as he stared at her, his brown eyes focused and his lips drawn back tight in concentration. Finally, he flashed her a wide smile, the freckles dotting his cheeks standing out. "You…you look *amazing*, Andrea."

Relieved and shy at the same time, she extended her hand to him. "Thank you. You look really nice as well. Come on," she said, "let's go meet the others."

Hand in hand, they left the bedroom and took their time walking down the steep, winding steps of the spire.

* * *

"Andrea! Kye! You two look wonderful!" Diana placed a hand on each of their shoulders after bounding up to them upon meeting outside of the Great Hall. Andrea had actually seen her outfit before—she had gone into the city with Diana to have the deep-blue coat and white, gold-trimmed shirt fitted.

She bowed her head. "Thank you, Your Majesty. You look lovely as well."

"Shall we go in?" Diana asked. "The others are already inside."

Andrea gestured ahead. "After you."

The two Legionnaires guarding the door noticed them coming and pulled the thick double doors open in unison with a swift movement. The Great Hall was just as huge as

Andrea remembered. Much of the decor mirrored the throne room—Legion banners and sigils from the various towns and sub-regions that made up the empire. An orchestra was set up in the corner and had just finished playing a traditional, upbeat Azgadaran song before starting another piece Andrea had never heard before. Moving across the dance floor were the highborn Azgadaran citizens, as well as the Royal Council members and those who accompanied them tonight.

She spotted Ithmeera at the far end of the Great Hall, a genuine smile on her face as she observed the scene before her. To her right stood a pretty young woman whom Andrea only knew to be Ithmeera's lady-in-waiting, and sitting in a chair to her left was a white-haired older man in dark robes. He was glaring at Jacob, who was surrounded by the other Guardians several paces away. She'd seen him earlier in the day walking (or as Elisa had put it, "skulking") around the palace but he did not acknowledge her, and even only gave Diana a stiff bow before continuing about his business. Behind them all stood General Veraun and a few other Legionnaires. Veraun was stone-faced as usual, and Andrea could see from the vigilant manner in which he watched over the royal family that he seemed content just carrying out his job tonight.

She tried to spot Cassie, but she couldn't seem to spot any of her companions in the crowd. Somewhere in the midst of their entrance Kye had been separated from them.

Once they crossed the spacious room, Ithmeera took notice and headed toward them. "There you are, Queen Lydia. And..." She acknowledged Andrea with an intense stare, though her greeting was quite pleasant. "Lady Andrea...or is it *Enchanter* Andrea now? Either way, welcome back to the Great Hall. I hear congratulations are in order for assisting with the Restoration."

Andrea had to fight to not look away. "T-thank you, Your Majesty. It is…nice to be back under better circumstances," was all she could get out, her knees threatening to give out. The only thing keeping her afloat was Diana's presence beside her.

She was grateful when Diana intervened. "Your son is wonderful, Your Majesty. He was just telling me about his adventures as a Legionnaire this past week."

The intensity of Ithmeera's gaze gave way to an amused smile. "Oh, dear. My apologies if he was bothering you. He got a new toy sword and he's been eager to try it out on everything and everyone in the palace." She tilted her head. "Actually, now that I think of it, I don't believe I've asked. Have you any children?"

Diana's laugh was not out of ridicule at the notion. In fact, its warmth had a calming effect on Andrea. "Jacob and I only recently married, and with all work that goes into rebuilding a kingdom, well, there just hasn't been any time to think of that…yet."

Ithmeera replied with what seemed like a heartfelt response to Diana that Andrea didn't quite hear, her eyes wandering in an attempt to find Cassie. Kye had disappeared and Elisa was nowhere in sight. *Perhaps they're hiding from all these people.* She wouldn't mind doing the same.

Diana and Ithmeera appeared very engrossed in their conversation, so Andrea took the opportunity to excuse herself. She wandered back out to the dance floor, hoping to spot Jacob again where perhaps Cassie might be with him.

"Enjoying yourself?" Recognizing Elisa's low voice, Andrea spun around. Her friend had dressed in full armor tonight, her daggers at her sides. She seemed tense, but as usual it was difficult to tell with Elisa.

"I've only just arrived. Where is Kye?"

Elisa shrugged. "Why would I know?" She looked down at Andrea's dress. Andrea could swear she saw Elisa's eyes widen, if only for a split second. "That dress suits you. You fit in well."

Andrea grinned. Elisa didn't often hand out compliments. "Better than last time?"

"That depends. Have you been arrested yet?"

"I have not," Andrea answered, getting a quiet laugh out of Elisa. "Not yet, anyway." She didn't hear the shift in music until the murmurings of the countless conversations amongst the guests died down. It was slow—a classic Gurdinfield waltz she had heard Kye perform before—and clearly a song intended to be danced to with a partner.

She was about to suggest to Elisa that they move to the side of the room in order to avoid the dancers when she noticed Elisa giving her a knowing look and staring at whoever was behind Andrea.

Afraid she would be confronted by Ithmeera again (or worse, a Legionnaire), Andrea slowly turned and just about passed out from relief when she saw Cassie standing before her in a rather expensive-looking charcoal button-down blouse and black pants. She looked quite good—no, *more* than good—and Andrea had to regain her composure before she could speak again without rambling.

"Oh! It's you. Sorry, I thought—I thought I was about to have a repeat experience of last year." Andrea waited for Cassie to laugh at her or tease her or say something that amounted to making her feel foolish for being worried.

Instead, Cassie simply stared at her with dazed blue eyes, lips slightly parted. Andrea's first thought was that something was wrong. "Are you all right?"

Cassie blinked and snapped out of her trance. "What? Oh, yeah…yeah, I'm fine." She gestured at the dance floor. "Let's go?"

She can't be serious. "Out—out there? To dance?"

"Yeah." Cassie offered Andrea her arm. "To dance."

She couldn't figure out just exactly how it happened, but before she knew it, Andrea was arm-in-arm with Cassie as they strode out to the dance floor, joining the dozens of couples already moving in near-unison to the peaceful, steady rhythm.

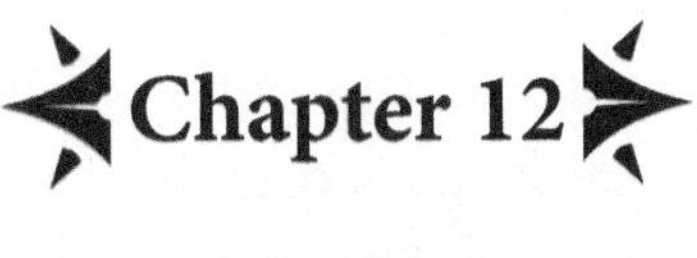

Chapter 12
Perfect

Andrea swallowed as she tried to think of a scenario where her standing around the center of the dance floor with Cassie could somehow not end in disaster.

Why couldn't Cassie have asked her to conjure a fireball or defend a city in battle? Andrea could handle those things. But *dance?* It was certainly not something she'd practiced at home or while living with Meredith. And yet Cassie's hopeful expression was making her want to try.

"C-Cassie, I don't know about this. I can't…" She took a deep breath as she held onto Cassie's wrists. "I can't actually dance."

Cassie's initial response was a quiet laugh, and Andrea's nervousness shifted to annoyance. *How in the world is this funny?* But then Cassie took her hand and arranged them so that Andrea's free hand was on her shoulder and hers around Andrea's waist. "Just follow what I do. We'll go slow," she said, leading them slowly in a lazy square across the room.

Too stunned for words, Andrea could only look down at her feet while she attempted to follow Cassie's more confident steps. Of course, her foot went down on one of Cassie's as she lost the rhythm of the song right after they started moving.

Damn it.

She rushed to apologize when Cassie faltered . "Sorry! I've never done this before and—"

"Hey." Cassie leaned in and pressed her forehead against Andrea's, the physical contact combined with Cassie's steady voice calming her down enough to try again. "I like your dress."

Andrea smiled and looked away. "Oh…thank you. I was hoping you would." As her confidence grew, she found the steps becoming easier the more they moved together.

"No, really," Cassie said, tilting her head to meet Andrea's gaze. "You look beautiful."

"Cassie." Andrea's cheeks burned. She never knew how to answer Cassie sometimes, especially when Cassie spoke with such sincerity. Her nervousness returned and for a dreaded moment, she was terrified she would wake up and that this incredible moment would be nothing but a dream. But Cassie's hold kept Andrea anchored to reality as she realized she wanted nothing more than to tell her all the things she was feeling—all the things she had kept to herself until now. "I'm sorry. I don't know what I'm doing and you—you're perfect." Her heart swelled when Cassie averted her eyes, accompanied by an even rarer shy smile. "How is it you dance like you've done this a thousand times?"

Cassie shrugged. "Would you believe my mother taught me? She used to give lessons out of our living room. She uh, had a lot of jobs." She sighed. "Money was hard to come by where I grew up. But I know she really liked teaching others what she knew."

Andrea gave her an encouraging smile, pleased that Cassie was opening up to her not just about her past, but about her *mother,* whom she never spoke of save one time after they met. "Really?"

"Oh, yeah," Cassie said. "I'd be home minding my own business and she'd pull me into her lessons as an example to her students."

Cassie's admission left Andrea with a hundred questions. "It's interesting that you know *this* particular dance."

"It's fairly common back…back home," Cassie explained before going quiet. The song continued and Andrea suddenly felt the eyes of others on them. Cassie must have sensed her self-consciousness because she spoke again.

"Serena."

"I'm sorry?"

Cassie chuckled. "My mother. Her name was Serena. I figured you wanted to know. She would, um…she never took any crap from me, even when I was really moody and insufferable."

Andrea gasped in faux-shock. "*You?* Moody and insufferable? I don't believe it."

"Yeah, yeah, you're hilarious," Cassie said, rolling her eyes. She glanced down at their feet. "You're doing really well, by the way."

Surprised and grateful that Cassie was sharing so much with her, Andrea could only think of one reply. "She sounds wonderful, Cassie. I'm…sorry she's gone."

Cassie tightened her hold around Andrea's waist. "Yeah. Me, too. I had to kind of take care of myself after…after she died. I really miss her." She bit her lip and Andrea could see that something was troubling her. *Maybe I shouldn't have said anything...*

"You know, I'm actually glad you brought me here. To Damea, I mean."

"You—you are?"

"Sure," Cassie said. "My life was *slightly* less exciting before I met you. It was the same thing every day. I mean, I could have done without almost dying all those times, but other than that it's been kind of fun." She pulled them closer together, their bodies nearly pressed against each other.

Despite the warmth their new proximity provided, Andrea shivered as she wondered what Cassie would say if she bared her feelings for her right then. "I'm—I'm glad you're happy here. I..." She looked down again. *Just tell her!* "I don't know what I would do without you."

"Andrea?" They stopped moving. Cassie released Andrea's hand and, with a gentle push, tilted her head to look at her. The anguish and regret in Cassie's eyes almost brought tears to Andrea's as she saw in them the remnants of Cassie's hopes and desires, the same ones which had crumbled to dust after her mother's death. But somewhere in there...*somehow,* she could see the feelings Cassie held for her—feelings more powerful than any magic in Damea.

"Yes?"

Before Cassie could answer, a roar rang out in the Great Hall, followed by the collective shrieks and screams of everyone in the room. Andrea jerked her head in the direction of the commotion and froze in terror. An armored Azgadaran woman was charging at them, sword held high as she bellowed her fury before bringing her blade down.

"Death to enchanters!"

The barrier came up fast, the magic coursing through Andrea as she pulled on every bit of energy she could find from the space around her and Cassie. She moved to fling the shield at their assailant just as her sword came down, but instead was thrown hard to the floor along with Cassie. The magic in her veins ceased with such abruptness that Andrea nearly fainted from the crippling sensation of losing so much energy at once. She watched in horror as her barrier wavered and disappeared.

"*Move!*" Victor leapt in front of them, sword drawn, and blocked the woman's blade before shoving her back and slashing at her, catching her upper arm. The assassin yelled and swung again in desperation. The blade cut into Victor's shoulder and sent him to the ground, writhing in pain. Cassie sped past him and tackled the woman, sending her sword flying from her hand and skidding across the floor.

More screams. Andrea struggled to overcome the dizzying side effects of her own failed spell. She needed to get up, needed to get to Cassie and help her. Most of the guests had scattered to the sides of the room. The Guardians and Legionnaires—including Jacob and General Veraun—were rushing to the center to help Cassie.

"*No!*" Ithmeera's scream drowned out all others as she shielded Marco from a second assassin who had ambushed them from behind. He charged, his blade aimed straight at Marco's heart.

A flash of steel. The assassin crumpled to the floor, throat cut, as Ithmeera covered her shaken son's eyes. Towering over the dead man's body stood Elisa. Her chest heaved as she clutched a bloodstained dagger in her hand and looked back at Ithmeera and Marco, who was now in tears.

The woman who had attacked Andrea tore herself from Cassie's grip and kicked out, leaving Cassie gasping for air on the floor. Andrea pushed herself up just in time to see the woman pull a knife from her belt.

"Cassie!" She was still weak and there was not enough time to get to Cassie before the assassin drove the knife down. *Have to get to her. Have to—*

Veraun's long sword sang as it cut through the air and into the woman's back, tearing a final surprised cry from her before she collapsed and lay still.

The heavy panting of those involved in the fight, Victor's groans of pain, and Marco's trembling sobs were the only things keeping the heavy silence that descended upon most of the Great Hall from enveloping the room completely. Andrea crawled over to Cassie. Her ragged coughs echoed in Andrea's ears as she fought to stabilize her breathing.

"Are you all right?" She helped Cassie roll over and sit up, but let out a choked cry when she saw the bloodstain on Cassie's sleeve. "Your arm!"

Cassie glanced at her arm and grasped Andrea's wrist, shaking her head. "It's not mine—I'm okay. Help Victor."

Andrea moved to Victor, who was surrounded by Jacob, Diana, and Roe. His face was pale, and beads of sweat dampened his brow. The others had removed his shirt, revealing the deep gash in his shoulder. Diana had repurposed her suit coat to help stop the bleeding, but most of the material was already wet .

Meredith had only taught her the most basic of spells for first aid, but Andrea had obtained some healing experience during their journey to Rhyad. She hoped it would be enough. "I need space," she said with as much authority as she could muster in her frightened state.

Andrea knelt and removed the rag from Victor's shoulder, biting her lip when she saw how deep the blade had cut him. "Hold on," she said, trying to be as soothing as possible. Out of habit, she tested the air around her to make sure there was enough magic for her to attempt the spell and found it satisfactory. *Then why did the barrier just...fail?* It made no sense. *Figure it out later.* Right now, she had to save Victor.

She placed a steady hand on his wound and had to fight to not pull away when the warm blood came in contact with her skin. She focused her will and energy toward closing the wound. Victor's head lolled back and his eyes fluttered shut soon after. The shallow gasps he had been taking turned to deeper breaths, and after several seconds his breathing seemed under control.

Andrea exhaled heavily as she removed her hand, relieved to see that the wound was all but closed. She stood up, her legs wobbly from the attack and the massive fluctuations of magic that had torn through her body. "He needs bandages still and careful observation," she told Jacob, "but he should be all right."

Jacob's shoulders slumped down as Roe took Andrea's hand, his eyes filled with relief. "*Thank* you."

She tilted her head down. "You're welcome. I should—"

"...shhh...it's going to be okay. He cannot hurt you." Ithmeera's soft voice was still the loudest in the room as she knelt next to a sniffling Marco, her arms wrapped tightly around him. "My poor boy!" She glanced up at Elisa, meeting her eyes for a brief moment before turning to Petra. "Take Marco to my room, Petra. *Please.*" Petra rushed to take the boy into her arms and carried him away, leaving Ithmeera surrounded by Veraun, Alden, Elisa, and the Legionnaires, the assassin's limp body only a few steps away from them.

Alden spoke up, the first time Andrea had heard his voice since their arrival. "Well done, General," he said, completely ignoring Elisa. "A pity there was no way to question them."

Ithmeera's gaze turned to the dead assassins. "Who are they? What did they want?"

"We can't be certain right now, but I did hear the woman very clearly announce her hatred for enchanters." Veraun walked over to the assassin he'd slain moments earlier and rolled her over with his boot. His eyes went wide as Ithmeera's hand went to her chest in disbelief. "No..."

Andrea's heart sank when she heard a similar exclamation from Cassie behind her.

"Look." Cassie pointed at the body. The woman wore the black, red, and gold uniform of the Legion.

"Legionnaires!" Diana breathed.

"Traitors," Ithmeera said. "I want double watch on all posts tonight and a full search of the palace," she barked at Veraun.

Elisa's voice was low and steady as she pointed at the dead man. "These assassins were Legionnaires. How are any of them to be trusted?"

Alden's lip curled up in disgust. "You of all people should not be questioning the empress's decisions."

"In case you hadn't noticed, the empress and her son were just attacked by Legionnaires!"

"Enough!" Ithmeera yelled, before turning to Veraun again. "I've made my decision. *No one* gets the night off. Do you understand, General?"

Veraun bowed, the shock of seeing his own soldiers turned assassins plain on his face. "Of—of course, Your Majesty."

Elisa stepped forward. "Allow me to stand watch over Marco tonight."

Ithmeera gave a vehement shake of her head. "Absolutely not. You saved his life, Elisa, and I am grateful, but that does not make you his bodyguard."

Andrea couldn't help but feel sorry for her, though she didn't understand why Elisa was so adamant about protecting Marco in particular. "But—"

"Her Majesty has spoken and your services are neither required nor desired, Elisa," Veraun interrupted.

Ithmeera buried her face in her hands before looking back at Diana and Jacob. "Forgive me. I must see to my son. Ben." She sucked in a breath, as though struggling not to cry. "Please, take care of this."

Veraun bowed again. "Right away, Your Majesty." He nodded at Diana before ordering his Legionnaires to corral the remaining guests and lead them out of the Great Hall. Ithmeera left with Alden in tow.

"We should get Victor to his room," Diana said in a hushed voice.

"Agreed." Jacob turned to the Guardians, including Cassie. "Guardians, stay for a moment."

"You should get some rest, Andrea," Diana said, placing a hand on Andrea's back. "You look exhausted." She scanned the room. "Where is Kye?"

Kye! Andrea realized she had not seen him since they arrived in the Great Hall. "I—I don't know. I haven't seen him. You don't think something has happened to him, do you?"

"He is fine," Elisa said. "He stepped outside for some air after the...well, you know." Her voice was hoarse and Andrea had never seen her so broken before. But as much as she wanted to know the deeper connection she was sure existed between Elisa and the Cadars, she agreed with Diana—she *was* exhausted.

Diana gave Elisa a pleading look. "I would be very grateful if you could find him for us, Elisa. Even a pardoned enchanter should not be wandering the streets of Azgadar alone tonight."

If Elisa was unhappy with the task, she did not show it. "I will do my best, Your Majesty."

Her legs feeling weaker with each passing moment, Andrea abandoned formalities as she took Diana aside. "I think I should rest—you're right. Would...would you please send Cassie up when Jacob is done?"

"Of course, Andrea," Diana said with a faint smile. "And thank you. For saving Victor." She glanced back at Victor and then at the dead Legionnaire with sadness in her dark eyes. "I just hope this isn't the beginning of something far worse."

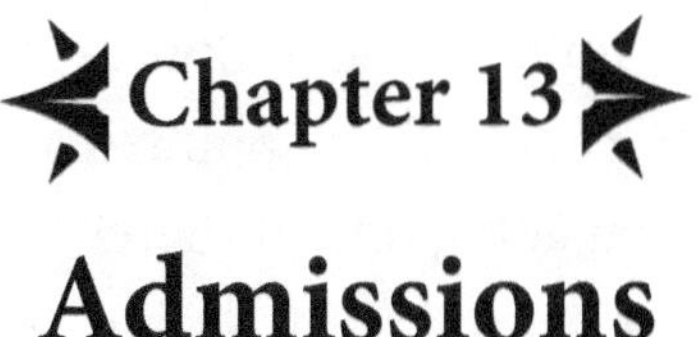

Chapter 13

Admissions

The silence hovering over Azgadar that night was unsettling. Not even the breeze sweeping through the capital could help Andrea relax as she sat on the deep red cushions on the bench next to the open bay window, looking out across the city. Wisps of smoke from the countless flames of the magically lit lamps illuminating the streets below rose up and filled the air with the clean, burning scent of magic. As hard as Andrea found it to believe, Azgadar had descended into an oblivious slumber tonight, the vast majority of its citizens not the slightest bit aware of the bloodshed that had occurred in the palace only hours earlier.

The heavy door to the quarters shut, startling her until she turned and saw Cassie's face illuminated in the dying candlelight.

"Sorry," Cassie said in a hushed tone. She fiddled with the lock. "These doors are a little…different and—there we go," she finished as the door locked with a solid metallic click.

"How are the others?" Andrea asked. She turned to face Cassie, smoothing out the plain grey tunic and leggings she had changed into after she returned to their room. The fresh air had worked well in helping her recover her strength after their ordeal, but her worry hovered just beneath her skin.

Cassie gave her a tired look, and Andrea could hear the exhaustion in her tone. “Upset. Confused. Angry. I’m glad Victor will be okay, though.” She pointed at the open window. “Anything interesting going on out there?”

“Thankfully, no,” Andrea said. She looked Cassie up and down, her gaze stopping at the bloodstain on Cassie’s sleeve, an icy chill running through her as the horrific events from earlier replayed in her mind. “You should…you should change your clothes.”

But Cassie shook her head. “Can’t. Need to grab my knife and take watch . You should get some sleep, though. It’s been a long day.”

“Watch?”

“Yeah, Jacob wants me guarding this room in case there are more of those crazies sneaking around the palace,” Cassie said, grabbing her pack from the chair nearest to the door. She rummaged through it, muttering to no one in particular, “Where the hell is it?”

Andrea frowned before hopping off the bench. “Even if there *are* others, which I doubt, there’s no way they could reach us this far into the palace.” She took Cassie’s arm in a gentle hold, making her pause the search for the weapon. “The empress has scores of Legionnaires on alert right now. Why don’t you get changed and get some rest?”

Cassie bit her lip, her discomfort obvious even in the room’s low light. “Andrea, I can’t. Jacob said—”

"*Jacob* knows that as an enchanter, I am perfectly capable of defending myself," Andrea said. She reached for Cassie's face and placed a hand on her cheek, forcing her to meet her gaze. "And you've been through enough tonight."

But Cassie looked away. "I know what you can do and it's irrelevant."

What is she talking about? "How are my abilities not relevant to my own defense? To *our* defense?" Confused, she shook her head and tugged on Cassie's arm. "We're *fine,* Cassie. Now can we please just get some rest and—"

"No!" Cassie yanked her arm away and took a step back, startling Andrea. They stood for a moment in silence, save for Cassie's quickened breaths. She pointed at the door. "That… was too close. What happened in Rhyad was too close. Same with Gurdinfield, when the Legion invaded. A-and before that, when Ithmeera captured you."

Andrea sighed. *This again?* It was a tired topic, but it was one she could handle. "Cassie, I've told you a hundred times, I'm *fine—*"

"Why? Because you're not *dead?*" Cassie cried. "Because by some stroke of sheer, dumb luck you didn't die in a dark forsaken cave in the middle of a wasteland? Or under a pile of rocks? Or at the hands of some Legionnaire?" Her voice had escalated to a pitch and volume that Andrea had not heard since the moments before the battle at the City of Towers. Cassie had been angry with Andrea before, but there was something different in her voice this time, and it tore at Andrea's heart.

"It wasn't luck," she said, trying to keep her voice as steady as possible with the hope that it would calm Cassie down at least a little. "You saved me, Cassie. We made it here, didn't we?"

Rather than calming down, Cassie clenched her fists, breathing shallowly and trembling. "You just don't…you don't *get* it, do you?"

"Then explain it to me, Cassie," Andrea pleaded, trying with all her willpower to understand what was going on inside Cassie's head.

Cassie turned away, her back to Andrea and her shoulders slightly hunched. *Why is she hiding?*

"Cassie, please?"

No answer. Cassie's breathing grew louder, the pattern more familiar. Andrea realized in her bewildered state that Cassie was fighting back tears. She reached out to touch Cassie's shoulder, her voice just above a whisper. "I'm here. I'm listening."

The distant sounds of the city crept into the room, dominating the air around them, and seemed to rise in volume until Cassie's voice broke through.

"I can't lose you."

Andrea was not certain she had heard correctly. She had never seen Cassie like this before. Angry, yes, but nothing like this. "What?"

"I can't…I can't lose you." Cassie straightened up with a sniff and turned around. Her gaze remained fixed on the floor.

Still puzzled, Andrea made an effort to keep her voice as comforting as possible. "Cassie, I'm right here. You're not going to lose me—"

Any progress Cassie had made toward calming down

unraveled as she met Andrea's worried eyes with angry, bloodshot ones of her own. "Don't say that! Don't make promises you can't keep!"

Andrea took a step back and folded her arms across her chest, her concern turning to frustration. "Why are you yelling at me? We're both alive, aren't we? The assassins are dead—what more do you want?"

"Those people knew exactly who you were. They knew who *every* enchanter in that room was."

"And we stopped them!" Andrea argued, yet she couldn't help remembering how her shield had fizzled out. Her chest and throat tightened. Arguments with Cassie were anything but enjoyable, and it did not help that Cassie was being especially evasive tonight.

Cassie threw her hands up. "For now! Until what—the *next* time someone or something tries to kill you for doing magic?"

Andrea could understand her partner's concern considering what had just happened, but she didn't know how to convince Cassie that she wasn't defenseless. "I don't—I don't know, Cassie. If that happens we stop them too, I suppose."

"Well, I'm not going to sit on my ass and wait for them." Cassie grabbed her pack and started searching for her knife again, making far more noise than Andrea felt was necessary.

She's being stubborn again. "Why are you acting like this? You don't trust my abilities?"

Cassie stopped. "No, that's not it—"

"This isn't like Rhyad, Cassie. I'm more than capable of defending both of us, so—"

Cassie growled before throwing her pack on the floor. She stood up and whirled around to face Andrea. "It's not the damn magic! I told you: I *can't* lose you."

Enough of this. "Stop it! That's not going to happen."

"Why not? It's happened to everyone else I've…" Cassie trailed off. She looked away and shrugged, but the confidence the gesture usually carried was missing. They both went quiet again.

Suddenly, Andrea knew. The discomfort in her throat and chest disappeared and was replaced with sorrow.

She reached for Cassie's hand, lacing their fingers together gently. "Tell me?" she asked with pleading eyes, looking to Cassie for the answer she already knew.

Cassie gave her hand a brief squeeze, her lower lip quivering as she spoke. "They were everything to me. And now…now they're gone." She swallowed, her eyes still brimming with tears.

Andrea wanted to hold Cassie, wanted to shield her and take her sadness away. But she knew she had to let Cassie finish. For both their sakes. "Your mother?"

Cassie sniffed. "Yeah. And…a friend. A good friend." She sighed. "I haven't…loved many people, Andrea. Just two."

Andrea could only nod in sympathy. She remained quiet, grateful that Cassie was being so open with her at last.

"Well, three." Cassie's voice broke the silence, a light laugh trailing the end of her admission. "But, uh…I guess it's a bit different this time."

Andrea's eyes widened as Cassie's free hand came to rest on her hip. *Oh…*

"Truly?" was all she could say. She realized after seeing Cassie's amused stare that her answer might have been a bit silly. But she was elated to see that there were no longer tears welling up in Cassie's blue eyes—eyes she wouldn't mind getting lost in forever.

"Yeah. I mean, uh…I'm not very good at saying stuff like this," Cassie said.

Andrea let her hand graze Cassie's arm. "I could go first if you like," she offered.

Cassie grinned. "Nah. You already did."

Wait…she knew? "You mean—"

"Back in Rhyad? Yeah, I remember." Cassie sniffed again, her voice no longer heavy with grief. Instead, the nervousness Andrea was getting better and better at detecting had crept back into Cassie's tone. "I would have said it back, but I wanted to be absolutely certain before I, well…"

"It's all right. I understand." *And we're still just* talking *about it.* She knew she was prone to rambling, but surely they would look back at this conversation someday and laugh about how long it took to happen. *I shouldn't push her like this. She'll say it when she's ready. She would do the same for me.*

"Andrea." Cassie surprised her by pulling her in close, the candlelight illuminating her solemn, intense expression. Memories of their dance only hours earlier surfaced in Andrea's mind. The shakiness in Cassie's voice was barely audible as she spoke.

"I love you." It took a few seconds for Andrea to register the words she had been longing to hear for months. They were simple—just three words. But if she had learned anything over the past year, it was that nothing about Cassie was simple.

She did not respond at first. There was no need—she was perfectly content just staring up at the young woman she had traveled, fought, and fallen in love with. But when Cassie arched her eyebrows a bit, Andrea figured she should probably say something.

"I love you," she said. Feeling vulnerable all of a sudden, she fumbled with her words. "For a while now. I—it's difficult to explain, and I'm not even sure I should try, but I know it was before Rhyad, when I thought I might lose you forever."

She saw the happiness flash on Cassie's face just before she was pulled into a soft kiss holding the countless words and thoughts Andrea could never hope to convey any other way. Leaning into Cassie's hold, she wrapped both arms around her neck, the kiss deepening until the tightness in Andrea's throat returned and she found herself blinking back tears. *Ugh. Of course I would cry.*

Cassie noticed right away and pulled back. She tucked a loose strand of dark hair behind Andrea's ear. "What is it? What's wrong?" she asked, her voice still softer than Andrea was used to hearing from her.

Andrea took a shaky breath. "I…nothing is wrong, Cassie." She smiled, allowing the tears to escape. "No, I'm—I'm *happy.*"

"You're crying."

"Because I'm *happy.* I promise." She allowed a quiet laugh to escape before kissing Cassie's cheek.

Cassie smiled before looking down at her arm in mild

disgust. "You're right—I should change." She unbuttoned the stained shirt and pulled it off before tossing it over the chair, leaving her in a dark, sleeveless undershirt.

"Much better and—oh! There." She headed for one of the ornate side tables next to the bed, where her sheathed dagger lay on top of the carved surface. She cast a guilty look at Andrea as she picked up the weapon. "I really should stand guard outside. Jacob said it's just for tonight, until we know for sure that it's safe."

"No." Andrea surprised herself with her own assertiveness. She closed the distance between her and Cassie and, after a moment's hesitation, took the knife from Cassie's hands and returned it to the side table.

Cassie blinked a few times before she answered. "Um, no?"

"No," Andrea repeated with another shake of her head. "If anyone tries to come in here tonight, I'll make them wish they'd never even *heard* of magic." Guided by an unexpected and inexplicable force that had taken root in her, leaving her unsteady, she took Cassie by the wrist and led her away from the table and closer to the bed. "Stay."

"This is a game, right? Where we try to see who can communicate better in vague, one-word sentences?" Cassie joked.

The dizziness and nerves that had been tugging at Andrea from every direction all evening intensified, and yet…there was a spark of confidence growing inside her. It started small, insignificant even, but soon spread throughout every fiber of her being. Although she had difficulty understanding what it was, she dared not question it, either.

Her hand shook where it gripped Cassie's wrist. "Stay…stay here with me." She swallowed, unable to recall exactly when her mouth had gone dry.

Cassie looked confused. "Andrea, it's just for tonight. You'll be fine sleeping alone for *one* night, right?" She nodded toward the bed with a small smile. "You can even have all the pillows if you want."

"No, it's not that, I just—I want…I want *you,* Cassie." Andrea took a deep breath and gave Cassie's wrist a brief squeeze. "Please?"

After a moment's pause, Cassie's eyes darkened with understanding and she cleared her throat. "Oh! I—uh, okay…" she stammered. "I mean, um, if that's what you want." Panic crept into her voice. "I mean, of course I would like that—it's just we've never, well, *I've* never—"

Andrea's newfound confidence grew even stronger. "Then stay with me," she said, taking a step back. Feeling the bed behind her, she braced herself as she sat on top of the soft mattress.

Unfortunately, in her anxiety, this did not work out quite like Andrea planned. She misjudged the space behind her and fell back onto the bed with a rather unflattering yelp—bringing Cassie down on top of her.

"Oof! Ow."

Andrea cringed as heat rose to her cheeks. "I'm sorry!"

Cassie glanced down at her for a moment before observing their predicament and let out a short laugh, then another. Andrea was confused at first, but a grin soon spread across her face when the laughter evolved into silent, hysterical wheezing, making her heart soar with joy.

"Why does this keep happening? First the wagon, then in Rhyad, and now this!" Cassie exclaimed once she had calmed down and could breathe again. Rather than get up, she rested her head in the crook of Andrea's neck.

"I can't take credit for the other times but for now I would say it's because I have terrible balance and even worse timing," Andrea said with a sigh that came out more content than resigned as she adjusted to the solid but not uncomfortable weight on her. She let her fingers comb through Cassie's disheveled hair, which had come undone from its hairband.

"You said it, not me. At least I'm not covered in bruises this time." Cassie lifted her head and chuckled again, but this time, Andrea could hear hints of unease in her voice.

"Are you all right?" she asked. Eyes locked with Cassie's, Andrea dragged her fingers from Cassie's head to her back, applying gentle pressure to the soft, thin fabric of her undershirt before moving back up to rest on either side of Cassie's face.

Cassie took a deep breath. "Yeah...yeah, I'm fine." When she saw Andrea's raised eyebrow, she clarified. "I promise. I just, um, I don't really know what I'm doing to be honest."

"That makes two of us." And it was the truth. They had shared a room, a tent, a bed for so many nights, and yet Andrea had never wanted to feel closer to Cassie than she did at that moment. But just admitting it was not enough. She wanted to be sure. *Is this what she wants? Is this what* I *want?* What if she did something wrong, fumbled in some awkward, terrible fashion? *I can't even sit on a* bed *without something going wrong.*

What if she said something inappropriate? What if it ruined what she and Cassie had? What if—

"Andrea." Fingers brushed against her cheek, Cassie's voice a low murmur near her ear that both soothed Andrea and sent shivers down her spine at the same time. "I know you. I can practically *hear* the conversation you're having with yourself right now." She planted a single kiss on Andrea's forehead. "I want to…be with you, but I need to know: are you sure?"

The discord in Andrea's mind eased. She knew she did not need to decide right now—Cassie had given her all the time in the world to do so, which made her even more certain of her decision. "I'm sure."

She watched Cassie's eyes light up and moved in to kiss her. When she heard Cassie's breath hitch, Andrea broke the kiss and stroked Cassie's hair again before whispering "I love you" in her ear, finding comfort in the fact that Cassie was just as nervous as she was.

"Love you." Cassie pushed forward and lifted Andrea up enough to slide her arms underneath her back, her fingers resting on the top of Andrea's shoulders. She leaned down, their trembling breaths intermingling right before she kissed Andrea hard. Safe in Cassie's firm hold, Andrea exhaled. Her heart still raced, but it only encouraged her to kiss Cassie back with everything she had. The last flickers of light in the room finally extinguished around them as she clung to Cassie's shoulders, never wanting to let go.

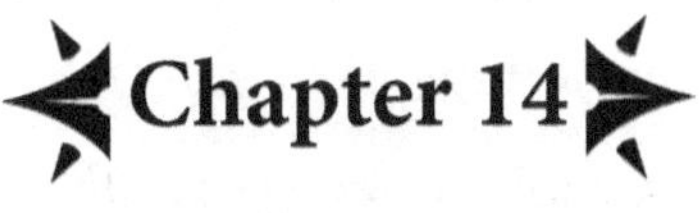

Chapter 14

Monster

Deep breaths. It was the only way Kye could keep the tears at bay as he took in the sight of the ashes that still coated the ruined foundations of the place he once called home. A sudden gust left a chill in him and he regretted tossing his coat on the ground when he'd fled the palace. But it had been too hot—the stress of what happened had been too much.

He gazed up at the stars even though he knew they would have no answers for him. It was here, in the charred remains of his childhood home, that his life had both ended and begun.

Quiet, cautious steps approached from behind, but Kye heard them with ease. Knowing when Legionnaires were nearby was a talent he had picked up while on the run. "Did they send you to bring me back to the palace?" he asked without turning around.

"They did, yes." Elisa took a spot next to him but avoided eye contact, instead looking out at the ruins with him. "I thought I might find you here when you weren't right outside." She paused and handed him the jacket she'd been holding. "You dropped this. We were worried."

"It's all right. You don't have to say that," he said as he slipped back into the coat. "I'll come back soon."

"I would not lie about something so simple."

Kye shook his head and turned to look at her. "No. But you would lie about other things."

Elisa sighed and rubbed her eyes with one hand. "It's late, Kye. I am tired and I've had to deal with many idiots this evening. What are you trying to say?"

"Before you left in the winter, you said you weren't going to Azgadar," he accused. "That you weren't going to see the empress. And yet you still got caught by the Legion."

"That was…not my intent."

"I don't believe you," he said. "I think you did it on purpose. I think you *wanted* to get caught."

Elisa raised an eyebrow. "I think your lack of sleep is encouraging you to hurl misguided accusations."

Her dismissiveness set him off. "Don't—don't talk to me like I'm a child, Elisa! Admit it. You *wanted* the Legion to take you to Azgadar. You were one of their best. You wouldn't let them catch you unless you planned it that way."

He held his breath, waiting for Elisa to yell at him. Instead, she just gave a quiet laugh. "And why would I do that?"

Why indeed? "You wanted to bring the general's sword to the empress yourself. But…why?"

"It belonged to Erik. Ithmeera is his surviving kin, so it was hers to have."

Kye folded his arms across his chest. "You could have just sent it to her when the queen sent his body. That assassin could have killed you tonight. But you jumped in just to save Marco," he said. "Why do you keep putting your life at risk for the empress? She invaded Gurdinfield, she wanted to kill you, me, our friends—"

"Because at the end of the day, boy, she and her son are the only family I have left," Elisa snapped. "So, yes, perhaps I could have simply had the sword sent to her, but I know that my brother would never have forgiven me if he was still alive." She turned to face him. "I swore a life oath to Ithmeera, and whether she acknowledges it or not, I *will* protect her and Marco until I no longer draw breath."

How can she just throw her life away for a family that doesn't want her when she has *one that appreciates and cares about her?* He couldn't understand it. How could she be so blind?

He decided not to press the issue further tonight. What was the point? "You should go back to the palace. I will return soon."

Elisa did not budge. "Why did you leave? We could have used your assistance."

He gave a harsh laugh. "I doubt that. Most likely I would have set one of the guests on fire. I'm still…" He wrung his hands. "I appreciate Andrea's help, but I don't think there's much point."

"She seems to believe you are making progress."

His eyes closed. "One barrier does not undo all the destruction I've done, Elisa."

Elisa gestured at the burned home before them. "Ah, I see why we are here."

Kye sniffed, ashamed to be seen in this state by Elisa of all people. "Those assassins—"

“Were clearly insane. But their actions do not justify the blame you are putting on yourself,” she finished for him.

“I—I killed my family. I killed all those Legionnaires in Gurdinfield.” He hung his head as his eyes welled up with tears. “I am a monster, Elisa. The empress should not have pardoned me.” He looked up when he felt a hand on his upper back and realized Elisa was standing closer to him.

“A monster does not regret his actions, Kye. Nor does he try to make the world a better place for the ones he cares about. The world is not that simple.” She patted his back. “As for your pardon, you will most likely have to file a formal complaint with Ithmeera about that.”

That got a broken laugh out of Kye. “Erm, I think I will pass on that. She’s quite scary.”

Elisa withdrew her hand. “She’s the empress of the Azgadaran Empire—what did you expect? Speaking of which, we should return to the palace. The others were looking for you.”

Kye smiled. “But not you, right?”

“Of course not,” she grumbled. “I have more important things to see to than babysitting you.”

“I appreciate that you do anyway,” he said, happy when his eagerness got a short laugh from her as they walked away from the house. “There’s no one else I’d rather have for the job.”

* * *

“You all right? You’ve been tossing and turning all night.”

Diana rolled over to face Jacob, the comforter shifting with her. The candles had all been blown out, and she had to strain her eyes to make out his face. "I can't get what happened out of my mind, Jacob. I knew the city was having problems, but this? Not even the palace is safe."

His large hand touched her cheek. "We are safe, love. Besides," he said, "no Legionnaire traitor is a match for you, me, Elisa, the Guardians, *and* two enchanters. They have their work cut out for them if they think otherwise."

She smiled despite knowing he could not see her. "Azgadar is unstable, Jacob. I could sense it during the talks with Ithmeera and her council today. Her people are unhappy with how the Restoration has been handled. The attacks on enchanters are only getting worse." She sighed. "She's got her own son to worry about and now *he's* a target. Then there's this mess with Elisa. She…is not certain she will come back to Gurdinfield with us."

"That is her choice to make, Diana."

Her smile faded. "I suppose it was too much for me to hope that Elisa would just renounce her oath to Ithmeera."

Jacob let out a frustrated noise. "You have an army of the best fighters in eastern Damea at your disposal, and yet you insist on pursuing Elisa. I…I don't understand it." He pulled his hand back, his tone sounding almost bitter to Diana. "She needs to find her own way, and we have to let her."

Annoyed, Diana threw the comforter off and sat up. She closed her eyes as the breeze from the open window cooled her face and shoulders. "She's my *friend*, Jacob, and as much a Guardian as you or I."

"She is my friend as well, but she has her own duties and they may not always line up with ours," Jacob told her. "We have our own issues to deal with back home."

As much as Diana hated the thought of leaving Elisa with these people, she knew Jacob was right. She covered her face with her hands. "The meetings today were exhausting. So many tedious details. It almost makes me wish I were back in the Southlands with you and Alexander. Life was so much simpler back then."

"Living in the forest, beating up bird scum, and being heroes, you mean?" Jacob said with a laugh. He sat up and put his arms around her from behind. "I miss it, too, love. But you're doing a fine job as queen and the people of Gurdinfield are better for it."

"You think so? I don't remember my parents, Jacob. I don't…I don't know what they would have done." She toyed with the stitching on the comforter's edge. "What if we're going about all of this the wrong way? Trade agreements with Gurith, alliances with Azgadar—they are all going to want things from us, and we're still rebuilding."

"That Balos is a strange fellow, that's for certain," Jacob muttered. "But it will be fine. Whatever happens, I am with you, Diana, and we will face it with our friends as we have always done."

She tilted her head to the side and kissed him before relaxing in his embrace. "Thank you. For listening and…for everything. We should probably get some sleep. I'm certain tomorrow will be even busier than today."

"What? *More* assassins?" Jacob exclaimed as they fell back onto the pillows together. "Send them to Roe. I'm sure he'll be more than happy to take care of them after today."

Diana's response was silence as the drowsiness she had been waiting for all night finally consumed her anxious thoughts. Content in Jacob's arms, she closed her eyes and hoped sleep would arrive soon.

Chapter 15
Departing Azgadar

A hawk flew past the open bay window, its powerful wings flapping hard as it worked to catch one of the thermals that would send it gliding across the city. The rustling of its feathers woke Cassie. The morning rays of bright light greeted her as they spilled into the room.

Ugh, that damn sun again. The Azgadaran sun had become Cassie's worst enemy, second only to the assassins who had attacked the palace. *Stupid assassins.* Not only had they caused trouble for everyone involved in the alliance negotiations, they also ruined what was supposed to be a nice, semi-normal date with Andrea.

When Cassie focused her eyes downward, a lazy smile spread across her face. *Well, not* quite *ruined.* Memories of the night before rushed to the surface of Cassie's mind, overwhelming her with bliss and a little disbelief that it had really happened. But Andrea was still sound asleep on her shoulder, her arms wrapped surprisingly tight around Cassie's waist.

She had to stifle a laugh at the sight of Andrea's wild strands of dark hair sticking out in several different directions. Seeing what form of animal nest Andrea's hair would try to mimic each day was always a new adventure, but Cassie decided that today's display was her favorite by far. But just *thinking* about the way Andrea's hair fell when it got in her eyes or even when it was in the way while they were kissing made Cassie's heart skip a beat. She sighed, not quite understanding how the stupidest, simplest things could make her so nervous when it came to the two of them, but also was more than happy to accept it.

She nuzzled the top of Andrea's head before planting a gentle kiss on her forehead. It wasn't her intent to wake her, but Andrea stirred anyway.

"...Cassie?" Andrea tilted her head up. The morning light caught her hazel eyes, leaving Cassie struggling to remember how to breathe.

"Uh, hi there."

Andrea gave her a lopsided smile. "Hello."

"You, um, you sleep okay?" *Perfect. I've lost the ability to speak normally.*

Andrea replied with a long kiss, pushing her into the bed. "Yes," she said when she finally pulled away—this time leaving Cassie entirely breathless. She let out a giddy laugh. "Did I make you blush?"

Yes. Cassie scoffed. "What? No."

But Andrea just grinned. "I did, didn't I? I've never seen you so red!"

Cassie rolled her eyes. "Okay. Time to get up, then." She started to sit up, but Andrea pushed her back down on the pillow.

"No! Stay." Andrea whining like this was probably one of

the more comical things that Cassie had heard since meeting her. But it was morning and the other Guardians would be expecting her at some point.

Her brow furrowed. "You used that line last night already, remember?" She rested her hands on Andrea's arms. "I need to get to the courtyard before Jacob sends a search party out for me. And uh…" She gestured at the two of them. "That might be kind of awkward."

"Fine." Andrea's defeated expression was almost enough to make Cassie decide to stay. But she figured they would have plenty of time alone together, especially after they left for Ata in a day.

"Besides, don't you get to talk to the royal enchanter today?"

Andrea looked at the ceiling in thought. "Master Tobias? Yes, Diana and I are to meet with him later."

"So, we'll both be busy," Cassie concluded. "But I'll see you tonight." She took Andrea's lips in another kiss. "Okay?"

"All right." Andrea gave her a hopeful smile. "I love you."

Jacob, I hate you right now. "I love you," she returned as she struggled to maintain their eye contact. The words still felt strange to say, but Cassie loved being able to say them. Her cheeks grew warm again, much to her dismay.

Sure enough, Andrea caught her. She grinned widely, touching Cassie's cheek. "I did it again!"

* * *

“Are you certain you have everything you need? You packed enough food?” Diana double-checked the buckle on the backpack before tossing it to Cassie, who caught it deftly and secured it to the horse with the rest of their supplies.

Their final full day in the palace had come and gone, with things for the most part back to normal as the Legion continued to investigate the source of the attacks on enchanters and Diana worked with Ithmeera and her council to flesh out the terms of their alliance. It was mid-morning when Cassie went to the palace stables to begin preparing the horse she and Andrea would be taking with them to Ata. Their tentative plan was to meet Andrea’s parents and stay in the Western Hills for a week before reuniting with their friends in Azgadar and then returning to the City of Towers.

“If we don’t, I guess we’ll know when we’re starving to death,” she said, earning a laugh from Jacob and a few of the other Guardians who had come to see them off. Even Victor, who was still recovering from his wound, had shown up.

Elisa picked up a particularly heavy pack and was about to toss it to Cassie when Andrea rushed between them. “Wait! Those are breakable.”

Elisa shook the bag a little anyway, the distinct clinks of glass against glass coming from it. “What’s in it?”

Andrea yanked the pack from Elisa’s hand, prompting a laugh from Kye who stood behind them. “Secret experiments,” she said with a pointed glare. “And they’re very fragile so please don’t throw them.” She turned on her heel and walked over to the horse where Cassie was.

Cassie grinned. “‘Secret experiments’, huh?”

"They're the potions I was working on in Gurdinfield," Andrea explained, though Cassie thought she heard some apprehension in her voice. "I…I thought maybe I could show them to Master Jheran."

"They're not going to explode or anything while we're traveling, are they?"

Andrea held her answer for longer than Cassie was comfortable with. She tried again. "Andrea…"

"I don't *think* so?" Andrea said, though it sounded more like a question than an answer. "Well, it's bottled magic and it *is* an experiment so…"

"Andrea!"

"It should be fine!" She held the pack out to Cassie, who took it after a brief hesitation.

"If this blows up on us," she said before securing it to the saddle, "I will be *very* upset."

Finally, they had everything they could think of packed. Cassie's sword and a few hunting knives had been hooked to the saddlebags, as well as the provisions Ithmeera had been gracious enough to give them for their journey.

Jacob pulled her aside and spoke in a quieter voice than usual. "Keep your eyes open. There could be more attacks on enchanters outside the capital city." His gaze gravitated to Andrea. "Do *not* let her out of your sight and if you do encounter trouble, guard her with your life. No matter how many times she tries to convince you she doesn't need protection, she is still your charge and therefore your responsibility." He placed a heavy hand on her shoulder. "We clear?"

Wow, no pressure or anything, right? She tried to sound as confident as possible. "I got this, Jacob. We'll be fine."

He smiled and slapped her on the back harder than Cassie felt was necessary, sending her into a short fit of coughing. "That's what I like to hear!"

Several steps away, Andrea frowned at her. "Are you all right, Cassie?"

Still coughing, Cassie could only lift a hand as she croaked out, "Fine! I'm fine."

"You're really going to ride the *entire* way to the Western Hills, Cassie?" Kye asked with an incredulous look as Andrea climbed onto the horse, with Cassie taking her spot behind her.

"She's going to try," Andrea said teasingly as she glanced back at Cassie.

Cassie shrugged. "Sure, just like I'm going to try to not throw up on you."

Diana crossed her arms and looked up at them, ignoring that particular exchange. "Good luck. I hope you find your parents well, Andrea."

"Thank you, Your Majesty." Andrea bowed her head. "We will see you soon."

Cassie felt a sickening jolt in her stomach as Andrea spurred the horse to take them out of the stables. *I don't know if I* can *do an entire trip like this.* Within minutes they had passed through the city gates, where they would soon head north and then west toward the forest that blanketed the knolls separating the Azgadaran Empire from the Western Hills. The journey would take them several days, and it was one neither of them had braved before.

“I can’t believe I’m really doing this,” Andrea said after they had ridden in silence for the first half hour. “I haven’t been back since…” She didn’t finish.

“You’ll be fine.” Cassie knew this trip was a long time coming and that Andrea would probably be nervous the entire way to Ata. *Meeting her parents can’t be any worse than taking on an army of Legionnaires…right?* “I told you I’d be there with you, didn’t I?”

“Yes, but…it’s been so long, Cassie. I don’t even know what I’m going to say to them.”

Pushing aside the nausea that came and went from being on horseback, Cassie squeezed Andrea’s waist in a quick hug. “Well, you have a while to figure it out.”

Andrea sighed. “You make it sound so easy.”

“It won’t be.” Cassie didn’t want to give Andrea false hope since she didn’t know what would happen. “But you’ll do it. I know you will.” She looked up at the rolling green hills in the distance—it would be a while yet before the dry grasslands they traveled across transitioned to the shady forest ahead.

She remembered Jacob’s words of warning and looked down at the sword that hung near their supplies. *Let’s hope her parents are the only scary thing we have to deal with on this trip.*

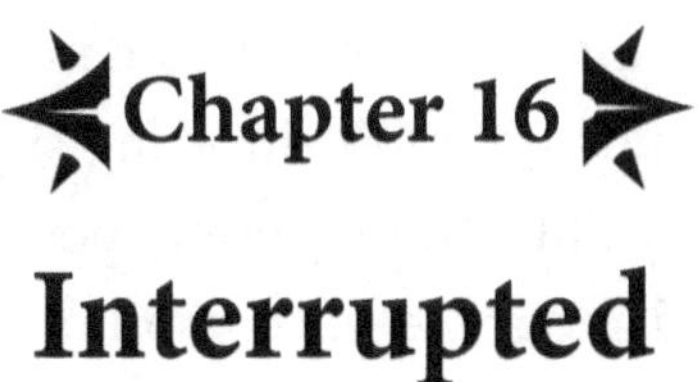

Chapter 16
Interrupted

Three days later

"They're fine. Stop worrying so much."

Andrea shook her head a few times, as though to free herself of some trance, before flashing Cassie a sheepish smile. "Am I that obvious?"

"Only a lot."

"Despite what you might believe, Cassie, you cannot, in fact, read my mind," Andrea said.

"Sure. So, you weren't just mentally going over all the horrible things that could possibly happen to Jacob and Diana without you around to protect them?" Cassie shot her a teasing grin, adjusting her hold on the reins as she guided their horse down the beaten path they had been walking on since dawn. The early morning fog had burned off and although the sun was almost at its highest point, the thick foliage of the tall trees they were under provided refuge from the heat as they neared the edge of the empire's realm.

As grateful as Cassie was for the shade, she could have done without the stupid bugs. Buzzing, crawling, flying—all varieties were unnecessary in her opinion. And the flying ones always seemed to zoom directly at her face.

"Given the circumstances, that should not come as a surprise to you," Andrea said, agitation shivering slightly in her voice. "In any case, it's my duty. I'd be a pretty poor royal enchanter if I wasn't concerned about the royal family's safety."

Cassie shrugged and kicked a rock down the path, chuckling when their horse snorted. "True, but what could you do from here?"

"If you're trying to comfort me, Cassie, you're doing a terrible job of it." Andrea glanced over at Cassie before looking up at the horse. "Also, we *do* have a horse. We would probably be out of these woods by now if you'd just let us ride her."

Cassie let out a harsh laugh. "Ha! Right. I'm sure your parents will find me incredibly endearing if I vomit on their doorstep after introducing myself." She altered her demeanor to a brighter, if unlikely, version of herself. "'Hi! I'm Cassie! Nice to meet you!'" she exclaimed before doing her best retching impression.

"You…you wouldn't actually do that, right?" Andrea said with a hint of fear in her voice.

Cassie stopped walking and gave Andrea a long, hard stare. "I might," she said in a low voice, leaning in close before pulling away. "But only if you make me ride the horse."

"Cassie…"

"Well you have to admit, it would make a better impression than 'Hey, I'm Cassie. I enjoy throwing myself into massive battles, going on suicide missions, and helping people set crap on fire! Oh yeah, and I'm dating the daughter that you haven't seen or heard from in over three years. Nice to meet you.'"

Andrea laughed as they picked up their pace. "That's all there is to you, hm? Massive battles, ever-present danger, and courting me?" She gave a dramatic roll of her eyes. "It all sounds rather *boring*."

Cassie scoffed. "For your information, I happen to know that saving your ass all the time is anything but boring. I mean, it's a full-time job!"

"Oh, so I'm a *job* now, am I?" Andrea said. She let out a melodramatic sigh. "Well, if that's all that I am, I suppose—"

Knowing when she should probably stop pushing, Cassie reached out and took Andrea's hand. "Did I say job? I meant that you're beautiful."

Andrea closed her eyes and shook her head, but she did not let go of Cassie's hand. They continued to walk under the trees, letting the chirping of birds and rustling of various animals hidden in the brush fill the air for a bit. "That's not a solution to everything, you know," she finally said.

"What's not?"

"Flattery. It doesn't work on me."

Cassie leaned in and placed a light kiss on Andrea's cheek. "Guess I'll just have to try harder, then." When she saw Andrea's face redden from the blush that spread across it, she considered teasing her some more, but decided that the simple closeness they had was worth hanging onto a little longer.

* * *

"There!" Cassie tossed the final pieces of deadwood onto the messy pile she had created once the sun had set. She gave Andrea a proud smile and dusted her hands off. "That should be enough for tonight."

Andrea seemed less than impressed. She was sitting on a short, rotted log, their backpacks and water canteens scattered on the ground next to her. "I hope so, considering you probably just alerted every animal and bandit in the area to our presence here by announcing that we had firewood." She stared ahead into the flames, their primary source of warmth in the clear, chilly evening. "Maybe we should have stayed in Azgadar."

Cassie groaned as she took a seat on the log next to Andrea, shifting a bit when she felt the decayed wood creak in protest. "Okay, now you're just finding things to worry about. I thought you *wanted* to show me where you grew up."

After propping her elbows on her knees, Andrea rested her chin in her hands. "I do," she said, half-sighing, half-sulking.

"Then lighten up!" Cassie told her, giving Andrea a gentle poke in the side, making her jump.

"Really?" Andrea said, eyebrow arched. "Ah." She ran her hand through her hair. "I'm sorry. You're right. And I *do* worry, but…no." She stopped and turned to face Cassie. "You're right and that's that. We're going to Ata and you're going to meet my parents and my friends and it's all going to be extremely awkward and uncomfortable, but...we're going to do it."

Finally. "That's better. Now," Cassie said, reaching for the bag containing their traveling rations—mostly bread, dried fruit, and cured meat. "Food?"

"Yes, please." Andrea moved over a bit to make some space while Cassie set up servings.

They ate in silence for the first several minutes, their appetites speaking for themselves. After inhaling her second serving, Cassie spoke up.

"So, your parents. They nice?"

Andrea seemed surprised at the question. She took a moment to wipe a few crumbs of bread from the corner of her mouth before answering. "Erm…what do you mean?"

"Well, you've never really talked about them except how you guys left things, which I know wasn't great." Cassie grabbed one of the canteens and took a long drink before offering it to Andrea. "I mean, come on. You haven't even told me their names."

Andrea blinked. "You of all people are getting on *my* case because I've held back about aspects of my life?" She took a drink as well and set the canteen back on the ground.

Laughing, Cassie put her arm around Andrea's waist and pulled her in close. "Consider it personal growth on my part."

Andrea gave her a sidelong look. "Right."

"Humor me. Please?" Cassie asked. She smiled when Andrea shrugged and leaned on her shoulder.

"Well," Andrea began, "you know they own a farm."

"Yeah. Vegetables and stuff, right?"

"Yes," Andrea said. "My mother's name is Isabel and my

father is Garrett." She let out an audible sigh, and Cassie could sense the hurt and disappointment in it. She tightened her hold on Andrea before asking another question. "No brothers or sisters?"

"Ah, no. Though I don't really know if they wanted more children. I suppose…I suppose they figured I would take over the farm once I was old enough, or when they couldn't manage it anymore." Andrea gave a soft laugh. "I wouldn't have minded the extra help with chores, that's for sure."

Cassie knew that talking about her own past was usually difficult for her, but Andrea did not seem uncomfortable, so she continued. "What are they like? Your parents, I mean."

Another shrug. "Well, I suppose my mother's always been rather serious. I think she worried about me a lot, especially after my abilities showed up." She paused. "We've never agreed on much, but she *is* my mother, and…I do love her. And miss her."

"And your father?"

Andrea rolled her eyes, but Cassie could hear the adoration in her voice. "Terrible sense of humor. I used to want to be just like him." She shook her head, smiling. "I'd follow him around *everywhere.* Nearly got myself injured more than once when I would try to 'help' him with some of the chores that required heavier lifting than a ten-year-old could manage. My mother would get so mad at him." She laughed again, but her voice carried a shakiness that Cassie recognized right away. "He was so angry when I told him I was running off with Meredith to be an enchanter."

Cassie refused to miss the opportunity when she saw

it. "But it worked out, right? You saved the world, *and* the mystery behind your underdeveloped sense of humor is finally explained!"

"You're hardly one to talk," Andrea exclaimed, sitting upright and giving Cassie a light rap on the shoulder.

"Ow!" Cassie gripped her shoulder, giving Andrea a look full of exaggerated grievance. "Definitely undeserved."

"I disagree," Andrea said, a smile tugging at the corners of her mouth.

Cassie leaned in and pressed her forehead against Andrea's temple. "Thank you."

"Mm? For what?"

"Talking about your parents. I know you don't like to."

"Oh." Andrea turned her head and pressed her lips against Cassie's. "I don't mind," she said between kisses. "It's nice that you want to know, even if it's a little strange to talk about." She reached around to place a gentle hand on the back of Cassie's neck.

"I know what that's…that's like," Cassie said, though it was getting harder to focus on the conversation and kiss at the same time. But when Andrea pulled her closer, Cassie made a fast decision. *Screw it—we can chat later.*

She liked it when Andrea took the lead—it helped her forget about the burden of responsibility she had been under since leaving Gurdinfield. The horrible events that occurred only days earlier could be put aside for now—only this mattered.

Only she *matters.*

An owl hooted, sounding rather close, and Cassie could swear she heard the distant howls of wolves, but overall the calls of the forest at night were dulled as she blocked out everything that was not Andrea.

Their moment had lasted for far too little when Andrea jerked her head back, her hazel eyes wide with alarm.

"What's wrong?" Cassie asked.

Andrea stood up and looked around. Her hands hovered at her waist, tense and ready to cast magic if necessary. Her voice was low, almost raspy. "Someone's here."

Cassie grabbed her sword and drew it, tossing the sheath on the dirt. "How do you know?"

The barrier went up before Andrea could answer—a flash of golden light blinded Cassie for a split second as the translucent shield formed a dome around them. The arrow that was headed straight for Cassie's head smashed into the barrier and bounced off.

Andrea lowered her hands. "Show yourself!"

Cassie tightened her grip on the hilt of her weapon, though she could already feel the metal growing clammy with sweat as her adrenaline fought her nerves. She swallowed hard as three armored men stepped into the clearing. Her breath hitched when she saw the color of their armor and the distinct coat of arms branded into it.

Brown. Gold. The scales of the Gurithian banner.

"Gurithians?" she whispered, standing as close as possible to Andrea. "What the hell?"

Two of the soldiers drew their swords. The third slung his

bow over his shoulder and drew a sword as well. "Take the enchanter alive. Don't worry about the other."

Cassie leaned back a little so that Andrea could hear her. "Get the horse and get out of here," she hissed.

But Andrea just glared at the intruders. "Leave or you'll be sorry."

The soldiers rushed forward, the tallest one in the middle heading straight for them with his sword held high. Cassie did the only thing she could remember from her training in that moment and jumped in front of Andrea, holding her sword out to block the attack.

The soldier yelled as his sword came down on Cassie's head. She froze, the fear anchoring her in place.

Suddenly the world grew hot and the scent of burning magic stung Cassie's nostrils. Lightning branched out from Andrea's outstretched hands and curled around them, searing and crackling. The leader and the man who had fired the arrow fell unconscious right away, but the third remained conscious, twitching in agony on the ground. Cassie remained beside Andrea as she approached the only conscious Gurithian soldier.

"Why is the Merchants' Guild after us? We had an accord," Andrea demanded.

Keeping her sword at the ready, Cassie was surprised when the soldier said nothing. He stared up at them, his face still contorted in pain from Andrea's spell. His eyes, though—it could have been the light from the flames of the campfire playing tricks, but the man's eyes did not seem to hold any contempt. In fact, Cassie thought he seemed more confused than anything.

But Andrea did not have the patience for any of this. She lifted her hand up, conjuring a ball of fire. "You have three seconds to answer my question or I use this on you. One… two…"

The man gasped and held up his hands, the veins in his neck popping and his eyes welling up with tears as he let out a ragged cough. "P-please! I yield! Don't kill me."

Cassie put her hand on Andrea's arm and gave it a gentle push, enough to make Andrea dispel the fire and lower her hand. "Easy. Something's weird here," she murmured.

The soldier struggled to push himself up. "I—I don't know how I got here. Honest!"

Andrea's brow furrowed. "The guild didn't send you?"

"No! All I remember is finishing my watch and then…" He trailed off. "I'm sorry. I truly don't remember!"

Andrea exchanged confused glances with Cassie before looking back down at the soldier. "Go back to Gurith. Take your friends with you." She turned to Cassie. "We need to leave."

They gathered their things, put out the fire, and were soon on horseback, Andrea using a conjured ball of white light to guide them through the forest.

"What if they follow us? What if that guy was lying?" Cassie asked.

"I don't think they will," Andrea said. "You were right—there was something strange about how that man was acting." She sighed. "I don't know what to do. Maybe we should report back to Diana—"

Cassie cut her off. "No way. We're close to Ata—we can try to send her a message when we get there, right?"

"I…I suppose that's true," Andrea said. "Fine. But we're riding the rest of the way. I don't think they will follow us, but I would feel a lot better if we had some distance between us and them."

Cassie made a face, even though she knew Andrea could not see her. "Ugh…yeah, okay." She paused and rested a hand on Andrea's arm. "Hey, are you all right? I know that can't have been easy for you. How did you know they were even there?"

Andrea placed a hand over Cassie's for a brief moment before returning it to the reins. "I'm fine, Cassie. And…I don't know. I suppose I could hear them? No," she muttered, "that's not what I mean."

"I didn't hear anything," Cassie said. Then she was reminded of something. "Could it have been like, a magic thing?"

Andrea was quiet at first. "I don't know." She sounded tense still, with tiredness creeping into her voice. Cassie considered offering to take the reins, but before she could, Andrea spoke again.

"I'm sorry we were interrupted. That was…really nice."

Cassie chuckled. "Yeah it was, wasn't it?" She wrapped her arms around Andrea tighter and relaxed as the stress and tension finally started to dissipate.

"Hopefully, we can make it through the rest of this trip without being attacked or killed," Andrea said, and Cassie was relieved to hear the calm back in her voice.

"With our record, that's asking for a lot," she said, hoping that Andrea was right.

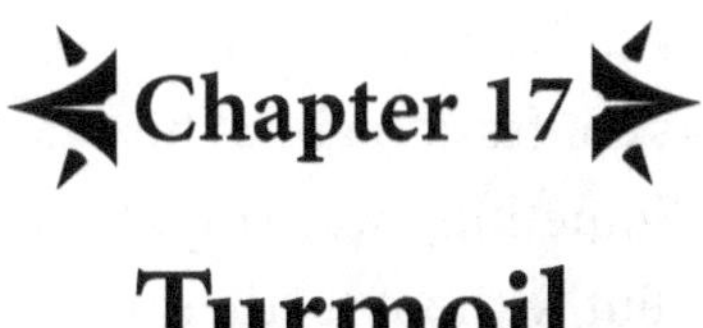

Chapter 17
Turmoil

“Your Majesty, your uncle is here to see you.”

Ithmeera was halfway finished with her edits to one of the alliance documents she would bring before the council for amendment in the morning when she heard Petra’s knock on her bedroom door. “Thank you, Petra. Please let him in.”

The double doors creaked as Alden entered the room. He bowed before speaking, his voice carrying a tone that had gradually become more severe in the months following his forced resignation. “Good afternoon, Ithmeera.”

She set her pen down next to a crumpled note which had been delivered to her earlier in the day. Amendments would have to wait. At least the meetings with Queen Lydia were finished for the day. “Hello, Uncle. Is there something I can do for you?” Ithmeera hated how strained their relationship had become since Erik’s death, but she still believed she made the right choice. War would not make the empire strong despite whatever Alden told her. Her father, Nardos, believed strong alliances with the other nations of Damea would make the empire more powerful, and she would see his vision through.

A tired smile flickered on Alden’s face. “I heard about the

attack on that enchanter in the city," he said. "It's the third this week, Ithmeera. The protests are forming almost daily in the marketplace. I cannot help but be concerned."

What will it take to keep him out of my affairs? Ithmeera was reminded of Petra's confession about his reaction to a letter she delivered to him. Something wasn't quite right with him—she knew that much—but without further proof she had no reason to investigate it further, and the fact that Alden was family made the situation even more difficult.

She took on the firm tone she was used to employing with him these days. "It is being handled, Uncle." She returned to her writing, hoping he would leave her in peace.

He took a step toward her. "I am concerned, Ithmeera, because the Legionnaires keeping the peace in the city are being told their fallen comrades sacrificed their lives for nothing when you invited the Queen of Gurdinfield into our home."

Ithmeera dropped her pen. "They're being told *what?* By whom?"

"By the very citizens who are protesting," Alden replied. "They say that none of this would be happening had the Restoration not occurred. And everyone knows Gurdinfield is responsible for *that.*"

"We were running out of magic, Alden!" She stood up and walked to the open window, gesturing to the city. "What would they have me do? Let our resources dwindle to the point where we cannot even power our cities? Our farms? Do they desire another centuries-long famine? Because that is what will happen if we do not let enchanters practice their craft."

Alden held his hand up calmly. "I agree with you, dear. I was merely reporting what I've been told by the councilors. They offered the information to me freely, by the way," he clarified.

Ithmeera fumed. *I will need to have a word with these councilors about the confidentiality of such reports, particularly around those who are no longer* on *the council.* "The people have a right to express their opinions, Alden. My father believed in fairness and openness with the empire's citizens." She closed her eyes. "If I silence the protesters it will only make matters worse."

"You are the empress of the Azgadaran Empire, Ithmeera!" Alden exclaimed. "The people will choose chaos over their empress if she does not assert her authority. You—"

She shot him a warning glare. "You will *not* remind me of my place, Alden. I do, however, feel it's been too long since you were reminded of yours."

Alden paled. "Forgive me, Your Majesty, I meant no disrespect. I only worry for your and Marco's wellbeing. *Especially* Marco," he added.

Ithmeera sighed. "Because of his abilities? Tobias is working with him every day."

"There are those…" He took a deep breath, and somehow Ithmeera just knew that his next words would anger her. "There are those who would not be pleased to see an enchanter sit on the throne. I would advise you to take these people seriously, Ithmeera, until you can find them and put an end to this nonsense. Bring back the laws on magic, send the Legion after these traitors, and order *will* follow."

For a moment, Ithmeera could only hear her own enraged breathing. She clenched her fists so hard her nails bit painfully into her palms. "That...will be all, Alden."

But Alden remained where he stood. "A dynasty cannot survive if it does not have the respect of its people. And right now, Ithmeera, the people are against you. Marco is—"

"Do not make me repeat myself, Alden," Ithmeera growled. "Leave me. *Now.*"

Alden stiffened, and Ithmeera was sure he would argue again. How *dare* he? She had half a mind to call the guards. With all that was happening in the city, the last thing she needed was her own uncle trying to meddle in her affairs again. Even if there was wisdom behind his words, *no one* told Ithmeera Cadar how to rule her own empire.

Instead his shoulders slumped, and he just seemed... Ithmeera could not put her finger on it. "Defeated" was not the right word. Rather, she spotted what almost appeared to be pity in his eyes. *But pity about what?*

"As you wish, Your Majesty. I will be in my quarters should you require anything at all from me." He grasped the door handle. "Please...please know that I love the empire above all else," he said before departing.

Ithmeera collapsed in her chair again. She looked up at the open window, the evening sun against the darkening sky a passive reminder that another day had passed without a solution being found.

"Is there no end to this?" she muttered and rubbed her temples.

"Your Grace?" Petra's cautious voice sounded from the doorway. "Do you need anything?"

"I don't know," Ithmeera whispered without glancing up. "Is

it too much to hope that *you* have a nice, simple solution for all of the empire's problems?"

Petra gave a soft laugh as she entered the room, carrying a cup of herbal tea. "You will find it, my lady, I am sure of it. In the meantime, I've brought you your tea." She set the cup down on Ithmeera's desk before biting her lip. "I should tell you that Marco hasn't touched his new sword since that night, Your Grace. I would be happy to get him something else if it is not satisfactory to him."

No. "You will not, Petra. This…this is my fault," she said, her voice breaking on the last words as the horrific realization that her son could not and would never be an ordinary boy sunk in. The anger she had hurled toward Alden returned, only this time, she was furious at herself.

Marco will never be normal as long as he wields magic. But the people of this empire will *bow to him.* She turned to Petra. "I will speak to Marco." She stood up, taking Petra's hand in a gentle hold. "You have been wonderful in all of this…this mess," Ithmeera told her sincerely. "Thank you."

If Petra was surprised by her actions, she did not show it. Graceful and dutiful as always, she bowed her head. "I am always here for you, Your Majesty. As are your people. We would do anything for you."

Ithmeera smiled as she released Petra. "I will go speak to Marco right now," she said. "In the meantime, I do have one thing to ask of you. It may seem like an odd favor."

* * *

"This hand goes here and—no, Elisa, *here.*"

Elisa let out a huff as she struggled to play a single chord on Kye's lute that did not come out sounding like a rusted iron gate. Why in the world was it so important that her fingers were in *that* exact position? She felt ridiculous, her hand was cramping, and Kye giggling every few minutes as she snarled at the instrument did nothing to help her situation. "I just *did* that, boy."

"You were too far up. The chord will come out wrong," he explained. Ignoring her frustration, he took her hand off the neck of the lute and repositioned her fingers against the strings. "There. Try that."

She gave it another tentative strum and her eyebrows went up in surprise when the sound emitted wasn't terrible. It wasn't *good,* but it didn't make Elisa want to smash the lute over Kye's head, either.

"Very good!" He gave her a brief round of applause that drew the attention of a few of the servants, guards, and visitors to the palace passing through the Great Hall, where Elisa and Kye had spent the last hour. Normally she would be with Diana in the negotiations, but when they had ended early for the day, Kye offered to give her a music lesson. She realized it was getting late when she noticed the servants begin lighting more candles in the room as dusk set in.

She gave a satisfied nod. "Perhaps someday I'll play a full song without causing anyone's ears to bleed," she said before handing the lute back to him. "I believe it is your turn."

Heavy steps approached as a shadow was cast upon them. General Veraun's large figure was formidable to many, but to

Elisa it was mostly just annoying. Kye must have fallen in with the former—his eyes turned to the floor as he set the lute down.

Elisa rolled her eyes. "Can we help you, Ben?"

Veraun wasn't amused. "You can start by addressing me properly. 'General Veraun' is very easy to remember." He pointed at the lute. "Didn't take you for a musician, Elisa."

"What do you need, *General?*" Elisa was not in the mood for small talk—especially not with *Ben* of all people.

Veraun grumbled something unintelligible before clearing his throat. "I can't believe I'm saying this but…the empress requests your presence, Elisa. Please, follow me."

Elisa gave him a blank stare. "Now?"

"Now."

She turned to Kye. "If Diana asks where I am, tell her that she and Jacob may need to get me out of prison again." When she saw his face lose some color, she sighed. "I am kidding. Just let her know where I am if she asks, yes?"

Kye's frightened gaze went from her to Veraun and then back to her before he mumbled his understanding. Minutes later, Elisa and Veraun walked up the stairs leading to the upper levels of the spire.

"Is he always so skittish?"

"Who?" she asked, already apprehensive about meeting with Ithmeera again and even less in the mood to chat like old friends with a man she despised.

"The smith's son. He looks like he wants to run away every time he sees me," he said as they turned the corner to head down another long corridor.

"Are you really surprised? Your men have tried to kill him on several occasions." Elisa observed their surroundings. She knew this hallway—she'd walked down it countless times. "Where are we going?"

His chainmail clinked against his sword as he walked. "Her Majesty has requested that you meet her in her quarters. I don't know why and to be honest, Elisa, I would have advised her against it."

Elisa stopped and faced him. "But you didn't?"

"No," Veraun said, scratching his head. "The other night…I strayed too far from the Cadars during that attack. I was so distracted I didn't see the second assassin." He seemed to struggle with his next words. "You were there, though. You protected the empress and Marco."

Baffled by his admission, her answer came out more monotonous than she intended. "I did my duty."

Veraun smirked. "You abandoned your *duty* the moment you knew your father broke the law and didn't do anything about it. However…" His voice softened. "Your actions the other night were still honorable." He motioned ahead. "After you."

Petra was waiting for them outside Ithmeera's bedroom, her lips set in a straight line as her dark eyes made contact with Elisa's. "Her Grace has asked that she be left alone with Elisa," she stated.

"I must object, Petra, if only for the sake of security—"

Petra held up her hand, silencing Veraun—much to Elisa's surprise. "Her Majesty's security is being seen to. Thank you, General."

Veraun held Elisa's gaze for a moment before leaving. Petra

waited until he was out of sight to speak.

"She is waiting for you." Petra reached for the door handle, distress clear in her voice. "*Please* listen to what she has to say, Elisa." She pushed the doors open.

Elisa took a deep breath and stepped into the room, uncertain and more anxious than she wanted to admit about what Ithmeera wanted with her.

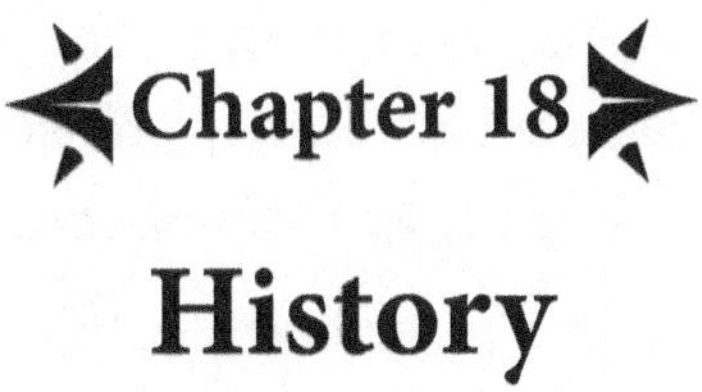

Chapter 18
History

She jumped when the door shut behind her, craning her neck out of instinct to see if Petra had followed her into Ithmeera's private quarters. She had not.

"Thank you for coming." Ithmeera's words were soft—softer than Elisa expected, considering how cold Ithmeera had been toward her ever since her arrival. But her tone today was different. There was agitation in it, and fear. Only one other time in Elisa's memory had she heard Ithmeera's voice like this—when Philip was found dead. She had been the one to break the news to Elisa—to tell her how her brother's body had been found beneath the remains of his splintered trading wagon.

Elisa recalled hanging onto reality by a thread when she heard the news—how she had sworn to find the bandits responsible and tear them apart piece by piece, and how angry she was when Ithmeera forbade it. She ordered Elisa to stay with her, to help her *mourn* Philip rather than avenge his death.

Her reclusiveness and the decline of her father's physical and mental health had been the catalysts for her downward spiral, ending in her exile from Azgadar.

The sight of Ithmeera sitting in quiet distress on her oversized bed, the dark red comforter bunched up at the occupied end, convinced Elisa to opt for a neutral response. A crumpled white piece of paper lay next to her. "You wished to see me, Your Majesty?" She noted a child's sword, still in its sheath, on the bed as well. She knew it was Marco's, but why was it here?

Ithmeera remained still, save the subtle movement of her lips. "Please, Elisa…don't."

Elisa wasn't sure *what* she should have expected when Veraun requested her to follow him to Ithmeera's bedroom but it certainly wasn't this. She tried again. "Is there something I can do for you?"

Ithmeera gave a slight tilt of her head. "There was another attack today."

"On an enchanter?"

"Yes." Ithmeera folded her hands together. "A young man, about the same age as your friend." She nodded toward the paper. "His murderers left this on his body."

Elisa closed her eyes before reaching for the note. Why Kye had agreed to come back to Azgadar was beyond her. She wished Diana had not brought him along—pardon or no pardon. "I'm sorry."

Ithmeera shifted on the bed so that she could look at Elisa. "They…" She gave a trembling breath. "They broke his arms, Elisa. Shattered his hands with—with hammers. He was just a *child.* Fifteen, sixteen at most!"

Elisa unfolded the note. "The Legion has apprehended them, though?" she asked, beginning to read the blotchy handwriting.

There were multiple ink stains on the paper that had spread to the actual note, but it was legible enough. "'We will purge this land of the unworthy. The empire shall never bow to an enchanter. Long live the New Legion.'" She looked up. "The New Legion? Who are they?"

"A very sick, determined group of scum who wish harm on enchanters."

Elisa placed the note back on the bed. "Is this all because you lifted the restrictions?"

"It doesn't matter," Ithmeera said, and stood up. "Between the attacks over the past few months and then what happened during the ball, I…" She met Elisa's puzzled gaze, her own eyes filled with what Elisa suspected was an internal battle. "I need to get the situation under control before it is too late. It may already be." Her voice dropped to a whisper as she turned her gaze to the window. "You should take Queen Lydia and leave as soon as possible. Azgadar is no longer safe."

Elisa's attention was drawn once more to Marco's toy sword. "Does Marco not like his new blade?" she asked.

Ithmeera chuckled, though even her laugh carried sadness. "He loves it. But he is scared and refuses to use it. After the other night…"

Elisa sighed and went to stand next to her. "For what it's worth, I am sorry for what he saw. But I would do it again if it meant keeping him safe."

"Marco is smart," Ithmeera said as she faced Elisa again. "He understands there are people who are trying to hurt him because of his abilities. A boy as young as he should not have to deal with this, Elisa!"

Elisa's eyes lit up as the strands of an idea began weaving together. She knew Ithmeera would probably be outraged at the very suggestion she was about to make, but it was probably the only way to guarantee Marco's safety short of locking him away at the top of the spire with constant guard supervision.

"There may be a way," she said. "Ask Lydia to take him to the City of Towers."

Ithmeera's jaw dropped and Elisa wasn't the least bit surprised. "Absolutely not. Have you gone completely mad, Elisa?"

"You said it yourself: Azgadar is no longer safe." Elisa pointed at the city below. "If it is not safe for me, then it is certainly not safe for Marco. Let her take him."

But Ithmeera backed away, shaking her head. "You're crazy."

"I trust Diana and Jacob with my life, Ithmeera. I know..." Elisa swallowed, her voice coming out raspier than she intended. "I know things are...what they are, but I'm asking you to trust *me*." She could only hope that Ithmeera would not let her emotions get in the way of reason when it came to Marco's safety.

But Ithmeera's dry laugh did not give Elisa much confidence. "Why in the world would I trust you after everything you've done?"

"Because I am still loyal to this empire." She tensed. "Just as I am still...loyal to you."

Ithmeera shot her a burning glare, her judgement cutting Elisa deep—into her very being, even. "You are not a Legionnaire anymore, Elisa."

I must try. For Marco's sake. And…for hers. "Maybe not, but you don't need a Legionnaire, Ithmeera."

"And just what *do* I need?" Ithmeera challenged as she stepped up to Elisa, their noses almost touching as Elisa felt the heat of Ithmeera's breath. "Since you seem to be the authority on what I require." The fiery gaze in her eyes did not waver and Elisa thought she would fall apart on the spot. "You abandoned us. You killed Erik. And now you want my *trust?*"

"He murdered my father in cold blood." The last fragments of confidence pushed Elisa to stand up to her. "I should have listened to Philip. I should have resisted the pressure when you asked me to become your guard!"

"*Don't* bring Philip into this!" Ithmeera cried. "Don't say his name. You have *no* idea what I've gone through—what *Marco* has gone through without his father."

"How can you say that?" Elisa crossed her arms over her chest as her last line of defense. "He was my *brother,* Ithmeera. There's not a day that goes by where I don't miss him. But *no.* You *let* him travel to the edge of Damea and back. He didn't have to go—"

Ithmeera's eyes widened and for a moment, Elisa was sure she was going to strike her. But instead she took a step back and began pacing. "I loved your brother. But I won't take the blame for his death. What happened was *not* my fault!"

"Why did you ask for me, Ithmeera?" Elisa demanded, her hands shaking as the tension between them escalated to dangerous levels. "You don't want my loyalty, my opinion, or my service. You don't give a damn about me—you couldn't care less if I turned up dead in some gutter in the slums come morning. You have Erik's sword now." She gave a mirthless laugh. "All I want is to mourn Philip and my father in peace. Why can't you all just leave me alone?!"

Ithmeera's eyes welled up with tears as something snapped between them and set her off. "Because you're not the only one who lost someone, Elisa!"

Silence. Elisa looked away, trying her hardest to not let Ithmeera's quiet sobs get to her. "I will leave you be," she mumbled. With a stiff bow, she walked past Ithmeera, wishing her hurried steps would carry her faster out of the room. She *needed* to be out of that room. Needed to be away from Ithmeera.

But Ithmeera's shattered voice stopped her. "Elisa…wait. *Please.*"

Stop going back to her. Stop giving her what she wants. If only she had stayed in Gurdinfield. At least then she could live out her life in relative peace without having to deal with Ithmeera… or any of this.

"Would he—would he be safe there?" Ithmeera, her fragile tone forcing Elisa to falter.

She couldn't do it. Couldn't walk away from Ithmeera, no matter how much she wanted to. Perhaps another day, a day when Marco's life was not at risk, she might but right now she needed to make sure her nephew would be safe. *If not for her, then do it for Philip.* "Yes."

"And his…abilities?"

Elisa slowly turned. "Andrea is a capable enchanter. She could help him until it is safe for him to return to Azgadar."

Ithmeera seemed comforted by this, despite having thrown Andrea in prison less than a year earlier. "Why would Lydia just allow him to live in her home?" She sat back down on the bed and after a moment of hesitation, Elisa joined her.

"Because she wants a strong kingdom. But Gurdinfield can only be strong with your help," she said. "You can trust her."

"And…" Ithmeera whispered. "And you?"

Don't. "That depends on what you would have me do."

Ithmeera waved her hand. "Whatever happened between you and Veraun needs to stay in the past. You may stay if you wish."

Elisa let out an exasperated huff. "I am not here on holiday."

That got a crooked smile out of Ithmeera. "Then…I wish for you to stay."

"All right, then." Elisa clapped her hands on her knees before rising from the bed. "I will go inform the queen then so that they can prepare."

"Elisa."

Halfway to the door, she turned. The anger in Ithmeera's face was gone, replaced with a blend of curiosity and something Elisa could have sworn was remorse. But this was Ithmeera she was dealing with, and so she remained cautious.

"Why did Erik execute your father?"

Elisa could only reply with a blank stare at first. The question was unexpected—she had assumed Ithmeera was uninterested in her side of the story. “Veraun…told Erik my father had been using magic to escape from his pain over Philip’s death. When Erik came to investigate, he ordered me to arrest my father. I refused, and Erik ordered my execution.” Her eyes burned, but she pushed back any tears that might have come. She would *not* cry in front of Ithmeera.

Ithmeera seemed disturbed by her recounting of the event. “That—that is not what he told me.”

“I know,” Elisa said. “My father tried to protect me and Erik ran his sword through him before I could do anything.” She waited for Ithmeera to lash out again, to tell her she was wrong or delusional.

But her response once again surprised Elisa. “Thank you. Please coordinate with Petra once you’ve spoken to Queen Lydia.”

Feeling exhausted and heartsick, Elisa could only give a short bow before leaving Ithmeera’s room.

* * *

“Are you certain you cannot accompany us back?”

Elisa lifted Marco up onto Roe’s horse before approaching Diana, who held the reins of her own. She, Jacob, and the Guardians were gathered under the dawn’s light by the Azgadar stables to prepare for the return journey to Gurdinfield. “I must remain here for now. I will join you once it is safe,” Elisa said.

Diana glanced at Ithmeera—flanked by Legionnaires and speaking to Roe in a hushed tone while he checked to ensure

Marco was secured in his seat and would be safe for the ride. "I understand." She tilted her head toward Ithmeera. "I hope you can bring a swift end to this madness."

"Will you be all right here?" Jacob asked. "I can spare one or two Guardians to stay with you, just in case." He frowned. "What of Kye?"

Elisa shook her head. "He wishes to remain in the palace with me, the fool. Says he wants to help." She sighed. "We will be fine. Please," she said and looked back at Marco. "Take care of him."

"We will protect him with our lives, Elisa," Diana assured her. "The City of Towers is the safest place in all of Damea."

Elisa reached out her hand and Diana took it in a firm grip. "Thank you. Truly. I will inform Andrea and Cassie of what's happened when they return from Ata." She released Diana's hand and went to join Ithmeera, who was attempting to ease Marco's fears as he begged her to let him stay in Azgadar.

"I don't want to go, Mother."

Ithmeera took his hand. "It is only for a little while, Marco. Think of it as an adventure!" She gave him a bright smile, but Elisa could see she was on the brink of breaking down. "And you'll have your sword with you." From behind them, Petra shot him an encouraging grin.

Roe laughed and patted him on the shoulder. "He will be an asset during our training sessions. We'll have a great time, won't we, Your Highness?"

But Marco refused to be distracted. "When will I see you again?" he asked in a small voice, and for a moment Elisa thought she was going to have to catch Ithmeera, who shook as though her legs were about to give out.

Ithmeera stroked his curly hair as he looked back at her with fearful brown eyes. “Soon, my love. Mind the queen and the Guardians,” she told him. “I will come and see you soon to take you home. I *promise*.” She planted a kiss on his forehead before stepping back from Roe’s horse to address Diana. “Safe travels, my friend…and thank you. I am in your debt.”

“And thank *you* for your hospitality, Your Majesty,” Diana replied with a subtle nod. “We will send word when we reach the capital.” She looked out at the road that would take them through the gates of Azgadar and then east, back to Gurdinfield. “Guardians, move out!”

In a thunderous roar, the riders took off, Diana in the lead with Jacob anchoring the end of the line of Guardians shielding Marco as they sped through the city gates. Marco looked back at them every few seconds, his eyes full of wonder and fright. Elisa stood with Ithmeera as they watched them disappear over the low, cracked dirt hills, Ithmeera’s choked sobs audible even though she covered her mouth with her hand in an effort to stifle them.

Elisa knew she should say something, but what could she possibly say to comfort a woman whose only child was just separated from her? *Better to be honest.* “He will be safe there.”

Ithmeera sniffed and wiped her eyes, her voice already calming down. “That remains to be seen. We must find out more about this ‘New Legion.’”

“Let me help.”

Ithmeera’s words were cold. “We will see.” She looked up at the brightening sky. “I need some time alone. With me, Petra.”

She excused herself, muttering something under her breath how Alden would no doubt be furious at what she had done...and how she did not care what he thought. Elisa watched the two head back to the palace along with their Legionnaire escorts.

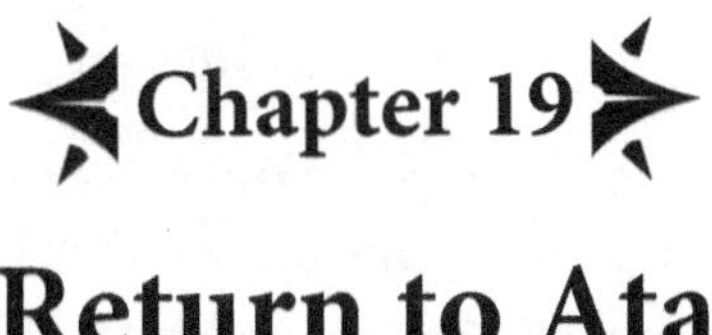

Chapter 19

Return to Ata

Ata, The Western Hills

Dawn was just breaking when Andrea and Cassie left the forest and crossed into Andrea's homeland—the Western Hills. From the peak of the hill where they stood, Andrea could see the lush, green valley below, where the largest town in the region, Ata, stood amidst the sprawling farmlands that blanketed the entire valley.

"Whoa," Cassie breathed, the light from the sun rising behind them illuminating her hair with a rich golden tone. "This is…you *lived* here?"

Andrea tilted her head. "Is that so surprising?" She took a moment to admire just how blue Cassie's eyes looked in the early morning glow before looking ahead. The temperature was already rising, and there were only a few clouds in the sky so far. Streaks of white collided with the red, orange, and deep blue hues of the morning horizon that Andrea remembered so well. For the first time in a long time, she was homesick.

Cassie's mouth was partially open as she took in the sight. "It's amazing. I've never seen anything like it."

Andrea laughed. "You don't have a sunrise where you're from?"

Cassie shook her head, and Andrea did not detect a hint of sarcasm in her reply. "No. Not like this."

Andrea smiled and took Cassie's hand. "Come on," she said, giving it a tug. "If we hurry, we can get to Ata in time for breakfast." Despite her homesickness, she was absolutely dreading knocking on the front door of her childhood home and having to explain to her parents where she had been for the last four years.

Cassie must have read her mind somehow, because she stood her ground. "Hold up. Don't you want to figure out what you're going to tell your parents?"

Not particularly. "I don't know, Cassie. Honestly, I don't know what I could possibly say that will make this any less awkward than it's already going to be." She looked up at her. "What would you say?"

Cassie hesitated. "Well," she said slowly, gentle teasing in her tone, "I mean—and this could be a crazy idea—but you *could* just tell them the truth."

"That's not what I meant."

"Oh, I know what you meant," Cassie said, "but I meant what *I* said, too. Tell them what happened." She pointed at the town below. "They're not stupid—they know magic's back. Their lives are probably easier now because of it and *you* made that happen."

"That was you…and Meredith. I didn't release the mag—"

But Cassie was not having any of her modesty. "As much as I'd love to stand up here, take in this amazing view, and argue with you all morning about how awesome I am, we probably want to make it down there before nightfall." She squeezed Andrea's hand. "Just say what comes naturally. I'll be right beside you if things go south, okay?"

Andrea looked down at Ata. *She's right.* She took a deep breath. Maybe if she was going home by herself this would be different. But if anyone could make a reunion with her estranged parents even the slightest bit less of a disaster, it was Cassie. "All right."

* * *

"Ugh! I'm *hungry.*"

"I'm not even going to pretend that surprises me." Andrea knew they had been walking for a while, and that it probably was a good time to stop and eat, but she was too distracted by their surroundings to make that call.

They entered the town of Ata not long after traversing the hillside to the bottom, where they finally arrived in the valley around mid-morning, stopping by the community stables first where they left their horse before heading into the village proper. To Andrea's delight, the town had not changed at all. The central marketplace they now walked through was dwarfed by the scale of Azgadar's or even Gurdinfield's market districts, but there was something about the scattered merchant carts, the dusty main road that led into the modest square, and the calm, slow pace of Ata's citizens going about their day that just made Andrea feel at *home* again.

She gazed out past the marketplace to the open fields that covered most of the valley, noting the deep green. It had been a good summer harvest this year—no doubt her parents' farm had done well, too.

The familiarity of it made homesickness rise within her once more. *It's like I never left.*

Cassie did not give up, however. "Something smells good."

Andrea smile grew broader. Her fear of seeing her parents again gave way to fond memories as she took in familiar, colorful banners hanging from many of the buildings and carts. There also appeared to be far more people than usual walking through town. "Oh! Yes, there's a festival happening right now. We have one in the summer and one in the fall. They're rather popular, actually—people from all over Damea come here for them." Pride suppressed her fear even more—she always enjoyed when she could talk about the *good* things Ata had to offer.

"But is there food?"

Really, is that all she can think about? "Erm, yes…of course there is." She narrowed her eyes at Cassie. "Did you actually hear anything I just said?"

"I did. But that doesn't change the fact that I just walked halfway across Damea and I'm starving. So, if we could *please* stop somewhere and eat, I promise I'll stop complaining and you can tell me all about this festival. Deal?"

Andrea relented and they stopped at a bakery in the square where, upon Cassie's insistence, they purchased one of every pastry the shop had to offer.

"But why? What if you don't like them all?" Andrea asked once they were seated at one of the many tables set up along the square for the festivities that would begin later in the day.

Cassie took a large bite out of her third sample before setting it down. "Because," she said, her words muffled from the food she was only halfway done chewing, "that's the best way to find out what I like—by trying everything out."

Of course. With her mood brightened, Andrea decided it had been too long since she picked on Cassie. "'Trying everything out'? Do you apply that approach across *all* aspects of your life?" she teased.

Cassie seemed to pick up on her jest right away. She finished off the pastry bite. "If you're asking me if that's how I pick my girlfriends, then no—that wasn't the case. And let's be honest—there weren't many options to choose from." She took a drink from her canteen.

Andrea laughed. "Oh? There were plenty. Elisa, Diana, Ithmeera..."

Cassie just about choked on her water. "Okay," she said, pointing at Andrea as she recovered. "First of all, Diana is married—and to my friend no less. So, that wouldn't work. Second, there's so much tension between Elisa and Ithmeera that I wouldn't dare go near *that* relationship...or whatever they are." She cleared her throat. "Now, there's *Meredith* of course, but I would hate to stand in the way of you two if there was a chance of—"

Andrea shot her a glare. "Don't even go there."

But Cassie was unfazed. "Me? You were the one who asked."

She took another sip of water while glancing at the crowds of people walking by them.

"Fair point. I suppose since you're out of options, you're stuck with me, then."

Another pastry made its way into Cassie's mouth. "I guess so," she said with her mouth full. "Good thing I like you."

"I'm so grateful." Andrea glanced down at the array of half-eaten pastries and tore off part of one she remembered liking. For the moment, she was content just sitting across from Cassie and people-watching. The nervousness she had been pushing down since they arrived in Ata refused to settle, however.

"It's going to be fine." Cassie reached out a comforting hand and placed it on Andrea's, giving it a short, gentle stroke with her thumb. "Come on. What's the worst that could happen?"

"I don't even know. I suppose I can only hope they scold me for being so far behind on my chores," Andrea said under her breath as she fidgeted with the hem of her cloak.

"*Ha!* Okay, that was actually funny."

"I'm glad you find this so amusing." She stretched before standing up. "I need to not…think about this for a bit. I'm going to go refill our canteens at the inn and see if Bill has any rooms available in case…well, in case things 'go south' as you said."

Cassie tilted her head. "Not sure how that will take your mind off it, but okay. You want me to go with you?"

"It's all right," Andrea said, shaking her head. "I'll just be a moment. I should probably say hello to Bill, anyway. You'll stay here?"

Cassie shrugged. "Well, I was thinking of running away, but I guess just this *once,* I can stay." She gestured at the carts behind them. "I'm going to go check out this festival. Don't worry," she added when she saw the alarm on Andrea's face. "I'll stay in the square."

Andrea raised both eyebrows as she grabbed the canteens and her backpack. "You can't fault me for worrying—you never actually listen when I ask you to stay put somewhere."

"That was *one* time," Cassie grumbled. While cleaning up her space, she continued. "And it turned out fine, right? We made some nice new friends!" She grinned. "And you got to go to a fancy ball!"

Andrea laughed, relieved that Cassie could finally joke about her capture in Azgadar. "I'm fairly certain it was more than one time, Cassie. The Gurdin Woods, the City of Towers…shall I go on?"

Cassie swept her hand across the table to take care of any remaining crumbs from her breakfast. "Nah. Go get the water. I'll hang out here." She followed up with a quick kiss on Andrea's cheek. "Promise."

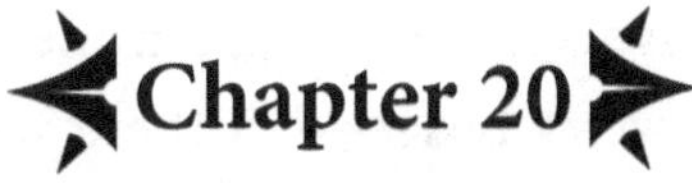

Chapter 20

Home

Wow, they really don't kid around with this festival stuff. Cassie couldn't help but be impressed by the sheer number of carts around as she wandered the square, let alone all of the decorations, tents, half-assembled stages for performances, and obstacles for the various athletic games that would take place in the evening. Everyone seemed to be selling something or shopping for something. Most of the merchants sold vegetables, fruit, alcohol, bread, or other baked goods. Others displayed weapons and armor forged in other regions, such as the empire or Gurdinfield. Cassie noted the nations' familiar coats of arms on the banners hanging from the carts.

One cart in particular caught her eye. The blood red fabric shading it was torn a little, indicating it was either old or the merchant had braved some harsh weather on the trek to the Western Hills. The gold accents and familiar double sword and shield on the cloth, coupled with the merchant's dark olive skin, made it obvious that the goods were from the Azgadaran Empire, possibly from Azgadar itself.

She pushed through the crowds toward the cart and was almost there when someone jostled her hard, knocking her off balance. She spun around to confront her assailant, but they were lost in the crowd before she could identify them.

"*Excuse* you, asshat," she muttered, and faced the cart once more. The goods on display were crafted ones—baskets, beaded tapestries, rugs, jewelry boxes—but there was one area of the shop that Cassie gravitated toward.

The threads, which hung alongside each other at the same length, gleamed in the mid-morning sunlight, a dazzling array of color that Cassie could not stop staring at. She reached out a tentative hand and lifted up a section of dark green threads, admiring the fine, silky material and the weightlessness of them.

"*The colors could mean anything, but they're really like a promise. They represent what you swore to protect in your lives. That's all the bracelet is, really. A promise.*" Jacob's words echoed in her head as she continued to inspect the threads. Her throat tightened and she swallowed to dislodge the nerves that had suddenly decided to rise up and bother her. *Not like I need to decide today. Don't even know if we're ready for that.* They had only been, well, them for less than a year.

Does that even matter? Cassie loved Andrea. She trusted her with her life. Andrea had this certain quality about her that Cassie could not place—she made Cassie feel like she could take on the world, even when the odds were stacked against them.

She smiled, the tightness in her throat receding as her nerves transitioned into the familiar giddy warmth that enveloped her whenever she thought of Andrea. The idea of giving Andrea a bracelet was nice, but as long as they were together Cassie would be happy. *But maybe it could help get the message across?*

"The green would complement her eyes." A deep voice startled Cassie from her thoughts, and she jumped as she dropped her hand from the thread. A tall man stood next to her, holding a thread that matched the one Cassie held a moment earlier. His dark, tousled hair and muscular figure contrasted that of the balding, heavier Azgadaran weaver he faced, and Cassie scolded herself for her paranoia when she realized that the two were working out a purchase.

He noticed her reaction, however. "My wife," he said, his voice calm and friendly. "She has the loveliest eyes. Not quite green or brown—something in between." He held up the thread, a mischievous glint in his grey eyes—he was probably old enough to be her father, but his mannerisms made him appear much younger. Judging by his strength and his sunburnt face, Cassie figured he worked on a farm or some other physically taxing job. "I stole her bracelet this morning and was going to get this woven in for our anniversary. Think she'll like it?"

Cassie blinked a few times before she remembered how to talk. "Uh...yeah! It's, um, it's a really nice green."

"That it is," he said. He pointed at the threads. "You looking yourself?" He turned back to the weaver and handed him the thread and a bracelet that Cassie noticed was adorned with a beautiful assortment of colors. "I'll take it," he said before turning expectantly back to Cassie.

Am I? Cassie figured she might as well be honest with the man. He seemed nice enough and after all, who was he going to tell? "I wasn't sure until I came over here to look, but I guess... yeah. I suppose I am." Just saying it out loud made her more certain of what she was doing…and why. *Maybe we should talk later. Or…maybe she's not supposed to know? How the hell does this even work?*

"Oh, I know that look. Pretty sure it's the same one I had when I got my wife's bracelet made."

Great. "Obviously, that worked out all right for you," she said. "To be honest, I have no idea how any of this works." She glanced back at the threads, wondering if she really should be talking to a complete stranger about this. "I mean, she has no idea I'm looking at these right now. I don't know what she'd say about it."

He handed the weaver some money and received the bracelet in return, its new green threading bright but blending well with the other colors. "If I may offer some unsolicited advice and share a poorly kept secret," he said as he pocketed the bracelet, "you won't really know until you ask."

Easier said than done. "Heh, yeah. Maybe I will." Cassie held out her hand. "I should get going. Thanks for the chat and good luck with returning your wife's bracelet."

He clasped her hand for a brief moment before releasing it. "My pleasure. And yes, hopefully she won't be *too* upset. Oh," he said, "and if you find the time, you should stop by our cart. It'll be here in the square tomorrow until the end of the week."

"Will do," Cassie replied with a nod and a half-smile. She gave the threads one last look before she sauntered off to find Andrea.

* * *

“There you are.” Andrea was out of breath when Cassie found her on the other side of the square. “I thought you’d run away again.” She handed Cassie two of the filled canteens she carried.

“Just wanted to see how long you would look for me before you started to freak out,” Cassie said. “Not very long, apparently.” She flipped open her backpack and stuffed the canteens in it.

“I don’t ‘freak out,’” Andrea protested, and Cassie could honestly not tell if Andrea was trying to convince her or herself. They left the square and were once again on the main road, this time headed in the direction of Andrea’s home. High noon had come, and Cassie was thankful for the distraction of teasing Andrea as the heat started to bother her.

“Of course you don’t. And Elisa loves hugs.”

“Someone should probably let *her* know that,” Andrea said, and Cassie was pleased to see she was once again in a joking mood.

“Ha, I know right? Where are we now?”

Andrea pointed down the long, dirt road they walked on, flanked by acres of rich farmland that stretched out to the horizon in a sea of green. “This road leads out of town and reaches most of the farms on the outskirts. That’s Bill’s inn. I used to deliver vegetables there for my parents.” She pointed at a large, rundown building. Patches dotted the roof, and the surrounding wooden fence was falling apart in some areas and missing entire sections in others.

“Looks rough.”

“Just a few minor repairs and it will be fine,” Andrea said. “It’s also where…where I met Meredith.”

Andrea’s voice was heavy with remorse. Cassie took her hand and they continued down the road, their fingers interlaced. “I’m sure your crazy mentor is fine,” she said, receiving a quiet laugh from Andrea in return. “She probably just went back to the Black Forest.”

“I wonder what happened to Richard. The magic we restored probably would have disrupted any progress Meredith made,” Andrea said.

“So, by that logic he probably died, then.”

Andrea responded with a grim nod. “Most likely.” She looked down. “I can’t help but feel sorry for Meredith. She spent twenty years trying to wake him. I don’t agree with the methods she used to try to cure him, of course,” she added and gave Cassie a quick apologetic look.

Cassie shrugged. “I’m not going to lie—what she did to me sucked. But I guess I understand why she was so desperate. Hell,” she laughed, “I might have done the same thing if it was you.” She paused and waited for Andrea to laugh with her or perhaps just smile. But Andrea just went quiet instead as an awkward silence descended upon them, something Cassie could not remember happening in months.

She squeezed her hand. “Hey. You okay?”

As though on cue, Andrea stopped and turned to meet her eyes. “Don’t compare yourself to her,” she said, the hardness of her tone catching Cassie off guard. "Meredith abused her power in the worst way. What she did to you was *horrible.* You—you could never be her." She released Cassie's hand and pushed on ahead.

Cassie stood there in momentary confusion before she quickened her steps to catch up. "Hold up," she called, grabbing Andrea's wrist and bringing them face to face again. "Did I say something wrong?"

Andrea held her gaze for a few seconds, looking as tense as she had been during their encounter with the Gurithian soldiers, before she let out a sigh. "I'm sorry, Cassie. I'm worried about seeing my parents and I'm still stressed about those soldiers the other night and then there was the assassin and…she—she *tortured* you, Cassie." She reached out and let her hand rest against Cassie's cheek. "She could have killed you. She's a disgrace to enchanters, and a terrible person."

Cassie's expression darkened. "Kye and I killed people, Andrea."

"You were *defending* us! Meredith had a choice."

Cassie shook her head. "There's always a choice. Take that soldier in the forest for example. You were about to roast him. Why didn't you do it?"

"It was a threat to get him to talk," Andrea mumbled and turned away. "I was never going to *kill* him."

But Cassie continued to push her. "I've never seen you threaten anyone like that before. Why now? Why that soldier?"

Andrea spun around, and pangs of guilt pricked at Cassie

to see the frustration on her face. "It's not about him," she said, voice shaking. "Ever since Rhyad, I promised myself I would never let you get hurt or used like that again. You never asked to be here and…" She trailed off and sniffed a little.

The pieces clicked together and Cassie took a deep breath. She wrapped her arms around Andrea, who did not object, and held her tight. "You," she began, "are the most badass enchanter bodyguard anyone could ask for. And I'm an excellent judge of character."

Andrea exhaled as she sank into Cassie's embrace. "Aren't *you* supposed to be the bodyguard?"

Cassie ignored her attempt to change the subject and hoped her next words would not scare Andrea away. "Andrea, if by some miracle a magical door opened up right here, right now, and I knew it would take me back…I wouldn't go through it." She put her hands on Andrea's shoulders. "I don't know how many times I have to tell you you're stuck with me to convince you."

Another smile from Andrea. *That's a good start.* "You—you're right. I'm sorry, Cassie." Cassie grinned when she saw Andrea's face turn pink. "Being here with you, knowing that you chose to stay with me, it's the greatest feeling in the world. And that night in…" She swallowed as she averted her eyes, her words escaping in a whisper. "In Azgadar—it was incredible and I suppose I'm still just afraid that this is all a dream and I'm going to wake up and be stuck *here* again or worse, be stuck with Meredith while she fails again and again—"

"Hey." Cassie knew from experience where this was going. "You know at this rate, I'm just going to interrupt you by kissing you, you're going to get all mad, and then we're going to laugh about how ridiculous we are and how we should stop putting off the inevitable which is going and seeing your parents, right?"

Andrea just stared up at her in disbelief before bursting into the laughter Cassie had been hoping for all along. "You are terrible at comforting people; do you know that?"

Cassie leaned in and kissed her anyway. "I love you, okay? Now, can we *please* go meet your parents and get this over with?"

"Yes, yes." Andrea broke away, making sure to take Cassie's hand again. "Let's go, before I change my mind."

With Andrea finally calmed down, they set off again, neither one of them saying anything for a bit until Cassie squeezed Andrea's hand and glanced over at her. "You know, for the record and in case it wasn't clear, I thought that night in Azgadar was pretty awesome, too."

Andrea just smiled and walked closer to her. Words were not always necessary and Cassie was relieved knowing things were fine—more than fine—between them.

They reached the end of the road, which branched off into a narrower, shorter path. A house of wood and grey stone stood at the end of the path, with a smaller structure next to it—a barn, Cassie suspected. Behind them were more acres of crop fields—the family's farm no doubt. The house's size could not match the spire in Azgadar or the palace in the

City of Towers, but something about its picturesque location against the stunning backdrop of the Western Hills gave Cassie a sense of belonging. Maybe it was because she knew Andrea grew up here, or perhaps it was the fact that she had taken an immediate liking to Ata. Regardless, this was the first time she had experienced the feeling of "home" in an actual place since arriving in Damea. And she liked it.

Hopefully, her parents won't be crazies. She figured they couldn't be too bad if Andrea was their daughter, but Cassie's record was not great when it came to meeting "normal" people in Damea.

"Well, this is it." Andrea made a sweeping gesture with her free hand as though she was presenting a grand tour of her childhood home. "That was a lovely journey. Time to go, then?" She tried to drag Cassie away.

Cassie snickered but stood her ground. "Nice try. Come on." She pointed at the barn. "What's in there?"

Andrea's eyes lit up and she let go of Cassie's hand. "Oh! Kira!" Without an explanation, she rushed toward the barn. Before following, Cassie scanned their surroundings to see if anyone had noticed them, but so far she had not seen a single person since they'd left the marketplace.

"Andrea?" she called as she took a tentative first step on the stray pieces of hay that were scattered all over the floor, snapping a few of them with the soles of her boots.

"Over here." She found Andrea near the back of the barn on the other side of a single stall, petting a chocolate-brown draft horse. A few workbenches lined the remaining sides of the barn, with sacks of soil, flour, and other supplies taking up most of the space.

She shook her head. "You and your horses."

Andrea ignored her remark. "This is Kira. She's my family's horse. She helps with a lot of the work here."

Cassie stared at Kira. "Hi."

Andrea gave her a disapproving look. "You don't have to ride her, but you can at least say hello properly."

Cassie rolled her eyes before turning back to Kira and giving her a few light strokes on the neck. "*Hi,* Kira. Nice to meet you."

"That's better," Andrea said. "I—I suppose we should go knock on the door."

"Why? It's still your house."

Andrea gave a half-shrug. "The way I left…I don't know if it would be appropriate." She met Cassie's gaze. "I'm scared," she said in a small voice.

Cassie reached her arms around Andrea for the second time that afternoon. "It'll be fine," she soothed, pressing her forehead against Andrea's. "I'm with you, all right?"

Andrea let out a trembling breath. "All right. Let's go so we can—"

The muffled thud of something solid and heavy being dropped on the dirt startled both of them, making them pull apart and face their intruder.

Cassie's jaw dropped at the slender, middle-aged woman standing speechless in the barn's entrance. Her features were much sharper, but with her wavy dark hair and hazel eyes, she could have passed for an older version of Andrea. The basket she had been carrying was now lying on its side, its contents—vegetables—spilling out across the dirt.

Cassie looked over at Andrea. All the color had drained from her face.

"Mother?"

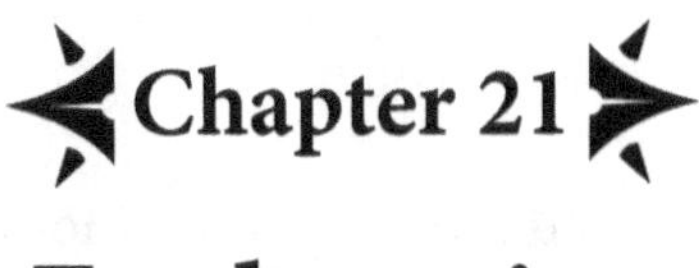

Chapter 21 Explanation

"A-Andrea…you're really here?" Isabel's fair skin had gone almost as white as her daughter's. Cassie could see her hands shaking from across the barn and worried that she might faint at the mere sight of seeing Andrea again.

She moved to take Andrea's hand—to give her any kind of support, even if it was just physical contact—but Andrea inhaled deeply and took a few steps toward Isabel. "Yes. I'm—I'm back, Mother."

Isabel remained frozen. "You're back," she repeated. Cassie was certain the poor woman would fall over. "I…"

Upon hearing her mother's choked words, Andrea rushed to close the distance between them, letting out a choked cry as she collapsed into Isabel's waiting arms.

Isabel's sobs reverberated throughout the barn as she clutched her daughter, one hand on Andrea's back and the other stroking the back of her hair as she repeated the words like a mantra.

Cassie could only look on at the two of them with mixed emotions. She was ecstatic that she had played a part in reuniting Andrea with her mother after so many years of guilt and regret. But the bitter reality that she would never see her own mother again gave rise to the grief that she had fought to keep buried for so long. She blinked back a few stubborn tears and sniffed. She refused to ruin Andrea's moment with her own problems.

Andrea finally pulled away from her mother's grasp, though she still held Isabel's arms. "I'm all right, Mother," she said, her face streaked with tears. "Really, I am."

Isabel's tone went from bewilderment to outrage. *"'All right'?* You most certainly are not." She reached out and grazed the scar on Andrea's cheek. "Where have you been? Why didn't you come home? And what is *this?*"

Andrea shook her head and took her mother's hand. "I'm fine. It's nothing, Mother. I'm here and that's what matters, right?"

"Don't 'nothing' me, Andrea. We've been out of our minds worrying about whether you were alive or dead." Isabel's voice escalated in both pitch and volume. "Your father looked up and down the hills for you for *months.* No one would take him to the Black Forest."

Andrea's eyes widened. "Father went to look for me?"

"I wasn't about to let him go off to the most dangerous place in Damea so that I could lose both my husband *and* my daughter." She released Andrea and wiped her eyes. "We waited for you, Andrea. We...we hoped you would come back. Jheran even went back to Azgadar. He made inquiries, asked around about you just in case you had ended up there and they said that—that you were wanted by the Legion!" She put her hands on her hips. "Really, Andrea? The *Legion?* What did you do?"

Andrea sighed. "It's not what you think, Mother. I—"

Isabel would not let her finish. "Don't dismiss this, Andrea. We were worried sick for years and the only thing we had from you was a letter with no more than a few sentences in it." Cassie cringed at the sudden shift to anger, suddenly wishing she was anywhere but there.

In a stroke of misfortune, Isabel finally noticed her. "And who is this?" she demanded, gesturing at her while looking to Andrea for answers.

Andrea hurried to Cassie and took her by the wrist in a gentle hold before guiding her over to where Isabel stood. Cassie found herself stiffening more and more with each step until she was face to face with Isabel, who looked her up and down with a hardened expression but otherwise gave nothing away.

If she had not been intimidated at the prospect of meeting Andrea's parents before, she certainly was now. But Andrea gave her wrist a reassuring squeeze. "Mother," she began, much calmer and softer than before. "This is Cassie." Another deep breath. "She's my—erm…we're together," she said, a shy smile tugging at her lips as she gripped Cassie's wrist tighter.

Nice. Cassie had to fight back a laugh and instead struggled to maintain a friendly smile at Isabel. As far as introductions to Dameans went, this was probably the most awkward she'd experienced yet.

Isabel rolled her eyes. "Well, I can *see* that!" She pinched the bridge of her nose and for a moment, Cassie marveled again at the uncanny resemblance between the two of them. "I need… please, Andrea," she said, her voice heavy with fatigue. "Can we go inside? I think—I think I need to sit down."

"We can answer any questions you have, Mother," Andrea said and let go of Cassie before offering Isabel her arm for support. Cassie nodded and hung back as she followed them out of the barn and into the house.

* * *

Not more than an hour later, the three of them sat in what had to be the tiniest living room Cassie had ever been in.

The house itself was much smaller than Cassie imagined it would be, but it was still a comfortable size and she had no trouble seeing herself living in a place like this should they ever decide to leave the City of Towers. The kitchen, equipped with a cast iron cooking pot over a low fire and a table with four chairs, was only a few steps away with no obvious barriers between the rooms. She had spotted a short hallway when they'd walked through the front door and figured it led to the bedrooms, giving her a moment's pause as she wondered what Andrea's bedroom looked like.

Isabel had informed them that Andrea's father, Garrett, had gone into town and would be home soon, before insisting that she put on some tea first.

Now, Cassie and Andrea shared a worn-out couch, which was little more than a rickety bench draped with thick fur blankets. Isabel sat across from them in a sturdy wooden rocking chair. The rough square table between them favored its left side, and Cassie couldn't help but keep looking back at it every few minutes or so to make sure her cup of steaming tea was not about to slide off it.

Not that she was really drinking much of it anyway. The leaves were far more bitter than anything she had tried in Gurdinfield or Azgadar, but what really kept her hesitating to drink more was Isabel's periodic glances in her direction. Her eyes held little emotion except perhaps a hint of curiosity, but that was enough to make Cassie more uncomfortable than she already was—if such a thing was possible.

"And Meredith? Where is she now?" Isabel asked. She leaned back in her chair, and Cassie figured she was still trying to absorb everything Andrea had finished telling her: the Black Forest, Azgadar, the civil war in Gurdinfield, and most of their trip to the Rhyadan Mountains. She had left out the parts where Cassie was not from Damea (apparently, they met in the Black Forest where Cassie had been traveling), Cassie having magical abilities, getting kidnapped by the Moores, fighting in the battle at the City of Towers (Andrea's battle scars were the result of an ill-fated experiment while still under Meredith's tutelage), and Andrea falling ill in Rhyad. Cassie almost objected when Andrea omitted these bits, but she figured they would talk later about it and Andrea would explain her reasoning.

"I'm not sure," Andrea admitted, wringing her hands. "We think perhaps she went back to the Black Forest to see to Richard."

Isabel gave a slow nod. "So, he is cured then?"

"I…don't know." Andrea shifted on the couch in obvious discomfort. "The magic—Richard's condition was so dependent on Meredith's experiments that exposing him to more magic could have destabilized him." She bit her lip and Cassie took her hand as she recalled their earlier conversation on the road. "He might not have made it."

Isabel's eyebrows raised at the two holding hands but to Cassie's relief, she was more focused on Andrea's answer. "And now you live in Gurdinfield? With…Queen Lydia? Or was it Diana?"

"She goes by both names," Andrea clarified. "We live in the palace. In the City of Towers." She seemed surprised at the fact as the words came out of her mouth. "I help her and Jacob with magic-related matters."

"And the magic itself? Am I to understand that there are no more dangers to…enchanters, then?"

Cassie noticed Andrea pause longer than necessary before she answered. "Yes, though we still don't know all the effects the Restoration—that is, the magic being released—had on the land."

"I see." Isabel took a cautious sip of her tea and directed her attention at Cassie. "And you? You are one of the queen's fighters?" She pointed at the sword that hung from Cassie's belt. "Or are you an enchanter, too?" Cassie could tell she wasn't used to saying the word.

"She's a Guardian, Mother," Andrea answered before Cassie could respond.

Isabel's brow furrowed. "I'm certain Cassie here can speak for herself, Andrea."

Andrea blushed and gave Cassie an apologetic smile while Cassie swallowed and worked up the nerve to answer the question. "Uh, right. I'm a Guardian, though I haven't been one for very long."

"So, you *do* speak." Isabel laughed, ignoring the annoyed look Andrea sent in her direction. "You'll forgive me if I'm suspicious. The last person Andrea brought home took her away from us without so much as a note."

"I told you I was leaving and why, Mother," Andrea said, sounding calmer than Cassie thought she'd be in this situation. "And Cassie isn't Meredith."

"The queen tasked me with protecting her," Cassie explained. "With all due respect, I've only known Andrea to act of her own accord. Even if I tried to make her do something, she probably wouldn't listen to me anyway."

"That is *not* true," Andrea protested.

"You either then?" Isabel said to Cassie before sighing. "It's admirable that you stand up for my daughter, and I apologize for my words earlier. But you have to understand, it was not all that long ago that we didn't even know whether or not she was alive." She faced Andrea again. "And all this about getting *arrested* by the Legion for stealing? I don't even know where to *begin* with that."

"It was only to help Elisa get the empress's journal," Andrea said, exhaustion apparent in her voice. Cassie stifled a yawn as the fatigue from the day's events set in. "Cassie and our friends helped me escape, and the empress has pardoned us for everything."

"Oh, well excuse me! I suppose it's all right, then!" Isabel said and Cassie had to hold back from laughing at her sarcasm.

Even Andrea appeared to be fighting back a grin.

"She was...in good hands." Cassie chose her words with care so as to not give away more information than Andrea was comfortable with. "She helped stop the civil war in Gurdinfield and brought back magic. She's done good things for a lot of people."

Isabel ran her hands through her dark hair, a fluid movement that Cassie had seen Andrea do countless times. "I just—forgive me, I'm still trying to understand all this." The whine of the front door swinging open interrupted her. A heavy slam shook the room, followed by a booming voice that Cassie found surprisingly familiar.

"I'm home, Isabel!" Garrett's weighty footsteps were felt through the wood floors several seconds before he made his entrance in the living room with a bracelet in his hand.

Cassie's eyes widened when she saw the dark green threads woven into the band. *The guy from the marketplace!* This man was Andrea's father. And she had talked to him about getting a bracelet for Andrea!

Ah, crap.

Garrett had eyes only for Isabel at first. "I know you were probably looking for this, but I wanted to get something added and I thought you might—" His eyes flickered to the couch, then to Andrea. He froze.

Isabel stood up and took his arm. "She just got here," she said, her tone low and gentle as she retrieved the bracelet from the hand that gripped it.

Garrett's mouth opened and closed but he seemed unable to

speak. Andrea let go of Cassie's hand and left the couch before addressing her father in what came out as a trembling whisper. "Father."

Cassie knew from what Andrea told her that they had parted on unpleasant terms and was ready to stand up to Garrett if necessary. She braced a hand on the couch, waiting for the worst.

Garrett glanced at Isabel, and she nodded and released him. He turned to Andrea—his grey eyes glossy with tears and filled with hope and fear—and held out his arms to her.

Andrea didn't need to be told twice. She bolted the few steps between them and leapt at Garrett, who took her into his arms and lifted her off the ground as she clung to him. They stayed that way, a respectful silence having descended upon the room, until Garrett spoke, his voice just as broken as Andrea's.

"I thought I lost you."

Andrea's words were muffled against his shoulder when he finally set her down. "I'm here, Father. I'm all right."

Cassie found herself fighting back tears again as she practically saw the weight of guilt lift from Andrea's shoulders. She looked over and saw Isabel clasping her hands together, fresh tears running down her cheeks.

It was then that Garrett noticed her and she cringed as he spoke. "Hello again?" He looked at Andrea and then back at Cassie. "You two know each other?"

"Wait—you've met?" Andrea asked as she pulled away from him. "Cassie's with me, Father."

"Yes," Isabel added, and Cassie could swear she heard

amusement in her voice. "They're *together,* Garrett."

"Well, yes. We met in the marketplace and—wait." Garrett stopped and blinked a few times. "Together?"

Oh, help me. Cassie stood up and approached them, hoping that Garrett would not mention anything about the bracelet. "Nice to see you again," she said, struggling not to let her nervousness show. *Please don't say anything.*

Garrett gave her a short nod and Cassie sighed with relief when she saw the understanding in his eyes. "Ah yes, very nice…was it Cassie, then?" He extended his hand and she shook it. "As I was saying," he said, turning back to Andrea, "we met in the marketplace. I was trying to get her to come to our cart this week, but…" He braced himself on the wall next to him, causing Andrea and Isabel to both start toward him out of fear he'd fall. "I'm sorry. This is just…you're home."

Isabel's voice took on an authoritative tone, one that Cassie suspected she used often and especially around her family. "Come and sit down, Garrett. I should start preparing dinner anyway." She took his arm again and led him to the rocking chair.

"Let me help, love. I…I need to do something," he pleaded.

But Isabel would not budge. "You can sit down while your daughter tells you where she's been the last four years. Cassie, would you mind helping me in the kitchen?"

Uncertain whether she should go and help or stay and support Andrea, Cassie looked to her partner for answers. To her surprise, a faint smile crossed Andrea's face. "I'll be all right, Cassie," she said, before retaking her spot on the couch across from Garrett.

Unable to keep from worrying about Andrea, Cassie followed Isabel into the kitchen with the full knowledge that she probably walking into yet another awkward conversation.

Chapter 22
Truths and Lies

"Well, erm, here we go. Mother said they didn't touch it much while I was gone," Andrea said as she guided Cassie by the hand into her small bedroom. There was one rectangular window near the ceiling—not huge, but large enough to let light in. In the far corner was the bed, which was clearly made for just one person. A chest of drawers stood up against the wall in front of the doorway. A few hand-carved wooden figurines of various animals—a wolf, a cat, a bird, and a bear—graced the top of the dresser, along with a few candles Isabel had lit shortly before dinner—the only sources of light in the room that evening.

"It's nice," Cassie said. She nodded at the figurines. "Cute."

Andrea gave a small laugh as she picked up the wolf and inspected it, feeling the intricate grooves and smooth surfaces. The detailing was rather impressive and Cassie made a mental note to remind Andrea to take the figurines with them when they left Ata. "Father made these for me after my abilities started to show. He tried to teach me how to carve them myself. I think he thought it would help distract me from the fact that I kept lighting things on fire." She cast Cassie a knowing glance. "I was very upset about having abilities at first."

Cassie grinned. “Wait, you can make this stuff?”

Andrea closed her eyes and shook her head before returning the wolf to its spot on the dresser. “I was never very good. Mine always turned out looking like little wooden lumps with cracks in them.”

“You’re probably giving yourself less credit than you deserve.”

Andrea shrugged. “Maybe. It’s been years since I’ve tried, so who knows.” She turned and closed the door behind them before facing Cassie again. “I’m so sorry about earlier, Cassie. I hope my parents didn’t interrogate you too much.”

Cassie shook her head. Dinner—a meat and vegetable stew that Andrea had practically inhaled—had been uneventful, to her and probably Andrea’s relief as well. Isabel had not asked her too many questions other than how she came to be a Guardian and what the training was like. Garrett was quiet while they were eating, although Cassie noticed the quick glances he’d give Andrea and her throughout the meal. If he had an opinion on their relationship, he wasn’t saying anything…yet. No mention was made of Meredith, magic, enchanters, war, or anything related, though Cassie wasn’t sure if that was the norm or if Garrett and Isabel were avoiding the topics on purpose. She and Andrea had excused themselves afterwards, and Cassie didn’t miss the pointed look Isabel gave her as they left the kitchen to go to Andrea’s bedroom.

“It’s fine. You’ve been gone for a while, so of course they’re going to be curious,” she said and took a seat on Andrea’s bed. “Speaking of which, why didn’t you tell them the truth?”

The bed gave way a bit as Andrea sat down next to her. “Did you see my mother? I thought she was going to faint when she saw us. How do you think she would have reacted if I told her I got my scars from a giant fireball crashing down on me?"

"Maybe let *her* handle that? You don't actually know what she would have done," Cassie pointed out.

But Andrea waved the topic away. "It's better this way. I—I'll tell her later. Eventually." She paused and took Cassie's hand. "Thank you," she said, "for being there for me. I wasn't sure how—well, you know what happened."

"You're welcome. I'm glad it turned out all right." Cassie stroked Andrea's hand with her thumb. "Your parents seem really great."

"Thank you, that's…I hope I can talk to them about magic eventually. I still think my father doesn't like it. After all, I left because of it." Andrea leaned her head on Cassie's shoulder.

"Hmm, you left and saved magic and became a royal enchanter. You help people. He can't fault you for that," Cassie said. She let out a long breath as Andrea's weight against her helped her relax for the first time since they arrived at the house.

Andrea smiled. "Maybe. But enough about that. I think I'd like to be done with stressing about this, at least for a bit." She sat up and leaned in, capturing Cassie's lips in a kiss.

Cassie hesitated but returned the kiss before pulling away just enough to speak. "Um…is this really the best idea?"

"What do you mean?" Andrea asked in a rather obvious playful tone as she tugged on Cassie's collar and drew her back in for another kiss.

Oh, please, like she doesn't know exactly *what she's doing.* "I mean…your parents are a room away and we only just got here and—" Cassie struggled to speak but it was getting difficult with Andrea interrupting her just about every word. Cursing herself, she pulled away and pushed herself up from the bed, bringing an end to the kiss before it could evolve into something more. "I think it would be best while we're here if, um, if I stayed in the living room or the barn or something. Your mother was giving me the eye when we left after dinner."

Andrea burst into laughter. "Oh, she was *not*." She reached for Cassie's wrist. "Don't go."

"Come, on—I'm serious," Cassie said, backing away. "Look, it's just for a few nights."

"But—fine, fine." Andrea rolled her eyes, but her smile remained. "Go on. I'll see you in the morning?"

The urge to stay was strong, but something in Cassie made her not want to jeopardize any good will she had earned with Andrea's parents just yet. She leaned down to kiss Andrea before uttering a final "good night" and slipped out of the room, closing the door behind her.

She padded back through the hallway and the living room, making sure to keep her steps quiet so as to not wake Garrett and Isabel. A few minutes later, she was outside under the stars, walking toward the barn once more. A cool, gentle breeze ruffled the blonde hair above her forehead—a welcome change from the summer heat they had endured earlier. Evenings in the Western Hills were much more of a dramatic shift from daytime than Gurdinfield, probably more comparable to those in Azgadar. Looking out at the fields, she took in a deep breath of the fresh air and understood why Andrea preferred this over the bustling cities they seemed to spend much of their time in.

Near the top of the closest low hill from the farm, something moved. Cassie couldn't be sure, but *something* in the distance caught her eye. It was only for a fraction of a second—a dark figure—but impossible to tell who or what it could be. When she blinked and squinted to get a better look, it vanished, as though it had never been there in the first place. *What the hell…?*

She yawned. *I think I'm losing it. I need sleep.* It had been a long day, an even longer journey, and now Cassie wanted nothing more than to collapse on anything that could suffice as a bed and get some much-needed rest. She debated between the couch and the barn and chose the barn.

Her shoulders slumped in disappointment when she spotted the warm light coming from the barn. *Great.* She considered finding a nice spot outside to get some sleep, but her curiosity to find out who was still awake won out.

She found Garrett alone (with the exception of Kira), moving canvas sacks from an old, paint-chipped wheelbarrow and tossing them on top of each other in stacks up against the wall. He didn't notice her—his head was down and his focus was on the task at hand. Cassie stood there for a few seconds, unsure of what to say, until an idea came to her and she cleared her throat.

"Want a hand?"

Garrett jerked his head up. His light work shirt was doused in sweat near the collar and his hair was matted to his forehead. He studied her for a moment before answering. "Much appreciated." He pointed to the sacks in the wheelbarrow. "These just need to get sorted and stacked."

She tossed her sheathed sword on the dirt, rolled up her sleeves and got to work. The sacks were heavy, no doubt about it, but her Guardian training came in handy and she was able to help him complete the task twice as fast.

"Perfect," Garrett announced once they had finished. He used his shirtsleeve to wipe the sweat from his brow before grabbing two cups from underneath one of the workbenches and filling them from the spigot of one of the nearby barrels on the ground.

"Here," he said and handed one of the cups to Cassie, who took it with a grateful nod. "Bill normally sends one of us home with a barrel once a month. I got this one today. The summer brew, apparently." He lifted his own glass at her. "To family, then?"

Cassie mirrored the gesture. "Sounds good." She took a sip and found the honey and citrus overtones to her liking. It was no Fimen's Fire, but it was good.

Garrett smacked his lips. "Mm. Not bad at all. No doubt he'll have this at the festival tomorrow night." He took a seat on one of the shorter stacks as Cassie found a stepstool to sit on.

She wasted no time as she knew what she wanted to say to him. "Thanks, by the way, for not saying anything to Andrea about, um, the bracelet."

Garrett chuckled and shook his head. "I won't lie—it's a little strange to even think of her as being old enough to consider such things. But I suppose she is grown now." He took another sip.

Cassie's words came out more defensively than she intended.

"Yeah. She is."

He raised an eyebrow, but did not seem offended by her declaration. "Indeed. Capable of making her own decisions and everything." He shrugged. "Even if they include keeping secrets from her father."

Cassie tilted her head. "What do you mean?"

"Oh, come now. You and I—well, you especially—both know there is more to the story than she told me," he said. "I know Andrea, even if she doesn't want to believe it. So." He shifted in his makeshift seat to get more comfortable. "What really happened, Cassie? Because I know you'll tell me."

Cassie scoffed. "What makes you think that? You don't know me."

Garrett gave a quiet laugh. "Because I can tell how much you care for her. Isabel told me how uncomfortable you looked when Andrea was telling her your story. Maybe you're just nervous, but…I think there's something more."

She groaned. She couldn't deny he was right.

"Please, Cassie. She's my only child and this…" His expression gave way to guilt. "You have no idea how many times I've thought about the night she left. The things we said to each other. How many sleepless nights I endured wondering if Andrea was alive. I need to know what really happened."

Andrea is going to kill me. But she couldn't stand the sight of this poor man practically begging her to tell him the truth. *Maybe if he knows, he'll understand why magic is so important to her.* "Okay. But not a word of this to Andrea. What do you want to know?"

Garrett's eyes lit up. "Everything."

Cassie shook her head before taking another long sip. "Start with a question."

"Gurdinfield," he said. "Merchants from there arrived in town for the first time in years after the battle at the City of Towers. They told us that Lydia Taylor was alive and that the Legion had been pushed back."

"Yeah, that sounds about right. What about it?"

Garrett bit his lip. "There…was a rumor. A rumor that a young enchanter held the gates while the armies of Gurdinfield and Azgadar clashed on the field." He looked away. "Andrea told me she works for the queen now, and—"

"She held the gates," Cassie said, her tone solemn as she recalled that terrible day. The gut-wrenching boom, the fear that tore at her when the Legion deployed the flaming meteors of magic that took down the gates of the City of Towers and left Andrea buried underneath a pile of rock and charred rubble. She wanted to forget it but she also knew that Garrett wanted—no, *needed* to know. "She used magic to protect the city until the Legion hit the gates with a—with a weapon."

Even in the low light, Cassie could see his face grow pale. He clutched the cup in his hand so hard she worried it would crack under the pressure. Still, she continued.

"It took out just about everything in that area. My friend Kye and I left our safehouse to take out as many Legionnaires as we could so that our other friends could find Andrea."

"You," Garrett said in what was almost a low growl, "were in a *safehouse* while she was on the front lines?"

"By the prince-consort's orders!" Cassie fired back, trying to defend herself but struggling to hide the guilt she still felt. "And we didn't want to be."

He closed his eyes for a few seconds, his breathing erratic. "Her face?"

"Yes," Cassie confirmed. "The scars are from the attack." Another sip. "What else?"

Garrett's expression hardened. "Rhyad?"

"What about it?"

"Andrea told me that you, she, and Meredith released the magic from that cave, and that Meredith left afterward without telling you where she was going. But," he said slowly, "you're not an enchanter. And you did not become a Guardian until after you returned from Rhyad. So, why were *you* there?"

Damn. You really need to get better at lying, Andrea. "Andrea… didn't meet me in the Black Forest. She and Meredith brought me to Damea with their magic. It was…an accident, I guess."

Garrett stared at her with wide eyes. There was a lot of information being thrown at him, but Cassie thought he had the look of a man ready to believe anything at this point. "If you are not from Damea, then where are you from?"

"I-it's not important. But—"

"No, I want to know. Where are you from?" he insisted.

Cassie could not decide if it was the drink, her fatigue, or maybe just the fact that she was tired of having to keep up the wall between her and these nosy Dameans. *At least I know who Andrea inherited her interrogation tactics from.* "It's not like Damea at all."

"Is it in the east? Beyond Gurdinfield?"

She shook her head again. "No, no. It's…only magic can get you here from there. At least, that's my understanding. I don't know. I never made it back."

"And Rhyad?"

"Right," Cassie said. "Andrea discovered I had…well, abilities of my own. She could use me to see where the magic was being trapped in Damea. Happened to be Rhyad. So, we went." She put her hand up before he could say anything else. "I'm not an enchanter, but I could give enchanters the energy to cast their spells."

"And you released the magic?"

"It wasn't that straightforward, but yeah, we did."

Garrett waved his hand. "I don't want generalities, Cassie. I want the truth."

"And what happens if you don't like the answers?" Cassie demanded.

Garrett sighed. "Please, Cassie."

Cassie muttered an apology to Andrea under her breath before answering him. "We found the magic and there was a cave-in. Andrea saved my life with her magic, but since everything was so unstable in Rhyad, she got sick." She finished her drink in a long swig before setting the cup on the ground.

"Sick? As in…?"

"That magic sickness that enchanters get. Or used to get. She…she got it," she said, doing her best to push down the horrible feeling the mere memory of Andrea's illness—and how close she came to dying—gave her. "Meredith and I took her into the cave and released the magic. Andrea woke up, everyone was fine, Meredith was gone, and we went back to Gurdinfield. End of story."

She observed Garrett to see what his reaction would be. He, too, finished his drink in a single draught and set the cup down before standing up and dusting off his pants. "Thank you for telling me," he said quietly.

She couldn't help but feel a little guilty for throwing so much at him. "If it helps, the whole time we were together she talked about wanting to help people. I wasn't always on board with her plans, but…I know she cares a lot about that. And about what you think of her."

He smiled, but Cassie could see from the strained lines on his face that her words had disturbed him. "I looked for her. I asked around about Meredith—no one had even heard of her. I tried to pay merchants to take me to the Black Forest, but none would brave the journey. I watched my wife cry night after night and wondered if perhaps we had made a terrible mistake by not sending Andrea to Azgadar or *anywhere* that could teach her to use her abilities properly, instead of—" His voice broke and he took a moment to collect himself before continuing. "Instead of pretending they didn't exist."

"We make mistakes. Hell, I've made a ton," Cassie said with a short laugh.

He looked up at the rafters hanging above them. "I don't even know how to begin again with her. I fear our relationship was ruined when she left."

"Maybe start by *not* lecturing her about how magic is evil.

That will win you some points, trust me." After sharing more than what Andrea probably would have approved of, Cassie figured she could make it up to her at least a little by making some demands on her behalf.

Garrett laughed and met her gaze. "You are a little strange, Cassie, and I like that." He rolled his shoulders back. "I should head to bed. Are you coming inside?"

"Oh," she said, the awkwardness returning. "Um, I think I'm just going to hang out here tonight. You know, fresh air and all."

"As you wish. Please don't feel that you aren't welcome, however. And," he added with a short bow of his head, "thank you for the assistance. And the truth."

Cassie returned the bow. "Anytime. Oh!" she called after him as he made to leave. "You, uh—you won't say anything to her about tonight…or the bracelet, right? That is, uh…" *Crap.* She wasn't sure how to handle this sort of situation. Obviously, he knew she and Andrea were together and that she was starting to look at bracelets, which meant something *bigger,* but—

Garrett just winked at her. "You don't need to worry about that. You seem a good sort, Cassie, and I see how Andrea looks at you. That's enough for me. Just…" His smile faded again. "Please keep her safe. That's all I ask. Good night."

"'Night," Cassie called back as she watched him depart, leaving her alone in the dimming light with only Kira for company.

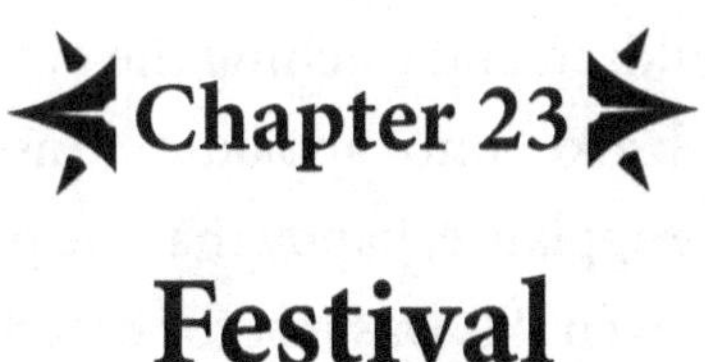

Chapter 23

Festival

One week later

The children of Ata yelled with glee as they watched the fireball shoot up into the smoky night sky and explode in a spectacle of light, the remains of it raining down as harmless specks of magic.

"Again!" one of them, a boy of six or seven, demanded.

"Again?" Andrea exclaimed as she dusted the ashes off her clothes. "I've done it five times now! Surely you're bored of it."

Cassie grinned up at Andrea from the low bench she sat on, surrounded by the group of eager children all waiting for Andrea to perform her next trick. Tonight's events had been going on for a few hours, and judging by the amount of people still competing in the various contests of racing, strength, puzzles, or guessing games, as well as eating, drinking, and dancing in the town square, Cassie figured it would still be some time before the town of Ata went to bed on the final night of the summer festival. "You heard them, Fire Lady! Again!" she yelled.

The children echoed her request, and Andrea gave her an

unimpressed look before turning back to her audience. "All right...one last time!"

Another fireball rocketed skyward, the explosion once again impressing the children and catching the eyes of several adults, many of whom broke into applause. Cassie found herself joining in with the applause, happy that the people of Ata could appreciate magic, even if it was just for entertainment. She had assumed the town would be close-minded or even fearful when it came to magic and enchanters, but she was more than happy to be proven wrong, especially if it meant seeing the look of pure joy that Andrea wore.

As Andrea gave a brief bow, Cassie stood up and waved the giggling children away. "All right, scram. Fire Lady's got other stuff to do tonight."

As they left, Andrea turned to her and raised an eyebrow. "'Scram?' That doesn't sound very nice. Also, *'Fire Lady'?*"

"It fits," Cassie said as she hooked her fingers on the end of Andrea's shirtsleeve and gave a gentle tug. "I believe *someone* promised me the walk-around if I sat quietly during that little magic show."

"You were shouting right along with them practically the entire time, Cassie."

Cassie just waved her hand. "Unnecessary details. Hey, I thought you weren't a fan of using magic for party tricks."

"That held true while we were in a magic famine." Andrea gestured around them. "No magic famine here."

"There'd better not be," Cassie said with a laugh. "Crippling pain and magically induced bruising is so last year. Now, *show me*. Please?"

With a broad smile, Andrea threaded her fingers with Cassie's before taking her on a grand tour of the various displays set up around the square and in the fields just beyond it. All of the businesses save Bill's inn had closed early that afternoon so their workers could partake in the evening festivities as well.

After sundown, Ata's marketplace lit up like a beacon. Tall torches surrounded the fairgrounds, and Andrea and her mentor, Jheran, who had returned from Azgadar shortly after the Restoration, had conjured light to store in glass orbs strung high between the buildings in the square. A stage was set up in the center of the square where a group of minstrels played song after song for the exuberant crowds dancing before them.

They walked for a bit, with Andrea pointing out the repeat visitors and exhibits—mostly the ones selling some kind of edible treat in a heavily fried form. Other displays were storefronts or carts, like the one Isabel and Garrett stood by for most of the evening.

Isabel was fretting about something—stress radiated off her while Garrett just seemed entertained. "*There* you are," she exclaimed. "Here, try this," and before Cassie could say anything, a thin wooden stick skewering a fried tomato was thrusted in her face. Cassie hesitated at first, but when she caught the teasing grin Andrea gave her, she took the stick and bit into the tomato. It was hot but delicious, and she savored the perfect combination of the light sweetness of the tomato and the salty fried batter.

"See? There you go, Garrett," Isabel continued while gesturing at Cassie. "If Lena wants to open her big mouth again about how much better her stupid shriveled tomatoes are than mine she can come over here and ask Cassie." She crossed her arms and looked to Andrea. "She's good with a sword, yes? We could take out an entire field before Lena can say 'tomato'. Isn't that right, Cassie?"

Andrea's jaw dropped. "Mother, Cassie is *not* going to vandalize our neighbor's crops just so you can win a contest!"

"Oh! You could always set *her* field on fire. Just a little spark and—"

"For a *tomato* contest?"

"All right, all right. And you were always saying you wanted to use your abilities for something useful," Isabel sniffed. "I suppose I'll just have to look elsewhere for help." She looked at Cassie, who was thoroughly enjoying her snack. "Especially if it means more fried tomatoes for Cassie."

Cassie mumbled in agreement and pointed at her new favorite snack. "This is *really* good. What did you need me to do again?" She coughed when a light elbow dug into her ribs. "Hey!"

"Let's go look at the other carts, Cassie," Andrea suggested, her tone a little too innocent, before dragging Cassie away from her parents.

"Have fun, you two!" Garrett called after them. Cassie shouted back her gratitude once more for the food as Andrea led her away. They took a seat on the edge of the field where an archery contest was underway.

Cassie applauded as one of the elimination rounds ended with the victor setting a new distance record. "Your parents are pretty laid back considering everything that's happened."

"I'm a little surprised, too." Andrea hugged herself—her cloak forgotten back at the house. "Maybe they're just trying to give me space? Or perhaps they don't know what to say to me." She shrugged. "Maybe they think I'll run off again if they say the wrong thing."

"That's not pessimistic at *all.*" Cassie was joking, but she was also reminded of her conversation with Garrett. *Maybe she's right.* Deciding that change of subject would be best, she pointed at the archers. "I'll bet Diana or Elisa would have loved this."

"Most likely," Andrea said. "Either of them might have even won." She frowned. "I hope they're all right."

"Oh, no," Cassie scolded as they set up the next round for the archers. "We agreed we weren't going to worry about that, remember?"

"Right. Sorry."

Cassie patted Andrea's arm. "Let's try to have fun, yeah?"

"I am," Andrea said. "Promise. This turned out better than I could have hoped for." Cassie relaxed when she heard the breath Andrea exhaled as she smiled, the flames from the torches and enchanted lights reflecting off her brightened eyes. They held each other's gazes for a very long but more-than-welcome moment until Andrea blinked a few times and looked out at hill in the distance. "What in the world?"

"Hmm?"

Andrea stood up. "There's—there's something out there." She pointed. "Or there was. I think it was a person. They were just…watching us."

Cassie jumped to her feet as well, feeling for the sword at her waist. "Damn it. I *knew* I saw someone the other night."

"Other night? You've seen them before?"

"Yeah," Cassie said. She grabbed Andrea's hand. "Come on. Let's see if we can catch them."

"You should have said something! What if they're hostile?" Andrea hissed, breaking into a run alongside Cassie as they headed in the direction of the mysterious figure.

"I was hoping you'd fry them or something," Cassie said when they had conquered the hill. "Look!" She pointed straight ahead, where the figure was disappearing into a small cluster of trees.

"It could be someone from the festival. Maybe they're drunk," Andrea suggested. She stopped and caught her breath. "I'd rather not accidentally hurt an innocent, Cassie."

But Cassie drew her sword, peering through the darkness. *Up ahead.* She could only make out the vague shape of the figure, but it was there at the tree line. Her voice dropped to a whisper. "Not taking chances. Be ready. If anything, we can try to scare them."

"Light?" Andrea asked.

"Not yet. Stay close." She struggled to ignore the pounding of her racing heart, focusing instead on the gentle straining of the tree branches in the soft wind, listening for any signs of whoever they pursued. She crept forward, remembering her Guardian training to keep her footsteps muted as they moved through the tall grass.

The silence was almost deafening as they passed into the woods. Cassie couldn't see Andrea, but she could hear her quiet breathing well enough to know she was beside her. She clutched at the hilt of her blade, hoping she wouldn't have to use it.

Movement. "There!" she shouted. The air around her lit up in a roaring orange blur as Andrea conjured a fireball—only to be snuffed out by an unknown force.

"*No!* Damn it!"

Cassie shut down her awareness to everything around her and put her strength behind her sword as she swung it downward. Before the blade could make contact with its target, a powerful force rushed at Cassie, throwing her to the ground and knocking her sword out of her hand.

"Cassie!" She heard Andrea but could not see well enough in the dark to get to her. Then, the forest lit up again—a barrier that spanned a radius large enough to protect several people, its brightness so intense that Cassie had to shield her eyes. The barrier shrank, leaving enough space for one person – its caster, who stood motionless as he observed them.

Cassie sputtered out a few coughs and let Andrea help her up. "I'm all right," she panted. "Can you *please* fry this guy now, And—" She stopped when she saw Andrea's eyes, wide and filled with shock. "What?"

Andrea just stared at the man before them. Cassie thought he seemed familiar, but it was hard to be sure. He was tall, though not as tall as Garrett. His brown long-sleeved shirt and black trousers fit him loosely, but he did not appear to be suffering from malnutrition. His blonde hair was short and blended into his even shorter beard. A woven bracelet hung around his wrist.

He smiled, the barrier accentuating the slightest of crow's feet around his blue eyes. "Evening." His voice was even and pleasant. He seemed calm for someone who had just been in combat.

Cassie glared at him. "Really? Is that your opening line to everyone or just to the people you make a habit of stalking and attacking?" She spotted her sword on the ground out of the corner of her eye, but it was too far out of reach for her to risk going after.

"Cassie…" Andrea's warning was hushed yet urgent.

"If I may, you attacked me first, Cassie," he replied, her name coming out softer than the rest of his words. He smiled at them, which Cassie found unnerving—but he also did not drop his barrier. He turned to Andrea. "It's good to meet you at last, Andrea."

"Don't talk to her like you know her," Cassie snapped, her eyes darting to her sword and then back at the stranger. "You've been following us. What the hell do you want?"

"Cassie," Andrea exclaimed. "It's Richard!"

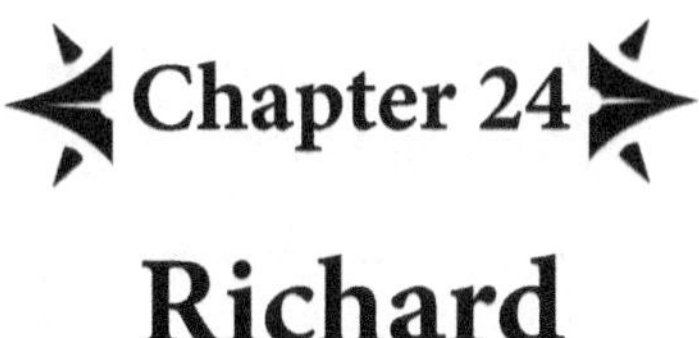

Chapter 24

Richard

Cassie stared hard in disbelief at the man standing before them. *This* was the mysterious figure who had been following them? For someone who had been spying on them for days, he seemed quite friendly.

But Cassie knew that like everything else in Damea, appearances could be deceiving. Meredith had appeared perfectly nice and well-mannered at first, too. *And look how she turned out.* "Richard? As in 'Meredith's dead husband' Richard?"

Richard scoffed, though it was one of amusement, not disgust. "Dead? I am very much alive, thank you. Wait." Stress edged into his voice. "Meredith. Where is she? Is she all right?"

Andrea shook her head. "We haven't seen Meredith in months. How are you—I mean, well, we assumed you to be dead from…from the Restoration."

"Restoration?" Richard stroked his beard, his other hand keeping the barrier up. "Is that what they're calling it, then?" He waved his hand and the barrier went down, right before an orb of white light appeared in the other hand, brightening up the woods around them and the grass where they stood.

"Hold up." Cassie moved forward. "You still haven't answered my question. Why were you following us?"

But Richard did not appear threatened by her. "Apologies," he said and gave a short bow. "It wasn't my intention to alarm you. I've been looking for you both."

Cassie wasn't convinced. "So you creep around farmhouses and festivals? That's your way of saying hi?"

Richard gave a short laugh. "Suspicious, are we? I understand. I had to make sure it was you."

"Why?" Andrea asked.

"Please, perhaps I can explain better over some tea. I'm staying at the inn and—"

"No," Cassie told him. "Talk now or not at all." She looked over at Andrea, who seemed unsure.

"Maybe we should hear what he has to say, Cassie," she suggested, her demeanor much calmer than Cassie thought reasonable.

Fat chance. Cassie laughed harshly. "After Meredith? No thank you. For all we know he's working with her on some crazy experiment."

Richard stood his ground. "I don't know all that transpired between you and my wife, but I implore you—I *must* find Meredith. I awoke on a metal table in the Black Forest—alone." He lifted his hand, and the ball of light floated upward, hanging in the air above them. "I found Meredith's journals and I read *every* entry. To discover that it has been *twenty* years since..." He fell silent for a moment. "Before I fell ill, enchanters were the pariahs of Damea. I'm a wanted man in the City of Towers.

Of course I am careful, but I do regret startling you."

"Magic is no longer scarce, and this isn't Gurdinfield," Andrea told him. "But we don't know where Meredith is."

"We thought she'd be with you," Cassie added. A shiver ran through her, though whether it was from the cold or their situation she couldn't tell.

"I...I see." Richard hung his head and sighed. "She wrote of you in her journals—both of you. I thought if," he said, meeting Andrea's eyes, "I found *you,* that you might be able to tell me where she went."

"You know what she did, then?" Cassie said, refusing to give him any quarter until she had all of her answers. "What she was trying to do?"

His eyes filled with guilt. "I do. I...don't have a good explanation for her actions. That's the truth."

All fell quiet once more, the only sounds coming from the forest and the dull, constant hum of the magic emanating from the orb of light.

"We might be able to help," Andrea said suddenly.

Cassie couldn't believe what she was hearing. "Andrea, don't—"

"For all her faults, she saved my life, Cassie," Andrea interjected before she could argue further. "And Richard is not Meredith. He deserves to know what happened to her."

Cassie couldn't believe what she was hearing. "What the hell, Andrea? What happened to 'Meredith's a terrible person'? You said—"

"I know what I said!" Andrea shouted, the rare outburst stunning Cassie. "I know what I said," Andrea repeated, more quietly. "But you know I'm right." Andrea looked at her with a pleading expression.

She threw up her hands in defeat. "Screw this. You don't even know this guy, Andrea. If you want to help him find his crazy wife, be my guest. Just…don't ask me to help." She walked over to her sword, picked it up, and sheathed it before stomping away, muttering, "I'll meet you back at the house."

"Cassie, wait!" Andrea called, but she ignored her, focusing instead on the torches lighting up the town at the bottom of the hill, guiding her back to the festival…and hopefully actual sane people.

* * *

"Your tea, friend." With a rough hand accustomed to heavy tankards, Bill set the ceramic cup down in front of Richard. Hot black tea sloshed around it, spilling over the edge and dripping a bit onto the table.

"Ah, perfect. Thank you, Bill."

"Yep." Bill then turned to Andrea, his bushy mustache twitching in a crooked smile. "You sure I can't get you anything?"

Andrea held up her hand. "I'm fine, Bill. Thank you."

Bill stood still for a moment and stared at her before he patted her on the shoulder. "It's good to have you back in Ata. Tell your parents hello for me when you see them."

"I will," she said as he walked back to the bar. Despite the late hour, the inn was still busier than Andrea had ever remembered seeing it, though the atmosphere of the establishment was somehow still the quiet she was used to. She figured most of the patrons were just visiting for the festival, but she hoped the inn was still doing well. The minstrel who normally performed at this time was missing. *Most likely still in the square with the others.* The familiar scent of Bill's famous stew was still there, as was the overpowering stench of whatever he had brewed or imported at the time. *Everything's the same.*

Only…it wasn't. Not really. Reconciling with her parents and introducing Cassie to them had seemed like such an insurmountable obstacle. Now, here she was—back in Ata, a royal enchanter, on speaking terms with her parents, and sitting face to face with Richard, a man she had never imagined actually being able to speak to.

And Cassie is once again angry at me. Andrea sighed. She knew Cassie would have a hard time going along with her proposal to help Richard considering the conversation they had a few days ago about Meredith, but she didn't expect her to just storm off like she had before Andrea had a chance to explain. *Clearly, I assumed too much.* She wondered if this was a bad idea. *Maybe I should go talk to her first.*

She noticed Richard was staring at her with a concerned expression on his face. Had he said something?

"I'm sorry?"

Richard chuckled and pointed to his cup. "The tea. It's good."

"Ah. I'm glad."

He leaned forward. “You’re worried about Cassie.”

How I wish I wasn’t so bloody obvious all the time. “Yes,” she said. “She—she wasn’t wrong. Meredith did terrible things to her. She’s right to distrust you.”

“And yet here you are—sitting with me, and with an offer of help no less.”

“I have only one suggestion and that is all I can offer,” Andrea said. “How did you find us, anyway?”

He gave her a tired smile. “Meredith’s journal. She mentioned you were from Ata and how she used that handy skill of hers to find you with your projection.” He shrugged. “I figured I’d try looking here first. And about the help—I am grateful for it. Make no mistake about that. Now,” he said, before taking a sip of his tea. “I understand Meredith was trying to…to wake me. But what is this about her saving your life? What happened?”

Andrea shifted in her seat and tried not to appear as uncomfortable as she felt. She didn’t like to think about Rhyad, let alone talk about the events in the mountains. “Cassie has—*had* an ability that allowed enchanters to draw on her for power.”

“Mm, yes. Meredith mentioned as much.”

Andrea continued. “Her ability also allowed me to see where the magic was trapped in Damea.”

Richard’s eyebrows went up at this. “Trapped? You mean to tell me that the magic was gathered in a single location all of this time?”

“Exactly!” Andrea tried to rein in her excitement, but it had been quite some time since she had conversed with an experienced enchanter other than Master Jheran. Talking to someone new, even if he was Meredith's husband, was a breath of fresh air. "It was in Rhyad. Cassie and I went there, along with some friends, and released the magic."

Richard's eyes grew wide as he took in the news. "But…how is that possible? How did you release it?"

"There was a—a device." Andrea tried to think of the best way to describe it but the fact remained that she had not actually been conscious to see it. "I became ill when we found the cave containing magic. Cassie had to carry me, and she and Meredith found the device inside the cave."

"Go on," he urged.

"I didn't really see it, but Cassie said that Meredith studied it briefly. I'm not certain of its purpose or how it got there but it had been gathering the magic in Damea for hundreds of years," she said. "They used Cassie's power to pour energy into the device to overload it."

"And so this 'Restoration' happened," Richard finished.

The whole situation made very little sense to Andrea. "I don't understand," she said. "We thought Meredith returned to the Black Forest to see to you. She wasn't there when you woke?"

"No," he replied. "If she did, in fact, return, then I was unconscious for it. When I awoke, I knew something had changed. The magic…" He stretched his arms out before returning his hands to the cup. "You can feel it, can't you?"

She grinned. "I admit, it's a little hard to believe myself sometimes."

He bowed his head. "The energy, yes, it's there again. Very rich, especially here. But," he pressed, looking her in the eye, "you and I both know that it won't last."

He knows. The sinking sensation in her stomach struck again and Andrea found herself pushing down the panic that had been closing in on her since Azgadar. "W-what do you mean?"

Richard took a final sip and placed the cup on the table before pushing it away. "That fireball you cast at me earlier—its dispelling was not of your control. And judging by your reaction to it, that was not the first time it happened, was it?"

Andrea swallowed as a lump in her throat formed. "I…I don't know…"

"I may have been out of commission for a few decades, Andrea, but if there's one thing I know, it's magic. I felt it in the Black Forest—the redistribution of magic is not even. This Restoration is destabilizing the energy in Damea," he said with such calm certainty that Andrea knew he was telling the truth. *Maybe I've always known and just didn't want to admit it.*

"There was a—an attack in Azgadar. I cast a barrier and something…wasn't right. It collapsed. Too brittle," she admitted. "Then in the woods on our way here, we were attacked by soldiers from Gurith. I think…I think they were under some sort of spell."

"A spell?"

"Yes," she said, recalling the brief fight with the Gurithian soldiers. "And even stranger—I could *feel* the energy from the spell before they got too close to us."

"Then my theory is only being proven correct," Richard sighed. "The energy levels in this region are much higher—more concentrated than in Azgadar, most likely."

Andrea groaned and buried her face in her hands. "This can't be happening." She looked up at him. "I thought we fixed this—truly, I did."

But Richard just reached out and took her hand, stunning her for a moment as he gave it a brief squeeze before letting go. "Meredith was right to choose you as her apprentice. You care just as she did."

"Thank you." Andrea didn't know how else to respond. Richard seemed nice enough, but she still didn't know him very well yet. The mystery of Meredith's whereabouts still hung in the air, and there were still many questions that needed answering. "About Meredith—I don't know where she is. But the royal enchanter in Azgadar might be able to help. Meredith visited Azgadar many times and if she ever registered as an enchanter there, they could know where else she might live. Cassie and I need to return to the palace there before we head home."

Richard laughed and banged on the table with his fist, garnering curious looks from the other patrons. "The palace? What in the world is an enchanter like yourself doing going to Azgadar, and to the *palace* no less?"

Andrea had to smile at his reaction. "I work for the queen of Gurdinfield as her royal enchanter. Cassie is a Guardian. We were in Azgadar helping work out an alliance with the empress when we left to visit my family here."

"*Ithmeera* rules now?" he gasped, though Andrea could tell his reaction was partly in jest. "And Gurdinfield has a proper leader again. My, how things change when you're in a magically induced slumber!"

They both laughed at this. "With your permission, I will

accompany you to Azgadar, then." He corrected himself. "Assuming that is all right with Cassie, of course."

Andrea took a deep breath. Convincing Cassie was not going to be easy. "I'll talk to her. She just needs some time. We leave the day after tomorrow."

Richard hesitated. "If I may be forward, I've never heard of a Guardian having equal pull in the decision-making of their charges."

Oh. Right. Andrea had forgotten that Richard could not have known. "Cassie and I are together. She's…" She tried not to blush, though the heat in her cheeks seemed like it was there to stay. "She's more than just a guard, and I care very much about what she thinks."

"Ah! It all makes sense now," Richard exclaimed. "Is she always so suspicious of others?"

Andrea shot him a dry grin. "Only the ones who watch us from afar and hide under the cover of darkness."

"Again, my apologies for causing trouble. But there's… something else I should tell you while we're here tonight, Andrea," he said, folding his hands together. "Something I think Cassie should know as well, although I'm not sure where to even *begin* telling her."

"What is it?" Andrea thought he seemed nervous and she couldn't fathom what could be so important and why would it be relevant to Cassie.

He looked down at the table. "I…don't know how to put this but…the place that you and Meredith brought Cassie from?"

Andrea tilted her head. "Yes? What about it?"

A pause. Richard looked at her. “I know it. Just as I know Cassie.”

Andrea thought she had misheard him. “What? What do you mean? How?” She waited for him to correct himself, to laugh and say that he was joking. But instead Richard leaned in.

“Because I’m from there, Andrea. And…” He exhaled. “Because she is my daughter.”

Chapter 25

Revelations

The short trip back to her parents' house was quiet, save for the low hum of the white light Andrea had conjured to guide her and the occasional scurrying of the nocturnal wildlife that lived in the tall grass around the dirt road. But Andrea's mind was anything but quiet. The wheels in her head turned still, her thoughts going over the news Richard had dropped on her again and again. He was from Cassie's world? And Cassie was his *daughter?* It seemed impossible—it *should* have been impossible.

And yet, I believe him.

He'd told her that he used to be a scientist—an enchanter of sorts as he described it—in the place he was from. A world where magic did not exist and in which energy was so scarce that he'd spent years of his life searching for an answer to keep his home—his civilization—alive.

"There were many others like me," he told her. "Men and women who dedicated their entire lives to finding an answer to our energy problem. Not unlike the situation you and Meredith faced before the Restoration."

She needed to talk to Cassie. She needed to figure out why

the magic was not being distributed properly and what that would mean for Damea. *So much for a break from it all.*

She wondered what Meredith would have done. How she would have reacted to finding out that her husband was indeed alive. Or when she discovered that he was not from Damea. But the questions fled from her mind as she approached the house and saw a dim light flickering inside the barn.

She found Cassie sitting on a stepstool next to the horse's stall, going through her backpack while muttering occasionally to Kira. A single lit lantern housing a nearly depleted candle hung nearby, the only source of light in the barn.

The crunch of the hay under Andrea's boots made Cassie look up. "Sorry," Andrea mumbled. "I didn't mean to startle you."

Cassie shrugged and put the bag down. "It's fine." She gestured at the bag. "I was just making sure we had everything for when we leave. Pretty sure your mother is going to try to make us take the farm when we go."

Andrea giggled, approaching Cassie slowly. "I'm certain she just wants us to have enough food on the journey back."

"Right." Cassie stood up and straightened out her clothing. "By the way, she said you're too skinny and that you have no excuse for not eating, considering we live in a palace."

"Did she now?"

"Yeah. She also told me that I need to make sure we come back here often. I don't know where she got this idea that I can influence what you do." Cassie looked away. "Not like you listen to me, anyway."

Andrea winced. She hated feeling guilty, especially when it came to their relationship. The days of their near-constant arguing were supposed to be over. She wished she could just take Cassie into her arms, and that they could move on. "I wish you had stayed. I would never endanger us on purpose. You know that."

But Cassie held up her hand. "It's fine, okay? I get it. Meredith helped you and you want to help Richard find her so they can be a nice, creepy magical family."

"She…she saved my life, Cassie. You both did."

Cassie jerked her head up, her words cold. "I remember what happened. We don't need to dwell on it."

"He's coming with us to Azgadar. I told him Master Tobias might be able to find out where Meredith went." She waited for Cassie to get angry at the news, to yell at her and perhaps even walk away from her again.

But Cassie just rolled her eyes. "Fine. Just don't make me talk to him."

I have to tell her. "Cassie…there's something else." When Cassie just waited for her to speak, she pushed her nerves away and continued. "It's about Richard. He said—he told me that he's from the same place you're from."

Cassie stared at her and blinked. Twice. Her eyebrows arched. "What?"

Andrea explained, her words coming out in a rush. "Yes, he said that—that he was a 'scientist' and he was working to find a solution to an energy problem…that you had an energy problem in your—where you're from."

“That’s impossible.” Cassie leaned against a wall, her voice flat.

“How? You came here, did you not?”

Cassie folded her arms across her chest. “He read Meredith’s journals. He knows how I got here. How do you know he’s not lying?”

“Why would he lie about something like that?” Andrea challenged.

Cassie brushed her words aside. “I don’t know—because he’s insane?”

Here we go again. “How many times—look, not all enchanters are like Meredith!”

“I know that!” Cassie said, throwing up her hands. “But I’ve got half of Damea telling me I need to protect you. I get that you’re trying to help, but you can’t blame me for being careful—”

“He’s your father, Cassie!” Andrea wasn’t sure how the words slipped out, but it seemed to be the only way to get Cassie to listen to her. She probably could have phrased it better, been more sensitive—but it was out and all she could do now was see how Cassie reacted.

Cassie’s arms dropped to her sides as she just stared at the hay-covered floor. *Maybe she didn’t hear me?* “Cassie? Did you hear what I said?”

“I heard you,” Cassie whispered. “No.”

“I’m sorry?”

“T-that…can’t be. My father—”

"Was missing," Andrea said, trying to keep her voice as gentle as possible. She closed the distance between them and put her hands on Cassie's hips. "That's what your mother told you, isn't it?"

Cassie still wouldn't look at her. "Yeah, but I figured he'd just left us. There's no way..."

"Cassie," Andrea said. "He was trying to get back to you."

"No." Cassie shook her head and Andrea could see her eyes glossing over with tears. "Either he's lying or he's an asshole."

"I don't...I don't think he's lying. He knew things about your home that only you have told me," Andrea said, her heart sinking at the crack in Cassie's voice. "Your cities—the buildings, the lack of mag—"

Cassie cut her off. "Well then, I guess he's an asshole because only an asshole would *leave* the mother of his kid while she was still pregnant just to screw around in some other world with a crazy enchanter who thinks *torture* is okay!"

Andrea fell silent, cringing as the remnants of Cassie's outburst bounced around the barn. Kira let out a quiet snort.

"Yeah, sorry. Forgot you were there," Cassie said to the horse. She sniffed and wiped her eyes. "Sorry," she mumbled, though this apology seemed more directed at Andrea than Kira.

Andrea saw an opportunity and took it. "She's used to it. My mother and I would bicker in here all the time." She leaned in and gave Cassie a tentative kiss, hoping she wouldn't push her away. "I'm sorry for forcing this on you. You're right to be cautious. I'll tell Richard that he'll have to look elsewhere for help."

"No," Cassie said with a heavy sigh. "It's fine. I—I guess I just need answers now. And he's going to give them to me whether he likes it or not. And," she added with regret in her voice, "I'm sorry for walking away from you like that. I don't—I'm still not very good at this yet." She bit her lip. "I love you a lot and I *really* don't want to mess this up."

Andrea could scarcely believe what she was hearing. A year ago, Cassie would have laughed at the very notion of hearing any side of the story other than her own and probably would have refrained from speaking to Andrea for days. Now, here she was apologizing *and* declaring her love. "You could never 'mess this up', though I appreciate the sentiment." She wrapped her arms around Cassie and kissed her again, this time for much longer. "And I love you. And I agree—you should definitely interrogate him on the way to Azgadar. I'll even supply fireballs if you wish."

"Perfect," Cassie laughed. She tugged on Andrea's shirt to pull them even closer together.

Damn it. The issue that had plagued Andrea's mind since Azgadar surfaced. She put up her hand just as Cassie was initiating another kiss.

"There's one more thing I need to tell you."

Cassie let out a frustrated noise. "Seriously? What *now?*"

"Last thing, I promise," Andrea said, her smile fading as the reality of what she was about to bring up set in. "It's about magic."

"I know," Cassie said. "Or at least, I think I do."

Andrea couldn't help but feel a bit foolish for not speaking to Cassie about this sooner. *Of course she'd notice.* "The magic we released…it's not being distributed evenly across Damea. I thought that it would flow back into the land naturally, but, well, you've probably noticed some of my spells haven't been working correctly."

"I've seen it. I guess I just didn't want to believe it. I figured *you* knew whether things were okay or not and that you'd say something if they weren't." Cassie met her eyes. "What do we do?"

"I—I don't know yet. I should tell Diana when we reach Azgadar, but aside from that..." She shook her head. She knew she couldn't solve this problem tonight, or while she was still in Ata for that matter. "We can figure it out when we get back. There's nothing we can do from here."

Cassie seemed impressed. "Wow. Did I hear right? You don't feel like worrying about *magic?*"

"Very funny. What was it you said? 'Personal growth'?"

"Sure, but you're not saying it right," Cassie said as she toyed with the light material of Andrea's shirt. "Not that it matters."

The flame in the lantern went out, leaving them in darkness.

"Heh," Cassie said with a soft laugh. "I guess that means it's time for bed."

"Mother usually kept the candles inside. I'll go get another so you have one tonight." Andrea moved to leave but was pulled back by Cassie's hand on her shirt.

"Or, you could stay a bit longer before I get some sleep." Cassie's voice was low, hushed, and suggestive, igniting the memories Andrea had been replaying in her mind since that night in Azgadar. She sank into Cassie's embrace against the wall and let out a shuddered sigh when Cassie nuzzled her cheek, breathing softly against her ear.

She decided to forgo a reply and let her actions speak for themselves as she pushed herself up against Cassie, giving her the rough kiss she'd been holding back since their arrival in Ata. Cassie had been hesitant to engage in any kind of public display of affection out of respect to Andrea's parents, and while Andrea understood, she couldn't help but be bitter at how life continued to interrupt them even after the Restoration. Magic, her parents, Diana, Richard, their duties—if they could all just leave her and Cassie *alone,* everything would be perfect.

Tonight, however, it was either late enough that Cassie was not worried about Isabel or Garrett seeing them, or she just no longer cared. She matched the kiss with equal force and ran her hands down Andrea's back, her fingers catching on the bunched fabric of the shirt, before she moved her lips down with slow precision toward Andrea's neck.

Upon contact, Andrea let out a quiet gasp and whispered Cassie's name, her breathing already so uneven and her legs weakening to the point where she was sure she'd need to sit down soon. The tension and stress from their brief fight in the woods dissipated, and for that moment, nothing could bother her. Abandoning all her inhibitions, she grasped at the front of Cassie's blouse and started to undo the small buttons near the collar. The first was easy enough, as was the second and the third, but she was stopped at the fourth by Cassie's hand clamping down on hers.

"A-Andrea." Cassie's stammer broke through her labored breathing. Startled, Andrea froze and looked up at Cassie with concern, despite it being too dark to really see her that well.

"Should I—was that not all right?"

"No, no! I mean, yes! I mean, damn," Cassie groaned. She took Andrea's hands in hers and kissed them. "It was amazing. *You're* amazing. But we…are clearly moving toward something that I don't think we'd be able to finish. Well," she said, looking around the barn, "not *here*, anyway. And, um, your parents—"

Andrea touched Cassie's cheek. "I understand." She gave her one final kiss before forcing herself to pull away. "I'll see you in the morning?"

"Count on it," were Cassie's parting words to her.

Wishing the night had ended in a different way but certainly not disappointed, Andrea walked back to the house with only the light from the stars and the glow of the candles within the house to guide her. She looked back every few seconds to give a small wave or shy smile to Cassie before stepping inside.

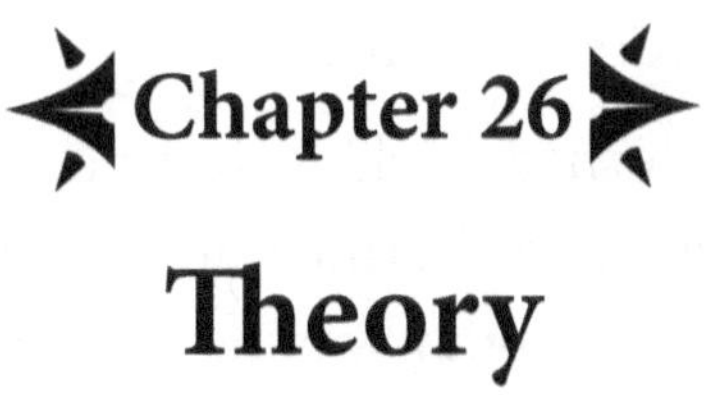

Chapter 26
Theory

"Here. Take these, too."

Andrea's eyes grew big when Isabel handed her yet another canvas bag of food. "Mother, we have enough food to feed the Legion. Please, you've given us more than enough."

Isabel clicked her tongue. "It's a long trip to Azgadar and I'll be damned if you return to Queen Lydia looking like you've been starving in the desert."

Cassie took the bag before Andrea could object and carried it over to their horse. She had fetched it from the village stables earlier that morning so that Andrea could have a little more time with her parents on their last morning in Ata. "Don't worry. If she doesn't eat it, I will."

When Isabel expressed her approval, Andrea rubbed at her eyes and gave up. "That's…I'm sure you will." She did a quick check to make sure they had everything they needed for the return journey to Azgadar. They planned to stop in town to meet with Richard before leaving the Western Hills together. Andrea still wasn't certain what Cassie would say, if anything, once the three of them met up, but she tried to put it out of her mind, at least until they were finished saying their farewells to her mother and father.

Cassie secured the fastenings on the horse's saddlebags before dusting her hands off and joining Andrea, Isabel, and Garrett. "I think we're good. You ready?"

"Yes." Andrea turned back to her parents as they stood in front of the house she'd grown up in, run away from, and was now leaving again, but planning to return to…eventually. "Well, then. I—I suppose this is it for now."

Isabel's eyes welled up with tears for the third time that morning. Garret put a comforting arm around her, though he had said very little to anyone since getting up before dawn and collecting all the supplies he could find that might be useful to Andrea and Cassie on their trip.

"Mother, I'll be back. I promise," Andrea said as she embraced Isabel, who held her with such force Andrea was certain she'd be sore later.

"You had better," Isabel sniffed. "Else I'll write the queen myself and demand she send you back."

Andrea gave a small laugh even though she had no trouble believing Isabel would actually do it. It took some wriggling, but she was able to free herself of her mother's grasp only to be swept up by Garrett, who held her even tighter.

"Be careful, Andrea. *Please,*" he begged, nearly making Andrea cry herself. "And write us. Don't make us worry for another four years."

"I won't, Father."

When they broke apart, he turned to Cassie and extended his hand. "Thank you, Cassie. For bringing her back to us and...for everything."

Cassie surprised Andrea by forgoing her usual humorous reply and clasped Garrett's hand. "You're welcome," she said sincerely, a knowing glance exchanged between them that made Andrea wonder if her father had had a private word with Cassie earlier. *I'll ask her about it later.*

They mounted the horse with Andrea in front and Cassie in the back, and gave Isabel and Garrett a final wave goodbye. Pushing down the urge to cry again, Andrea spurred the horse and they set off down the road toward Bill's inn, the overcast skies doing nothing to help her already somber mood.

It only took a few minutes before she was huffing in annoyance as her vision blurred again and again despite how many times she wiped her eyes. Finally, she felt Cassie, whose arms were around her waist, lean in and press a comforting kiss to the back of her shoulder. "You want to talk about it?"

Despite the temptation of Cassie's rare offer to actually *talk* about something, Andrea shook her head. She didn't understand why leaving Ata *now* was more painful than when she had left with Meredith, but it was, and part of her wished she didn't care so much. "T-thank you, but I'll be all right."

"Sure?"

She nodded and tried to focus on the path ahead. "I'm good, Cassie. I just—I need time is all."

"We'll come back once we figure out the magic issue, okay?"

Andrea didn't answer, and Cassie seemed to understand because she didn't say anything else. The remainder of their trip to the inn was quiet with only the heavy thuds of the horse's hooves to help her drown out her thoughts. She tried not to dwell on wondering where her home truly was now—and when exactly she would be able to return.

* * *

Richard met them with his own horse outside the inn. It only took one look at Andrea's sullen face and Cassie's scowl for him to decide to keep his greeting brief. "All set, then? Thank you again for meeting me."

"I can get you an audience with the royal enchanter. Beyond that I'm afraid you're on your own," she replied as they left Ata and made their way toward the steep hill that would lead them back to the forest bordering the Azgadaran Empire.

"I appreciate the help," Richard said. They rode with Richard in front (at Cassie's request) and Andrea and Cassie following behind in silence, with Cassie shooting Richard the occasional dirty look whenever he looked around to observe them.

"Hopefully we can steer clear of bandits or any other trouble along the way," he called back. "Not sure if you noticed, but I'm a bit out of practice when it comes to self-defense."

"Good thing you're up in front, then," Cassie grumbled loud enough for Richard to hear. "They can pick you off first."

Andrea thought about asking Cassie to refrain from antagonizing Richard, but she held back when she remembered their conversation the other night in the barn. If he truly had abandoned Cassie and her mother, Cassie had every right to be angry at him.

Richard answered, his demeanor almost jovial, "Ha! They can try. I might be rusty, but I'm not so useless that I can't take out a few idiots with swords."

"Shame," was Cassie's dry comeback. Andrea stifled a laugh. When Cassie disliked someone, she was *not* shy about showing it.

He continued. "I'm going to go out on a limb and guess that your girlfriend here told you everything we talked about."

"That I did," Andrea said.

"Good!" Richard slowed his horse and waited until they were beside him to start moving again. "Then we can stop pretending we don't all know exactly what's going on here."

But Cassie just turned her head away from him. "I'm not interested in a conversation with you right now."

Richard shrugged. "Suit yourself. You're going to want to hear the truth eventually."

Andrea's temples began to throb and she sensed a headache coming on, no doubt from the combination of crying and stress. She decided to interject before a fight between Cassie and Richard made it worse. "Have you given any thought to what we spoke about the other night? About the magic?"

Richard gave her a wry smile, letting her know he was aware she was trying to change the subject, and for the first time since meeting him Andrea noticed the slightest hint of family resemblance between him and Cassie. *Not that I'll tell her that.* "I have, actually," he said. "There is, of course, research to be done and studies to conduct, but the answer could be as simple as redistributing the energy ourselves."

Andrea frowned. "Ourselves? How would that be possible?"

"Oh, it's quite possible, believe me. How do you cast a fireball? Or a barrier?"

She wasn't sure what he was getting at but the question seemed familiar, almost like something Meredith would ask during one of her teaching sessions. "It's a conversion. You use magic from nature or an object and you manipulate it into a form you can use and control."

"Precisely. Just a conversion. Glad to see someone still knows the mechanics of it," Richard said. Andrea could swear she heard Cassie mutter some choice words under her breath behind her. Despite Cassie's protests, she couldn't help but admit to herself how eager she was to learn from an experienced enchanter again.

"Many enchanters are terribly inefficient in their spellcasting, though—we waste a lot of the magic we gather because we're just concerned with getting that barrier up or making that fireball to take out the bandit. If they haven't already 'picked me off', that is." He grinned at Cassie, who ignored him. "Lots of wasted potential, and the magic's dirtied just enough that it's not very viable for the next person to use, at least not for some time." He shifted in his saddle as they climbed the path going up the hill. "When an enchanter looks for that energy to convert, it's usually there. Sometimes, though, we get too much of the leftovers or not enough magic at all. You cast the spell but there's an imbalance—not enough 'good' magic. The energy for the spell has to come from somewhere, and it usually ends up being the enchanter, unfortunately."

"You get sick," Andrea concluded.

"You get sick, correct," Richard said. "A most unpleasant experience, as I'm sure you'll agree."

Andrea grimaced. "I'd rather not think about it, to be honest. But what does this have to do with distributing the magic?"

"Right. So, what we need is a way to transfer more of the 'good' magic to the regions where it's not as saturated. This area, for example, is quite rich with magic. Azgadar, on the other hand, has always lacked resources. Likewise, we need to remove it from some of the oversaturated regions, as both over- and under-saturation will result in instability, causing things like say, fireballs, to fizzle out or explode in our faces." His explanation sounded so *simple* to Andrea, even though she had no idea how he planned to accomplish it.

"We could enchant objects, couldn't we?" she suggested, and didn't hide her satisfaction when Richard appeared to consider it.

"We could," he said. "Enchanters have done it for centuries. It might not be ideal, however. Objects have a saturation point, so we would need multiple artifacts. And transporting so many objects back and forth across Damea would take a long time, time that I'm not so sure we have."

"Why? What could happen?" Both Andrea and Richard exchanged surprised glances when Cassie spoke up.

"Ah…well," Richard said slowly, as though choosing his words carefully, "I imagine something similar to what happened during the Starving, only much worse."

Tendrils of dread enveloped Andrea as the sinking feeling in her stomach returned. He didn't need to answer—she knew.

But Cassie should know. "How?"

His tone grew dark. "Because this time, there is no device to destroy. There would be no magic to release, because you already released it. The energy will continue to distribute unevenly. Eventually, any magic will be too unstable for an enchanter to use."

The end of magic…of enchanting as we know it. Andrea's mouth went dry as the throbbing in her temples intensified. What had she missed? Releasing the trapped magic in Rhyad should have fixed the effects of the Starving, not caused a new one.

Did we destroy magic? Did I *cause this?* "You said transferring magic to objects wouldn't be ideal," she began. "What about the device we found the magic trapped in? Something like that could hold more energy."

Richard barked out a laugh. "Is that so? And did you study it? Do you know how to build it?"

Andrea winced. Had her question really been so naïve? "Well, no, but—"

"And since you destroyed it, we can't exactly go back and learn how to replicate it. No, this is going to take more than simple enchanting to solve."

"Hey, lay off," Cassie snapped. "Andrea didn't blow the stupid device up—your crazy wife and I did."

Richard sighed. "I get that you aren't a fan of Meredith, Cassie, but could you at least—"

"Nope," Cassie interrupted. "Listen, I don't like you. If you thought leaving your family behind was a good idea—fine.

You're an asshole. But don't start blaming other people for trying to solve this screwed-up world's problems." She pointed an accusatory finger at him. "And don't you dare try to justify the evil things people did to us. You have *no* idea what we went through."

Richard pulled on the reins to stop. Andrea did the same. She held her breath, waiting for him to lose his temper and prepared to employ magic in the event he lashed out.

"I did not *leave* my family," he said through clenched teeth, letting one hand off the reins and pinching the bridge of his nose. He turned to Cassie. "I was trapped here!"

Cassie shot him an icy glare. "Why should I believe anything you say?"

"Please," Richard said, looking at Andrea for help. "I can't explain myself if she won't let me."

Another throb in her head. *Enough.* "Stop it! Both of you!"

Cassie and Richard stared at Andrea after her outburst.

"But—" Cassie protested.

"*No.*" Andrea was done. She eyed Richard. "If you have something to say to Cassie then just bloody say it. Otherwise, quit toying with us and tell us what we have to do to fix this problem before it becomes *everyone's* problem!"

A flock of birds took off from a nearby field and headed for the forest ahead. Richard's horse whinnied, the only other noise filling the stillness between the three of them.

Richard rubbed the back of his neck and cleared his throat before speaking again, this time in the calm tone Andrea had grown used to expecting from him in the short time she'd known him. "I am—was a scientist, Cassie. Serena and I were already separated when she told me she was pregnant with you." He pressed his lips together. "She was the one who left me."

Cassie maintained her glare but waved for him to continue.

"I worked in energy. Resource conservation. We were running out of power, Cassie, and we were running out fast," he told her.

She shrugged. "I don't remember any of that being a problem."

"You wouldn't have noticed," Richard said. "We predicted a few decades left before resources in the cities started to become scarce."

"How did you come to Damea?" Andrea asked, the pain in her head easing now that they'd all stopped yelling. She nudged her horse's sides with her heels, Richard did the same, and they continued toward the forest on the hilltop.

"I built a...machine," Richard said. "We were running out of time and I needed something that could detect energy—*any* kind of energy—and harvest it. The sun was gone, our water supply was all underground—"

Andrea tilted her head. "The *sun* was gone?"

"Not *gone.* Just...covered," Cassie clarified. "Not completely. There was a lot of dust in the air."

Andrea finally understood. *The sunrise in Ata...no wonder she'd never seen one like it!* How much dust would it take to block out the *sun,* though? When she first met Cassie, she remembered wanting to learn as much as she could about where Cassie was from. Now that she knew more, Andrea wondered if Cassie and Richard's world was really worth going back to.

"We couldn't produce enough power to sustain our population, so we got it from wherever we could," Richard said. "One night, the machine I built detected traces of an energy so incredibly powerful I didn't believe it myself. I tried to tap into it, but there was some kind of surge from a storm outside and when I awoke, I was on my back in the middle of a farmer's field on the outskirts of Gurdinfield."

Andrea remained quiet upon the completion of Richard's story. She watched Cassie's neutral expression change to apprehension as she took in his explanation.

"But...you're an enchanter," Cassie pointed out.

"I am. I learned about magic—about energy—here in Damea very quickly. I discovered I could harness magic on my own. I knew I had to get back to you, Cassie, but I didn't have the means to do it. So, I enrolled at the Enchanters' Academy in the City of Towers." He looked out at the forest ahead, a proud smile crossing his face. "I was an excellent student."

"You met Meredith there," Andrea said.

"Yes." He suddenly hung his head, his pride giving way to shame. "I hoped that somehow I could use magic to recreate my experiment and return home to you, Cassie. But," he said, "magic was still scarce. Meredith...she was so *passionate* about her cause." He chuckled. "She wanted to save magic and bring peace to Damea. She wanted to save the world."

Andrea found herself smiling as she recalled the early days of her tutelage with Meredith, when she was convinced her mentor really was trying to save Damea.

"I fell in love with her," Richard continued. "I knew I'd have to tell her where I was from eventually. I was going to help her. We were going to bring back magic. And then we were attacked in our own home."

"Meredith told me," Andrea said. "So, your plan was to help Meredith fix the magic problem, and then you were going to work on getting back to Cassie?"

He nodded and then looked back at Cassie. "Please believe me when I say that I'm truly sorry."

Andrea half-expected Cassie to snap or yell at him again. But instead she just shrugged. "Yeah, well…we'll see. Just—just tell Andrea how to fix the stupid magic issue we have now."

Richard gave her a pained smile. "I understand. I was thinking about what you said regarding enchanting an object, Andrea."

"And?"

"And…as I said, I believe that method lacks the efficiency and speed we need. However, a *person* as a vessel would allow us to store *far* more magic and transport it much more easily."

Andrea stared at him with her mouth partly open. *Is he really suggesting what I think he is?* "I'm sorry, are you mad? Using a *person?* A human being?"

Cassie fumed behind her. "Here we go again—I *knew* it."

But Richard put out his hand as though to prevent her from jumping to conclusions. "Not in the way you're thinking! Please—this is different."

"Talk fast, then," Cassie ordered. Andrea wondered what could possibly be different about it that didn't result in the same monstrous technique Meredith had tried.

"Based on Meredith's journal and your personal account, Andrea," Richard said, "Cassie was capable of providing immeasurable amounts of energy to any enchanter that made physical contact with her, provided they drew upon that energy well. Is that correct?"

"Erm…yes, that's correct," Andrea said with hesitation, "though I wouldn't describe Cassie's ability quite as…coldly as that."

"Forgive me. I've done too many experiments, I'm afraid," Richard said, bowing his head.

"After the device was destroyed, Cassie no longer had her ability," she added.

With renewed excitement, Richard pointed at Andrea. "Ah, but you couldn't be more wrong!"

"And that means what, exactly?" Cassie asked with growing impatience.

Richard continued. "I can't explain your ability, Cassie, only that from what I've read it's nothing I've ever seen or experienced before. But here's the thing—you had what was essentially stored energy within you. You poured it into that device and overloaded it, right?"

"Sure, but it hurt like crazy. I mean, unless Andrea was doing the, uh…energy-taking," Cassie said.

"Did you ever try to absorb more?" he asked, paying no attention to her fumblings .

Andrea's heart skipped a beat. *I am such an idiot.* "It works both ways," she gasped.

Cassie frowned. "What are you talking about? What works both ways?"

"Your ability, Cassie!" Andrea said, her mind racing at top speed. "If Richard's correct, you could theoretically absorb the magic where it's more saturated and then release it in places where it's lacking."

Richard seemed so enthusiastic Andrea thought he was going to burst into applause while riding his horse. "Yes! Exactly!"

"A-absorb? Release—Andrea, you would still be doing all the work," Cassie said.

"We don't know that for sure," Richard chimed in. "I think you should try to absorb the magic yourself, Cassie. As I said, I've never heard of your ability, but as an enchanter myself perhaps I could help guide you."

Andrea couldn't see Cassie's face, but the sudden silence made her wonder whether Cassie was nervous. And while she was sure Richard was excited about the prospect of being able to solve this problem with the help of the daughter he'd been separated from for so long, she wanted to make sure Cassie was completely comfortable with the idea. "You don't have to do any of this if you don't want to, Cassie."

"Of course," Richard agreed. "We can always try to find another way. Don't let me pressure you."

They waited for her answer. Up ahead, the summit had grown closer—it would not be long before they reached the forest.

When Cassie did speak, she seemed the calmest she had been since leaving Ata. "I'll try it."

Andrea's worries ate at her. What if Richard's idea didn't work? And even if it did, the fact remained that none of them had any idea how absorbing magic would affect Cassie. "Cassie, we don't really know how this will work. It's all theory."

"Can *you* absorb energy?"

Andrea sighed. *She's right.* "No. Enchanters can only manipulate it. No one else has your ability."

"Then I'll try it," Cassie repeated. "If it works, we grab some magic here and take it to Azgadar. If it doesn't, we figure something else out."

"A risktaker." Richard gave her a warm smile. "Very admirable."

"You'll forgive me if I'm not excited," Andrea said. That he was so eager to try this experiment bothered her, but she could sort of understand now why Meredith had been so attracted to him. *He's a bit obsessed...just as she was.* "Cassie's idea of taking risks has historically involved her nearly getting herself killed."

"I'll be fine," Cassie insisted and rested her hand on Andrea's arm. "Promise."

Andrea shook her head. "You can't promise something like that."

"Then *trust* me, Andrea. I want to fix this as much as you do. If we don't do something now, you're just going to get sick again. I won't let that happen."

Between Cassie's hand on her arm and Richard's encouragement, Andrea wanted so much to believe that everything would be all right—that they would be able to do this without Cassie getting hurt. They could redistribute the magic in Damea and all would be well. But she knew better than to hope for the best. Cassie had been right to worry back in Azgadar. There had been too many close calls, too many brushes with death, for her to be comfortable taking risks like this. *But someone has to do it. Who else will, if not us?*

She looked over her shoulder at Cassie, who wore a hopeful smile on her face. A year ago, Andrea would have been completely on board with this plan—no questions asked. Now her contingency plan to run off to some remote coastal village with Cassie was looking more attractive by the minute.

But Cassie was right. *Can't run off together if I'm dead, I suppose.* "All right," she said, hoping she was making the right decision. "Let's try it."

Chapter 27

Reversal

It was early evening, the day steadily growing chillier, when Richard suggested they stop and make camp, where he would attempt to show Cassie how to absorb magic with her dormant abilities. Dark clouds had grown to cover the Western Hills, and Andrea could smell the rain that would most likely move in later that night. Finding an ideal spot to set up a fire and tents proved difficult, as the forest was thickest in this part of the Western Hills. They were still a few days' travel from the western border of the Azgadaran Empire, and it would take them even longer before they reached the capital city itself.

Andrea was in earshot of Richard and Cassie's exchange as she took inventory of their food rations. She just hoped that Cassie would not lose her patience and do something reckless, such as kill Richard, for example.

"So, I am to just freeze to death is what you're saying?" Richard sounded more amused than annoyed, which seemed to get on Cassie's nerves even more.

"I didn't say that. I said I didn't want you anywhere near our tent," Cassie said, gesturing to the tiny canvas tent, warmed by the campfire Andrea had assisted her in lighting. "The fact that it happens to be near the fire just means that it sucks to be you right now."

"What about here? Would that be permissible?" He pointed toward an area of dirt near the fire opposite from where Andrea and Cassie's tent had been pitched.

"No," Cassie said. "What part of 'near our tent' did you not understand?"

A smile tugged at the corners of Richard's mouth as he began the process of setting up his own tent. "Who in the world raised you? Your mother was never this bitter."

Andrea froze, tensing as she waited for Cassie's anger. But Cassie just glared at him. "Shut up. You don't know me and you *don't* get to talk about her." She shot him a final disdainful glance before ducking into their tent.

Richard shook his head. "Suit yourself."

The sky had not gone completely dark yet, and Andrea figured they still had a few hours left before they would have only the campfire to rely on as a light source. Once she finished her inventory, she went to join Cassie in their tent. She found her setting up their makeshift bed, smoothing out the blankets with more care and attention to detail than she'd ever seen Cassie apply toward making a bed.

She decided to try her hand at cheering Cassie up before they were all in for a miserable evening. "You've been holding out on me."

Cassie stopped fixing the bed. "What?"

"The bed." Andrea pointed at the blankets. "You're usually intent on making sure the comforters and sheets stay as tangled as possible."

She'd hoped that would have gotten a smile or at least a snort from Cassie, but if Cassie was offended she didn't show it. Instead she grabbed the last blanket next to her and began to unfold it. "I can be neat when I want."

Andrea sat on the ground. "He shouldn't have mentioned your mother."

"No wonder she left him," Cassie said as she finished with the bed. "But I think he's telling the truth about the magic." She rubbed her eyes. "Will all that he said really happen if we don't fix it?"

"The end of enchanting? Possibly. His theory makes sense, but of course we can't be certain until it actually happens." Andrea knew that she would feel a lot better about all of this if Meredith, despite her terrible flaws, was there to give her opinion.

Cassie exhaled heavily and clapped her hands together. "Okay. We should probably go test out this theory about me, then, before he tries to be my friend again."

The disappointment in Cassie's voice made Andrea wince with guilt. "Are you all right?"

"I'm good. I guess..." She closed her eyes and took another breath. "I never hoped I would meet him, honestly. I'd had it in my head forever that he must have been a terrible father to just leave his family like that. And even now, knowing the truth..." She lowered her head. "Your parents are awesome. Seriously, they're great people and they love you. They were nothing but welcoming to me."

Andrea smiled. "They know you're important to me."

"I know," Cassie said, "and I guess I can't help but be a little jealous. Even if they don't understand what you do they're still grateful you're alive and okay." She jerked her head toward the tent flap. "He doesn't seem very interested in me at all. Just wants to find his crazy wife."

"He is interested." The words were out of Andrea's mouth before she could think them through.

"No, he's interested in what I can potentially do," Cassie corrected.

Andrea reached for her hand. "Maybe. But in his defense, you're not exactly easy to talk to sometimes, Cassie."

Cassie gave her hand a squeeze and released it. "Look at you, trying to be all diplomatic. Come on, let's get this over with so we can save the world again. Honestly, it's getting old now."

* * *

"Ready, then?"

Another gust of wind prompted Andrea to push her hair behind her ears, if only to defend her eyes from the strands that blew in front of them. A few drops of water tapped the top of her head and she looked skyward. The rain would be there soon—it was already starting, in fact. Rain wouldn't interfere with magic, but she wasn't in a hurry to get her clothes drenched. Hopefully, Richard's attempts to get Cassie to absorb magic would conclude quickly and successfully.

If it didn't work, well, they would just have to find another way.

She observed the two as Cassie rolled her shoulders back. "Yeah. What do I do?"

"Put your arms out like this," Richard told her, demonstrating. "Now, this might be difficult since you've never been the one executing the magic before. You're going to try to detect the energy around us." He closed his eyes and breathed deep. "There's a lot of it here—I'm sure you can feel it too, Andrea."

"I can."

Cassie looked back at her, and Andrea gave her an encouraging nod.

"The best way I've found to do this is to simply close your eyes and relax, as odd as that might sound," Richard continued. "You'll want to eliminate any distractions from your mind. Absolute focus is the number one rule for an enchanter."

Cassie raised an eyebrow. "I thought it was, you know, not hurting people."

Richard did not take the bait. "That attitude is precisely what you need to avoid if you're going to do this successfully, Cassie."

She crossed her arms. "Fine. What else? I've closed my eyes lots of times here and I've never felt magic."

"You need to reach for it. The energy exists in nature. Calming your mind is key to being able to harness it." He lowered his arms and took a few steps back. "Try it now."

Cassie gave Andrea an uneasy smile before extending her arms as Richard had done. She held still for several seconds before dropping her hands to her sides with a sigh. "Right. *That* was pointless."

"You're tense," Richard explained. "I can see it from here. What are you worried about?"

Andrea nearly laughed out loud at the disbelieving look Cassie gave him. "Uh, that this won't work?"

"No. You're worried about *her.*" He jabbed a thumb in Andrea's direction. "Stop thinking about her and *focus.* Otherwise, we're all wasting our time."

Maybe I should have stayed in the tent. But she also didn't want to leave Cassie alone—not when there was magic involved.

"All right, all right." Cassie raised her arms again. After another few seconds Andrea saw her shoulders go limp as her hands began trembling. "I…I think I feel it," she said, her voice beginning to waver. "It's—it's weird."

Richard perked up though his voice remained low and calm. "That's normal. Are you in pain?"

Andrea almost interfered when she heard the strain in Cassie's answer. "No. I think…I think I can get it."

"Reach out for it," he urged. "It will come to you."

Another gust of wind snapped several small branches as the trees swayed hard against their protesting roots. A low hum carried through the air and descended into a rumble that shook the very ground they stood on. Cassie's sudden, sharp cry sent a cold shiver running through Andrea. She moved to help Cassie but stopped when Richard's hand shot up, his eyes ordering her not to sever Cassie's connection with the magic.

She loathed how helpless she felt as Cassie let out a strangled gasp, her shoulders heaving from what Andrea suspected was an intense connection with the magic in the area.

Her face. Those bruises she had every time anyone but Andrea had used her ability. The fine dust that had covered the heavy, dark overshirt Cassie wore when Andrea found her in Meredith's home, sprawled out on the bed. The fear in Cassie's eyes when Andrea woke her. *She just wanted to go home. Wanted to be anywhere but here. But we needed her*—I *needed her.* Andrea wouldn't put Cassie through that again. She couldn't.

"*Stop!*" She rushed to Cassie's side and grabbed her arms. "Enough! Cassie, *enough!*"

Cassie's eyes flew open, their usual blue flaring unnaturally bright. Her face contorted and she gasped for air, falling to her knees in the grass and grabbing Andrea's arm.

"Cassie!" She wrapped her arms as tightly as she could around Cassie. "You can stop. It's all right," she murmured as she stroked Cassie's cheek, repeating the words until her breathing returned to normal.

She realized Richard was still standing motionless with his hand on his chin as he observed, almost as though he was intrigued by it all. His inaction set her off. "Are you just going to sit there and do *nothing*? What kind of father are you?"

His hand dropped, his face immediately shifting to something that might have resembled shame if his next words had not been so abrupt. "I will be in my tent." Without further explanation or even checking to see if Cassie was all right, he turned and headed back toward the camp, leaving Andrea still holding a very exhausted Cassie.

Another tap on her head. Then another. The intervals between the drops grew shorter, and soon the rain was coming down in hard sheets.

"Are you all right?" she said, holding Cassie as close to her as possible. A familiar buzz emanated between them as Andrea realized she could once again draw on energy from Cassie if she desired. Something was different this time, though. The magic *burned,* the concentration so high and so aggressive she had to push it back with her own ability. "We should get to our tent."

Cassie's eyes, having returned to the blue Andrea was so familiar with, fluttered as she let out a long exhale, rivulets of water running down her face. "I'm…I'm fine. I'm just tired." She grimaced. "It's raining."

Andrea bit her lip. She wanted to cry, but she knew it probably wouldn't help Cassie. "Are you hurt?"

Cassie gave a brief shake of her head. "Tired. It was just…a lot. Did I…did I do it?"

Andrea forced a smile as she tried to appear less worried than she really was. Why was the magic so much stronger this time? What would happen when they released it? *So many unanswered questions. I shouldn't have let her do it.* "You did it. But we can talk more about it tomorrow."

Now completely soaked, she hooked her arm around the small of Cassie's back as Cassie leaned on her shoulder for support. Stumbling a bit, it took most of her strength to get Cassie back to camp, where she pulled them both into their tent without a word to Richard, who did not emerge from his own.

She helped a barely conscious Cassie change into dry clothes and lie down on the pillow before drawing a blanket over her.

The guilt, the helplessness, the regret—it all came down on Andrea as she took responsibility for this, even though it had been Cassie's choice. It was all a mess. Magic, enchanting—Andrea had in her idealism tried her hardest to make the best of her abilities in a time where so many people distrusted them. And now, like so many of Andrea's actions before, Cassie was paying the price for what she'd done. For the first time since she was a child, Andrea saw her abilities not as a gift, but as a curse. And nothing, not even the grand title of royal enchanter could make up for everything Cassie had gone through and continued to go through because of magic. Fantasies of running away seemed more real with each passing minute as Andrea made her decision.

She was done. Once the magic was redistributed, she would renounce her title in Gurdinfield and take Cassie away from this. Diana would probably insist she stay, but Andrea would stay true to this promise she was making to herself. She was done being a royal enchanter. She wanted to go home.

With Cassie asleep, the tears came fast and hard. She placed a soft kiss on Cassie's brow, whispering the only words that could come close to conveying how she felt, even though they still seemed inadequate.

"I'm so sorry."

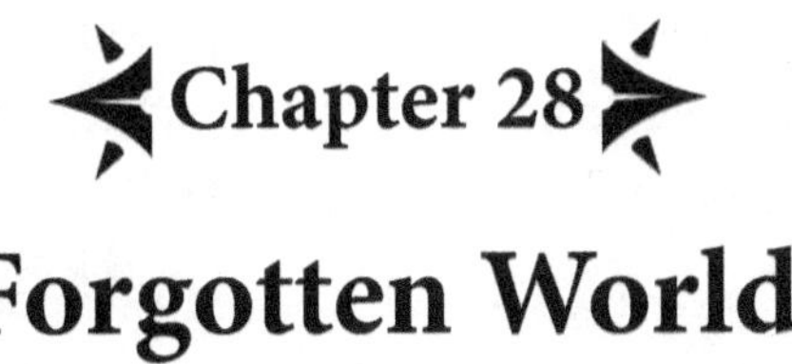

Chapter 28

Forgotten World

When Cassie woke, the first thing she noticed was how rested she felt. The events of the previous night were a haze, but she remembered Andrea holding her, taking her back to their tent so she could change and—

The magic! She bolted upright, the blanket falling into her lap. She didn't feel any different, but then again, she'd never have known the magic was even there had Meredith, Andrea, and Kye not drawn it from her. But even though she couldn't detect the magic in her now, *something* had changed—almost as though she had unlocked some aspect of herself she never knew existed.

The strange, wet and burned scent of magic as it had mingled with the rain. How the transfer had not really *hurt*—in fact, she couldn't really describe how it felt. There was no pain as there had been with Meredith or Kye. The power had been a shallow touch at first, seeping into her outstretched arms and building up pressure until finally something within her just…gave. Was this what Andrea felt every time she conjured a fireball or constructed a barrier? Even with a fuzzy memory, Cassie remembered the sheer, indescribable force of the energy as she absorbed it. *I did it.*

Her dislike of Richard aside, his plan had worked. Now they could go to Azgadar and release the magic she had gathered and then…what? She cast a longing stare at Andrea, who was still fast asleep under the blanket. Although Cassie couldn't recollect everything from the night before, she did remember Andrea being worried, maybe even…sad?

Deciding it was time to get up, she buckled on her sword before pushing open the flap of the tent and heading outside. Upon standing, she took a deep breath, the clean air of morning refreshing after a heavy rain. The sky, dotted by the remaining puffy clouds from the rainstorm, still had the orange glow of sunrise, and Cassie wanted to get a good view of it before it was over.

She saw the small grassy hill not far from the campsite and headed straight for it. As she approached, though, she gave an inward groan when she saw it was already occupied.

"Sleep well?" Richard asked from his cross-legged position in the grass.

It was too early to answer with anything but the truth. "I guess. Yeah, I did."

"I was concerned for you." Richard patted the ground beside him. After giving him a suspicious look, she took a seat. "We both were. Andrea—she, well…it's pretty obvious how much she cares for you."

"I'm fine. And yeah, she does." She stared out ahead and tried to focus on enjoying the remaining beautiful blend of colors in the sky, hoping he would take the hint.

Much to her dismay, he didn't. "You never really got to see these back home, did you?"

Cassie let out a sigh before turning slightly to look at him. "I don't really feel like chatting it up with you, honestly."

He chuckled. "You're not at all interested in what happened to me? Why I couldn't be there for you when you were growing up?"

"You haven't asked once about my mother, so no."

Nodding, he chewed on his bottom lip. "You were already bent on not speaking to me other than to accuse me of purposefully leaving you. I figured asking about her was off the table."

She picked a few blades of grass from the dirt and began tying them together in an attempt to keep her hands busy. "She was sick. She died."

Richard swallowed, his voice cracking just enough that Cassie had to look at him. "When?"

"Years ago. I was fifteen," she said.

He placed a gentle hand on her shoulder, and she surprised herself by not flinching. "I'm sorry, Cassie."

Heat rushed to her eyes. *Stupid. Don't cry.* "It was a long time ago." They sat without speaking for a while, and Cassie was grateful he did not press her for more information as she watched the sun climb higher and the blend of colors fade to blue.

"Cassie," he said. "There is something I need to tell you. It… may be hard to believe. But I need you to trust me."

Great. More secrets. At least the tears were gone. "What?"

He folded his hands together. "Beyond Gurith, past the Sea of Gurith to the west, there is an ocean. As of today, it's unexplored. The boats on the Gurith Coast don't wander too far from their fishing spots."

She gave him a blank stare. "Um…okay? I've seen maps of Damea, too."

He smiled. "That was definitely your mother talking right there. But," he continued in an oddly careful tone, "there is land on the other side of that ocean." He took a shaky breath. "Two hundred years from now, brave people from all over Damea will migrate across the ocean. They will find that land and they will call it Tarrasha."

Cassie let the grass slip from her hands. "W-what? Tar—but that's—"

"Our word, yes. It's millennia old." He met her eyes and for a surreal moment, it was like Cassie was staring at her own reflection. "You know what this means."

No. It couldn't be. "That's impossible."

"What?" he said, leaning back. "That we named our world, or that the old word for the world was lost thousands of years ago?"

She scrambled to her feet, her thoughts overloaded from what he was telling her. "There's no way. There's no magic back home. Plus, never mind the whole thing about *time travel*—we would have had *records* of magic!" She gestured around them. "Of Damea! At least—at least the name!"

Richard also stood up. "If the magic ran out, Cassie—if something happened that was so catastrophic it wiped out every city, every building, and every record of Damea, enchanters, magic, the Starving…ask yourself: would we know about it thousands of years later?"

Cassie just gaped at him. This wasn't possible—it couldn't be. "Y-you said millennia?"

"I did," he said.

"But...our language. I can understand everyone perfectly here. I shouldn't be able to. Wouldn't the language have changed over so many years?" She felt short of breath—she was most likely still exhausted from the night before—and she wished she hadn't gotten up so fast.

He laughed. "Cassie, you absorbed magical energy from *nature* last night. You watch your girlfriend cast barriers and throw fireballs like it happened every day when you were growing up. You don't think magic can affect how we communicate?" He placed a hand on his chest. "I don't understand everything about magic, but I know that there is *something* that tries to keep everything here in some kind of equilibrium. Even us."

Her hand went to her mouth. *This is crazy.* "What...what happened to the magic?"

"I have many guesses," Richard replied, "but no answers, I'm afraid. Perhaps it gets manipulated to the point where it no longer becomes viable for us to use. Or..." His tone darkened. "We fail in our own endeavor to redistribute it."

She shook her head. "No. We'll do it. We've already started." She looked out at the path before them. They were still far from Azgadar, but the magic wasn't going anywhere yet. There was still time to fix this. "How did you know?"

"That I had gone back to the past?" he said. When she nodded, he shrugged. "Geography. I'd been to Gurdinfield before when I was younger. Of course, it was a very different place in our time, but there's nothing quite like the sight of the

Rhyadan Mountains in the distance."

"I can't believe no one back home knew."

His hand returned to her shoulder, the gesture surprisingly comforting. "It's been a very long time, Cassie. There aren't even any ruins remaining. The records are gone—no doubt destroyed in whatever terrible event happened here." He began to walk down the hill and she followed alongside him.

"If we get this right—if we redistribute the magic—will Damea be okay?" she asked.

"I couldn't tell you," he admitted. "We're talking about changing events in the past that could affect the future. Maybe something else happens to magic, but it's so far in the future that we won't live to see it. Oh." He stopped and began fishing into his pocket. Cassie watched with interest as he pulled out a thick silver chain. On it was a pendant Cassie didn't recognize—overlapping semi-circles framing a diamond-shaped centerpiece.

He presented it to her. "This was Serena's. She gave it to me long ago as a way to remember her, even when we parted. And now it's yours."

The metal of the pendant felt oddly cool against her palm when he dropped the necklace into her hand. She ran her fingers along the cold metal grooves of the design, unable to hold back a crooked smile as she held the last remaining possession of her mother's. "Thank you," she whispered, before putting it on. The chain and the pendant were much heavier than they looked, but she found herself taking comfort in that fact.

He beamed at her. "Perfect. It looks lovely on you. I spent a few days at least searching for it in Meredith's house. Would have been terrible had she gotten rid of it. Now," he said as they approached the campsite, "if it's all right with you and Andrea, we should get going. The sooner we get to Azgadar the better."

Cassie agreed, at the same time wondering how in the world she was going to explain all of this to Andrea. She looked at Richard. Despite the fact that he had not chosen to leave her, something held her back from just forgiving him. He was, after all, married to Meredith. *What does he think will happen, that we'll find Meredith and be one big happy, screwed-up family?*

She couldn't worry about it now. She needed to wake up Andrea, and they needed to leave the Western Hills. *One thing at a time.*

* * *

Azgadar, Azgadaran Empire

"I am sorry, but I'm going to have to see some sort of proof. A letter with the Azgadaran seal on it would be a good start."

The Legionnaire before them stood resistant to both Andrea and Cassie's persuasions. Andrea had explained more than once who she was and how they were there to meet with Diana and Jacob in the palace. But he still refused them entry.

"Like we said," Cassie tried again, "we were just here. We work for the queen of Gurdinfield. The empress knows we're coming—they're in the palace negotiating an alliance." She pointed to her sword. "Look, this even has Gurdinfield's crest on it!"

But he just shook his head. "The city is closed to outsiders.

No one is to enter without the empress's explicit consent. So, unless I see some *written* proof of your claim, I'm afraid Azgadar is closed to you."

Cassie rolled her eyes and spun around to face Richard and Andrea. "This isn't working."

Richard stroked his beard. "Perhaps we can send a letter in to Ithmeera?"

Andrea gazed up at the iron gates. "Something's not right. The city wasn't closed when we left."

Another attack? Cassie had no idea why Ithmeera had closed the city, but speculation wouldn't get them anywhere. She was considering Richard's idea when she heard someone call out to her.

Three armored soldiers of the Legion approached, their leader a tall, muscular, short-haired woman who seemed *very* familiar to Cassie.

Oh, crap. "Taryn, right?" she asked with a sheepish grin.

But Taryn narrowed her eyes. "Ah, so you remembered! I'm flattered. Or are you just trying to get in my good graces so you can deceive me again?"

Trying to ignore the amused glances from Andrea, Richard, and the Legionnaire guarding the gates, Cassie cleared her throat, attempting to salvage what she could from what was already an awkward situation. "Who said anything about deceiving? I mean, I just asked you some questions. It was a nice conversation!" A roguish grin spread across her face. "I mean, if this is about me not going to your room—sorry, but like I said, I'm spoken for," she said, giving a quick wink at Andrea, who crossed her arms and suddenly seemed more annoyed than entertained.

Taryn's fellow soldiers exchanged grins, and one of them nudged her teasingly with his elbow. "That's quite enough from you two," she scolded before rounding on Cassie again, her voice softening enough so that only Cassie could hear her. "So, what you're telling me is that Elisa escaping that *very* night after we spoke was a complete coincidence, hm? Is that what you're trying to say?"

Cassie chuckled. *This is going to be interesting.* "Oh, I totally helped her escape. My question is: can you help me get into the city to see her? Or…" She nodded in the direction of the other Legionnaires. "Should I ask them? Of course, I'd have to tell them everything that happened. Wouldn't want them left in the dark."

Taryn's jaw set in barely contained anger. "Espionage *and* blackmail? Such class," she sneered. She noted the Great Lion sigil on Cassie's sheath and shook her head. "A Guardian. I should have known."

"Guilty." Cassie waited for her answer, but she was confident enough to know what it would be. "I really do like your hair, though."

Taryn looked past Cassie to Andrea. "A fine catch you have here, friend. Well done." Then to Cassie, "Follow me and don't say a word. Also, don't bother me again or I *will* have you arrested."

Cassie dropped her bravado and held up her hands. "Don't worry—we're even," she promised as Taryn signaled for the guard to open the gates.

"You have a strange definition of 'even'. Oh, and when you see Elisa, tell her we all still hate her, would you?"

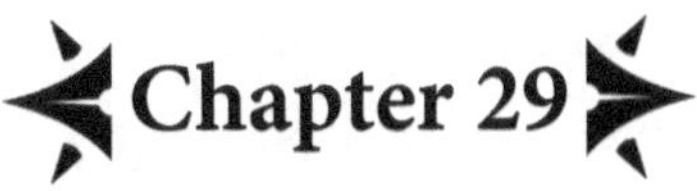

Chapter 29

Promises

It was near dusk when they arrived back at the palace. Andrea had never really enjoyed Azgadar as a city—too loud, too crowded, and too busy. But as they walked down the main road, she could tell something was different. There were less people in the streets than she expected to see in the evening. Merchants who would normally be open later had already closed up their shops. *Maybe it's quieter in the summer.*

Elisa met them at the palace entrance along with General Veraun. Andrea still wasn't certain of their history, but seeing them standing together and *not* seconds away from killing each other was an odd sight to witness. Then again, normal hadn't been in the itinerary for a while.

She was beyond grateful that Cassie had made a speedy recovery from her ordeal—she had been the one to wake Andrea the morning after their attempt to absorb the magic. But when Cassie sat Andrea down and told her the very strange truth—that she and Richard were, in fact, Damean but from another *time,* she worried perhaps the event in the clearing had affected Cassie's mind.

What worried her even more was the dark future in store for Damea if they failed to get the magic settled properly again across the land. And even that wasn't certain.

A year ago, Andrea would have been ecstatic to learn the answers to all her questions. But now it seemed the more she knew, the more she wished she didn't.

"Welcome back." Elisa's voice was cool as usual. *No surprises there.*

Andrea caught Veraun's gaze before turning back to Elisa. "Thank you. This is Richard," she said with an open hand by Richard. "Meredith's husband. He's come to speak to Master Tobias about finding her."

Elisa's eyebrows went up with mild interest. "Very well. The empress is waiting inside. Shall we?"

They entered the palace, with Andrea walking next to Elisa and Cassie and Richard following and Veraun trailing behind. The palace was almost eerily quiet, the only sound coming from the click of their boots against the floor.

"Where is the queen?" Andrea asked. "And why is the city closed?"

"She and Jacob left for Gurdinfield days after you departed for Ata," Elisa said as they passed into the throne room. "The empress can explain in more detail."

Sure enough, Ithmeera sat on her throne at the end of the enormous room. Being there reminded Andrea of when they first arrived in Azgadar with Diana and Jacob, only now she could clearly identify Petra and Alden as they stood behind Ithmeera. Kye was nowhere to be found, and neither was Marco.

Ithmeera stood as the group bowed before her. "Welcome back, friends." There was warmth in her voice, but Ithmeera did not appear happy to see them. In fact, Andrea thought she looked quite distraught.

"Elisa may have briefed you, but Queen Lydia and your other Guardians departed with my son days ago," Ithmeera explained. "There are some…threats to the safety of enchanters in our city, and Lydia agreed to take Marco to the City of Towers until the situation here is contained."

A moment of silence passed until Andrea realized Ithmeera was waiting for her to answer. "A-apologies, Your Majesty. I… understand the situation. Our companion here wishes to find his wife, who is also an enchanter. We were hoping Master Tobias could perhaps lend a hand."

Richard immediately bowed his head. "Richard of Gurdinfield, Your Majesty. An honor to meet you."

Ithmeera didn't seem very impressed, but she gave a nod acknowledging him anyway. "Very well. You three are welcome to stay, although I believe your queen requests your presence in the City of Towers. It was my hope that," she said, focusing her eyes on Andrea again, "you might be able to tutor my son until such a time as he can resume his lessons here. That is, of course, if you are willing."

The safety of enchanters…threatened? Andrea wondered what had passed while they were in Ata. The attack during the ball had been bad enough, but what else could have possibly happened to convince Ithmeera to send the heir to her throne and her only child to live with a former enemy of the empire? "I would be honored to assist him, Your Majesty," she said. *Maybe at first.* The promise she'd made to herself had not changed. She would need to tell Diana her plans eventually. *The sooner the better.*

"Richard, one of my servants will show you to your room. You may speak to Master Tobias in the morning. Enchanter Andrea, you and your Guardian are welcome to the room you occupied before," Ithmeera finished. "I must see to other affairs now. I bid you a good evening." Before she left, however, she spotted Cassie's new necklace. A pleasant smile flickered on her face, as though she were recalling a fond memory. "That is a lovely necklace. Was it a gift?"

Andrea saw Cassie's eyes widen as, in what was probably self-consciousness, she grasped the silver chain. "Yes. Yes, it was."

"Ah. Well, I commend their taste in jewelry." She squinted at the circular pendant. "I wonder if…no." She shook her head a few times. "It probably would not be very becoming of me to offer you a trade for your fine gift," she said, garnering quiet laughs from everyone in the room. "Good evening, everyone."

* * *

"You're back!" Kye chased after them, jumping over stairs to catch up to Andrea, Cassie, and Elisa as they climbed the torchlit stairs of the spire to their room. "How was Ata? Did you find your parents?"

Elisa stopped and turned. "Where have *you* been hiding all afternoon?"

"Honestly? The kitchen," Kye replied. Even in the dim, flickering light Andrea could see his freckled cheeks turn a bit pink. “There is some wonderful food coming out of there. You should try it—the cooks are so kind.”

“I’m in,” Cassie said immediately. “Come get me in the morning and we’ll check it out.”

“The trip was fine, Kye. My parents are well,” Andrea said, adjusting her pack over her shoulder as they reached their floor. She yawned—the day’s travel had tired her, more than she thought it would. “Why aren’t you back in Gurdinfield with the queen?”

Kye shrugged. “I wanted to stay with Elisa.”

Elisa made a long-suffering face. “He insists on being my shadow.” To Kye, “You should go with them when they leave. It’s safer out there than in here, trust me.”

“About that,” Andrea said. “What happened while we were gone? Another assassination attempt?”

Elisa halted. She looked around as though to make sure no one else could hear them before speaking in a hushed voice. “There is a group of fanatics here in the city calling themselves the New Legion. They hate enchanters and have killed one already.” Her eyes flickered toward Kye before returning to Andrea and Cassie. “The victim…he was fifteen.”

“That’s why she sent Marco away,” Andrea concluded, her heart sinking. *Fifteen.* She wondered what his family had done when they discovered him—how horrible it must have been for them to find their child dead for something he hadn’t even asked for. What would her parents had done if the same fate had befallen her? Her decision to retire from enchanting seemed even more attractive now.

Elisa motioned at their bedroom door. "Your companion will be allowed to speak to Tobias in the morning. You should probably go with him, Andrea."

"Of course. We have a few things we need to take care of before we leave Azgadar, but they can be done after the meeting," Andrea said, placing her hand on the door handle.

"So…are you working for Ithmeera again or something?" Cassie asked Elisa, who immediately shook her head.

"I was asked to help track down the idiots running this New Legion. Once that is taken care of, I will probably leave Azgadar." Andrea could tell from her terseness that Elisa did not want to be pressed about the matter. "I shall leave you two for the evening. Good night."

"'Night." Cassie gave a small wave as Elisa left with Kye in tow, and Andrea pushed the door open.

"I'm *exhausted*," she moaned before dropping her backpack on the ground. "Honestly, I just want to sleep for days."

Cassie used her foot to kick the door shut behind her. "Yeah, I think after we get back I'll be crossing 'walking across Damea' off my list for good." She unfastened her sword and leaned it against the chair and tossed her own pack on the ground before going to join Andrea on the bed—where she had already claimed an entire side as well as three pillows.

"Right, so you *do* realize you don't get to keep all those pillows to yourself, right?"

"I don't know what you're talking about," Andrea said with an innocent smile. "I had this side last time and it just *happened* to come with these pillows. If that is how the empress designed this room, who am I to argue?"

A rush of air hit her face right before the pillow did and she cried out. Composing herself, it took her a few seconds to realize what Cassie had done. "You…you hit me!" But her protest fell on deaf ears when Cassie smacked her again with the pillow. On the third attack, she cast a small barrier which successfully blocked the pillow but made Cassie frown in disappointment.

"No fair," she whined. "Magic's not allowed!"

Andrea giggled and dispelled the barrier. "I don't remember there being *rules* to this. And you started it!"

"Hey, hey." Cassie put her hands up. "At least it's not mud." She collapsed on her back and inhaled deeply. "That's something to be grateful about, right?"

"Hmm. Right. Of course." Andrea gave a final short laugh before leaning back to join Cassie. She wasted no time in finding her favorite spot—Cassie's shoulder—and nestling her head on it while wrapping an arm around Cassie's middle. "This. This I could do for a while." She sighed in contentment when she felt Cassie's arm settle around her waist.

"Much better than walking across Damea," Cassie agreed. "And far more comfortable."

Andrea closed her eyes. *It's time to tell her.* "Cassie?"

"Yeah?"

"What were your plans when…when you were back home? What were you going to do?"

Andrea felt Cassie's chest jerk a bit when she cleared her throat and she worried she had made her uncomfortable with the question. "Uh, well I guess I didn't have a lot of long-term plans. Was kind of just focused on making it to the next day to be honest." She tilted her head down until their eyes met. "Why?"

She'll understand. She has to. "You know, being a royal enchanter was something I wanted for a long time," she said.

Cassie chuckled. "How else are you going to save the world *and* do weird experiments?" She suddenly went quiet, and Andrea figured Cassie must have realized she was trying to tell her something.

"But…then I met you and we went to Rhyad and, well, you were there."

Cassie's hold around her tightened. "I was."

The next words were harder and Andrea couldn't explain why. Perhaps it was because if she actually voiced her promise to give up enchanting, that might make it more real. "I think—no, I *know* there's something I want more than to be a royal enchanter."

"Let me guess. You want to be a royal enchanter with a *very* attractive bodyguard who also happens to have a great sense of humor?" Cassie laughed at her own joke. "Because you already have that."

"Very funny. No, what I want is really to not be a royal enchanter at all." She looked up at Cassie again and her heart began to race. *I can do this. Tell her.* "I want to just be…me. And for you to be, well, *you*. And maybe when we're done fixing Damea's magic, we could just leave all of this and go somewhere else where we don't have to worry about magic or enchanters or empresses or any of that." She clung to Cassie. "What do you think?"

The rise and fall of Cassie's chest ceased for a moment. *Was that too much? Am I asking too much of her?* But when Cassie finally responded, she sounded...*relieved.* "When we were trying to get to Rhyad, all I could think about at first was getting the magic so that I could go home. And then it was one thing after another and when it was all over...I didn't want to go home, because I *was* home."

She sat up and leaned back against the dark wood headboard of the bed. "Being with you," she said, taking Andrea's hand, "*that's* home for me. But...I think you're right. Maybe that's all we need, you know? Just a place we can go to finally get away from all of...*this.*" She turned her gaze toward the window. "Where I'm from, Andrea...the people I was around." She sighed. "There were a lot of promises made, and a lot of disappointment afterwards. Even by me."

"I'm sorry," Andrea whispered.

Cassie opened her arms, and Andrea was more than happy to fall into her embrace. "It's not your fault. Just—after my mother died, I had to fend for myself and I was around some not so great people for a few years. Some were worse than others. But...I guess promises are a lot easier to make when you don't know if you'll live to see tomorrow."

Andrea clutched at Cassie's shirt as though her life depended on it. "You're stuck with me," she said, echoing Cassie's own words. "I love you and I want to spend every minute proving that to you that instead of enchanting."

Cassie grinned. "That sounds exhausting."

Andrea reconsidered. “Maybe not *every* minute. I might need to employ a fireball or two for bandits.”

“Bandits? There are bandits now?”

“Oh, yes,” Andrea informed her. “They’ll try and steal our crops.”

Cassie’s brow furrowed. “We have crops?”

“We’ll try. I’ve heard the coast isn’t favorable to them. But we can always have a small garden at the house.” All of Andrea’s worries surrounding the topic had faded, and for once, she was perfectly comfortable talking with Cassie about the future like this.

“We have a house on the coast?” Cassie gave her a perplexed look.

Andrea leaned in and kissed her. “We will.”

“You don’t have to prove anything to me, Andrea,” Cassie said as she rested her head against Andrea’s. “I want this as much as you do.”

All-too-familiar heat spread across her face, and Andrea was sure her heart would burst from how happy Cassie’s words, her actions, *everything* made her. She pressed her lips against Cassie’s again, the kiss harder and more desperate this time as they fell back together on the stack of pillows. She was so focused on kissing Cassie for as long as possible that she was unprepared when Cassie grabbed her and rolled them over. The newly absorbed magic thrummed between them as Andrea let out a shuddering gasp.

“That okay?” Cassie whispered.

Andrea took a few seconds to catch her breath. “Y-yes.” But

when Cassie bent her head down to kiss her again, the fatigue from earlier caught up to her.

She put her hand on Cassie's chest and gave it a gentle push. Cassie froze, querying Andrea with concerned blue eyes. "No?"

Andrea ran her fingers over the scar above Cassie's brow. "Would you be terribly disappointed if I told you I'm about thirty seconds away from passing out from exhaustion?"

A soft smile crossed Cassie's face. She placed a final kiss on Andrea's forehead before rolling off to lie beside her. "The only disappointment tonight is that you've stolen most of the pillows."

"I told you," Andrea said as she let Cassie pull her close. "They are here by design." She felt lips press against the back of her neck and relaxed even more, closing her eyes as sleep claimed her.

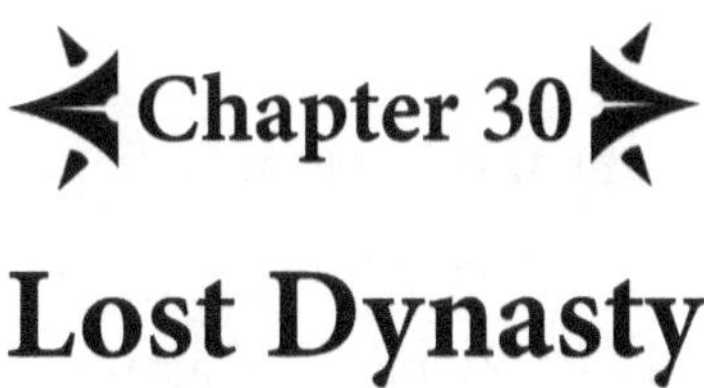

Chapter 30

Lost Dynasty

Andrea had finished stuffing the last of her clothes into her backpack when the bedroom door swung open. "How was breakfast?" She figured she didn't need to look up to know it was Cassie. But when she was answered with silence, her eyes darted upward.

Cassie stood in the doorway, hesitating until Andrea asked, "Are you all right?"

"Hmm? Yeah!" Cassie said, smiling. She patted her stomach. "Food was good—Kye was right. We took a walk around the marketplace, too."

Andrea fastened the buckle on her pack. "You sure that was wise? With this New Legion threatening enchanters and all?"

But Cassie just waved dismissively. "I had my sword and Kye could probably have set half of them on fire if he wanted to. We were fine." She moved into the room and took Andrea's arm. "I promise."

While she wasn't exactly thrilled Cassie had taken Kye into the city without her or other protection, Andrea felt some comfort knowing the two were more capable of defending themselves than they had been a year ago. "All right, but... perhaps I could go with you next time?"

Cassie nodded. "We about packed? Kye says he's ready to go when we are."

"Yes. They brought the horse to the palace gates, so that should make things a bit easier."

"What happened with Richard?" Cassie seemed apprehensive about even asking the question, and Andrea figured she was still debating just how much she trusted her father after all that had happened.

"Nothing, I'm afraid," she said. "Master Tobias has no record of Meredith anywhere in the empire's ledger."

"Oh," was Cassie's empty response. "So what's the plan, then?" She went to her own pack, which sat on the chair, overflowing with unfolded clothes, and checked inside it before pressing down on the contents, attempting to compress them so the bag would close.

Andrea slung her bag over her shoulder. "I'm going to prepare the horse and let Elisa know we're leaving soon. Richard actually wanted to talk to you, though. He's waiting for you outside."

"About what?"

"He didn't say," Andrea replied, picking up Cassie's bag. "My guess is that he'll try to find Meredith on his own. After we release the magic, of course."

"All right. Um, maybe afterward I can talk to you about something?"

Andrea frowned, her thoughts returning to the previous

night's discussion. "What's wrong?"

Cassie laughed, and Andrea found it odd at how *nervous* her laugh was. "No! No, nothing—I just wanted to talk to you. But I'd rather not do it with *him* waiting for me downstairs."

What could she possibly want to discuss? "Oh. All right, then. Come find me after?"

"Can do." Cassie suddenly pulled them close together in a deep kiss that left Andrea dazed. "I love you."

"I—I love you too," Andrea panted once they had separated, fighting to regain her composure. "What was that for?"

"I can't just kiss you? Actually, I appreciated our talk yesterday." Cassie winked at her. "I'll see you in a bit," she said, before leaving Andrea alone again to try to figure out what Cassie could possibly be thinking.

* * *

"About time." Richard squinted as he glanced up at the sun, which had already climbed to mid-morning, bringing the heat of the region with it. He gestured at the horse next to him as Cassie clattered down the palace steps to meet him. "Come on. Let's go for a ride. There's something I want to discuss with you."

She backed away. "Why do we need to be on a horse? Just tell me."

"Ah, yes, my apologies. I heard about your dislike of riding. It will be fast." He hesitated. "It's about your mother, Cassie, and…well, I would prefer to speak outside the city if we can.

The spire is quite lovely from a distance and we were in such a rush to get here that there hasn't been much time to take in the sights."

I guess if it's something only he *can tell me.* "They won't let us back through the gates once we leave."

"Don't worry," he assured her. "General Veraun was able to get me a letter with the empress's seal on it. We'll be fine." He extended a hand to her and she finally took it, allowing him to pull her up onto the back of the horse. "Ready?" he asked.

"Yeah, just go," she grumbled. "This had better be fast, though."

"It will be. I'll try not to go *too* fast, however," he joked as he spurred the horse on, cantering down the main city street before heading through the gates and toward the rolling fields outside of Azgadar. The ride was shorter than Cassie feared it might be, and to her relief, Richard reined the horse in near a cluster of low mounds with sparse vegetation. The city of Azgadar was still very much visible in the distance. Further away were the hills they had ridden across on their way to Ata, while the terrain in the other direction seemed to be nothing but desert.

Richard examined the area and made a satisfied hum. "I think this will work."

Cassie jumped down from the horse and Richard followed suit. "You wanted to talk?"

"Yes. Just over here," he said, leading them several paces away from the horse to the tallest of the mounds. "Interesting. The magic here is thicker in concentration, and it's flowing quickly."

He turned to her. "Thank you for trusting me. I know things haven't been easy for you."

Cassie tried to shrug off his attempts at comfort. She wasn't entirely sure if she trusted him. *I didn't trust Andrea at first, though.* "Honestly, you were the last person I expected to meet in Damea."

"I have been worried about you for a very long time, Cassie. All I ever wanted was to return home to you. You and Andrea may not believe me, but I hope…I hope that someday you will," he said, and returned to looking at the city in the distance. The sun was reflecting off the spire, illuminating it like a beacon that could be seen for great distances, guiding travelers to the heart of the empire.

"Do you love her?"

"Andrea? Yeah." *Why are we talking about this?*

"Believe it or not, Serena and I were very much in love once." He hung his head. "But life is unpredictable. You put plans in place and you think to yourself, 'This is going to work'. But then it just…doesn't."

* * *

Andrea wiped her brow as she headed back inside the palace. The heat was already starting to get to her, but she knew it was in everyone's best interest if they returned to the City of Towers as soon as possible. *And we still have to release Cassie's magic.*

She shook her head. It was time to find Elisa and let her know she and Cassie were departing Azgadar.

She thought perhaps she would find her friends in the Great Hall, so she went there first. As she passed into the room where only weeks before she had felt the magic around her crumble, her mind became so preoccupied with how exactly they were going to execute their plan that she nearly barreled into none other than Ithmeera herself.

"Oh! My apologies, Your Majesty!" she stammered, almost losing her balance. "Please forgive me—I wasn't looking!"

But Ithmeera just seemed amused at Andrea's flailing. "Relax, Enchanter Andrea. I will not lock you up for not watching where you were going."

Completely flustered, Andrea was even less impressed with herself when her words came out in a squeak. "Of course, Your Majesty. I do apologize still."

Ithmeera gave her a cool smile. "I understand you will be leaving us soon?"

"Y-yes. I was actually looking for Elisa, and…" She stopped when the banner caught her eye. *What in the—*

She hadn't noticed it before—really, she hadn't taken note of any of the banners that hung from the ceiling other than the ones boasting the primary sigil of the empire and assuming the others had represented the various towns and sub-regions around Azgadar. But the white overlapping semi-circles, the diamond in the middle—it was *too* familiar on the faded black banner which almost appeared to be hidden behind the others.

"Your Majesty." She pointed above. "That sigil. What town is it from?"

Ithmeera followed Andrea's gesture, eyes lighting up

with recognition when she saw the banner in question. "Ah! No wonder your Guardian's necklace seemed familiar," she exclaimed. "That is the emblem of the dynasty that came before the Cadars. Interesting that she would have a necklace with their sigil on it. I've always thought it was beautiful, despite its dark reputation."

"Dark reputation? What do you mean?" Why would Richard give Cassie a necklace bearing the sigil of a dead Azgadaran dynasty? More importantly, why would he tell Cassie it belonged to her mother?

"They ruled before the Starving happened," Ithmeera said. "They were quite powerful—conquered most of Damea, actually. You see, their last generation only had one heir and she disappeared. Then we had the Starving and, well..." She shrugged. "You know the rest I suppose."

Something seemed off to Andrea. The sigil was from a family that lived over two hundred years before Richard arrived in Damea. *How is this possible?* "What happened to the heir?"

"Unfortunately, the records are a bit incomplete," Ithmeera said. "A lot was lost during the Starving, and there was quite a bit of...purging when my family took power." She took another look at the banner. "Some say she died in an accident, while others believe she ran away with a lover. Actually," Ithmeera continued, "she was an enchanter as well! Of course, this was before all the laws the empire put in place later to restrict magic usage."

Andrea couldn't explain why, but she felt compelled to know more about this lost heir. "Is that why it has a dark reputation, Your Majesty? Because the heir was an enchanter?"

"Oh, no!" Ithmeera chuckled. "Being an enchanter was quite common back then. But this heir was something different—the records say she used her abilities to actually *control* others. It was rare even during that time for any enchanter to wield such power. It's…a popular theory on how Azgadar became so powerful. There were even rumors that she could enchant objects to control her enemies with. But when she left, her mother—the empress—had no heir." Her smile faded. "When you abandon your title—your post—you condemn yourself and your family to a life of dishonor and shame."

No wonder Elisa never spoke of her past. But something still nagged at Andrea. This necklace, and this heir who was also an enchanter so powerful she could control people and conquer Damea—she knew there was something else, some other piece of a puzzle in her head that until now she didn't know she was struggling to solve. She suddenly wished Cassie was there with her. "Your Majesty? One more question, if you don't mind."

"Not at all, though you'll forgive me if I'm not an expert on every detail of the empire's complex history. We do have a library if you're interested in learning more, however," Ithmeera offered.

"Just a final question. The heir—what was her name?" Andrea asked, and on some deeper, terrifying level she somehow *knew* what Ithmeera's answer would be.

Ithmeera smiled as though Andrea had asked the simplest question of all. "Serena, I believe. I think the library might even have some sketches of her."

No. Andrea saw the room spin around her as Ithmeera's answer echoed in her mind again and again. *There's no way—*

that was hundreds of years ago. But the necklace, the *name,* the Starving, magic disappearing…

If Ithmeera was right, if Serena had been a powerful enchanter with the ability to enchant artifacts that could control other people, then why would Richard give a necklace with her sigil on it to Cassie—a sigil that was over two centuries old?

Did we destroy magic? Richard had been so eager—too eager, even—to have Cassie absorb magic…to the point where he had turned down any idea Andrea had to offer.

The device in Rhyad. How he had snapped at her for even mentioning it.

"And since you destroyed it, we can't exactly go back and learn how to replicate it."

The Western Hills, in the forest. Cassie—absorbing the magic, gritting her teeth as the energy rushed into her. Richard—calmly observing as his own daughter attempted a feat that most would consider impossible, or at the very least dangerous. But he had just looked on, as though she were nothing more than an experiment.

"I built a…a machine." He had said he was trapped here. *"… you destroyed it."*

The sphere. She never saw it, but some part of Andrea still remembered how it felt as she lay dying on the cold, rocky floor under the pulsing light that had slowly siphoned magic from Damea over…hundreds of years. *The Starving.*

"We were running out of time and I needed something that could detect energy—any kind of energy left—and harvest it."

It had taken an enormous amount of energy to bring Cassie

to Damea. Andrea had always suspected that there would have been no way to send her back without replicating the exact conditions of the experiment that had brought her here...or having a nearly unlimited pool of magic to draw from.

"Harvest it." The words repeated over and over in her mind like a terrible chant, splitting apart and fusing together again until the final piece snapped into place. In one horrific moment of clarity, Andrea finally understood *everything.*

No.

Cassie.

She had to get to Cassie. Without a word to Ithmeera, she bolted out of the room at top speed, flying past confused Legionnaires and almost colliding with Elisa, who shouted at her, "Where are you going?"

"Where's Cassie?"

Elisa shook her head in confusion. "Why are you—"

"Elisa, she's in danger. *Where is she?*" Andrea yelled.

Elisa pointed at the doors. "Richard took her to the fields—what is going on, Andrea?"

Andrea yelled back as she took off again. "Richard's a traitor—get everyone to safety, *now!*"

Through the open doors she ran, leaping down the last few steps, the sting in her calves making her grunt in pain when her boots hit the ground. Her horse was just ahead and Kye stood next to it. His eyes widened in alarm when he saw her running toward him.

"Andrea? What in—"

“Cassie’s in trouble,” she gasped. “We have to stop Richard!”

Kye swung himself onto the horse before helping Andrea up. “Let’s go!”

Chapter 31

The Fields of Azgadar

Cassie wasn't sure why Richard wanted to talk about love and other matters that really were none of his business, especially when it came to her relationship with Andrea.

But he continued to stand there, arms crossed, looking at Azgadar with a tenseness about him that made Cassie wonder what else he was hiding from her.

"What did you want to tell me?" she asked again.

His hands fell to his sides. "I wasn't honest with you before. Serena and I…she wasn't pregnant when we separated, Cassie. She'd had you months before."

That was the deep, dark secret? Cassie grew annoyed at what was starting to feel like a waste of her time. "Okay? Why would you lie about something like that?"

"Serena, your mother—she wasn't from our time, Cassie." He turned back to her. "She was from Damea. I met her the first time I came here, not more than a few steps from where we stand, in fact."

Wait. "The—the first time? You mean you'd been here before?"

"My machine allowed me to travel between our time and Damea. Once I secured a power source—magic—I could create a return door—a portal that would allow me to come and go as I pleased. Serena taught me everything I ever wanted to know about enchanting." He pointed at the necklace Cassie wore. "That necklace is actually enchanted. *She* enchanted it. And..." He rubbed his eyes. "We fell in love and you were born here in Damea."

It took Cassie a moment to register what he'd said. "H-here?"

"Well, not *here*," Richard said with a sad smile. "Actually, you were born in the City of Towers."

Cassie touched the pendant out of instinct as her legs began to feel weak. "W-what happened with you two?"

He exhaled. "I have always had one goal, Cassie—to save our home. Serena was supposed to help me get magic to Tarrasha through the machine. I brought her there. I even taught her our language. She saw firsthand what was happening to our world—how it was dying—and swore to help. She even left her own people for me. For *you*. But...at the end..." He trailed off.

Cassie was losing her patience. "What. Happened?"

"She abandoned our cause—told me that the magic was too valuable to take from here. She took you and went through the portal and...she *destroyed* it. She *left* me here!" His final words came out in a rough growl as he stood there, fists clenched, shaking with anger. "She destroyed the machine and any hope our world had for surviving. But I refused to wait here to die. I used every resource available to me and everything I had learned since arriving in Damea, and I built another machine—one that would give me enough power to open a new portal."

Fiery blue eyes met hers. "One that would take me back to you. But it would take a long time to gather the energy I needed." He smirked. "I am nothing if not patient."

Cassie felt a lump in her throat. What he was saying…it couldn't be true. Although, if everything else he was saying really happened…

No.

"*You* built that device in Rhyad!" she cried, pointing at him. "You caused the Starving and all those wars, all those deaths!"

Richard nodded, speaking with a calmness that angered Cassie even more. "Creating a drink that could sustain me in sleep for hundreds of years and slow the aging process was possible with the knowledge combined from Serena and myself. It wore off eventually and when I awoke, I found that the device had worked! But…more magic was needed." He crossed his arms. "When I met Meredith, it brought me hope. I knew she could help me."

"You…you used her?"

Richard shook his head. "I care deeply for Meredith. But I did what I had to do to get back to you, Cassie. I did what I had to in order to *save* us."

"No!" she shouted. "You're a liar. You *knew* what taking all the magic would do to this land." This man was a mass murderer. Everything that had happened—the disappearance of magic, the Starving, the famine, the wars, Andrea and Meredith bringing her to Damea and everything that had happened after—it was all because of *him*.

She drew her sword. "You're going to come back to Azgadar

with me and tell them everything."

Richard cast her a defiant look. "Our world is dying, Cassie. The device I built in Rhyad would have saved us had you and your girlfriend not interfered."

Enough. She charged at him with all her strength, forgetting most of her Guardian training in her anger. He cast a quick barrier and hurled it at her, throwing her to the ground.

"You may not understand my reasons now but you will, Cassie," Richard said. He strode over to her, kicking her sword away as she coughed up dirt and struggled to push herself up. "Your ability turned out to be a very well-timed gift. For that I am sorry, but I am also grateful." He waved his hand before closing it in a tight fist, emitting a dull hum that rippled through the ground where they stood and ended in an earth-shaking boom.

The silver chain suddenly burned around Cassie's neck, searing the skin beneath it, branding its symbol into her chest as she screamed. She clawed at it as she writhed on the dirt, trying with all her might to pull it off, but it refused to budge.

Then it was over. The chain fell off and rolled onto the dirt, shattering into a million pieces on impact. Her neck felt raw and her chest still throbbed with white-hot pain where the pendant had been. She looked up, gasping for air, and mentally prepared to attack Richard again. But she had no weapon and they were too far away from the city for anyone to hear them. Tears rolled down her cheeks from the pain as well as the paralyzing regret she felt for letting her guard down around Richard.

Andrea. Cassie wanted more than anything for Andrea to show up and save her—to take her away to that house on the coast she had spoken of the night before. But Andrea wasn't there. She had no idea where Cassie was or that she was in danger, and she wouldn't be coming to help.

Never before had Cassie felt so alone.

Richard spoke again. How she hated the sound of his voice—how smug and calm he was about the terrible things he had done and how he justified them. "That was…more intense than I suspected it would be. But it seems to have worked." His tone went cold and he waved his hand again. "Now, get up."

"Go to hell," Cassie wheezed.

Pain slammed into her again, her entire body seizing with it. She cried out, her vision blurring as she tried to convince herself she could take it, she could resist. She would *not* give in to him. She couldn't.

But it was too much. The wound on her chest burned, and it was less than a second before her cries became screams again.

Get up. She thrust her hands to the ground and pushed. The moment she climbed to her feet, the pain stopped. She spun around, her knees wobbly, and glared at Richard with as much defiance as she could muster.

He studied her. "Interesting. The soldiers in Gurith were able to shake off the effects when I tried to control them from a distance. It appears the trick is to have the subject actually *wear* the necklace."

Soldiers? "Y-you sent those fighters after us?!"

"I used Andrea's projection to find you. A clever trick I learned from Meredith, actually." He shrugged. "Your girlfriend still carries the markers from the device you so unhelpfully destroyed, so finding her was easy enough—she has quite a bit of potential as an enchanter, you know."

"You tried to kill us!" Cassie swung a weak fist at his face but Richard disabled her with a single swipe of his hand before another barrier sent her flying to the ground again.

"Actually, the Grandmaster himself allowed me the use of a few of his men if I promised him a strong enchanter in return," he explained. "So it was a win for everyone. Well, until the spell broke, of course."

She coughed. "You're *insane.*"

He ignored her comment. "The necklace appears to be working as expected. Now." He tilted his head toward the horizon. "Let's finish what we started. Absorb the magic."

She must have heard wrong. Her ears began ringing. "What?"

"You heard me. Absorb it. *All* of it."

* * *

Wind whipped at Andrea's hair as she and Kye raced across the fields searching for any sign of Cassie or Richard.

She hoped she was wrong, that she had missed a piece of the puzzle. Cassie would be fine, and they could finish redistributing the magic before returning to Gurdinfield.

But she knew she was right.

If Richard had built the device in Rhyad, how had he survived for so long? Why was he trapped here? How did Serena end up in Cassie's time? Did Meredith know? The questions provided no comfort, but they kept Andrea from completely falling apart while they searched for Cassie.

Up ahead.

"I see them!" Kye cried, pointing at the two figures in the distance.

"Go!" *We can make it—we have to.*

She could hear the horse's heavy panting, the hurried rate of its breaths matching the pounding of her heart as everything she knew was put into question. If Richard built the device—if he caused the Starving—the answer was clear. Damea had never seen a greater criminal.

Using Cassie's ability had never been about fixing Damea's magic. This was about him taking the magic for himself—for what, Andrea couldn't say.

"There they are!"

She could see Cassie standing next to Richard, facing away from them. *Just a bit further.* They could make it.

"We're almost there. Cassie!" Kye shouted.

No.

Cassie's arms went up.

"Stop!"

Blinding, burning—her vision was useless as the shockwave of white light slammed into them. She had only a moment to realize she was airborne before the ground rushed up at her… and then there was nothing.

* * *

There we go. Finishing up a letter to Marco in her study, Ithmeera signed the parchment and began to fold it so that she could have it sent off to Gurdinfield with the remainder of the negotiation papers for the alliance. She preferred to deal with these things in person, of course, but with the situation being what it was she had to make do.

A quick dip in blood-red wax and a hard stamp sealed the letter with the Azgadaran emblem. She was reminded of how oddly Andrea had behaved after their brief history lesson. It wasn't often one of her guests just ran out on her, but she recalled Andrea being a bit strange. Still, she had seen the reflexes with which she deployed her spells during the attack weeks ago and felt confident Marco would be in good hands with her as a teacher.

Marco. She had to resist the urge to cry again. How she missed him. She had caught Petra wandering the halls as though searching for Marco only to remember that he wasn't there. Even the Legionnaires who would humor him with pretend duels seemed more severe without him around to bother them. But Elisa—*Elisa* of all people—had been right. Marco was not safe in Azgadar.

"Is that for Marco?"

She glanced up at the open door. Alden stood with his arms crossed and a sad smile on his aging features. "How did you know?"

"You always get that look when you think about him. I think

we all worry." He took a seat in front of her. "He will return before you know it."

Her eyebrows went up. It wasn't like Alden to be so optimistic about issues where Gurdinfield was involved. *Perhaps he's finally decided to stop meddling and just be supportive as an uncle should be.* "Thank you, Uncle. It's just hard not hearing him run around the palace or being able to hold him. He is too young to have to deal with this."

Alden snapped his fingers. "You should have another ball, Ithmeera. Show these fools that we refuse to live in fear."

She sighed. "I don't know, Alden. After what happened last time…"

"With all due respect, the palace has become a tomb since Marco left. Your enemies will take advantage of every weakness."

There's the Alden I know. "And grief can be a weakness," she concluded, stacking up her papers. "Thank you, Alden, I will… consider it."

He gave an eager nod. "Of course, my dear. I'm here to help with whatever you need. Now, then, could we perhaps talk about—"

A low warbling sound rang out, shaking the room as crumbs of plaster fell from the ceiling. Ithmeera and Alden both stood up slowly, having only a moment to exchange wary glances before the window behind Ithmeera shattered and they were thrown forward like ragdolls. Ithmeera hit her desk with a solid thud and rolled onto the floor, while Alden was tossed against the wall. The desk lurched forward and books toppled violently from the shelves.

Head throbbing, she grasped for the edge of her desk and hoisted herself up. Her eyes widened when she looked out the broken window. The previously bright room had gone dark as the blue skies had warped into a swirl of pale green and dead grey. The sun was gone, covered in a dark haze that obscured it from the world.

Then, on the horizon—her lip quivered when she saw the bolts of white lightning lancing down from the dark clouds concentrated in the fields beyond the city.

Chapter 32

Exiled

The crackling static overhead lifted the hairs on the back of Andrea's neck, beckoning her to open her eyes. The world was blurry as she sat up, her body crying out in protest. Her eyes gravitated toward the source of the noise and she paled.

Dark clouds gathered above, the lightning chaining them together in a roaring storm as the scent of magic pervaded the air around her.

To her left, Kye lay on the ground, unmoving. The horse lay on its side—she couldn't tell if it was breathing or not.

Someone was screaming. Not out of shock or fear, but pain. And perhaps…denial? *Cassie.*

She could see them ahead. Cassie—arms extended, her body stiff and muscles straining as the magic flowed into her from the maelstrom above. Richard—mouthing words that Andrea couldn't make out over the noise of the storm.

They were *so* close. She had to get to them. Had to save Cassie. Had to stop this.

She fought through the pain and forced herself to stand before breaking in an unsteady jog, her teeth clenched as she pushed away any kind of sensation other than her adrenaline-driven need to get to Cassie.

"Cassie!" She stumbled, corrected herself, and kept going. *So close. Have to keep...going.*

She was just steps away. The static was stronger now, pulling on her from within, threatening to rip out everything she was. She staggered, holding her side as it burned with the ache of the fall and her ragged gasps.

Save her. She cast a barrier with the intent to throw it at Richard. She could see Cassie's eyes blazing with magic, the blue glow in them almost white. Her face was twisted as her screams continued.

A pause. *Throw the barrier. Save her.* She tried to get Cassie's attention, to let her know everything was going to be all right. But when their eyes met, Cassie let out a broken sob, crying out, *"No!"*

Andrea launched the shield at Richard. A spark ignited in her hand, dispelling the barrier and sending charged energy up her right arm and shoulder. The force of it stopped her in her tracks. She dropped to her knees, clutching her arm—the sensation of being ripped apart sent lances of unbearable pain through her arm, shoulder, and chest as her shrieks of agony carried across the field.

The air was empty—the very thing that kept the land feeling alive was gone, leaving nothing but the fine charcoal ash that coated her and everything around her. She couldn't remember when she stopped screaming because the pain refused to stop. When she managed to look at Cassie, she had collapsed, eyes closed, chest barely moving. Richard was holding her with one arm, his other outstretched. His gaze met Andrea's and his lips curved in a final, contemptuous smile before his hand closed.

They were gone. It was impossible—it *should* have been impossible for them to just *vanish* like that.

Andrea collapsed to the dirt as the ash continued to rain down on her. The pain hadn't lessened, but her throat was so raw from screaming that she could only groan, her body wracked by occasional tremors. She was weak and getting weaker—she knew that much.

Her arm…

There was no sensation—she was terrified to even *look* at the damage. She could feel her heartrate dropping, and the desire to close her eyes and let sleep take her grew urgent. She could remember feeling this way only one time before—in Rhyad.

No. Not again.

The magic was gone—Cassie had absorbed it all…and Richard had taken her. Where they had gone, Andrea had no idea. *He took her. We failed.*

I failed.

She needed magic—something to balance out the spells she had cast to overdraw. But the magic was gone, torn from the very earth she lay on. Torn from within her.

Cassie.

"Andrea!" *Kye.* She could feel arms rolling her over and lifting her up but his voice sounded so far away. Her body still seized from her injury. *Need magic…something to—*

She held out her unblemished hand, her voice coming out in

a raspy whisper. "Potion, Kye. My bag…there are…vials."

She didn't actually hear him acknowledge her, nor could she recall when exactly he had left her to grab the bag, but at some point she felt the cold opening of a glass vial against her lips.

"H-hold on, Andrea," he pleaded, and even through her blurred vision she could see his brown eyes were bloodshot. "You'll be all right. Drink this."

The liquid hit her stomach with such force that she was sure she'd vomit. Her insides were on fire with the potent magic spreading to every limb, every finger, every nerve ending—each sip of the potion worse than the last. She gagged and coughed but Kye held her close, forcing her to drink it as the world went white and she went numb—the echoes of Cassie's final cry the last thing she heard before she passed out.

* * *

A muffled groan from behind made Ithmeera tear her eyes away from the phenomenon in the sky. Her headache had worsened and something slick ran down from her hairline to her brow.

"Alden!" She rushed to his side and slid her arm underneath him.

He gave a few haggard coughs as she helped him to his feet. "I'm all right. I'm fine, Ithmeera but what…what was that?" He glanced out the window and his face trembled when he saw the fading sky. "What has *happened?*"

Ithmeera was about to reply when Alden gave a sudden

choking gasp, his eyes bulging out. She cried out in shock as the blade impaling him punctured through his shirt, the blood spreading out across the fabric in a deep red blotch as his eyes rolled back and he collapsed at her feet.

"*Enchanters* are what have happened." Petra yanked her sword back before staring in disgust at the remaining blood that coated the blade. She turned her attention to Ithmeera, who staggered back against the crooked desk, her eyes on Alden's lifeless form.

"P-Petra! What have you *done?*"

Petra stepped toward her. "I am bringing order to the empire."

Ithmeera gaped at her with wide eyes. "You murdered him!" she screamed. "*Traitor! Guards!*"

A cool smile spread on Petra's face as two Legionnaires ran into the study with their swords drawn.

Ithmeera thrust her hand out, pointing at Petra. "This woman murdered my uncle! Arrest her!"

But the Legionnaires did not move.

Ithmeera shot them a fatal glare. "Did you not hear me? *Arrest her.*"

Petra gave a soft laugh. "These soldiers swore an oath to the New Legion, *Your Majesty,*" she mocked. "Much of the Legion has, in fact. They are tired of citizens not respecting them and they have had enough of enchanters running around unchecked, endangering everyone."

Ithmeera flew into a rage as she looked around for something—anything—that she could use to defend herself with. "You're behind the New Legion? It was you this entire time? Petra, how could you do this? How could you...*betray* the empire? Betray *me?*"

But Petra just shook her head. "The only traitor here is you, Ithmeera. Allowing enchanters to rule over us and cause another Starving—have you learned nothing?" She nodded at the broken window. "And now look where we are. Magic did that." She lifted her sword, preparing to drive it through Ithmeera. "And it's all because of you."

Blocked by a rogue Legionnaire on either side, Ithmeera could only hold her arms up in what she knew would be a vain effort to stop the blade. She closed her eyes...but it never came.

Her eyes flew open as the Legionnaire on her left crumpled, a clean cut across his throat. Petra jerked her head up in surprise before Elisa yanked her back and threw her to the floor. The remaining guard charged but was too slow—Elisa slashed his arm before driving her other knife through his upper chest.

She pulled out the knife and turned to Ithmeera. "*Go.*"

Petra jumped up and narrowed her dark eyes at her. "I am surprised you still remember how to fight without your sword, Elisa."

Elisa ignored her, keeping her daggers at the ready. "Ithmeera, go! *Now!*"

But Ithmeera stood firm where she was. "I'm not leaving you. She's a traitor!"

Petra just laughed. "There's an army of Legionnaires waiting for you both. All I needed to do was give them a reason to join our cause. Azgadar's new cause."

"Why? Why would you do this?" Ithmeera cried. "I've given you everything you need here, Petra!"

"You care nothing for the plight of your citizens, Ithmeera," Petra snapped. "You forgot all that we've overcome as an empire the instant magic was returned to us. You forge alliances with the enemy when all we ask is that you bring back the restrictions on enchanters before another catastrophe can happen. And now look what they have done!"

Ithmeera could only scowl at her. "Elisa, arrest her."

"No!" Petra threw herself against Elisa, swinging her blade down and forcing her to back away. Elisa darted forward to slash at Petra when her boot slipped on a pile of torn pages which had fallen from the shelves during the earthquake. Petra moved in with a mighty slash which Elisa failed to dodge. Clutching her side, Elisa slipped again, letting out a pained grunt as she smashed into the desk.

"Elisa!" Ithmeera yelled. She moved to help, but Petra once again stood in front of her.

"No more games, Your Majesty." Her blade drew back, but was stopped by another: Veraun had leapt between them and blocked Petra's sword with his own.

Ithmeera feared the worst. "Ben?"

Holding Petra at bay, he spoke through a clenched jaw. "I'm with you, Your Majesty, but the Legion has turned on us—we need to get you out of here!"

Ithmeera looked out the open doorway and saw a large group of Legionnaires approaching, their weapons all drawn and their expressions determined. "Ben, there are more coming!"

"Can't even keep your own men loyal, can you General?" Petra said, pushing him back. Veraun charged but she was too fast, too nimble, avoiding every cut of his sword.

Elisa climbed to her feet, holding her side.

"Elisa!" he barked once their blades crossed again. "Get the empress out of here, *now!*"

Elisa hesitated as the death march of the Legionnaires grew closer. "Ben…there are too many—"

"Just *go!*"

Ithmeera barely had time to process what was happening as Elisa's hand clamped around her wrist. The next thing she knew they were tumbling out the broken window, the short drop feeling much longer than it actually was. Elisa twisted her body and took the brunt of the fall before they rolled apart on the garden soil in the courtyard of the palace.

"We have to help Ben!" Ithmeera declared once she recovered.

A panting Elisa pushed her down. "Get down," she hissed. "We need to get out of here. What's the fastest way out of the city? Is the courtyard grate still connected to the sewers?"

"I am *not* leaving my own city—"

Elisa clamped her hand over her mouth and held her close, her whisper fiercer than anything Ithmeera had heard from her. "You want to die? You want Marco to be an orphan? Because that's what will happen if we do not leave Azgadar." She glanced up at the shifting sky, and Ithmeera could feel her shiver. "Is the grate still connected?" she repeated.

Ithmeera could only nod.

"Then let's go. We can take the sewers." She was still panting—whether it was from adrenaline or something else Ithmeera could not tell as they crept through the hedges and rosebushes to the edge of the courtyard.

Elisa pulled up the grate. "After you," she said.

Ithmeera backed away. "I cannot just *leave,* Elisa."

"Over here! They went out the window!" The shouts of Legionnaires followed by armored footsteps on brick approached.

Elisa's bright green eyes met hers, the fear in them matching her own. "Go. Now."

Taking one last longing look at the palace—her home—Ithmeera could only wonder what had happened to get them to this point. Had Petra been right? Had she ignored the pleas of her own people?

Ben. She knew he had probably gone down fighting his own traitorous soldiers. *And Alden.* His lifeless eyes were branded in her memory forever.

She grasped the grimy metal bars and lowered herself down the ladder to the sewer tunnel below as the question she was desperate to know the answer above all the rest to finally came to her.

How could this have happened?

Chapter 33

Oaths Taken

"This should be it." It took Elisa a few pushes before the iron door would budge. The rusty hinges groaned in protest, but a solid shove later and the door finally swung open. "Had I known the courtyard was still connected I might have considered using that entrance last year."

"How many times have you done this?" Ithmeera asked as they stepped through, with Elisa few steps ahead. She bit her lip as the shallow water seeped into her shoes, instigating a chuckle at herself for being annoyed at her shoes at a time like this.

Elisa looked back. "What's so funny?"

Ithmeera shook her head before absentmindedly touching the shallow cut on her head she had acquired when she hit the edge of her desk. "I was getting angry at myself for wearing the wrong shoes."

"The wrong...*shoes?*"

Ithmeera sniffed. "Judge all you like—it was not on the agenda today to go crawling through these filthy sewers."

"Technically they're *your* filthy sewers. And," Elisa said, "I've done this more times than I've counted if I'm being honest. It was the only way I could get in and out of the city without anyone recognizing me."

"You were here that often?"

Elisa cursed under her breath as she stumbled into a deeper pocket in the ground, causing water to splash up from her boots. "I had to get my information somehow."

"The information you *stole* from me, you mean," Ithmeera corrected. Then, without thinking, "I am surrounded by traitors and spies." She regretted her words instantly, even if they were true.

Elisa stopped. "How long has Petra been a Legionnaire?"

"Since before she started working for me. Her background made her a...a good choice. I wanted someone protecting Marco at all times."

"One personal guard was not enough?" Elisa's question was an obvious mask for another—one that Ithmeera could already hear in her head. *Was I not good enough for you?*

She had no desire to get into this topic with Elisa, especially not now. "Who I choose to defend me is my choice and my business." A small, dark creature scurried by her feet, startling a shrill cry from her throat. She huffed when she saw the smug grin on Elisa's face. "Don't give me that look—you know I hate rats! Ugh!"

Elisa stifled a laugh. "Sorry."

The lightness of their exchange reminded Ithmeera of happier times, times when she would tell Elisa everything and would even welcome the teasing Elisa would often throw her way. But when the cold realization that they were trudging through a sewer while escaping for their lives set in once more, the tears Ithmeera had been holding back since Petra's betrayal surged forth and broke free. She braced herself against the stone wall and cried into her arm.

A tentative hand rested on her back. "We really should move," Elisa said, in a quiet voice that Ithmeera knew was designed to not attract attention to them in case they had been followed.

Ithmeera spun around and pushed Elisa away. Her head still hurt, she was covered in filth, her uncle and general were dead, her son was on the other side of Damea, and a woman she had thought to be her friend—her confidante, even—had been scheming behind her back for months and turned most if not all of the entire Legion against her. She was tired of people telling her what she should and shouldn't do. "You know what I want, Elisa? Do you? I want to march back to the palace and make her pay for what she's done. Those assassins? My boy being sent away? It's *her* fault and yet she sits in *my* home. Why?"

Elisa could only stare back at her before she staggered and held her side again, the look on her face telling enough that Ithmeera understood. "You're hurt!"

"I'm fine."

"No, you're not. Let me see." Ithmeera bent down and slapped Elisa's hand away. "Move your hand so I can look at it—oh…"

She was certain the wound was from Petra's sword. It did not appear deep at first glance but the blade had punctured through Elisa's armor and clothing. "We need to get this bandaged."

"I'll be fine," Elisa repeated, giving Ithmeera's shoulder a gentle push. "Let's get out of here so we can figure out a plan. We have to get to the City of Towers."

Marco. "And how do you expect us to do that?" she demanded. "We have no horses, no supplies, and no food." As much as Ithmeera wanted to get to Marco, she knew that without supplies and with Elisa injured, their chances of making it to Gurdinfield alive were slim.

They reached the sewer exit, a half-rotted panel of wood on algae-coated hinges. Elisa fiddled with the old lock before opening the door, revealing the grasslands outside the city walls. There was no one in sight. "Sadford isn't too far and they won't be expecting us," she said as they stepped out into the open.

Ithmeera squinted as her eyes adjusted to the strange, greenish tint in the sky. The sun was still covered and if she hadn't known already, she would never have guessed it was early afternoon. "And where are we supposed to stay?"

"I still have a house there. That is, if news of the pardon made it all the way to Sadford, and news of your exile has not," Elisa said as she shut the door behind them. "Otherwise, I'm friends with the innkeeper. Maybe he can give us a room." She looked Ithmeera up and down. "Though bringing the exiled empress of Azgadar into a common inn is probably not the best way to maintain cover."

Relieved she was done walking through ankle-high sludge, Ithmeera shook her foot in disgust, sending a spray of water in Elisa's direction. "I am *not* in exile."

Elisa looked down at her splattered greaves and sighed. "Was that really necessary?"

Ithmeera was about to answer when she heard the cries of

someone calling Elisa's name accompanied by hooves trampling across the grass. Kye was riding at a rapid pace from the peak of the closest hill, holding an unconscious Andrea on the saddle in front of him.

Elisa ran up to him as he slowed the horse. "What happened?" She took one look at Andrea, her lips parting and eyebrows arching in fear. "Where are Cassie and Richard?"

A wave of fresh sorrow hit Ithmeera when she saw Kye's tear-stained face. He was covered in dirt and his clothes were torn. Charcoal dust streaked his face and his curly hair was peppered with the same black ashes.

Andrea looked even worse—she was pale, with dark bruises circling her eyes and her brow doused with sweat, although her breathing seemed stable.

Kye coughed hard as Elisa helped him move Andrea off the horse before he climbed down himself. "Richard...is a traitor. Somehow he—he made Cassie do this and then they disappeared." He pointed at the sky. "It's gone. *All* the magic. All…gone. And s-so are they! I'm so sorry! I'm sorry!" His voice cracked at the end as he broke down, covering his face with his hands.

Elisa gasped. "*Cassie* did this?" She gently set Andrea down in the grass.

"Andrea tried to save her, and I couldn't get to them in time," he wailed. "I *tried!* I—"

"Kye." In a fluid movement that made Ithmeera almost start crying again herself, Elisa took Kye into her arms and held him in a tight embrace as he sobbed into her shoulder. "This is not your fault."

Ithmeera felt Andrea's forehead with the back of her hand, finding her burning with fever. "What is wrong with her?"

Kye lifted his head. "She was hit by some sort of lightning when she cast a spell. I gave her a potion which seems to be helping, but she won't wake up." He looked to Elisa. "Can you help her?"

"The Legion has mutinied. Petra is behind the New Legion." She averted her eyes in shame, a sight which stunned Ithmeera. "We barely escaped."

He pulled away. "W-what?"

"Elisa and I need to get to Sadford and then to Gurdinfield to find my son," Ithmeera said, the words not sounding real, even as she heard her own voice say them.

Elisa put her hand on Kye's shoulder. "You said they disappeared. How?"

"I don't know. Magic, but I've never seen anyone use magic to vanish into thin air!" He looked at Andrea. "I need to help her. I need to—I don't know what to do, Elisa!"

Ithmeera watched as Elisa gave a long, hard stare at Andrea before glancing back at her. "We must move quickly, but I don't know how to help her if magic did this to her." She swallowed. "She needs an enchanter."

Kye shook his head a few times before his face lit up. "Master Jheran! Her old mentor. M-maybe he can help." He wiped his nose with his sleeve. "I'll take her to Ata."

"The Western Hills are far," Ithmeera said. "Are you certain you can make that journey alone?"

Elisa answered for him. "He has no choice." She looked at the sky, as though she were contemplating a painful decision.

Then she grabbed Kye's collar. "You *will* make it to Ata and help Andrea. Then you will both come find us in Gurdinfield."

"I—I will. I promise."

She shook him hard. "Don't make a promise if you cannot keep it. Without you and Andrea we don't stand a chance of fixing all of this."

His lower lip trembled. "I will find you, Elisa."

She released him. "We'll see you soon. Here." She drew one of her daggers, twirling the blade around to present the hilt to him. "Take this, and whatever you do, don't cast any spells."

A hot wind rustled the tall grass around them. Even though she was not an enchanter, Ithmeera could not deny the sheer *emptiness* the wind left in her as it ruffled her tangled dark curls. She had lived her entire life in Azgadar, and never before had the air felt so…dead. "We need to go, Elisa."

"Good luck." Fresh fear rose in Kye's eyes as he suddenly seemed to realize that he was in an empress's presence. He rushed to bow. "I—I'm sorry, Your Majesty, I—"

But Ithmeera stopped his stuttering with her hand. The devotion Kye had shown to his friends was admirable and Ithmeera could see how Elisa cared for him. Part of her felt guilty for not investigating his family's death personally, but she knew she could not change the past. The thought brought back her inner turmoil from earlier as Petra's bitter words ate away at her. *Perhaps I am not as connected to the people as I thought.* An idea came to her. She removed the gold band from her right ring finger. The ring had been a gift from Erik, and had the swords and shield of the Legion engraved across the metal. She knew what it represented, though, and hoped it could be helpful here.

"Formalities mean nothing if Azgadar falls, Kye." She took one of his rough hands in hers before placing the ring in it, his eyes going wide as she gently closed his fingers over it. "And without a loyal Legion, the empire cannot defend itself or its allies. A Legionnaire's oath is not just to Azgadar, but to Damea." She met his terrified yet determined gaze. "Will you take that oath, Kye?"

Kye's eyes blazed with resolution and Ithmeera could not help but swell with pride as his determination gave her a small glimmer of hope that Azgadar—no, that *Damea* would somehow be saved. "I will, Your Majesty."

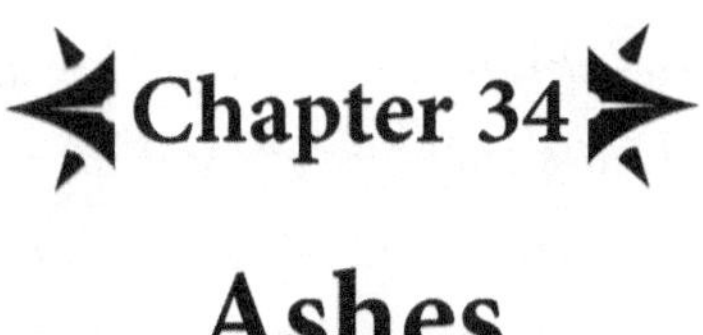

Chapter 34

Ashes

Cold. But also, familiar.

She should have been dead. But instead she hovered on the precipice of where she should have been and the void that pulled at her.

It was just a tug at first, then another. Someone screamed at her—desperate, angry, and on the brink of being lost to that same void forever with a single spark. She knew the scream—she'd heard it before. She just needed to—

The spark. The unbearable pain as the bolts tore into her flesh returned, carving out the paths on her skin that would be with her forever. Not as guides, but as a reminder…

"NO!"

Cassie. *But Cassie was gone. She had tried so hard to reach her in time…and failed.*

Another tug. Stronger this time. Something whispered at her, urging her to look, although she wasn't sure if she should. Curiosity won as her eyes slowly moved through the blackness, those dark clouds circling overhead as the ashes of a future she would never see fell around her, mocking her.

How did I not see it?

“I guess promises are a lot easier to make when you don’t know if you’ll live to see tomorrow.” Cassie. *She stumbled and fell on her back, her cries unanswered as she lay at the bottom of the rocky crater. The clouds raced overhead on the backdrop of the green haze that had become the sky as she stared up in horror at what the magic had done to Cassie, to her, and to Damea.*

“The magic is right there! Use it and fix this!”

I failed.

“Andrea…”

I failed her. I failed Damea. I failed everyone. *She closed her eyes. She could have left it alone. Could have run away with Cassie where they could live out their lives together before it was too late. But she hadn’t.*

She had destroyed magic. The world was broken. Damea would wither and die because of her. She stared back into the void as it hurled Cassie’s anguished scream at her again and again. She was done.

Let it take me.

* * *

At first, Andrea only felt light pressure. A cold, damp cloth was pressed against on her forehead. Her eyes were heavy and she struggled to keep them open as she became aware she was in a bed. The soft pillow underneath her head felt vaguely familiar as the scents of melted wax, burning wood, and her mother’s stew swirled together, wrapping her in a warm cocoon she had no desire to leave. It was almost enough to make her fall back asleep.

A deep, aching throb in her arm changed her mind.

She forced her eyes open and had to blink a few times to regain focus on the world. The cloth left her head as she heard the strangled cry of…her mother?

"Garrett! Garrett—she's awake. Get in here!" Solid footsteps hammered across the hardwood floors. Her head hurt and her lips were cracked—she felt as though she hadn't eaten or drank anything in days

She spotted the dresser, bare except for the candles. The figurines were missing—had Cassie remembered to take them before they left?

But we already left. Andrea tensed up as confusion set in. She was in her own bedroom, in her own bed. Her mother and father stood over her. *They both seem terrified. What am I* doing *here?* She tried to recall what had happened to lead to this but her memory was fuzzy.

Where is Cassie?

Her voice came out in a hoarse whisper. "Mother?"

Isabel's tired eyes welled up with tears as she pressed the cloth back down on Andrea's forehead, her voice so soft and soothing Andrea worried she might fall asleep again. "Shh. Try not to talk."

Andrea inhaled to speak again—a mistake. Her lungs and chest burned as she was pulled into a fit of deep coughs that shook her entire body and made her right side explode in pain.

Garrett grew very pale. "I—I'll go get Jheran." Isabel looked after him as he hurried out before turning back to Andrea. "It's all right, Andrea. You're home now."

Cassie. "Wh-where is Cassie?"

The sorrow in Isabel's face told her everything as the events outside Azgadar came back to Andrea in a frenzied rush.

Her arms outstretched, shoulders tense as lightning from above fused with her hands—her screams echoing across the fields of Azgadar under the black clouds and fading sky of a land whose lifeline had been severed. Save her. Have to get to Cassie. *Have* to. *But they were gone—*she *was gone. The tiny rocks in the dirt cut into her skin as she lay crying on the ground—*

She shot up, gasping for air. Isabel set her hands on Andrea's shoulders, trying to calm her down. "Andrea, lie down. *Please.* You must rest!"

"I have to find her!" she cried, struggling against Isabel's hold, her throat stinging as though she'd swallowed broken glass. "I have to get her back. I have to—" But she was weak—too weak. Isabel somehow managed to push her back down on the bed.

"You are *hurt,* Andrea!" Isabel grabbed her hands and squeezed them. "Jheran is on his way and he's going to look at you, but you must stay in bed, *please.*"

Andrea stopped thrashing. "Hurt?" She looked down at her right arm for the first time since waking up. Someone had removed her button-down tunic, leaving her only in an undershirt and leggings. She knew if the undershirt was removed she would be able to see more of the wound, but what she saw was more than enough to make her stomach churn.

Thin, dark streaks resembling the very bolts that hit her had been burned into the skin from the top of her right shoulder and the right side of her chest all the way down to her hand. She could tell without looking that that the wounds reached down to her ribs and waist and wrapped around her back. A sickening hue hovering between purple and black, the burns varied in thickness but none were open or raw. As hideous as they were, the pain was nothing compared to what Andrea had endured when she acquired them.

The magic. She could feel its absence around her. Throwing the barrier had been a mistake. A stupid, amateur mistake that could have killed her, had Kye not given her the potion that—

The potion! It must have saved me. An unexpected result, but then again, she hadn't planned on actually *using* the potions. And…something else. There was a new, foreign sensation Andrea hadn't noticed before, a strange tingling that spread to her fingertips and pulsed in her arms. The power was much stronger on her left side than her right, but it was still there. It took her a moment to understand—the potion was giving her a supply of magic despite the lack of energy around her. Her experiment had worked. *But…* "Where is Kye? How did I get here?"

Isabel's shocked expression made Andrea wonder if she had asked the wrong questions. "Andrea, what has *happened?* The sky…there was this horrible sound, and then the sky changed color. We've all been so frightened and there was word it came from Azgadar and we hoped you weren't involved but then your friend told us—"

"Mother!" Andrea's side gave another spasm as she cut Isabel off. "I need to talk to Kye."

"Your friend is asleep in the other room. The poor boy has been recovering since he brought you here a few days ago—how he managed to get you here on his own is a miracle," Isabel said, glancing at Andrea's arm. "He told us everything. About Cassie and that man…Richard?"

Andrea seethed with anger at the mere mention of Richard. She started to get out of bed, frustrated that she had no memory of the journey from Azgadar to Ata or even what had happened to the rest of her friends. *Did Elisa know? Diana? Are they all right?* "I need to speak to Kye." Her own weakness became apparent as she fought to push herself up again. "Help me."

But Isabel would not budge. "Absolutely not. You're injured, Andrea," she exclaimed as she pointed at Andrea's wounds. "Was Jheran right? Did magic really do this?"

"Richard forced Cassie to take all the magic, Mother. I need to stop him and get her back. Please," Andrea begged, "help me."

Isabel looked away, but Andrea could still see the hurt in her mother's eyes. "You lied to me, Andrea. You lied to your father. He said…he said that Cassie told him everything." She sniffed as tears began to roll down her cheeks. "The battle… and Rhyad."

"I'm sorry," Andrea whispered, the sadness in her mother's voice adding to the already staggering burden of guilt on her conscience. "I need to see Kye, Mother. If we're to have any chance at finding Cassie I need to find out what happened after I…" She trailed off as she remembered passing out, and the dream that had followed as she plunged into the darkness. *You failed her.*

Isabel remained firm. "You need to *rest,* Andrea and so does he." Her eyes traveled to the window above the bed and Andrea's gaze followed. The sky was still the same green it had been when she lost consciousness in Azgadar. *How in the world are we going to fix* that?

Isabel must have thought the same thing because she took Andrea into her arms. "I know it's frustrating to just sit here, but you must get better first. You can't help Cassie in this state."

Andrea stiffened in her mother's hold. She knew she was weak—her side still hurt and she could feel herself growing too tired to even speak. "I…have to save her, Mother."

"You have to get better." Isabel helped Andrea get as comfortable as she could before she laid a blanket over her. "Your father and Jheran will be here shortly, and Jheran will check on you. Rest for now. Please."

Andrea's eyelids grew heavy once more as she began to lose the battle of staying awake. "I'll try." She sank back into the pillow, her mother pressing a light kiss to her temple just seconds before she slipped away again.

* * *

"More?"

"I'm not very hungry."

With a shrug, Elisa set the small metal pot back over the

fire, its contents sizzling as the flames licked underneath them. She took a bite of the second helping she had scooped out for herself and watched in silence as Ithmeera seemed mesmerized by the flames and the thin plumes of smoke wafting into the night sky.

After a few mouthfuls, she pointed with her fork at Ithmeera's half-empty tin bowl. "You've barely touched it and we've got another long walk ahead of us tomorrow."

Ithmeera tucked her knees against herself, her gaze never leaving the fire. "I appreciate the concern, Elisa, but I will be fine."

Elisa took one last bite before setting her bowl and fork down on the ground next to her with a clatter loud enough to interrupt Ithmeera's concentration. "All right. What is it?"

Ithmeera rolled her eyes and lifted her hands. "What is *what?*"

"Your issue. You've been sulking like this since we left Sadford. At least Andrea and Cassie were somewhat entertaining what with their nonstop bickering."

Ithmeera gave a bitter laugh. "Oh! My apologies. Next time I am banished from my own empire I will be sure to maintain a more chipper mood when I am in your presence." She put her hand to her head, her fingers running over the scabbed wound below her hairline. "Please, just leave me be."

Elisa frowned when she saw the guilt Ithmeera had been carrying with her since leaving Azgadar fill her eyes again. She scolded herself for being insensitive, but she was not good at comforting people and her traveling companion being

Ithmeera did not help make things less awkward at all.

Still, there was no harm in trying. What could Ithmeera do: get angry and exile her? *Say something.*

She crawled from her seat on the ground to sit next to Ithmeera, who glanced up in surprise.

Elisa settled in. "It's not your fault, you know." *Not a great start, but it's something.*

Ithmeera cast her a suspicious look. "Not now, Elisa."

"I've had a long week." Elisa gestured to her side, where her bandaged wound was healing nicely. "The sky has turned green. My friends could be dead. I've been injured, jumped out of a window, crawled through sewers, walked to Sadford, and now we have to walk all the way to bloody Gurdinfield because you keep picking terrible bodyguards. If I have to complete the rest of this journey in silence, Ithmeera, I *will* go insane." She wondered if perhaps she'd gone too far with her stab at Ithmeera's choice in bodyguards, but her worry disappeared when Ithmeera gave a quiet laugh. Then another—covering her mouth as the short laughs turned into stifled giggles.

She's lost it. "What in the world is so funny?"

But Ithmeera could barely get a word out between her laughs. "You...you of all people...are mad because I don't want to *talk?*" She started to calm down. "I must send word to every village and city in the empire. Elisa of Sadford, the surliest woman in all of Azgadar, wants to have a civil conversation!"

The sight of the empress of the Azgadaran Empire rolling on the ground laughing was enough to make Elisa grin. *At least she's distracted.* "Very funny." She began picking up the bowls so she could wipe them down.

"Elisa."

She stopped and turned her head right as Ithmeera's deep green eyes met hers. She half-expected Ithmeera to make another snide comment about her complaint and was caught off guard at the solemnity of Ithmeera's expression. "You've always been arrogant—so certain that you were *right* all the time." Her eyes flickered to the fire before going back to Elisa. "But you're wrong. My bodyguard was the best Azgadar has ever seen. And she saved my and my son's life more than once. I…never thanked her for that."

Elisa's lips tightened as the two stayed as they were—just staring—until she finally broke free of whatever hold Ithmeera seemed to have on her in that moment. "You're welcome." She looked down at the bowl in her hand. "Are you sure you don't want more?"

Ithmeera held out her hand. "I'll have a bit. But only to get you to stop complaining. Whining never suited you."

Elisa let through a smile as she gave the bowl back. "Duly noted, Your Majesty." She reclaimed her seat next to Ithmeera, relaxing as her attention wavered between Ithmeera eating and the calls of wildlife in the distance.

Ithmeera shivered. "Marco…he must be so frightened." She put the bowl back down and wiped her eyes. It was not the first time Elisa had seen her cry that day, and she knew it would not be the last. "I need to see him." She sniffed. "He needs his mother."

"Marco is brave." Elisa's tone sounded more confident than

she felt. But she knew what Ithmeera needed right now was hope; otherwise they stood a slim chance of making it to Gurdinfield, let alone taking Azgadar back. "He's probably less afraid than we are, honestly." She hesitated before reaching out and placing a cautious hand on Ithmeera's shoulder. "You will see him again soon."

Ithmeera choked out another laugh but did not pull away—instead she gave Elisa a grateful smile. "Somehow, I believe you."

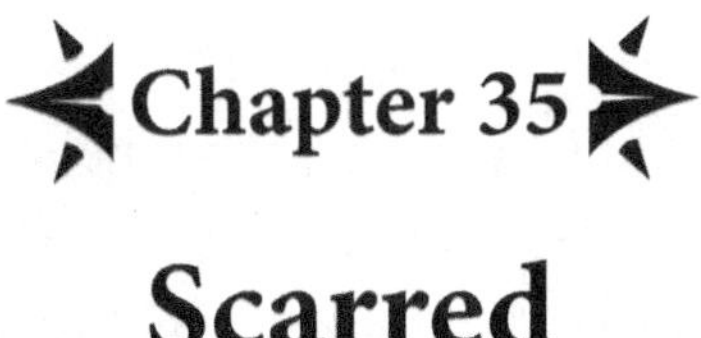

Chapter 35

Scarred

Andrea woke with a muffled cry, her body feeling like it was on fire. She immediately rolled onto her side and curled up as waves of nausea washed over her. Her injured side gave a deep throb and out of instinct she gripped her arm in a vain attempt to stop the burning.

Of course the potion would wear off. She just needed to get to her pack, although she couldn't remember just how many of the vials she had brought with her from the City of Towers.

She tried to keep her steps quiet as she shuffled across the hardwood floors of the house in the dark, using the doorframes and walls to keep her balance. The last thing she wanted to do was wake her parents, who were already sick with worry.

Where is it? She passed by the living room, not bothering to see if Kye was there or not, before pushing the front door open and heading out to the barn, where she and Cassie had kept their supplies during their last visit.

Her stomach lurched again as she crossed the grass between the house and the barn, forcing her to stumble while holding her side as her gaze turned up. There were no stars tonight—the night sky was dark, but rather than the deep blue or blackness it should have been, it carried the anemic greyness she had seen during the day with a tinge of green that even at night was a visible reminder of what Damea had lost.

As she dragged herself into the barn, Andrea heard Kira give a quiet snort of acknowledgement while she searched in the darkness for a light. Her side quivered again in pain and she gritted her teeth as she conjured a ball of white light out of desperation. It flickered a few times but stayed lit. She found the lantern hanging in a corner and hobbled over to it before lighting it with the smallest spark of fire she could muster in her crippled state.

There. As she suspected, her, Cassie, and Kye's packs were piled up on the hay just a few steps away. Their horse, however, was nowhere to be seen.

She fell to her knees and began rummaging through their supplies. Her heart pounded in alarm when she discovered that the contents of the packs had been mixed up, with several items that should have been in her pack missing.

What if they were lost during the trip here? Had Kye administered them all to her and she somehow didn't remember? If he had, what would she do?

She panicked.

"No, no, no, *no*—where *is* it?" The pain caused her to forgo any shred of patience she had left as she tore through the backpacks, their cookware, rations, and clothing flying everywhere. Frantic thoughts of what would happen if she couldn't find another vial ran through her mind, the possibilities terrifying her. The illness would return and she would die, without ever seeing Cassie again…

Cassie. Was she all right? What was happening to her? What would happen to all the magic?

But Andrea knew from experience the answer to most of these questions. Tears pricked at her eyes. She would die. Her body was already unbalanced from the overdraw of energy. Coupled with what the lightning had done to her, she would soon be too weak to fight for much longer.

And this time, Cassie wasn't there to save her.

"Andrea?" Kye's soft voice came from the wide doorway. She looked behind her as he hurried to her, looking tired but no worse for wear. He knelt next to her, a gold ring hanging from a thin chain slipping out from under his shirt. "What are you doing?"

Andrea resumed her frenzied hunt and tossed one of the empty bags aside. "I need another potion, Kye."

Kye seemed confused. "Another? But we're here now and you're awake! Why do—"

"*Where are they?*" She didn't mean to raise her voice at him. She just *needed* that potion. She needed to not die so that she could find Cassie.

Kye nearly fell backwards, stammering with fear. "I-in this one!" His hand shot out and grabbed the pack at the bottom, the one containing Cassie's clothes. "I moved them in here so that they wouldn't break."

Andrea tore the bag open and dumped out its contents on the straw-littered floor. There were six vials, four of which contained her potion.

Kye must have seen the dread in her eyes because he put his

hand on her shoulder, his voice shaky but fighting to remain calm. "I had to give you another one while we were traveling here. Y-you were delirious and you asked me." He looked at her arm. "I-is that from…?" He didn't finish.

She took one of the vials and ripped off the cork before downing the harsh liquid in a single gulp. The nausea that had somewhat subsided while she was distracted returned with a vengeance as the potion left a horrible, acrid taste in her mouth. She doubled over with a moan and fell face first on the floor. Her insides felt as though they were melting, and in that moment, she would have gladly taken the sickness over this torture.

She was sure she would pass out—she wished she would—but the burning began to wear off. Kye lifted her up so she was sitting on the floor, clutching her knees, head hanging down. The pain was fading as she'd hoped it would, and the tingling sensation she'd felt earlier returned as the liquid magic began spreading throughout her body. "Pleasant" was the wrong word to describe it, but Andrea found herself taking some small comfort in the compact, concentrated power that pulsed within her. It was, in some ways, similar to what she experienced when she drew energy from Cassie, though nowhere near as intense or potent. In other ways, it left her wanting more, just in case this one wore out.

"Easy," Kye murmured, stroking her back. "It's going to be all right, Andrea. I'm…" His voice cracked. "Your arm!"

She looked at where he was pointing and gasped. The jagged wounds that ran up and down her arm and under her clothes were *glowing*. The light, obviously fueled by the magic she had consumed, came in pulses—a bright blue shifting to white before ebbing back to blue again. "The potion…"

"Why is it doing that?"

"I—I don't know, Kye. Maybe—" And then she saw it. In her fevered state she had missed it but it must have fallen out of Cassie's bag when she emptied it. Dark green threads wove together with blue and red ones into something Andrea had seen countless times in her life.

She picked it up, hands roaming gently over the fusion of colors as she silently admired the way the threads shone when the light from the lantern hit them.

She could hear Kye swallow. "She bought it our last day in Azgadar, right before…before *it* happened."

Andrea's lips remained slightly parted as she continued to marvel at the bracelet in her hands. It seemed delicate upon first glance, but she could *feel* the energy that radiated from it. Somehow, its magic had not been taken. Whether or not that was the case for all enchanted objects, she didn't know.

This…this was what she wanted to talk to me about. She was suddenly reminded why she was there, holding the bracelet Cassie had intended to give to her. She set it back down. The tears came back in full force as all the frustration, the anger, the rage she had bottled up while she was weak erupted. She grabbed the two empty vials and stood up before hurling them at the wall across the barn, the glass shattering on impact as she screamed. The magic in her flared up, the bolts of light along her arm gleaming as white as the pain that had accompanied their creation, and then she spun around and flipped over one of Garrett's workbenches. Kye jumped back in fright and called out for her to stop, but she ignored him. She swore she heard the cries of her mother but it mattered not to her.

Nothing matters anymore. Everything Andrea had ever wanted, everything she'd dreamed of—becoming an enchanter, saving magic, living in a palace and allying with the most powerful people in Damea—meant nothing if Cassie was lost to her.

Cassie. She shouted her rage as strong arms wrapped around her from the side. She struggled and kicked, ignoring the hushed murmurs from Garrett, who sounded near to crying himself as he held her close to him while Isabel stood a few steps away, hands covering her mouth and tears rolling down her cheeks.

"I've got you," Garrett whispered while Andrea continued to thrash in his arms. "It's going to be all right. I promise."

No. It won't be. Regret found its place in her anger as the magic within her cooled down. *I should have just stayed here. I should have never gone with Meredith. Cassie would never have come to Damea and then she'd be fine.* But she also wanted nothing more than to just collapse in Cassie's arms in their bedroom in Gurdinfield—messy blankets and soup-stained rug and all—and just cry her eyes out on Cassie's shoulder.

The glow in her scars faded as she finally crumpled in her father's hold, reduced to heaving sobs. Isabel bent down and picked up the bracelet. She and Garrett exchanged looks of understanding.

He kissed the top of her head. His soothing voice reminded Andrea of the time he had comforted her when she was eight years old and had been traumatized after she'd accidentally set a field of crops on fire. "Why don't you get your bracelet and I'll take you back inside, hmm?"

Without saying a word, Andrea untangled herself from his arms and took the bracelet from Isabel's offering hand. Still saying nothing to either of them or Kye, she started to leave the barn when she froze at whom she saw standing in the doorway.

She wore her dark brown cloak's hood over her head, covering up much of the grey-streaked dark hair that framed defiant grey eyes. She seemed thinner, frailer than she had when Andrea last saw her, but it was difficult to tell.

Meredith smiled at her. "Hello, Andrea."

* * *

Hours later, the warm, comforting scent of Isabel's homemade stew floated through the house, despite it being past midnight. The lantern in the barn had been put out, the bags reorganized, and everyone had returned to the house for the remainder of the night. Garrett and Isabel stayed in the kitchen with Kye to give Andrea and Meredith some privacy as they sat beside each other on the living room couch.

Andrea stared at the floor, twisting the bracelet in her hands.

"How did you find me?" Her voice was rough, her throat still raw from screaming. She wanted to go back to bed and sleep for eternity, but Meredith had insisted they talk, much to her parents' disapproval.

Meredith gave a low hum. "Actually, I didn't know you would be here. I was going to ask your parents if they knew where you were before moving on, just in case you had decided to resolve things with them after all." She sipped the hot tea from the small cup in her hands. "Then I meant to travel to Azgadar. That is where it happened, yes?"

Andrea didn't respond.

Meredith set her cup down and observed the bracelet Andrea held with heightened interest. "It's lovely. But it hasn't been bound yet. You haven't put it on."

"I know."

"Ah. Still deciding then?"

Andrea gave a half-hearted shrug. "No. It doesn't matter." She looked up. "Why are you here, Meredith? Richard went looking for you after he woke up in the Black Forest and you weren't there."

A long sigh. "After Rhyad, I could no longer manipulate magic or cast spells. I failed Richard, and so instead of returning home I went to Gurith." Meredith folded her hands together. "A few months later, my abilities slowly returned. I meant to go to the Black Forest to…to see to Richard's body." She shook her head. "I was so convinced I'd failed that I never stopped to consider how the Restoration might have helped him."

That struck a nerve. "I don't see why you care. He's a traitor—a murderous monster."

Meredith chuckled. "Because you think he single-handedly caused the Starving? Listen to yourself, Andrea. It's obvious that this…Serena woman—a legendary enchanter—built that device. Why you continue to vilify Richard and me is something I will never understand."

Andrea jerked her head up. "He has Cassie. He *forced* her to take all the magic. Kye was there, too—he told you the same thing I did!"

"Andrea." Meredith put her hand on Andrea's bare arm, her eyes traveling over the broken skin. "All I know is that the magic—*most* of the magic, anyway—is gone." She bowed her head. "We can only hope that all the other enchanters in Damea know better than to try any spells. Not all of them are as fortunate as you."

Andrea scoffed and pulled her arm away. "You think *this* is fortunate? Look at what it did to me, Meredith!"

"But you can still cast spells?"

Really? Is that all she cares about? "I don't see how that's relevant, but yes."

Meredith went quiet, but Andrea could see the wheels turning in her head. "What?" she asked. "Why does that matter?"

"When the sky went dark, I was out for a stroll along the docks." Meredith lifted her cup again. "I could feel the magic leaving the land, Andrea. It was…terrible. But also impressive." Excitement crept into her voice. "That Cassie is capable of that kind of power—"

"Don't." Andrea began to seethe again. "Don't talk about her like that."

But Meredith was unfazed. "I wanted to investigate, but I didn't want to go to Azgadar alone if I could help it. Obviously, I couldn't use your projection to find you so I came here."

Andrea stiffened. "What did you say?"

"Your projection?" Meredith repeated, giving her an odd look. "Without magic I risked getting sick myself."

Yes. It had never occurred to her before—Andrea had never imagined she would be able to do it, but maybe now, when there was no other choice…

"Teach me."

Meredith lost the grip on her cup and a few drops of tea spilled into her lap. She set it back down on the table. "What?"

"Projections. Teach me to read them." She expected Meredith to refuse her request before dragging them both into a long, dull lecture about the dangers of attempting a feat like this when Damea was devoid of magic.

Instead, Meredith laughed, loudly enough that Andrea was certain her parents could hear the commotion. "You must be joking!"

Andrea rolled her eyes. How was this funny? "I'm not. We can use it to find Cassie…and Richard."

Meredith held up her index finger. "First of all, reading projections is almost impossible to teach—people are born with the ability to do it. It is not like casting a simple light. Second, even if I could teach it to you, why would I? So you can go off on your own and kill my husband before I have a chance to question him?"

"I wouldn't do that, Meredith. I just want Cassie back," Andrea said, gripping the bracelet tighter. Then, in a whisper, "I just want to *fix* this so we can be left alone."

"Left alone?"

Must she poke her nose into everything? "I'm done enchanting,

Meredith." Her gaze dropped to the floor again. "I was going to take Cassie to the Gurith Coast, maybe Onede, and we were going to just…live." She ran her fingers around the bracelet again. "You said most of the magic was gone—not all. Where is the rest?"

"Buildings. Artifacts. Those horrid potions you somehow thought were a good idea to drink—honestly, what were you *thinking*, Andrea?" Meredith scolded. "Taking untested potions into the field? I taught you better than that."

But Andrea just glared back at her. "I was trying to stay alive so I could help Cassie, something *you* don't seem to understand!"

The awkward silence between them returned. Andrea could hear her parents and Kye talking in low voices in the kitchen. The stew smelled delicious and she was surprised she was hungry at all after everything that had happened.

Meredith's shoulders tensed as her normally cool and confident voice descended to a shaky whisper. "The land is unstable, Andrea. Damea's source of life *is* its magic. You're right—we do need to fix it."

Andrea felt the tears coming back. "What will happen if we don't? I…" She wiped her eyes. "I still don't understand how all of this works."

Meredith took her hand with unexpected compassion. "The sad truth is that we *don't* know. Not really. Our magic can light up even the darkest of nights, Andrea, but it takes incredible power—*terrifying* power—to consume the source of it all. Once the light has been snuffed out…" She shuddered. "…forever, *that* is when we'll know." She released Andrea's hand. "All right.

We can try this. But you must swear to me that you won't harm Richard if we find them."

"I swear it." Andrea wasn't sure who she was trying to convince more—Meredith or herself—but she knew that if they found Cassie and Richard, she wanted to have more than words with him for the atrocities he had committed.

And here we are again. She knew having Meredith as a teacher again would be difficult, especially given that Meredith could not actually demonstrate to her exactly how to read Cassie's projection. But Andrea would try. She owed Cassie that much—and more.

She slipped the bracelet onto her right wrist, savoring the magic as it flowed through her before looking down at her scars, the memory of Damea descending into darkness still fresh in her mind. But Andrea would not allow scars or a dying sky to deter her. She *would* find Cassie, no matter the cost.

And she would save her.

Chapter 36

Broken

Rain pelted down on what should have been an abandoned mansion in the Black Forest. The windows were dark—most of what Richard needed was in Meredith's laboratory in the basement. There was no need for him to waste candles.

Still, the thunder was loud enough to startle him from his work whenever a bolt of lightning hit particularly close. The broken equipment on the floor was an unfortunate mess, but there was no time to clean now. He needed to confirm the results of his test.

"Damn it," he muttered when he heard a soft groan and suddenly remembered that Cassie was still in the room. "Oh, you're up." He turned from the old wooden table which served as a desk and walked over to the wall, where he had discovered the heavy iron shackles that had come in handy upon their arrival to the house. He didn't want to use too much of their gathered magic by fighting Cassie's willpower with commands, and the shackles had been an easy, if temporary solution.

Cassie lay on her side on the rough stone floor, the shackles around her wrists hooked to chains anchored to the floor. Her face was stained with tears—she had alternated between crying and raging at Richard since she woke up, but he very quickly decided that he would rather deal with the crying. One of the more curious side effects of the absorption had been the amplification of her strength—as evidenced by the additional broken machinery and pieces of shelving strewn about the room—and he had no desire to be on the receiving end of that strength whenever she got angry, which was most of the time.

"That can't be comfortable," he said as he stood over her. "Are you sure I can't get you a pillow or a blanket or something?"

She refused to look at him, though he could see the soft blue illumination in her eyes—another interesting side effect he still wanted to research. "Get away from me."

He crossed his arms. "I thought you might be interested to know that we'll be leaving soon. We need to find more magic. We would have gotten it all, but Andrea interrupted us. Fortunately, we won't have that problem anymore, but we'll have to leave regardless."

Cassie glowered with uncontrolled fury before she leapt to her feet, the chains and their anchors straining against the tremendous force with which she pulled. "I'll *kill* you! I swear!"

"The only thing you're going to do is calm down, Cassie," Richard said, taking a step backwards. "You'll see. It's all going to be okay. We're finally going to get to go home!"

"I'll die before I go back there with *you,*" she sneered, giving the chains a hard, but futile, tug.

He smirked. "You'll change your mind. We were never meant to be here, Cassie. You know that." He clapped his hands. "I'm going to make something to eat and then we can discuss where to go next. I'd like to see you try to eat something, but I don't suppose that will happen, now will it?"

Cassie just stared at him, the hatred in her face telling enough.

He put his hands up in surrender. They weren't going to get anywhere tonight. "Fine, fine. I'll be back. Try not to break anything while I'm gone, please." He turned on his heel and stopped by the desk to jot down a few more notes before heading upstairs.

Before he left, he heard the heavy clink of the chains as Cassie collapsed to her knees. As she hung her head in momentary defeat, her quiet sobs echoing in the cellar, Richard almost felt sorry for her enough to say something. But he knew once they returned to where they belonged—once he fixed Tarrasha's energy problem for good—she would be much happier, and in time would forget about this accursed place.

He was *so* close to escaping Damea at last. And with Cassie's help, they would get home...together.

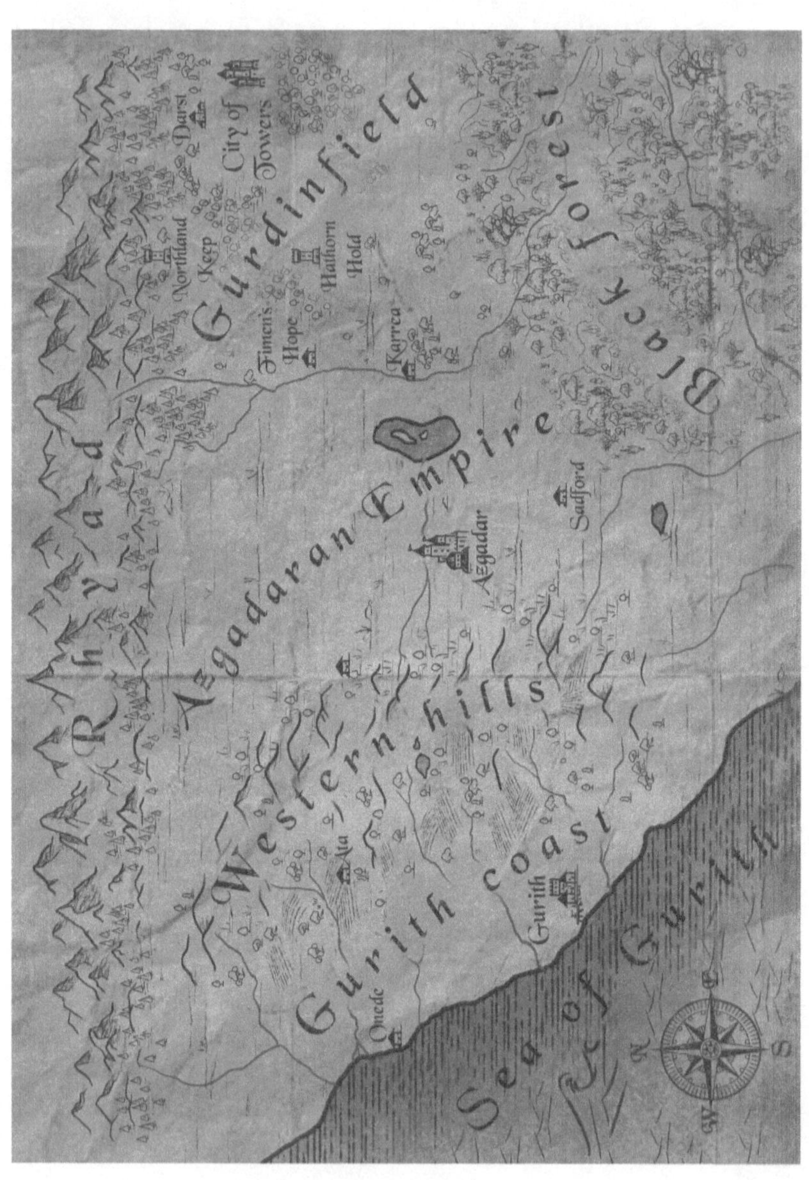
Northland Keep
Darst
City of Towers
Gurdinfield
Hathorn Hold
Fimen's Hope
Karrea
Black forest
Ægadaran Empire
Ægadar
Sadford
Western hills
Ata
Gurith coast
Gurith
Onede
Sea of Gurith
N
E
S
W

Appendix

A Brief History of Damea

Although the specifics surrounding how the explorer Dameas and his companions arrived in the land now known as Damea are debatable among the land's historians, it is generally accepted that the first permanent settlements were established roughly one thousand years before the Second Era. The earliest cities and towns were spread across the land, with ruins still being discovered today from the rocky shores of the Gurith Coast in the west to the still mostly uncharted forests in the far reaches of the realm of Gurdinfield in the east. Scholars (particularly in Gurdinfield) mostly agree that Dameas was declared king and ruled over the land until his death. As Dameas had no heirs, the most influential of his companions and their children set out to stake their claim on the land, eventually forming the nations and regions of today—The Azgadaran Empire, Gurdinfield, the Gurith Coast, and the Western Hills—and marking the beginning of the First Era.

Before his death, Dameas encouraged his companions to harness the land's natural energies whenever possible and to share the knowledge of spell casting with the future generations.

While certainly not as prevalent as it was hundreds of years ago, magic is still relied upon to power Damea's way of life—farms, cities, militaries, research, and even its structures— and the great spire that is the Azgadaran Palace was in fact built with magic. The origin of magic is unknown and the explanation as to why magic began to decline is almost as mysterious as its origin. Perhaps more time dedicated to magical research could have been invested by Damea's nations during The Starving and might have provided such answers, but there was no such effort recorded among the many wars and famines that followed that historic and sudden decline of magical energy.

Climate

Damea plays host to a variety of climates. To the west lies the Sea of Gurith, a cold, deep body of water rarely explored beyond the immediate waters near the Gurith Coast. The fertile Western Hills act as a wall between the coastal villages and the Azgadaran Empire and is called home by many who live in its farming towns and a few wealthy landowners. The Azgadaran Empire stretches across the drier, warmer lands of central Damea, its northern border touching the foot of the treacherous Rhyadan Mountains and its southern border just on the edge of the Black Forest. On the eastern side of the Rhyad River lies Gurdinfield, a colder realm that also shares its borders with Rhyad and the Black Forest, two regions of Damea that few have explored and even fewer have returned from.

Timeline

Pre-1st Era – Damea founded as one nation under the leadership of the explorer, Dameas, and his companions. Exploration continues until his death. His companions and their children established the nations and regions of today.

1st Era – Study of enchanting artifacts and harnessing the land's magical energy continued. Magic usage is at an all-time high.

1st Era – Crops and infrastructure begin to fail as magic becomes scarcer. Enchanters across Damea grow ill when exposed to unstable levels of magic or when overdrawing on the land's energy. Thousands perish from famine and sickness. The event is dubbed "The Starving" and marks the end of the First Era. It would last over two hundred years.

200, 2nd Era – Damea's energy begins to stabilize, although its distribution across the land is inconsistent. Nations enact laws restricting the use of magic. The Starving is declared over.

200, 2nd Era – Per King Caleb of Gurdinfield's orders, the Enchanters' Academy in the City of Towers closes. Students and teachers take to the streets in protest, but the school remains closed.

202, 2nd Era – House Taylor is attacked at night in their castle in the capital city of Gurdinfield. King Caleb, Queen Helen, and their three children are murdered. Houses Moore and Harrington plunge the nation into a bitter civil war.

220, 2nd Era – Events of Enchanters begin.

223, 2nd Era – Lydia Diana Taylor is revealed to have survived the attack in the City of Towers and is crowned Queen of Gurdinfield, ending a decades-long civil war.

223, 2nd Era – Andrea of Ata, an enchanter's apprentice, leads an expedition into Rhyad where a device designed to siphon Damea's magic is discovered in one of the caves of the Rhyadan Mountains, its origin unknown. The device is destroyed, and the magic is released back into the land. The event is dubbed "The Restoration".

224, 2nd Era – Events of Conduit begin.

Regions of Damea

Azgadaran Empire

The largest nation in Damea by far with borders touching the frigid wasteland of Rhyad and the northern edge of the Black Forest, the Azgadaran Empire (or just "Azgadar" as it is commonly referred to) has withstood centuries of war and famine while still maintaining the most powerful army in Damea.

While there are divides of rich and poor, particularly in the capital city, the empire's middle class is quite large and growing. Most Azgadarans that are not of the nobility find their calling as craftsmen, farmers, or merchants. The Market District of Azgadar is the center of trade in Damea, with goods imported and sold from all over the land. The nobility, however, is a different story. Citizens born into the upper castes of Azgadaran society enjoy comforts and luxuries that the middle and lower classes can rarely afford. Grand balls and royal parties at least twice a week are typical for an Azgadaran noble, with most families vying for a coveted spot on their ruler's advising council.

The mighty Azgadaran Legion remains the common tie throughout society. Citizens of all social and economic classes often enlist once they are of age, regardless of their social status.

The climate of Azgadar is hot and dry, and its northern region is for the most part desert.

Black Forest

Located in southern Damea, the Black Forest is a dark, labyrinthian collection of woods and tributaries. While there are some who take up residence in the forest, it is not a well-traveled region and it is not uncommon for a merchant to take a shortcut through and never come out. The Black Forest does not fall under any nation's rule. For those who can survive its dangers, the forest can be a peaceful retreat—especially for enchanters who wish to perform their research in isolation.

Gurdinfield

Gurdin, the older of two brothers that served under Dameas took his family and armies east and founded the City of Towers, now the capital of Gurdinfield. Sprawling grasslands and patches of forest of cover most of Gurdinfield, which claims most of eastern Damea up to the Rhyad River and its several farming and fishing villages. The region's summers tend to be hot and humid while its winters see snow most years. The City of Towers was once home to the Enchanters' Academy, and while its doors have long been closed, the nation was one of the last known places to find significant sources of magic in Damea after the Starving.

Most Gurdinfielders enjoy nature and prefer to live closer to it, taking care not to let their villages grow too large. Citizens from Gurith and Azgadar tend to look down on Gurdinfielders for their isolated and slower-paced way of life.

Gurith Coast

The Gurith Coast starts at the merchant-ruled city of Gurith and spans north along most of the western coastline of Damea. Named after the younger of two brothers that served under Dameas, the Gurith Coast has a milder climate than the rest of

Damea, with wet, rainy winters and dry summers. Temperatures stay consistent throughout the seasons. Smaller towns dot the coast north of Gurith—the largest being the fishing town of Onede. The port city of Gurith itself has no king, but is governed instead by the Merchants' Guild, an exclusive group of tradesmen, craftsmen, and other influential figures in the economy of the city.

Perhaps the most noteworthy thing about the city of Gurith is the infamous Shadow Arena. The annual Grandmaster's Tournament is a highly publicized event where gladiators, usually enchanters, can sign up to duel other challengers in a battle for money, property, and glory. Nobles from other regions are often heard criticizing the event for its violence and the risk it poses to the participants, who are often injured and sometimes killed during the matches. However, the very same nobles have also been seen attending the event when they think no one is watching.

Rhyad

The northernmost region of Damea as well as the least populous, Rhyad is a cold and mostly mountainous place. Rarely traveled due to its extreme weather conditions and treacherous terrain, Rhyad is not under the banner of any Damean nation. The occasional traveler might use Rhyad's mountain passes to avoid crossing the desert in northern Azgadar, but the risk is so great that most will not risk the journey.

Snowstorms, avalanches, wild animals, and more are what await those who travel to or through Rhyad. The more careful adventurers stick to the foothills of the mountains but are often attacked by the mostly unorganized groups of bandits that plague the region, waiting for an easy opportunity.

Western Hills

To the east of the Gurith Coast is a barrier of tall, rolling green hills in which several farming villages have sprung up over the last few centuries. Most of the people of the Western Hills are farmers or own shops in their village and it is rare for its citizens to leave the region. They enjoy longer, hot, and dry summers and shorter, wet winters. Several rivers run down the hills on both sides and keep the farmlands irrigated. Most of the villages are settled in the valleys while larger villas belonging to the more secluded nobility rest in the higher altitudes. The Western Hills are not ruled by any government or monarch and most of its residents prefer to think of themselves as from their town as opposed to from the region itself.

Glossary

Alden Cadar – The younger brother of Emperor Nardos Cadar and Ithmeera and Erik Cadars' uncle. Alden served on Azgadar's royal council for most of his life and provides guidance to Ithmeera on all ruling matters.

Alexander Telman – A former Guardian, or royal guard, of Gurdinfield's ruling family. Escaped during the assassination of House Taylor in 202, 2nd Era. Adoptive father of Lydia Taylor. Led the Guardians as a militia during the Gurdinfield Civil War.

Andrea of Ata – An enchanter from the village of Ata in the Western Hills and the apprentice of Meredith of Darst as well as the Royal Enchanter of Gurdinfield. Known for her role in the defense of the City of Towers during an Azgadaran invasion and for leading an expedition into Rhyad that resulted in the Restoration. Originally a farmer, she is the only child of Isabel and Garrett of Ata. She is romantically involved with Cassie and close friends with Kye of Azgadar.

Ata – The largest village in the Western Hills and famous for its festivals which occur in the summer and fall.

Azgadaran Empire – The largest nation in Damea, centrally located with its borders touching the southern edge of the wasteland of Rhyad and the northern edge of the Black Forest. Colloquially known as "Azgadar", its climate is hot and dry with its northern region being mostly desert.

Azgadar (city) – The capital city of the Azgadaran Empire and home to the ruling family, the Cadars.

Azgadaran Legion – The standing army of the Azgadaran Empire as well as the largest and most advanced military force in Damea.

Black Forest – Located in southern Damea, the Black Forest is a dark, labyrinthian collection of woods and tributaries.

Cassie – A Guardian of Gurdinfield and romantically involved with Andrea of Ata as well as close friends with fellow Guardians Jacob, Victor, and Roe. Brought to Damea via an experiment performed by Meredith and Andrea. Known for her ability to absorb and store magic as well as her role in the Restoration.

City of Towers – The capital of Gurdinfield, famous for its three white towers and home to the famed Enchanters' Academy. Notable for also being the site of the start of the Gurdinfield Civil War.

Darst – A small town, populated mostly by nobility, in the northeast corner of Gurdinfield at the foot of the Rhyadan Mountains.

Elisa of Sadford – A veteran Legionnaire and former Royal Guard of Empress Ithmeera Cadar. The only daughter and youngest child of an Azgadaran merchant and a Gurdinfielder seamstress. Sister of Philip of Sadford and aunt of Marco Cadar. Was charged with treason and exiled by Erik Cadar upon refusing to arrest her father for illegal consumption of magic.

Enchanters' Academy – Located in the heart of the City of Towers, this prestigious school opened in the First Era to all who possessed the ability to connect with and manipulate magic. Per the orders of King Caleb of Gurdinfield, it was closed after the Starving was declared over to reduce the amount of enchanting done in the city.

Erik Cadar – Second child of Nardos Cadar. Younger brother of Ithmeera Cadar and former general of the Azgadaran Legion. Slain by Elisa of Sadford during the Azgadaran invasion of the City of Towers in 223, 2nd Era.

Fimen's Hope – A village located on the western border of Gurdinfield. Origin of the famed whiskey-based drink, Fimen's Fire.

Gurdinfield – A kingdom spanning most of the eastern side of Damea, covered mostly by grasslands and patches of forest. Gurdinfield was plunged into civil war in 202 2nd Era when its ruling house was assassinated. The war lasted until in 223 2nd

Era, when Lydia Taylor reunited the kingdom under her house once more. Gurdinfield's summers tend to be hot and humid and the region typically sees snow most winters.

Guardians of Gurdinfield – Once the royal guards of the ruling family of Gurdinfield, the Guardians became a militia after the start of the Gurdinfield Civil War. After the war ended, they returned to serving the Queen of Gurdinfield. Today, all members of Gurdinfield's army are called Guardians.

Gurith Coast – The westernmost region of Damea and home to the fishing city of Gurith as well as several coastal villages. Starting in Gurith and spanning north along the western coastline, the Gurith Coast has a milder climate than the rest of Damea, with wet, rainy winters and dry summers.

Gurith – The capital of the Gurith Coast and home to the Merchants' Guild, a group of influential figures govern the region and often fund gladiator matches in the city's infamous Shadow Arena.

Hathorn Hold – A military fortress built in the First Era and the primary base of House Moore during the Gurdinfield Civil War.

Ithmeera Cadar – The eldest child and only daughter of the late emperor, Nardos Cadar, Ithmeera is the Empress of the Azgadaran Empire. She began participating in meetings with the empire's royal council when she was only fourteen, and quickly impressed her father's advisers with her quick thinking, calm demeanor, and confidence in handling any diplomatic issue thrown at her. Was married to the late Philip of Sadford, she has one son: Marco.

Jacob of the Southlands – The son of traders, Jacob was

rescued by Alexander Telman and the Guardians during the Gurdinfield Civil War when bandits ambushed his family's caravan. A skilled swordsman and experienced leader, he is married to Queen Lydia Taylor and commands Gurdinfield's army.

Karrea – A fishing town located on the border of the Rhyad River in Gurdinfield. Destroyed by House Moore's army during the Gurdinfield Civil War.

Kye of Azgadar – The son of the Azgadaran Legion's primary blacksmith. Became aware of his magical abilities when he was seventeen when he accidentally set his family's home on fire, killing them all. Played a critical role in the battle during Azgadar's invasion of the City of Towers and later joined Andrea's expedition to Rhyad. Is close friends with Andrea and Elisa.

Lydia Diana Taylor – Going by "Diana" when among friends, Lydia is the Queen of Gurdinfield. The youngest child of Caleb and Helen Taylor, she was rescued by Alexander Telman during the assassination of House Taylor in 202 2nd Era and raised by him and the militia Guardians of the Gurdinfield Civil War. Married to Jacob of the Southlands.

Marco Cadar – The only son of Ithmeera Cadar and Philip of Sadford. Marco is the heir to the Azgadaran Empire.

Merchants' Guild – The governing body of Gurith and led by the Grandmaster, the Merchants' Guild is an exclusive group of tradesmen, craftsmen, and other influential figures whose day-to-day dealings have a significant impact on the economy of the city.

Meredith of Darst – Born to a noble family in the city of Darst, Meredith was sent to the Enchanters' Academy in the City of Towers as soon as she developed magical abilities. She quickly rose to the top of her class but was forced to leave the academy when the city closed it down due to the magic shortage. Married to Richard. Mentor to Andrea.

Nardos Cadar – Late and previous emperor of the Azgadaran Empire. Father of Ithmeera and Erik Cadar. Brother of Alden Cadar.

Northland Keep – Located in the Northlands of Gurdinfield. The stronghold of House Harrington, one of the two warring houses during the Gurdinfield Civil War.

Onede – A small fishing village located on the west coast of Damea.

Philip of Sadford – A merchant, Elisa's older brother, and the emperor consort of the Azgadaran Empire. Philip was married to Ithmeera Cadar and is the father of Marco. He was killed by bandits while on a business expedition.

Rhyad – The northernmost region of Damea as well as the least populous, Rhyad is a cold and mostly mountainous place. Rarely traveled due to its extreme weather conditions and treacherous terrain, Rhyad is not under the banner of any Damean nation.

Roe of the City of Towers – A veteran Guardian and close friend of Victor, Jacob, Lydia, and Cassie.

Royal Enchanters of Azgadar – A small group of enchanters dedicated to researching and understanding magic. The infrastructure of the Azgadaran Empire's farms and cities were designed and built by the royal enchanters.

Sadford - Located just south of Azgadar, Sadford is one of the empire's most populous towns and is home to a Legion fort as well as The Dusky Ale, a favored tavern and inn among Legionnaires.

The Restoration - The redistribution of magic in Damea after a machine in Rhyad which had been slowly siphoning the land's energy for the last 200 years was destroyed in 223 2nd Era. The Restoration also caused an uptick in the number of potential enchanters across Damea.

The Starving - A decline and destabilization in magic in Damea at the end of the First Era, marked by the deterioration and subsequent failure of farms and infrastructure as well as the rise in illness among enchanters who were exposed to unstable magic or overdrew on the land's energy. Lasted until 200 2nd Era and resulted in nations placing heavy restrictions on magic usage.

Victor of Fimen's Hope - A veteran Guardian and close friend of Roe, Jacob, Lydia, and Cassie.

Western Hills - A fertile region west of the Azgadaran Empire, populated mostly by farmers who live in the collection of villages dotting the valleys. The Western Hills boasts longer, hot and dry summers and shorter, wet winters.

To Readers

Thank you for reading Conduit! While every effort has been made to edit and find all the typos in the book, it is entirely possible some were missed. If you have found an error and would like to report it, please email it to contact@enchantersnovels.com.

If you enjoyed this book, please consider posting a review on Amazon, Goodreads, Tumblr, Facebook, Bella Books, Kobo, or your own blog if you have one. I often host giveaways and updates about new and upcoming works so be sure to sign up for the newsletter on my website (kfbradshaw.com) where you can also subscribe to my blog.

- K. F. Bradshaw

About K.F. Bradshaw

K. F. Bradshaw is the author of the Enchanters Trilogy. She loves fantasy, science fiction, and writing epic stories about women who save the world. Growing up, she was often frustrated that there were not enough of these stories that starred realistic female characters, and even less that depicted LGBTQ representation as normalized. While she agrees that "coming out stories" are hugely important, she believes it is just as important to have queer characters in stories where their motivations, desires, and plot arcs have absolutely nothing to do with their orientation or identity.

She lives in California with her wife, who is a lot better at video games than she is, and she would love it if you stopped by her website (kfbradshaw.com) and said hello.

www.ingramcontent.com/pod-product-compliance
Lightning Source LLC
Chambersburg PA
CBHW051212120726
47905CB00004B/1085

* 9 7 8 0 9 9 8 7 5 1 8 3 2 *